PRAISE FOR #1 *NEW YORK TIMES* BESTSELLING AUTHOR ROBYN CARR

'The Virgin River books are so compelling—I connected instantly with the characters and just wanted more and more and more.'
—#1 *New York Times* bestselling author Debbie Macomber

'Insightfully realized central figures, a strong supporting cast, family issues, and uncommon emotional complexity make this uplifting story a heart-grabber that won't let readers go until the very end.... A rewarding (happy) story that will appeal across the board and might require a hanky or two.'
—*Library Journal*

'Robyn Carr has done it again.... *What We Find* is complex, inspirational, and well-written ... ly inspires read...

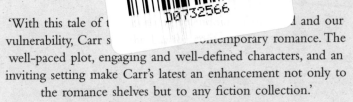

'With this tale of t ... d and our vulnerability, Carr s ... ontemporary romance. The well-paced plot, engaging and well-defined characters, and an inviting setting make Carr's latest an enhancement not only to the romance shelves but to any fiction collection.'
—*Booklist*

'A satisfying reinvention story that handles painful issues with a light and uplifting touch.'
—*Kirkus Reviews* on *The Life She Wants*

'Carr's new novel demonstrates that classic women's fiction, illuminating the power of women's friendships, is still alive and well.'
—*Booklist* on *Four Friends*

'A thought-provoking look at women...and the choices they make.'
—*Kirkus Reviews* on *Four Friends*

Second Chance Pass

Robyn Carr

MILLS & BOON

Mills & Boon
An imprint of HarperCollins*Publishers* Ltd
1 London Bridge Street
London SE1 9GF

www.harpercollins.co.uk

HarperCollins*Publishers*
1st Floor, Watermarque Building, Ringsend Road
Dublin 4, Ireland

This paperback edition 2021

First published in Great Britain by Mills & Boon,
an imprint of HarperCollins*Publishers* Ltd 2021

Copyright © Robyn Carr 2009

Robyn Carr asserts the moral right to be
identified as the author of this work.
A catalogue record for this book is
available from the British Library.

ISBN: 9781848458857

MIX
Paper from
responsible sources
FSC
www.fsc.org
FSC™ C007454

This book is produced from independently certified FSC™ paper
to ensure responsible forest management.

For more information visit: www.harpercollins.co.uk/green

Printed and Bound in the UK using 100% Renewable Electricity at
CPI Group (UK) Ltd

This novel is dedicated to Valerie Gray, my editor and friend.
Your commitment and support has made everything possible.
Your dedicated work has made everything better.
Your affection has made everything sweeter.

Second
Chance Pass

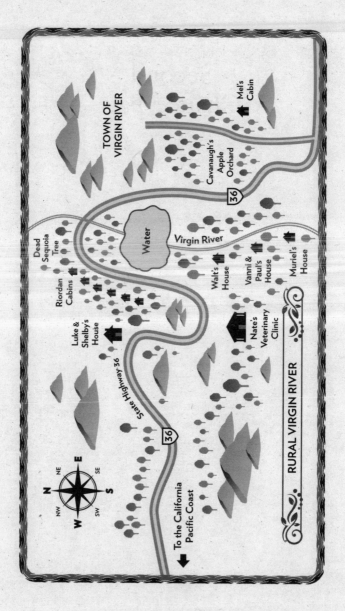

TOWN OF VIRGIN RIVER

Prologue

Paul Haggerty was finally back in Grants Pass after almost six months in Virgin River and there was an ache in his chest he just couldn't ease. The last six months had been hell.

Paul had gone to Virgin River back in the autumn to help finish Jack Sheridan's new house. Much to his surprise, he discovered Vanessa Rutledge was living in Virgin River with her father and younger brother while her husband, Matt, served in Iraq. She was pregnant with Matt's baby and looking more beautiful than ever. Seeing her had reminded Paul of the serious "thing" he'd had for Vanessa since first laying eyes on her all those years ago. But his best friend was the one she had married. Then life went into fast forward.

Just before the baby was born they all had a video conference with Matt. The call was mostly for Matt and Vanni as it was the first time in six months they'd seen one another. Then everyone else got to say a quick hi and when it was Paul's turn Matt had said to him, "If anything goes wrong over here, look after Vanni."

It couldn't have gone more wrong. Matt was killed in an explosion in Baghdad the first week in December. It had been a terrible time and Vanni had asked Paul to stay until the baby came—another two months. Of course he agreed, and all that time he held it together so Vanni could lean on him. But the strain of the situation, his secret love for Vanni and his grief for his best friend ate him alive.

He thought going home to Grants Pass would ease the pain or at least distract him from it, but instead the pressure continued to build. A night out drinking with some of his construction crew and getting painfully loaded, only added a miserable headache to his breaking heart. He felt like a dead man, slogging through the days, tossing through the sleepless nights.

Without thinking too much about it, he called a woman he'd been out with a couple of times. Terri. He needed the distraction of someone who wasn't already caught up in his drama. What qualified Terri was that their friendship had been easy; there was no clinging, no expectations. Plus, she used to make him laugh. She was simply a nice young woman, twenty-nine years to Paul's thirty-six. Terri was the only woman he'd been out with in a couple of years, and he hadn't talked to her in six months. That, if anything, should have told him something, but he hadn't been paying attention.

He started out the conversation with, "Hey, Terri. Long time." He asked her to dinner, but first confirmed that she wasn't in a relationship—he didn't want to complicate her life.

She laughed at that. "I wish," she said. "No boyfriend, Paul. In fact, I've hardly gone out in the past few months. Let's go someplace quiet and low-key, just catch up." This was just the response he'd been hoping for and he'd been so grateful.

Paul rang her doorbell and when she came to her apartment door, he realized he had forgotten how pretty she was. Small of stature with shoulder-length dark brown hair and large eyes, she flashed him the bright, sexy smile that first got his attention a year ago. She laughed that wild laugh of hers and threw her arms around his neck. "God, it's great to see you! I can't wait to hear your excuse for disappearing for months!"

"Hey, remember Rosa's? That hole-in-the-wall Mexican place? How about we go there?"

"Love it," she said.

Paul stared straight ahead as he drove them to the restaurant, his jaw locked. He tapped his fingers on the steering wheel and shifted in his seat; *maybe this wasn't such a good idea,* he thought. When they walked in the door, Terri pointed to a dark, corner booth and said, "Back there." And when they sat down she said, "You're not a real talkative guy, Paul, but it's obvious something's wrong."

"I just got back to town from California. I'm a little behind on everything."

She was shaking her head. "No, it's more than that. You're upset and nervous, and I wasn't going to say anything, but you have dark circles, like you're not sleeping. Since I haven't seen or heard from you in a long time, I know it isn't anything I did. You act like you just got out of prison. Go ahead—I'm a good listener."

That was all it took. He ordered himself a beer and a glass of wine for Terri and let it spill. Best friend, dead. Best friend's wife pregnant. Him hanging around, trying his best to hold her up.

"Good God," she said, shaking her head. "You could have called me, you know. I mean, going through something horrible and not having anyone to talk to can make things so much worse."

"I feel like a real jerk dumping on you now," he said.

"Well, save it. I'm a girl, girls talk about their tragedies and heartaches. And if you don't get it out, it's going to eat a hole in you."

"That's how it feels," Paul admitted. "Like I swallowed acid. Matt and I became best friends in junior high. I have two brothers but Matt was an only child, so he spent more time at my house than his own. We served in the Marine Corps together—he stayed active while I went to the reserves. I think my mom and dad were hit as hard by his death as I was. But his wife… Aw, Terri. I've never seen anything so painful. Here she was, about to have their first child, and she would cry until she was weak and dry. All I could do was hold her. But it was worse at night when the only sound in the house was Vanni sobbing in bed."

Terri reached for his hand. "Paul…"

He held her hand while he talked. "When the baby came, she wanted me with her. Because Matt couldn't be, I guess. It was the worst and best thing I've ever done, seeing that baby being born. It made me so proud to hold Matt's baby." He looked away and blinked back emotion. "On his headstone they put Matt Rutledge, beloved husband, father, brother, son, friend. That brother part— that was for me, for us, the brothers in arms. It just doesn't feel like he's gone. But he's so gone and I just can't seem to get over it. And if I'm feeling this way then Vanni must be torn to pieces."

Right then the food was delivered, but they didn't eat much. Paul had another beer and told her stories of growing up with Matt, playing football, driving their parents' cars too fast, trying to hustle girls with little success, enlisting in the Corps after two years of college and Matt's parents going absolutely, totally, cosmically nuts. "My parents weren't happy, but Matt's were out of their minds. Matt's mother was convinced that I'd talked Matt into it, but the truth is, that's what he wanted. Period.

I went along because I didn't want him going in alone. Or maybe I didn't want to stay behind without him. My mom used to say we were joined at the hip."

Their plates were taken away, and they lingered over coffee while Paul continued to reminisce. Pretty soon they'd been in that corner booth for a couple of hours.

"I've never lost anyone that close," Terri said, her eyes liquid. "I can't imagine how hard it must be. You should have called me, Paul. You shouldn't have shouldered that alone, without support."

He squeezed her hand. "When I called you, I didn't have any intention of dumping all this on you. At least not consciously. I thought you'd take my mind off it for a while. But talking to someone who isn't in the middle of it helps," he said. "The whole bunch of 'em in Virgin River are so frickin' torn up—Vanni, her dad, her little brother— I couldn't let down my guard for a second. Even around my own family—my mom starts crying the second Matt's name comes up."

"You must feel like you're going to explode," she said.

"You know what I wish?" Paul said. "I know this is nuts—I wish I'd been there with him. I wish it had been me instead of him."

She was shaking her head. "No. Oh, Jesus, no."

"He's got a family. He should be with them. You just have no idea the kind of man he was—he took loyalty to the next level. I could always count on Matt."

"He counted on you, too. He asked you to look out for his wife…"

"He wouldn't have had to ask."

"Paul, you did for Matt what he would have done for you."

Paul was reflective for a few moments realizing that this woman he'd been out with a few times, slept with a couple of times on a mutually agreed to "friends with privileges" status, could bring him this degree of comfort and understanding. "I owe you, Terri," he said. "I didn't realize how much I needed to talk to someone about this."

She smiled. "Men," she said, shaking her head. "All that stoicism wrecks your stomach. And usually causes migraines."

He grinned at her, feeling almost human. "I've never had a migraine, but I think my headache's letting up. For the first time in a while."

"Look around," she said. "There's only one other couple in here, and they're eating. Let's get out of here before they start putting the chairs upside down on the tables and mopping the floor."

"Yeah," he agreed. "I've put you through enough. And thanks. For listening."

When he walked her up the stairs to her second floor apartment, she turned and asked, "Would you like to come in?"

He shook his head immediately. Terri had done a lot for him tonight, just giving him a place to unload. He wasn't about to take advantage of that. "I don't think so. But thanks."

She smiled up at him. She pulled on his hand, drawing him into the apartment. "I'd better not," he said again, but he said it more softly. And when the door closed, he found his hands were on her waist, his mouth seeking her mouth. And just like the last time he'd been with her, she was up on her toes to reach him, circling his neck with her arms, leaning in to him.

"No," he said against her mouth. "I'm all screwed up. Tell me no."

She pressed against him, tonguing his lips apart. "I would hate doing that."

And he was gone. Brain freeze took over. He had no judgment, no willpower. He was all raw need and pain and gratitude. This was as unburdened as he'd felt in months and he was weak from having carried that grievous load for so long. Before a whole minute had passed, he had Terri down on the couch, kissing her, touching her, hearing her say, yes, yes, yes, yes.

He had one moment of sanity before he slipped his hand under her knit shirt. "Terri, this isn't a good idea… I didn't call you for this… I didn't plan on this…"

"I didn't, either," she whispered, letting her eyes fall closed. "God, I missed you."

Paul's brain took a hike. He was all physical sensation. He was hard; she was soft. He was desperate, she was hot and willing, and beneath him she seemed as needy as he felt. He ground against her, her bare breast in his hand, his tongue licking its way along her neck. Her hands were on his belt buckle, then his zipper; his hands were tugging at her clothes while she squirmed and moaned. His lips were on her nipple; her hand wrapped around him and he almost lost it. He grabbed for his pocket, pulled an old condom from his wallet and, in a hoarse, desperate whisper he asked, "You have your side covered?"

"The pill, remember?" she answered breathlessly. "Oh God, oh God, oh God."

Paul felt his pulse slow just slightly. The gentleman in him had to be sure she wasn't left hanging so he took a moment, slid a finger along that erogenous knot in her very center while his lips tugged at her breast and when her sighs turned into near cries, he entered her, pumped his hips, waited for pleasure to lock her hips against him and steal her breath away, and he let months of misery spill out of him.

The first thing he felt, while he panted and tried to catch his breath, was overwhelming relief. Basic, primal,

physical relief, as potent as a narcotic. The next thing he
felt was regret. He shouldn't have done that. Even though
they had an understanding he could sense that she cared
about him. Why else would she listen to him with such
sensitivity; draw him inside and welcome this encounter.

But he loved someone else.

Haggerty, you are a brainless fool! he thought to
himself.

But he put a hand against the hair at her temple and
brushed it back over her ear while she drifted slowly back
to earth and her eyes opened. "Okay?" he asked.

She nodded and smiled. "God, I missed you so much."

He gently kissed her lips. "I shouldn't have let that
happen. I'm too messed up. But thank you."

She put a palm against his cheek. "My pleasure," she
said softly, smiling.

He held his weight off her and even though he felt
stupid and guilty, he managed to smile at her. When a respectable length of time had passed, he said, "I'm sorry,
but I can't stay. I'd better get going."

"I know. But maybe it won't be six months until you
call me again."

"It won't be," he said. He would call her again, take her
out for a drink, and try to explain that even though he
didn't have any reason to be optimistic, his heart was tied
up elsewhere. And as long as that was the case, it was
wrong for him to be intimate with Terri. She was a good
person. She deserved better.

One

Vanessa Rutledge stood in front of her husband's grave, her coat pulled tightly around her against the crisp March breeze, red hair billowing in the wind. "I know this is going to seem like a strange request—but I just don't know who else to ask. Matt, you know I love you, that I'll always love you, that I see you in your son's eyes every day. But, darling, I'm going to love again, and I need your blessing. If I have that, I'd like you to give the man who is to be my future a little nudge. Let him know it's all right. Please? Let him know he's so much more than—"

"Vanessa!"

Her father was standing out on the deck behind the house holding the baby away from himself, like he'd just pooped on his mess dress. It was past time to leave. Little Matt had been born six weeks ago and this morning they were both seeing Mel Sheridan for their first checkups since his birth. Her father, retired general Walt Booth, was acting as chauffeur so that he could watch the baby while Vanessa had her exam.

"Coming, Dad!" she called. She looked back at the grave. "We'll have a real conversation about this later," she told the headstone. She blew a long kiss in that direction and hurried down the little hill, past the stable and up to the house.

The last place Vanessa ever expected to find herself was in a tiny mountain town of six hundred. When her father chose this property a couple of years before his retirement from the Army, she and Matt had taken a look at it. Matt fell in love with it at once. "When I go," he had said, "plant me on that little hill, under that tree."

"Stop it!" she had laughed, slapping his arm, neither of them realizing how prophetic his words would be.

There was a time, years before she met Matt, that Vanni had envisioned herself as a high-powered news anchor; using her degree in communications. She decided to take a year before pursuing an eighty-hour-a-week career path and, on a whim, went to work as a flight attendant. One year turned into five because she loved the job, the travel, the people. She'd still been working for the airline when Matt left for Iraq. It was her loneliness and advancing pregnancy that had sent her packing to Virgin River. She had thought it would be temporary—she'd have the baby, wait for her husband's return from war and move on to his next assignment with him. Instead Matt was brought here, to that little hill with the tree on it.

She didn't cry as much anymore, though she missed him; missed the laughter, the long, late-night talks. Missed having someone hold her, whisper to her.

Walt had the diaper bag slung over his shoulder and was headed for the car. "Vanessa, you spend too much time talking to that grave. We should've put him somewhere else. Out of sight."

"Oh, dear," she said, lifting a curious eyebrow, the corner of her mouth twitching. "Matt hasn't been complaining that I'm bothering him, has he?"

"Not funny," he said.

"You worry too much," she told her dad, taking the baby from him to put him in the car seat. "I'm not brooding. There are some things no one but Matt should hear. And gee, he's so handy…"

"Vanessa! For God's sake!" He took a breath. "You need girlfriends."

She laughed at him. "I have plenty of girlfriends." She had lots of girlfriends from flying days and, even though they didn't live nearby, they were great about visiting and staying in touch, giving her every opportunity to talk about Matt, about grief, then about the baby and recovery. "You'll be happy to know Nikki's coming up for the weekend," she said. "A girlfriend."

Walt hefted himself into the driver's seat. "We've been seeing a lot of Nikki lately. Either she can't stay away from the new baby or things aren't going so well with her and that… that…" Walt couldn't seem to finish.

"She can't stay away from the baby and no, things aren't going well with Craig. I smell a split coming," Vanessa said.

"I never liked him," Walt said with a grunt.

"No one likes him. He's an ass," Vanni said. Her best friend, too sweet for her own good, wanted a husband and children, but instead was stuck with a live-in arrangement that had gone flat years ago, leaving her almost as alone as Vanni.

Vanni had other friends besides fellow flight attendants. She'd begun to grow close to some of the women in town—her midwife, Mel Sheridan; Paige, who worked alongside her husband in the only bar and grill in town; Brie, Mel's sister-in-law. Still, there were some things only Matt would understand.

When you live in a place like Virgin River where the doctor's office only makes appointments on Wednesdays, it's a pretty good bet there won't be any waiting around. Sure enough, Mel was standing in the reception area right inside the door waiting for them to arrive. Her face lit up in delight as they walked in and she immediately reached for the baby. "Ooooh, come heeeere," she sang. "Let me look at you!" She lifted him as if weighing him. Then she cuddled him close. "He's looking good, Vanni. Getting nice and fat on the breast." She looked at Walt. "How's Grandpa doing?"

"Grandpa could use more sleep," Walt grumbled.

Vanessa made a face. "There's no reason in the world he has to get up. He certainly can't help me nurse the baby."

"I wake up, that's all. And if I'm up and Vanni's up, I might as well see if she needs anything."

Mel smiled at him. "That's a good grandpa," she said. "He'll be sleeping through the night before you know it."

"When did David sleep through the night?" Vanni asked of Mel's one-year-old.

"The first time or the last time?" Mel asked. "You might not want to ask that—we have sleeping issues at our house. And now Jack lets him in the bed with us. Take my advice, don't start that!"

Vanessa peered at Mel's growing tummy. David had just turned a year and their second baby was due in May. "I hope you have a really big bed," she said.

"There will be plenty of room when I kick Jack out of it. Come on—let's look at Mattie first and take care of his shots." Mel carried the baby back to the exam room with Vanessa following behind.

Mel had delivered little Matt right in Vanessa's bedroom and their bond had grown deep and strong. It didn't take long to determine the baby was at a good weight and in excellent health. "I'll take him out to Walt while you get into a gown, how's that?"

"Thanks," Vanni said.

A few minutes later Mel was back. "Your dad took the baby over to Jack's for a cup of coffee. And some male bonding, I suppose."

Vanni had taken her place on the exam table, and Mel checked her heart, blood pressure, and got her in position for a pelvic. "Everything looks great. You had a wonderful delivery, Vanni—you're in excellent shape. And boy, did you lose weight quickly. Isn't breast-feeding a miracle?"

"I'm not back in my old jeans yet."

"I bet you're close. Go ahead, sit up," Mel said, offering a hand. "Anything we should talk about?"

"Lots of things. Can I ask you something personal?"

"You can always ask," Mel said while writing in the chart.

"I know that before you married Jack, you were widowed…"

Mel stopped writing. She closed the chart and looked at Vanni with a sympathetic smile. "I've been expecting this conversation," she said.

"How long was it?" Vanni asked, and Mel knew exactly what she was referring to.

"I met Jack nine months after my husband's death. I married him six months later. And if you confer with the town historian and gossips, you'll learn that I was at least three months pregnant at the time. Closer to four."

"We have a town historian?"

"About six hundred of them," Mel said with a laugh. "If you have anything you'd like to keep secret, you should consider moving to another town."

"Matt's only been dead a few months, but he's been gone almost a year… Mel, he wasn't on a business trip. He was in combat, out of touch. I talked to him a total of three times, saw his face once on live video cam. The letters were short and sparse. It's been a really long time since—"

Mel touched Vanni's knee. "There's no rule of thumb on this, Vanessa. Everything I've read, and I've read a lot about widowhood, says that when people enter new relationships relatively soon after losing a spouse, it indicates they had happiness in their marriage. Being married was a good experience for them." She smiled.

"I didn't even know for sure I was pregnant when Matt left for Iraq last May. I'm not thinking about another marriage, of course," Vanni said. "But I am thinking about— Well, what I'm thinking is that I don't want to be alone forever."

"Of course you shouldn't be alone forever. You have a lot of life to live."

Vanni smiled. "Should I be thinking about birth control?"

"We can talk about that. You wouldn't want to be as unprepared as your midwife. Especially with having a baby to take care of. Believe me." She took a breath and ran a hand over her big belly. "I wouldn't *let* myself think ahead! I remember when my sister said, 'I know widows who have remarried, and are happy.' I almost took her head off. I was appalled. I wasn't at all hopeful life could go on."

"It sure went on for you," Vanni said.

"Boy howdy. I came here absolutely determined to live out my days lonely and miserable, but that damn Jack— he ambushed me. I think I fell in love with him the minute I met him, but I fought it. As though I might somehow be unfaithful to my husband's memory by moving on, which was absurd. I had the kind of husband who would have wanted me to have love in my life, and I bet you did, too."

"You don't send a man off to war without talking a few things through—my parents taught me that. One of the first ways Tom and I figured out the general was headed for a possible deployment was when the paperwork came out. Wills, trusts, etcetera. Not just in case something happened to him, but what if he was away in some jungle or desert war zone and something happened to Mom?" She smiled a bit wistfully. "Matt didn't dwell on the worst-case scenario, but he was quick and to the point. He said I wasn't the type to wallow and he'd be disappointed in me if I did. He had a few requests—where he wanted to be buried, what to do with his favorite personal items, to make sure his parents got regular visits especially if we had children. And—if a good man showed his face, I was not to hesitate." She took a breath. "My requests of him were almost identical." She straightened. "If I'm lucky enough to run into another man half as wonderful as Matt, I should be ready."

"Absolutely. It's not at all impossible, even in little old Virgin River. Let's get you something reliable while you're considering all this. You want a pill you can take while breast-feeding? Can I hook you up with a diaphragm or IUD? Have you given the options any thought?"

Vanni smiled gratefully. Of course she'd thought about it. "Yes. IUD please."

"Let's go over the models," Mel said. Then she smiled. "By the way, you're all cleared for intercourse. Should you find…"

Vanni laughed. "Thanks," she said.

"You have good judgment. Make sure there's a condom involved. We don't want the transmission of any—"

"I have good judgment," Vanni repeated. "And extremely good taste."

There *was* a man on Vanessa's mind, he was the reason she'd found herself imploring Matt for help and blessings. Matt's best friend; her best friend. Paul.

He spent months in Virgin River, supporting and comforting her, spending Christmas away from his parents, brothers and their families. They spent a lot of time talking about Matt; crying about Matt, lost in hours of sentimental remembering. Without Paul's strength, she'd never have gotten through the worst of it. He was her rock.

Her relationship with Paul went back much further, of course. It wasn't as though they became friends because of Matt's death. In fact, that night long ago when she met Matt, it had been Paul across the room who'd first caught her eye. He was so tall, his legs so long and hands so big, it was hard for him not to stand out in a crowd. There was that willful, sandy hair that had to be kept short because it would defy any kind of styling. Not that Paul was the kind of man to fuss with his hair—it was obvious even from a distance that he stuck to basics. It was his masculinity she noticed; he looked like a lumberjack who'd cleaned up to go into town. He had an engaging smile; one tooth in front was just a little crooked and he had a dimple on the left cheek. Heavy brown brows, deep chocolate eyes—details she discovered a bit later, of course. She hadn't even noticed Matt…

But it was Matt who put the rush on her, swept her off her feet, made her laugh, made her *blush*. While Paul hung back, shy and silent, Matt charmed her to her very bones. And shortly after the charm, he made her desire him madly, love him deeply. He was hardly a consolation prize—he was one of the best men in the world. And a devoted husband, so in love with her.

She loved Paul before Matt's death, grew to love him more deeply afterward. When little Mattie was born, she said to Paul, "I will never love anyone but Matt." But as the weeks passed she realized that she didn't have to stop loving Matt any more than Paul should. Matt would be with them both forever. And it was like the natural order of things that Paul should step in now. But there was no indication from him that he felt anything more than a special friendship. She had no doubt that Paul loved her, loved little Matt, but it didn't appear to be the kind of love that could warm her on cold nights.

She'd called him several times since he'd returned to Grants Pass; polite and entertaining conversations about the baby, the town and his friends here, about her dad and brother, even sometimes about Matt.

"The baby's gained a pound and a half already," she told him. "He's already changed so much."

"Who does he look like?" Paul asked. "Is his hair still dark or does he have a patch of fire on his head, like his mom?"

"Still just a little Matt," she said. "I want you to see him. Hold him." *Hold me!*

"I'll have to try to get down there."

He hadn't visited yet. And he never betrayed any longing. Not a whiff of desire came through those phone lines.

She felt like a fool for even wanting him. But there was no denying it—she missed him so much. And not the way a young widow misses having a man in her life. The way a woman longs for a man who stirs her, moves her.

When Mel walked Vanni out to the clinic's waiting room, Vanni spied her younger brother's girlfriend waiting there. "Brenda!" Vanni said, going to her, giving her a hug. "I guess if there are only appointments on Wednesdays, there's a good chance you'll run into all your friends here," she said with a laugh.

"I guess." Brenda shrugged, blushing a little.

"I have to rescue my dad before he runs into a messy

diaper. He's got the baby at Jack's. I'll see you later—probably tonight at dinner?"

"Sure," Brenda said. "Later."

Vanni blew out the door and Brenda sank into her chair. The waiting room had been the old house's front room and was decorated exactly so. Heavy cream-colored velvet draperies covered the front windows. They were pulled back with sashes and always remained open. An ancient sofa and settee, upholstered in burgundy velvet, were flanked by two wing chairs with curved wooden legs. The fabric on the chairs was yellow brocade that had long ago lost its luster. A few Gisele chairs with cane seats were spotted around the room, which, itself, was rarely full. There was only Mel and Doc Mullins to see patients, so unless someone wandered in, the appointments were spaced comfortably apart.

Brenda had an elbow on her knee and her forehead rested in her hand. "Whew," she said weakly. "Of course I'd have to run into Vanessa. Crap."

Mel grabbed Brenda's chart. She just chuckled and went to her, pulling her to her feet. "Don't worry about that. Come on, let's check you out."

"But it's Tommy's sister! What if she asks me why I was here?"

"Brenda, Brenda, that's not going to be a problem." Mel pulled her along to the exam room. While Brenda stood by the door, Mel stripped off the disposable paper from the exam table and refreshed it. Then she handed Brenda a gown. Mel flipped open the chart and said, "So—you're here about concern over heavy periods…"

"Yeah, but…"

"I know," Mel said. "Except, they're fine."

"Fine," Brenda said shyly. "I need birth control pills…" She looked down and Mel just lifted her chin with one finger.

"Sure. I know," Mel said. "But if Vanessa ever asks you why you were here, you just say you were concerned about your periods and I checked you, told you everything was just fine. How's that?"

"Really?"

"I don't talk about patients' business," Mel said. "Put on the gown. We'll have a checkup. We'll talk about why you're really here. And Brenda—everything is going to be fine."

"My mom doesn't know I'm doing this," she said. "She thinks it's my periods."

"Okay," Mel said, but she knew Sue Carpenter was pretty sharp. Chances were good she knew exactly what was going on. After all, Tommy and Brenda had been steadies since the start of school and there was no question they were real serious. "I'll be back in five," Mel said, leaving the room.

Few seventeen-year-old girls felt comfortable discussing birth control with even the closest of mothers. When Mel returned and Brenda was gowned and ready, she said, "I'll need to update your pap and, if you don't mind, I'd like to do a check on you for STDs to be sure there's nothing we should treat. Should we talk about emergency birth control?"

"Huh?"

"Have you recently had unprotected intercourse?"

"No," she said. "Thing is, Tommy won't come near me without my own birth control, even though he has…you know…"

"Condoms," Mel supplied.

"Yeah. He says that's not good enough."

"Well, God bless him," Mel said. This darling girl, a gifted student who would very likely get lots of offers for full-ride scholarships, had been the victim of a sexual assault less than a year ago, before Tom had moved here. She'd gone to a beer party in the woods with a bunch of teenagers, intending to have one sneaky beer, and three months later, discovered she was pregnant without having the first idea how that could have happened. If that wasn't bad enough, Brenda had had a raging case of Chlamydia, which may have contributed to a spontaneous miscarriage.

Mel performed her examination, did some tests, gave her a three-month supply of contraceptives and a prescription and said, "I want to commend you for taking care of your health, Brenda. I know it can be scary to ask for this kind of help when you're young. But you're wise to take precautions."

"What if my mom asks you about this?"

"She probably won't, but if she does, I'll tell her that you're doing just fine."

"You think that'll do it?"

"Oh, honey, I've gotten very, very good at not telling things. Ask Jack," she added with a laugh. "You can start taking these right now, but they won't be effective for two weeks. Try to remember to take them at the same time every day—like right before bed or as soon as you get up in the morning. That will increase the reliability."

"He's going away, you know," Brenda said a little emotionally. "Right after graduation he goes into basic, then West Point."

Mel put a hand against the girl's soft, pretty hair. "First of all, you wouldn't want any other kind of boyfriend—he's an overachiever and will be a huge success. Cream of the crop. Second, just because you have pills doesn't mean you have to do anything that you're not ready for. With me?"

She nodded.

"He'll be back for leave and vacations. There will be lots of letters between you—wonderful letters."

She nodded again but said, "E-mails."

"Just as good. These pills are for your health and safety, Brenda. You don't have to send him off with something to remember. Don't be pressured."

"Oh, I'm not. I understand what you're saying," she said softly. "Tom would never pressure me. Besides, I love him."

Mel smiled. "How nice for you. He's a very special young man. And you, my dear, are a very special young woman. You're completely in charge of your body—always remember that."

Nikki Jorgensen pulled up in front of the Booth ranch and gave the horn a toot before getting out. When she let herself into the house, Vanni was sitting on the floor beside the baby. Little Matt was lying on a small baby quilt with toys he was entirely too young to enjoy spread around him.

"Hurry up," Vanni said. "He's *smiling!*"

Nikki threw her purse in a chair and knelt on the floor opposite Vanni. They were so unalike—Vanni being a statuesque redhead and Nikki small and dark, her black hair falling down her back almost to her waist in a straight, silky sheath. Vanni was bold; Nikki was quiet and hated confrontation. Nikki liked to say that while she was studying the latest hairstyles in high school, Vanni, the military brat, was learning to pack a house in six hours and navigate Customs in foreign countries.

They spent a few minutes making faces at the baby until Vanni finally said, "I can't wait to tell Paul he's smiling for real."

And that alone plunged them into silence. "Have you heard from Paul?" Nikki finally asked in a gentle voice.

Vanni shook her head, looking away. "Well, I call him. A couple of times every week. But he's only called here once."

"Oh, Vanni," Nikki said, sympathetic.

"Never mind. He's probably relieved he doesn't have any obligation to the Widow Rutledge anymore…"

"I'm sure that's not it," Nikki said, giving Vanni's thick, red mane a stroke.

"A couple of months ago it never occurred to me I'd have feelings for him. I mean, these kind of feelings. I thought of him as my ballast, my rock. And then slowly, he started to mean more to me than that. Since he left… I miss him so much. And not just because he was a supportive friend."

"Who more likely for you to be attracted to than someone who misses Matt as much as you do? Who loves little Mattie as much as Matt would himself? Besides, it's not like you just met him—he's been around since the day you met Matt! You know him better than anyone. You certainly don't have to wonder what kind of man he is."

"I'm just afraid… I'm not sure I'm ready to really let go of Matt."

Nikki laughed. "Vanni, you don't have to let go of Matt any more than Paul does. He'll be part of you and Paul forever."

Vanni gave her a thankful smile, lifting a tawny brow. "That's what I've been thinking lately. It's not like it has to be a choice, does it?"

"No way, babe."

"So, how are things with you and Craig?"

Nikki's smile vanished. "The same. Not good. I gave him an ultimatum. Commitment or we're over. He just keeps saying he needs time. But how much time? It's been five years. He knows I want a family, and my clock isn't standing still."

Vanni shook her head, doubtful. "He'll never give you up," Vanni said, but truthfully, she feared Nikki would never leave him even if he didn't give her a tenth of what she needed.

Nikki lifted her chin. "Oh, yeah? You a betting woman?"

"Nikki, do you mean it this time? Really?"

Nikki touched the baby's foot. "I'm not going through life without at least a shot at this," she said. "I'm selfish. I want it all. And things have been nonnegotiable with Craig on all of it."

Paul had been back in Grants Pass for just over six weeks. He'd had that evening with Terri and had promised her he'd be in touch. When she came to him at work and asked if he could sneak away for a conversation, he figured it was about the fact that he hadn't called as he'd promised.

But no.

He folded his long legs up into her little Toyota parked in front of his office and said, "What's up?" Through some nervous tears, she explained that she was pregnant and hadn't been with anyone but him.

"Pregnant?" he repeated stunned. "Pregnant?"

"Yeah," she said. "It happened that night after you got back to town. You remember. It was a pretty intense night. You can't have forgotten."

"How in the world did that happen? You said you were on the pill. I wore a condom."

"I don't know," she said, sniffing. "It's probably my fault. I'm sorry."

"Your fault?" he asked. "How?"

"I haven't had a boyfriend in so long, I got a little sloppy with the pills, missing them sometimes. Your call— it came as a surprise. I hadn't heard from you in such a long time and I couldn't pass up seeing you. But you had the condom and I was sure we'd be okay… I don't know what went wrong. It must have been me missing pills, you having a faulty condom... I can't think of any other explanation..."

"Aw, man," he said. He took a deep breath. "Okay," he said, getting a grip on his panic. "Okay, tell me what you need," he said, taking her hand and holding it in both of his.

"Any possibility marriage might come to mind?"

He didn't even have to think about it. There was someone else; there'd been someone else for a long, long time. "God, Terri, we can't get married. What did you call us—friends with benefits? We're consenting adults who like and respect each other and that's a lot, but at the same time, not enough. You're important to me, but we don't have the kind of relationship that would get us married. Keep us married."

"That's a little beside the point right now," she said.

"We don't really know each other. Not really."

"We know each other well enough that I'm pregnant."

"I take this to mean you've decided you want to have the baby?"

"I'm almost thirty," she said, bristling. "I'm not getting rid of it."

"Okay, okay, good," Paul said, relieved in spite of common sense telling him this could be taken care of; it could disappear. He did *not* want to be in this position, but he didn't want this baby erased, either. "I can help financially. I can do my best to support you emotionally. I swear, I'll stand by you. But, Terri, anything more than that would be a mistake for both of us."

"Why?" she asked, tears springing to her eyes.

He put an arm around her and held her against his shoulder as much as he could, given the tight space in her car. "Lots of reasons, starting with, before anything happened between us, we had a conversation about us—neither of us was looking for anything serious. We've been together, what? Three times in a year? Four? God, I'm sorry, Terri, but the night this happened, that's the closest we've ever been, and that happened because I was messed up and you were sweet enough to give me an ear. Honey, we're just not in love."

"How do you know I'm not?" she asked.

"We've spoken once in the last six months. If you had those kind of feelings, I never suspected." He tightened his arm around her. "Terri, you're so special and wonderful. But here we are, two people who can go six months without talking, without seeing each other." He shook his head. "I knew that night was a mistake. I went too deep into my feelings and you got too attached. But it's just not the real thing. It was my crisis, your compassion that got us where we are today. Marrying you now would only get in the way of you finding what you really need. And believe me, you don't need me."

"What am I going to do?"

Selfishly he thought, *what am I going to do?* "Whatever you want to do, I'll help in every way I can. I'm sorry, but you deserve a husband who loves you as much as you love him."

"But I'm having your baby!" she said desperately.

"I'll do whatever I can, Terri, except marriage. It wouldn't last. It could make us enemies and we have to do better than that."

"Would I be such a terrible choice for a wife?" she asked pitifully.

There was absolutely nothing wrong with Terri, nothing. The problem was with *him*. He found Terri attractive, desirable, funny and sweet, which was how he'd ended up with her at the time Vanni was married to his best friend. He'd have given anything to fall in love. When he thought of Vanni his blood pressure shot up and his heart pounded. When he thought of Terri, a smile came to his lips because she was so cute, because she made him laugh and because she was just plain good people. When he thought of Vanni, he was filled with fear and lust and ridiculous hope. He liked Terri; he was totally crazy for Vanni and had been for years. He didn't know why. He suspected an evil curse made him want something he could never have.

It wasn't fair to Terri; it wasn't right, nor was it the easy way. But it was what it was. His testosterone kicked up when he was with Terri because she was seductive, pretty, available and he was alone. He was just a man; sometimes it was nice to have a woman in his life. Calling Terri after Matt's death when the only woman in the world he wanted to be with was Vanni had been a critical mistake. But he'd been so desperate for understanding, for friendship.

"I think you'll make someone a wonderful wife, when you find the right man," he said. "I'm not the guy, but I'll do whatever I have to do to be a part of this, Terri. I won't run, I won't hide. And God, Terri, I'm sorry. I sure didn't mean for this to happen."

Joe Benson had been designing houses for Haggerty Construction for about ten years, and he was a little worried about his friend Paul. He'd seen Paul on a couple of job sites and they talked about getting together for a beer, but Paul had been evasive, distracted, morose and probably depressed. Small wonder—Paul had been through a lot with Matt's death. Joe suspected a pressure cooker. So he did what a good friend does—he pushed. It was time for Paul to let it out, so he could move on.

Joe went to a small, dark, quiet bar and waited for Paul to meet him. Joe had picked the place—somewhere a man could talk privately about the stuff that was eating his gut. He looked at his watch several times, wondering if Paul would be a no-show. Joe had a beer and was thinking about either trying the cell phone or just leaving when Paul finally lumbered in, head down, looking like he'd looked for too long now. The man was hurting all over.

"Beer," he said to the bartender before he even said hello. "Heineken."

"So," Joe said, picking up his almost empty beer. "You're in lousy shape."

Paul was quiet for a moment, waiting for his beer. When it came he took a long drink before he said, "Lousy."

"Listen, I thought maybe if we had a beer together, talked about it…"

"Believe me, you don't want to talk about this, Joe."

"Business okay?" Joe asked, nibbling around the edges of this situation. Paul's family business was a good little company that did quality construction. While Matt might've been Paul's best friend since they were kids, Joe had been closest to him since Desert Storm when they joined the same Marine reserve unit. They'd worked together since then and had gone back to Iraq together.

"Business is fine," Paul said. "That's not the problem."

Joe clamped a strong hand on Paul's shoulder. "You're not yourself lately, bud. You're having trouble moving on after Matt… He wouldn't want this, you know."

"I know…"

"Maybe it's more than Matt," Joe said. "I get the feeling something's really eating you."

"Yeah?" he asked with a somber laugh. "Jesus, you're psychic." He took another long drink of his beer.

"Any chance you could just go ahead and get it out

where we can look at it? Because if you're gonna drink that fast, you'll leave me in your dust pretty quick."

Paul shook his head. "I fucked things up pretty bad, Joe. I got myself in a mess I'm not gonna get out of."

Joe stared at him a long moment. Then he banged his glass on the bar and when the bartender came over he said, "Gimme another one of these, huh?" While he was waiting for a new brew, he turned to Paul and asked, "You have any idea how confusing you are right now?"

"Yeah. You should find more stable people to drink with."

"Well, until I do…"

It was a moment before Paul finally said, "I got someone pregnant…"

"No," Joe said, stunned. "No, you're too smart for that…"

Paul laughed. "I guess I'm not. Maybe I should sue Trojan, huh?"

"Oh, Jesus," Joe said. "Oh God. Someone special? I hope?"

"Nice girl," Paul said with a shrug. "But it wasn't… Aw, man. It was… We aren't… Shit. It was just one of those things. You know? I've known her about a year, but I've only been out with her a few times. We really didn't have anything going on except…"

"Oh, Jesus," Joe said again.

Paul turned toward Joe. "While I was in Virgin River last fall I didn't talk to her once during that time—that's how casual. I came back here all the time to check on the company, my dad and brothers, but I never even called her. And she didn't call me. But…"

"But…?"

"But I came home with my gut in a knot after everything that had happened in Virgin River and I called her. On instinct, probably. And guess what happened?"

"Oh damn," Joe said. "What are you gonna do?"

"What are my choices?" Paul asked, hanging his head. "I'll take care of her, of my kid. What else do you do?" He shook his head sadly. "I want it," he said. "I know— it's stupid. I should probably try something, like buying her off or something. Get her to make it go away—but if I have a kid coming, I want a part of that. I'm nuts, right?"

Joe smiled patiently. "I don't know. Maybe you're not nuts about that—but what about the mother? Is she someone you're going to be able to work with on that?"

"No telling," he said. "She wants to get married. I can't do that. I'm only planning to do this marrying thing once, and then it's going to be to a girl I love so much I can't stop myself. If I married this woman, it would really fuck her up, worse than she already is. I can't fake it—not something like this. I'd be the worst husband. You don't marry someone that fast."

"It's a big, permanent step," Joe said. "Only you know if you can make something like that work. If you can't, you do the next best thing," Joe said. "Man up. Take care of her."

"It's just that I slept with her when I love someone else. Why the hell did I do that? What kind of sorry bastard does that? What was I thinking?"

At this point in the conversation Joe was completely lost. Paul loved someone? It wasn't as though men got together and talked about women they had crushes on— they just didn't. They rarely said how they felt, period. He'd known Paul a long time and there'd been very few women. He was the quiet one; he kept back. Even when they were abroad together, at war, with a lot of tension to unload, Paul never hustled the women.

The bartender delivered Paul another beer, from which he took a deep drink.

"Love someone else?" Joe repeated.

"I'm such a screwup…"

"You love someone?"

"It's wrong, that's all. I had no business…"

"Paul. You *love* someone?"

"Yeah. I was a real horseshit best friend for years. Vanni. I just couldn't help it. I didn't want it to be that way, but—"

Joe drank a big gulp. He was prepared to help Paul through just about anything, but he never saw this coming. And why hadn't he? Probably because he'd have done for Paul what Paul did for Matt—stay with the widow through everything. "Whoa," he finally said. "Oh, shit."

"Oh, shit," Paul echoed.

"Vanni?"

Paul nodded grimly. "You wanna try to imagine how guilty I feel about that? I tried like hell to talk myself out of it. Sometimes I got damn close. I stayed away from them, you know? Because I could talk to Matt just fine, but if I saw Vanni, my heart wanted to explode… Aw God." He put his head in his hand. "And now I've got someone else pregnant. Think I could've messed things up any worse?"

Joe shook his head, but he was thinking—yeah. You could've been the dead guy. "You sure this baby is yours?" Joe asked. "Maybe it's not yours."

"I thought about that," he said. "Then I decided that was probably wishful thinking on my part. She said there hadn't been a guy in a long time, which is why she got lazy on the pills. And what did I have? Some poor old condom in the wallet that thought it was never gonna get out of that package. I probably wore a damn hole in it just getting in and out of the truck. Nah, it's mine."

"But you're gonna find out for sure before you set up the college fund, right?"

"Yeah. Sure. Right now, though, I don't want to push on her too hard. She's a wreck—a crying, miserable wreck. If she gets the idea I'm not going to step up—who knows what she might do. I don't want her to get an abortion just out of fear that I won't be responsible. I'm just going with the assumption it's mine, since it most likely is. We'll sort out the details later."

"What are you gonna do about Vanni?"

"Hell, what can I do? Vanni's in a lot of pain right now. You think I could help that pain go away by telling her I've loved her since the first second I saw her, but I went ahead and got some other woman I barely know knocked up?"

Joe smiled in spite of himself. "We might have to work on your delivery a little bit there, bud. Paul, keep your head here—it's not like you cheated on Vanni. Huh?"

"Why do I feel like I did?"

"You've got your feelings all mixed up in guilt and regret, that's all. You have to let yourself off the hook about Matt, for one thing. The way you feel about Vanni—it never messed with their marriage or your friendship."

He slowly turned his eyes toward Joe. "Even though I don't stand a chance with Vanni, I have to come clean about how I feel. It's still too soon after Matt. You gotta believe me, I never wanted anything bad to happen to Matt."

Joe gripped Paul's biceps. "Of course you didn't. But this business with Vanni? You owe it to yourself to know where you stand before you borrow all this trouble."

"Yeah," he said, hanging his head. "I'm sure she'll just try to let me down as easy as she can…"

"Then again, you never know," Joe said with a shrug. "Maybe it'll go your way for once. In which case, right after she says, 'I love you, too,' you're gonna have to say, 'I'm going to be a father pretty soon.' Whew." Joe gave a short, unhappy laugh. "That's gonna bite. I think, my friend, your ass is grass. Either way."

Paul leveled his gaze at Joe. Then he said, "We're gonna need a lot more beer."

Two

Mike Valenzuela was the Virgin River town constable and, as such, he spent a great deal of time driving the back mountain roads surrounding the town, taking in the lay of the land. It was important to know the people, the structures, the vehicles. There was no better way to identify something unusual. He got out of his Jeep and walked among trees and shrubs for a while, staying mostly out of sight. He came upon a half-buried semitrailer and metal storage unit that he'd seen before and had been keeping an eye on. There was a generator between the building and the trailer and camouflage netting stretched over the tops, strung between the trees, which identified it as a cannabis operation, but he'd never seen any activity around it. Mike kept his distance—they were sometimes booby trapped.

This time he happened to see a vehicle departing, and he recognized it—a Ford truck, dark, tinted windows. The driver was known around these parts as an illegal grower.

This guy had been seen around here a few times in the past couple of years. The bills in his pocket were large and carried the stink of freshly cut marijuana. When Mel had barely arrived in Virgin River, he had hijacked her out to a trailer, to an illegal grow like this one, to deliver a woman in childbirth, in trouble. Not so long after, Jack's cook Preacher's wife, Paige, had been abducted by her abusive ex-husband, and this guy had stepped in, whopped him over the head and facilitated Paige's rescue. But most significant, Mike had seen him just a few months ago meeting a Sheriff's Department detective in an isolated location. It had been a sheer accident that Mike had seen them. But the two men had probably handpicked the place—Virgin River had a reputation as dope free—there weren't any illegal growers nearby that Mike or anyone else knew about. It was a good place for a secret meeting.

Mike decided to check out the trailer. The guy had a relationship of some kind with a cop and Mike wanted to see what he had going on in there. From twenty feet away he could see that the padlock on the semi's door was left unhitched. Sloppy, was his very first thought. He stepped slowly, carefully, listening for a click, a trip wire. One rule of thumb—growers want to protect their crop from other growers, but really do not want to hurt or kill anyone from law enforcement, not even lowly, nonofficially recognized town constables like Mike. It brings a barrage of cops down on the area, busting up everything that might have otherwise been missed or ignored.

But Mike saw nothing; no trip wires, so he slipped off the padlock and slowly opened the door. The place was almost empty. There were a few medium-size plants right inside the door, so few he could grow that number legally with a prescription and permit. But, all the equipment was there for a large grow—pots, irrigation tubing, lights, fertilizer. The guy obviously bought what a grower would need for a large operation, but there was no real crop. So, he looked like a grower, but he wasn't growing.

Jesus, Mike thought. The guy was a narc. He was either

undercover police or a confidential informant. He'd set up something to look like an illegal grow, but it was a ruse. There was only one reason to establish oneself as a grower when you weren't—to search for other growers.

It took a long time to form even a nodding acquaintance with other growers, and even when they got friendly, they kept a safe distance unless they were doing business together, and they never showed each other their hidden grows. They spotted each other at the hardware store, the nursery, buying supplies, carrying around bags of chicken shit in the back of pickups. But they didn't have dinner parties with each other at their grow-sites.

The other reality was that local law enforcement couldn't keep up with the illegal crops; their resources and manpower were limited. They let a lot of cases slide when they were too small to make an impact, or to get a conviction. When a call came in about a hairdresser who was driving a Hummer and had a generator behind the house and a couple of windows blacked out, it was pretty obvious what she was doing, but the cops had bigger fish to fry—they were looking for over a thousand plants to press for a conviction or ten thousand plants to drive it into a federal crime, otherwise it was a waste of their precious time.

So—this guy, planting himself in the area, making himself known as an illegal grower… He must be looking for something. Mike slowly exited the trailer and once outside, looked around cautiously. Then he looked at the padlock. It had obviously been an oversight on the part of his buddy, the guy in the truck. If he didn't think it would compromise his operation, he'd find him, tell him he understood what was going on and to be more careful. Instead he removed the lock and pocketed it. He'd think about all this for a while before taking any action.

* * *

Paul sat in a small Italian restaurant in Grants Pass, staring into a cup of coffee, waiting. He looked up to see Terri enter the restaurant and he frowned slightly; there was no reason not to be attracted to her. She was a beautiful, tenderhearted girl. She had a very attractive figure that would soon blossom with motherhood.

When they connected eyes, he smiled and began to rise. Yes, she was a lovely girl, but she just didn't do to his blood pressure what Vanni did to him. The chemistry between them was nice, but it wasn't explosive.

He held a chair out for her to sit down. "Everything all right, Paul?" she asked a bit nervously.

"Sure," he said. "Fine. We haven't talked since last week. I apologize for that—I meant to get in touch sooner."

"That's all right. What's up?"

"I thought we should have a conversation. I think the shock and tears kept us from getting anything resolved the last time we saw each other." He reached across the table and gave her hand a pat. "I don't know how we could have avoided that."

"Resolved?" she echoed.

"You haven't really explained what you think I can do for you right now."

"Well," she said, "I just found out myself, so I haven't given it much thought, either. I mean, the best-case scenario didn't work out for me."

He held his tongue, not willing to go there again, but he looked down uncomfortably. Even if things never worked out with Vanni, which was what he feared, he didn't have the kind of passion for Terri that was required to take on marriage—it would rob them both. Yet, he was going to end up committing most of a lifetime to her because of the child. "How about insurance benefits? Financial obligations?"

"I have a good job, Paul. My benefits will see me through the pregnancy, though I haven't told my boss yet. I don't think that's the kind of help I'm going to need."

"How are you feeling?" he asked.

"Good," she said. "Excellent."

A waiter came to their table, offered menus, took drink orders, disappeared again.

"Go ahead," Paul said. "Take a look, see what you feel like for lunch."

"I'm, ah, not real hungry right now," she said.

"Well, you have to eat, Terri. You're supporting more than one body. One of them's growing." And then he smiled kindly. "I know—I'm a little nervous, too. I think we're going to have to try to get past the jitters if we're going to make this work."

"Sure," she said, looking into her menu. She lifted it up so he couldn't see her face and he noticed a movement behind the menu that suggested she wiped her eyes before lowering it again. "I'll just have a salad," she said. And then the waiter was beside them with water and iced tea.

"I'll have lasagna," Paul said. "And bread. And bring the lady a minestrone soup with her salad." When the waiter had gone he said, "Don't worry, Terri. This will get easier."

"I don't know about that."

"Have you told your parents yet?"

She looked down. "I told my mom. She and my dad are divorced and I haven't had that much contact with him." She looked up shyly. "She'd like to meet you sometime."

"Sure," he said, sitting back in his chair. "When we've had some time to sort things out a little, huh?" And she nodded. This woman was a far cry from the little pistol he'd met a year ago. She was subdued, self-conscious and submissive today. He didn't know her well but, at the moment, it was as if he didn't know her at all. As much as he wished this wasn't happening, he couldn't help but see it was harder for her than him. She'd been so good to him; he hated that he'd hurt her.

"Have you told your parents?"

He laughed a little. "No," he said. "I think I might hold off on that a while."

"Will they freak out?"

He chuckled again. "Oh, I think it'll surprise them. In fact, maybe I should brush up on my CPR."

"Ew," she said, a hand going to her tummy.

Paul immediately reached for her other hand and held it supportively. "Terri, you don't have to worry that they'd be a problem for you. My parents are real decent people. Even if they were thoroughly disappointed in me, they'd treat you and your child with kindness. Respect."

"Our child," she said softly after a moment of silence.

He was quiet, not responding to that. He might get there eventually, but he wasn't there yet. He kept thinking of this as her baby or his baby but not *their* baby. "You've seen the doctor?"

"Just once, to confirm what I already knew. I'm not very far along, you know."

He knew *exactly* how far along. Almost to the minute. "And you're due…?"

"November. The twentieth."

"Are you happy with the doctor?"

"She's nice." Terri shrugged. "She was recommended…"

To Paul's great relief, the food arrived. He waited for Terri to take a couple of bites before he started on his; he found himself watching her to be sure she was eating. They sat in uncomfortable silence. After a few minutes, he pulled a card out of his shirt pocket, turned it over to be sure it was the right one and slid it across the table. "My home, work and cell phone numbers," he said. "I have your home phone, but I don't know where you work. Secretary, isn't it?"

She nodded. "Legal secretary. I'm thinking about applying for a paralegal course."

"Hey, that's great," he said.

"Well, I was thinking about that, before…"

He liked that she had goals for herself, something to look forward to, since he wasn't giving her much in that department. And she would improve her earning potential, he thought. Because she was going to be a working mother. Or… Maybe she shouldn't have to work. His head started to spin. "Listen, it's hard to make long-term plans when you have a short-term complications, but if that's something you really want to do, don't give up on the idea. Not yet. Things always seem to work out the way they're supposed to. You'd be surprised."

"Right now it's a little hard to figure things out. Things like that…"

"What other things have you concerned?" he asked.

"Well, I live in a one bedroom, upstairs apartment. It's a nice apartment—you've been there. Single women like the upstairs—it's safer. Fewer means of entry, for one thing. But single mothers probably have a hard time with things like that. Babies come with a lot of gear. You know?"

Stroller, diaper bag, car seat, swing, Port-a-Crib, etcetera. He'd spent years watching his brothers tromp into their parents' house, hauling all the baby stuff. The stairs to her apartment were steep. She should live in a house, he thought. In a safe neighborhood. He thought he felt a migraine coming on. The first one of his life.

"I don't have any savings," she said. "I make a decent

living, not a great one. My office has paid leave for six weeks and optional time off without pay up to six months. I already feel like six weeks isn't enough. Not for a new baby. And then—what about child care? I haven't even felt this baby move—and I'm already worried about leaving him with some stranger. Or her. Him or her."

Paul smiled kindly. "Try not to worry about things like that yet, Terri. You're not going to have to make those decisions alone. Don't let it keep you up nights. I'll be pitching in."

"Pitching in? How?"

"Well, financially and, hopefully, with child care."

"Helping me pay for childcare? Is that it?"

"And with actual child care," he said, smiling.

"You thinking of sticking your mother with a baby?"

"I'm pretty good with babies," he said. "I was thinking of having my time with him. Or her."

"Oh," she said. "Thanks. That's nice of you."

Nice of me, he thought shamefully. She was talking like she expected to go it alone if he wouldn't marry her, and that almost made his cheeks flame. He had at least as much responsibility here as she did. She might've been lazy about those pills, but he'd used a condom he'd been carrying around for months, rubbing it thinner every time he slid into a chair. "I told you—you're not in this all alone. Can you think of anything I can do to help right now?"

"To tell the truth, just having you show a little interest helps a lot. Moral support, you know." And then for the first time since they sat down, she smiled.

"Ah," he said. "There it is. I know you don't think you have that much to smile about right now, especially where I'm concerned. I'll do whatever I can. It'll help if you tell me what you need."

"Right now? I want my baby to have a father. A good father. I just need someone to care."

"I care about what's happening with you and the baby. I'm kind of clumsy with words, Terri. I might've been a little too shocked to give you the kind of comfort you needed when I first found out, I'm sorry about that. Here's how I feel—I think it would be a mistake for us to try to make a marriage out of a very nice friendship, but if I'm having a child, I'm committed to the child. For life. I'll do my part because I want to. You can rest easy about that."

"How will your parents feel about that?" she asked.

"They'll feel the same way," he said. "Terri—I'm thirty-six. I'm past asking my parents for approval. What we're going to have to do here is find a way to work together." He swallowed. "We have to put the needs of the child first."

She sighed. "God," she said, tears sparkling in her eyes. "I never expected you to act like this. I thought you'd take off or deny it. But you're a good man, Paul. A real good man…"

If I was worth a damn, you wouldn't be unmarried and pregnant, he thought. "I'm sure I'll fall short a lot, but I'm going to do my best."

"Thanks," she said. "You have no idea how much that means to me."

When their lunch was over, he walked her to her car and she hugged him. "Just having you nearby—that's very re-assuring," she said. "I thought I'd never hear from you again. Sometimes this feels so lonely." Then she looked up at him and said, "Although I might not have a husband—I feel like I have a partner. Thank you, Paul."

"Um… Yeah. We'll work together on this, make sure everything is covered…"

Her arms still around his waist, looking up at him with

those large, sad eyes, she said, "Maybe I could make you dinner this weekend…"

He was shaking his head before she even finished. "We have to keep this in perspective, Terri. We're going to be parents together, I guess. But that relationship we had, such as it was? We're not going to have that relationship anymore. We can't. It'll only complicate a situation that's already complicated."

Her face fell. She looked down. "I see," she said.

He put a finger under her chin, lifting her face so their eyes met. "We're in this together, but we're not a couple. We never were."

She took a breath. "If I'm going to carry the baby, it would be nice if I also had some affection."

He put a small kiss on her brow. "You have that. As the mother of my child."

"You're absolutely sure nothing could grow between us? As we have this baby together?"

"Terri, my intention is to be good to you and be a good father. But if there was something more between us, we both would have known before this, before now. I think what we can be is good friends, good parents. Let's shoot for that, huh?"

"Sure," she said with a sad smile. "Sure. That's something, I guess."

"I'm sorry, Terri. That's all I have. And until that night I called, I think that's all you had. Think about it—we never even had phone calls. We just weren't that connected. Let's move ahead. Let's see if we can make this work for the child."

"Then I guess it'll have to be enough," she said, pulling her arms from around him.

For the first time he thought, what if she takes this child away from me? What if she finds someone else, some guy, willing to be that husband and father? And it puts me in the way? I have to know more about this kind of thing, he thought. I have to know what I can do about this.

"That's all I can ask." He gave her shoulders a brief, friendly squeeze. "I'll be in touch."

Vanessa had almost every piece of clothing she owned spread out across the bed. She was trying to pack for a trip to Grants Pass to visit Matt's parents and she wanted to look her best. She had asked her mother-in-law, Carol, if she would please invite Paul to dinner. She hadn't seen him since the baby was born and she'd so like to get his attention. But when Vanessa looked in the mirror, she saw a waist that was still too thick, breasts too heavy for her tops and thighs that felt like tree trunks. She couldn't get into any of her old clothes and she'd be damned if she'd wear maternity clothes. The baby was almost two months old.

Vanessa had always been sure of herself. Her mother had called her feisty, her father proclaimed her a handful, her best friends from the airline told her she was a fearless extrovert and counted on her to handle difficult situations with pilots or passengers. Matt had called her his fiery-haired vixen.

Around Carol, however, she lacked confidence. Carol was chic, perfect, successful and took self-assurance to the next level. Vanessa and Carol seemed to disagree on everything, and Carol managed to get her way at all times by wearing the most engaging smile. Carol Rutledge was possibly the only woman alive Vanessa had trouble standing up to. On top of that, Vanni felt she looked *fat*.

Frustrated, she pulled on a pair of jeans with an elastic waistband and her riding boots. She found her father in the great room. "Hey, Dad. Matt's asleep and should be down for another hour or two. Can you listen for him while I take a short ride? I won't be long."

"Take your time," he said, barely looking up from his book.

"Thanks."

At least she was finally cleared to ride again. The exercise and glorious spring weather was good for her spirits. When she got to the stable, she noticed the door to the tack room was ajar. She heard something, hopefully not a mouse. She pushed the door open a bit further and saw her younger brother Tom sitting on the bench, paging through a book. "Whatcha doin?" she asked.

He jumped in surprise, slammed the book shut and hid it behind his back. His cheeks brightened and he looked like he wanted to die. She walked into the room and reached behind him, grabbing onto the book. She withdrew *The Joy Of Sex.*

"Is this mine?" she asked.

He shrugged.

"This is *mine!*" she said.

"Come on, Vanni. Be a sport, huh?"

"Where did you find this?"

"I had to clean out the garage for Dad," he said.

"But this must have been packed up in my stuff," she said. "You're not, you know—using this to— You know."

"What?" he asked, brows drawn together in confusion. Then he caught her meaning; she thought he was using the pictures to beat off. "No! Jesus, no!"

"Well, then what?"

He shrugged. "I was just a little curious. That's all."

She flipped through the pages. It was an old book, but quite graphic. "You and Brenda aren't having enough joy?"

He frowned. Sometimes he hated his sister, and this was one of them. "No, if you must know."

"She suggest a little homework?"

"Vanni, we haven't done it, all right?"

Her head snapped up in surprise. She smiled wryly and lifted a brow. "Really?" she said, grinning.

He hated her. "Really," he said.

"You're a virgin?"

"Vanni, so help me—"

He was. He'd made it all the way to eighteen with his virginity intact? Whew, she thought. Either he wasn't as motivated as most boys his age or he was awfully well mannered. "Hmm," she said. And then it hit her—she and Dad were going to Grants Pass with the baby for the weekend. "Oh-oh."

"Don't start," he warned her.

"You have a date this weekend, Tommy?" she asked him.

He put his head in his hands. "God, why couldn't I have had a big brother…"

"I presume you're totally covered?" she asked him.

"I swear, if you say anything to anyone, especially—"

"*Are* you?" she asked a little hotly.

He looked up at her, almost bored. "Ask yourself—does the general's boy have the facts about sexual responsibility? Does he have a drawer full of rubbers and all the birth control information available to the entire U.S. Army? Does the kid know anything about STDs? You wanna give me a frickin' break here? Who is your father, huh?"

"Yeah, okay," she said. Dad probably started talking to him about this stuff when he was three. "I'll give you that one." She flipped through the pages. She held the book open, turned it around toward him and gave it back to him. "Read this page. Memorize this page. I'm going for a short ride."

She saddled up and took one of the horses out on the

trail along the river, thinking about how long it had been since she'd even anticipated making love. Matt left almost a year ago and didn't come back. She envied Tom, and she was frankly very surprised he was still untouched.

Well, if they were going to do it, she hoped her little brother would do a decent job of it. Vanessa's first time had been a waste of time. But hopefully Brenda would fare better—the page she had shown Tom was all about the clitoris.

Carol and Lance Rutledge had been down to Virgin River twice in the past few months. First, last December to bury their son on the general's land, an event that was understandably painful. If it wasn't bad enough that they'd lost their only son, they had nothing to say about where he'd be laid to rest, and Carol had been stiff and angry about the decisions she felt Vanessa had made alone.

The Rutledges came back right after the baby was born to see their first and what would be their only grandchild. Those visits had been tense until Carol softened toward the baby. Lance, however, was very like his son had been— laid-back, cuddly, humorous. Carol was cool; a well-decked and still sexy grandmother who said, "Ew," when the baby spit up on her blouse.

Now that the baby was almost two months, Vanni and Walt were going to them for the first time. Vanessa had always hated these visits, even when Matt was alive. Lance Rutledge was so easy to get along with, so unflappable. And, as men will do, Matt and his dad had hung together during visits and either ignored or were oblivious to any discord between the women.

Vanni wasn't the only one who had trouble getting along with Carol. She and Matt had laughed about how Carol blamed Paul for talking Matt into quitting college to join the Marine Corps. Paul had gone back to college and received his degree in engineering while Matt stayed with the Corps.

The Rutledge home was very large for only two people, up on a hill with a long driveway. Lance was an endodontist and Carol had been in real estate for many years and was a real mover and shaker in the business world of Grants Pass. They were certainly successful enough to retire, but they both enjoyed their work, social lives and vacations.

Carol Rutledge didn't look her age. She was fit and trim with thick auburn hair that she kept short, manicured nails, a drop-dead wardrobe and, though this was supposed to be a secret, a woman who had benefited from a face-lift that made her look more a youthful fifty than sixty. Before pregnancy and childbirth, Vanni felt equal by comparison, but at the moment, breasts straining at her shirts, hips too wide and waistless, nails trimmed down short, she felt dowdy and insecure.

When they arrived, Lance grabbed the baby immediately, thrilled to be nuzzling him, while Carol stood beside him, giving the baby a few pats. Vanni wandered into the house, so large and richly decorated. Eventually she moved down the hall to peek into the room Matt had used as a teenager, looking at all the memorabilia. It was everywhere—pictures, letters from high school teams, trophies, posters, airplane models. It hadn't been preserved, but restored, like a shrine. A small framed picture of the baby now rested on the bureau, as though Matt would be back directly. It almost made Vanni cry.

That evening, as Lance turned steaks on the grill with Walt and the women keeping him company on the deck, Vanni learned that Carol had at least one surprise in store for her. "I've invited another guest to dinner tomorrow night, Vanessa," Carol told her. "A friend of ours—a young doctor I met through work. His name is Cameron and he's just darling."

"Carol, you're not fixing me up, are you?"

"Of course not! But I didn't think it was too soon for you to meet someone. If you two get along, maybe sometime in the future…"

"She's fixing you up," Lance said.

"That's what it sounds like," Walt agreed.

"Oh God," Vanni said miserably.

"Stop it, all of you. We've had Cameron to dinner before, and he's charming. I happen to like him."

"But, Carol, Paul will be here, too."

"I know, honey," she said brightly. "I'm sure they'll hit it off. I know if Matt were with us, *he'd* like Cameron."

How could she do that so well? Make Vanni feel guilty, as though Matt would want her to meet this Cameron? Vanni's pants immediately began to feel more snug, her belly rounder, her breasts bulkier and nails choppier. Not only would she look plump and awkward to Paul, but to *two* men. She tried to be ready for anything with Carol, but hadn't counted on something like this, a new widow with a baby just two months old—and two bachelors at dinner. One of whom she had been missing. Missing so much.

"We should talk about what you're going to do next, Vanessa," Carol said smoothly. "With just the smallest interest in real estate, I could take you into our firm. Your hours would be flexible for the baby, the market is good right now and it would set you up for a successful career." She beamed. "I could work alongside you until you get your sea legs."

Vanni wanted to die. She'd rather have an ax firmly planted in her skull than work with Carol every day. "I'm…ah…afraid real estate doesn't appeal to me much."

"You can't be thinking of flying again," Carol said. "Really, I could help. At least give it a fair chance."

"Thank you," she said. "It's too soon for me to think about that now. I'll let you know."

"Good girl," Carol said, patting her knee and smiling.

Vanni was a long way from having Carol figured out. She seemed to be trying to be helpful, but she plowed through every polite, "No, thank you," and did as she pleased. She'd made Vanni's wedding a nightmare with her interference. Vanni's mother had been deceased only a short time, and Carol had wanted to step in and help in that role, but she took over. Carol had not liked the colors of the bridesmaids' dresses; she preferred coral to pale green. She thought that by getting a consensus from the bridesmaids and paying for the ones she liked, the problem was solved, but Vanni had *hated* them. When she had appealed to Matt, he had said, "What's wrong with orange, or whatever that is? They look nice and the girls like them."

"They clash with my hair!" Vanni had tearfully argued. "There will be pictures…"

"Look," said Matt, the peacekeeper. "She doesn't have a daughter—why not let her have her way about some small things?" So Vanni let it go and Carol changed the flowers from Vanni's favorites of calla lilies to white roses and baby's breath. She added a hundred names to her guest list and presided over the parties and wedding reception as though it was her wedding, cracking the whip over caterers and florists like an Egyptian pharaoh. "Try not to worry about little things," Matt had said. "Really, she's only trying to help. She just wants everything to be beautiful for us." It left Vanni in the uncomfortable position of fighting it out with her future husband or future mother-in-law.

As for Saturday night's dinner, Cameron arrived a good half hour before Paul for drinks. Vanni suspected Carol had told Cameron six and Paul six-thirty, and because of that, Vanni didn't give Carol any credit at all for coming up with a perfectly nice man in her attempted setup.

But the man who stood before Vanessa had absolutely no excuse for being thirty-five and single. He was so good-looking, he could make a woman pee her pants. He was six feet with dark hair, heavy, expressive brows, sexy dimples in his cheeks when he smiled and teeth so white that they almost made you gasp when he grinned. And he grinned hugely when he met Vanessa.

"You're a doctor, I'm told," Vanni said.

"Uh-huh. Pediatrician," he answered, and she thought— Carol has outdone herself. What is sexier than that? Gorgeous, hot and loves kids.

"And yet, you don't have children?"

"I couldn't work that in. But now that I can, all the good women seem to be taken. But hey, I still have time to father children. Don't you think?" Grin.

Oh, yeah, she thought. He could probably father them like mad.

Carol directed them to a pair of chairs in the living room—soft comfortable chairs that faced each other at angles, separated by a side table, where they could sit and get to know each other. Walt and Lance resumed their positions on the deck after initial introductions so the couple that was not being fixed up—ha!—could have this intimate little session to themselves. Carol delivered them drinks and then pleaded business in the kitchen, leaving them alone.

So Vanni had what turned out to be a very pleasant conversation with Cameron Michaels. She would have taken him for a doctor at once—though he was broad shouldered and nicely muscled, he was dressed like an ad for *GQ*. But a children's doctor? He should have some spit-up on his shoulder or poop on his shoe to be convincing.

He worked with a group of pediatricians in town and had just bought his first real house—through Carol of course. It was much too big for just him, but he couldn't resist it. And he didn't think it was too late to fill it with family, if the right woman came along. He asked about Virgin River and the baby, and was fascinated by her home birth with a midwife. She relented to herself that there was nothing about him not to like when the doorbell rang and she began to rise.

Carol flew out of the kitchen like a rocket, aimed at the door. "Stay put—I've got it. That will be Paul. Cameron, you're going to *love* Paul," she said on the fly.

Vanni looked around. This pair of chairs was isolated from the rest of the room; a cozy little corner. There was no place for Paul to sit and join them and again she thought—*I always underestimate my mother-in-law. She has everything worked out. She must plan to shuffle Paul out onto the deck with Walt and Lance right after introductions.* But that's not what Vanni had in mind.

She stood. "Excuse me," she said to Cameron. She walked toward the door just as Paul was coming in.

The minute she saw him, she felt more alive. Paul was not as pretty as Cameron, nor even Matt, for that matter. Paul had rougher good looks. He was probably six-two, his arms so strong thanks to years of physical labor in home construction, thick sandy colored hair still cut short in that military fashion. He was tan, had big, gentle hands, a strong jaw and when he saw her his dark eyes sparkled. She nearly ran to him, hugging him close. He lifted her off the ground.

"God," he said. "It's so good to see you." He put her on her feet. "Let me look at you. Aw, Vanni—you look fantastic. It's like you never had a baby!"

"You're such a liar," she laughed.

"Can I see him?"

"You bet," she said, grabbing his hand and dragging him right down the hall, leaving Carol standing at the door, her greeting ignored. Although little Matt was asleep, she picked him up and presented him to Paul. "Here you go," she whispered.

Paul didn't hesitate. He took the baby into his arms, holding him close. "He's so big." Then he met Vanni's eyes. "He looks just like him, doesn't he?"

"He does." She smiled. "I've compared their baby pictures and it's just a little Matt all over again."

Carol's head popped in the room. "Come on, you two," she said cheerily. "We have company." Then she quickly withdrew, clearly expecting them to follow as ordered.

Paul questioned with his eyes and Vanni sighed. "Carol's trying to fix me up," she whispered.

"Really?" Paul said. "How do you feel about that?"

"Not thrilled. But it's not the guy's fault—and he seems like a perfectly nice guy. Still…"

"Just not ready?" he asked.

"Not for him," she said, frowning. "Come on, we'd better be social or we'll be punished. Paul," she said, touching his arm, "I've missed you so much. Tommy misses you, too. You have to come to Virgin River soon. Will you?"

"Sure," he said with a smile.

She took the baby from him and put him back in the crib. Then, pulling him by the hand, took him to the living room. When they got there, Cameron stood. Carol intercepted Paul, taking his hand out of Vanni's to pull him forward. "Cameron, this is Paul Haggerty—he was my son's best friend. He and Vanni are like brother and sister."

The men shook hands, but there was obvious and

instant reticence in the postures of both—Carol wasn't fooling either one of them. Vanni took it upon herself to drag a chair across the room so that Paul could join them, catching her mother-in-law's frown out of the corner of her eye. And when they were all called to dinner, Carol seated them according to her plan—she and Lance occupied the heads of the table, Paul sat beside Walt, Vanni beside Cameron. And that's how they remained.

Another of Carol's talents was to grease the conversation and she got people talking quickly so that there was no tension at her table. She might as well have had a notebook beside her with specific questions and topics for each person at her table, so that each one had his turn to talk. She did drop into the conversation several times that Paul was Matt's best man, Paul and Vanessa had been friends for years, Paul worked construction and oh, yes, Cameron was a *doctor.*

One topic Carol couldn't control was Virgin River, and at her table were three people who loved it there and extolled all its virtues—from redwoods, mountains, valleys and rivers, to the little bar and grill run by Jack and frequented by friends and neighbors, reuniting Marines, playing host to hunters and fishermen.

After dessert and coffee, Paul was the first to leave, which Vanni thought must thrill Carol. But that was all right, because Vanni walked him outside. They hugged. "I don't think of you as a brother," she said.

He laughed. "And I don't think of you as a sister."

"I wish she hadn't done that."

"Carol does as she pleases. She always has. We understand that," Paul said.

"I wanted to spend more time with you. How are you, really?"

"I'm doing okay. And you? Really? How are you doing with missing him?"

"I'll always miss him. I miss him as much as you do, Paul."

"Yeah," he said, hanging his head for a moment. "Can't really help that, can we?"

"But I don't cry about him so much anymore. Matt wouldn't want that—and he said so—he made me promise. Plus, Mattie takes a lot of energy, and gives me so much joy. I'm riding again—which is a wonderful diversion. Come down, Paul. For a weekend. Soon. Ride with me…play with the baby."

Carol stuck her head out the front door. "Vanessa? I think I hear the baby."

Vanni took a breath. "Well, Carol, you can pick him up if he's crying. Or you can tell my dad—he knows what to do."

"Oh," Carol said. "Sure. But you'll be in soon?"

"*Soon,*" Vanni said, an irritated edge to her voice.

The door softly closed and Paul chuckled.

"God," Vanni said, rubbing her temples with her fingertips. "That woman…"

"It's just Carol. No one takes her seriously."

"To their peril," Vanni said. Then she looked up at Paul. "Please—come to Virgin River soon. We all miss you. Especially me."

"Yeah, I should do that. So—what do you think of that guy? At least she found you a doctor."

She laughed. "She should get credit for that, huh?" She shrugged. "He seems pretty nice—and it's not his fault he got fixed up with someone who isn't interested."

"You'll be ready one of these days."

I'm ready now, she wanted to say.

He kissed her forehead. "I'll give you a call. We'll set something up—get together soon."

"Please," she said, very conscious of the fact that she had been the one calling him since the baby's birth. And then she watched him go. So, I may not think of him as a brother, but he still thinks of me as his best friend's wife. She feared that might never change.

Tommy and Brenda had gone to a lot of trouble to arrange a whole night alone at the Booth house while the general and Vanni were both away in Grants Pass, but all that preplanning backfired. Brenda was edgy. Maybe scared. Not ready for it. Tom could tell after fifteen minutes that this wasn't going the way he thought it would. The way she had said she wanted it to.

So, he throttled back. "Relax," he said. "We'll just watch a movie. We don't have to do anything."

"You'll be disappointed," Brenda said.

"No, I won't," he lied. "I told you a hundred times— we're not going all the way until you're ready. We'll just watch a movie and curl up. We'll sleep in our clothes. I'm not going to push you."

"I'm sorry. I don't know what makes me like this. I thought I'd made up my mind."

"You don't have to apologize, Bren. Not to me. I like that you're giving it a lot of thought. I want you to be sure, because afterward, you have to be happy about it, not all screwed up and guilty. There's no other way it can be, not for us. Since we're in for the night—should we pilfer a couple of the general's beers and put on a movie?"

"Yeah," she laughed.

"You pick the movie, I'll pick the beer."

Of course it had to be a chick flick; a real groaner at that. But what the hell, if it made Brenda happy, it made him happy. Halfway through the movie and the beer, the kissing started and he thought, God bless chick flicks. They might be boring, but they sure did warm up the girls.

They reclined on the sofa and pressed their bodies

tightly against each other, kissing wildly, openmouthed, tongues going nuts. He got hard, of course. By now she was used to that and she liked it, grinding against him very nicely, getting some good feelings of her own. This sort of thing had been happening between them for a while now, and it was extremely satisfying. And while Tom didn't want her to do anything she'd regret, he definitely wanted to try out what he'd learned on page ninety-seven. Shew— the magic button. He just wanted to touch the magic button one time. Just for a second. Just to see what happened.

He lifted her shirt, unhooked her bra and felt her soft breasts. She loved it when he did that—it caused her to moan and wiggle. She was getting so hot that he wondered... "Bren," he said breathlessly. He put a hand over her crotch on the outside of her clothes. "Can I just touch you here? Just with my hand? Nothing else—just my hand?"

"Uh-huh," she said against his lips. "If you want to."

He thought he might die, he was so excited. He opened the snap on her jeans and slipped his hand down and down, slowly and gently, over her flat tummy, over her soft mound, just a little further, into a place that was dark, secret, hot and damp, looking for a spot described on page ninety-seven as the trip-wire for the female orgasm. He felt a small, hard knot and when he made contact she gasped and pushed against his hand. The very second he made contact, it electrified her. "Tommy," she said in a weak whisper.

"Yeah, baby," he whispered against her lips. "That feels nice, doesn't it?"

"Ooooh," she moaned, moving back and forth, up and down. "God..."

Go for it, Brenda, he thought. Just go for it. He rubbed a little harder, reached a little further, making contact with her opening with one finger just as his other finger stayed with the magic button. He gave it a great deal of personal attention—teasing her, softly touching, roughly rubbing, all according to the suggestions in the book. The whimpering sounds she made were almost as if she was crying; panting, squirming, writhing. And then, *kabam!* She froze, her breath caught, and against his hand he felt the most amazing clenching sensation. "Oh God," he whispered. "Oh my God."

"Tom," she said in a breath. An exhausted, happy breath. She collapsed in his embrace. "How did you know to do that? That wonderful thing you just did?"

He was not about to say his sister tipped him off. "Everyone knows," he lied. He wondered if half the male population was as dismally uninformed as he had been. "Come on," he said, getting off the couch. "We're going to get more comfortable and do that some more."

"I'm not sure I can even stand up," she said, limp and satisfied.

"Come on," he laughed, pulling her up.

He took her to his room, the chick flick still playing in the background. They fell onto his bed, kissing. He pulled off his sweater and then hers, holding her close with her breasts against his chest and thought—I have waited forever to feel this. It didn't take him long to coax her out of her jeans, because she wanted his hand on her again. His pants coming off was another story. When he started to remove them, she said, "I'm not sure."

"Let me know when you're sure, because I'm pretty much past sure…"

"Maybe you could just put it close. Touch me there a little bit. I mean, don't put it in yet, but touch it there a little bit, let me get used to the idea…"

"I can do that," he said, but he was positive what she was asking for was beyond the realm of possibility. Whatever, it got him out of his pants, and he was desperate.

They'd never gotten this far before, but she had always said she wanted the first time to be special and if what she had out on the couch wasn't special, he just couldn't imagine how much more special it could get.

He got a condom out of the drawer and ripped it out of the package. "Brenda, we're gonna play it real safe, honey. We don't want to get too close and not be double safe, huh?"

"Okay," she said, laying back, eyes closed, ready to be pleasured again.

He laughed in spite of himself. "You like that, don't you?"

"I like that."

Sheathed and ready, feeling as if he didn't unload this gun he'd be walking on three legs for the rest of his life, he lowered himself to touch her in the place where he might enter her if he ever got permission, and then he put his fingers on the magic button and went to work. This thing was like a miracle, he thought. Response was instant. Faster than instant. She was moaning, writhing, panting. And he was dying, barely touching her, holding out, holding back. The strain was starting to make his head pound. He was in complete misery while she clearly neared ecstasy once again. Finally he just lost his mind. "Let me," he begged. "God, Brenda. Let me in."

She tilted her pelvis up a little and he slid forward. He put a hand under her bum while he massaged with his fingers. "Okay," she said. "Okay."

"You're sure?"

"I'm sure," she said.

He slid into her slowly and discovered it was everything he dreamed it would be. He was surrounded by this tight, hot, wonderful body, cinching down on him. But he wasn't crazy, he wasn't letting go of that miracle button.

He worked it, and beneath him she went crazy. It didn't take long before she rose against him, froze, gasped and the spasms he had felt against his hand before were nothing compared to what he felt when she tightened around him while he was right there, inside. She went off like a missile and, although she might have been totally unaware, so did he. It was the most amazing experience of his young male life. It shook him up so bad his whole body trembled. He pulsed until his brain was emptied.

"Ooooh," she said.

That was how much more special, he thought. And he croaked, "Good God."

"Oh, Tom," she said, not unhappily. "We did it."

"We did," he said, breathless.

"That was… Holy cow, Tommy. That was awesome."

"Awesome," he agreed, almost faint.

"Let's do it again," she said.

And that's when he learned that for women, all things are possible, and for men, time is required. There was recovery involved. Women, apparently, could just hop back on that bus, while the men were left to deal with a flat tire. He committed that to memory—these gorgeous creatures needed no time to get ready again. "You might have to give me a couple of minutes."

"How long?" she asked impatiently.

"Well, Brenda, we could always time it…"

She giggled. "Did you know it was going to be that wonderful?"

"If I had known, I don't think I could have waited as long as I did."

"I love you," she whispered.

"I love you, too," he said, kissing her softly. And what he thought was, who knew? This girl who had been saving it, waiting for that special moment, so nervous about the whole thing—well, once she was a little stimulated, she was hot as a pistol. On fire. Completely and totally into it, giving and giving, trusting, wild and wonderful. And people said the first time wasn't that great for a girl. Hah.

She snuggled closer to him and giggled.

"What's so funny?" he asked.

"In the end, you begged."

He sighed. "I did. I begged. I'm sorry—I swore to you I'd never beg."

"I'm okay with it now," she laughed. "I don't think you'll have to beg again."

"That's a relief." He kissed her again. "I want to tell you something." He brushed her hair back from her face. "When I go into the Army, I'm planning to be faithful to you while I'm away. Until you tell me you want to be free of commitment or have somebody else or something, I'm going to be thinking that you're my girl."

"Aw, Tom. Are you sure you want to do that?"

"Baby, I'm totally sure. I was sure a long time ago. I didn't just say that to get into you, Brenda. I think you know I'm not the kind of guy who wants to screw around. This means something to me. I love you a lot."

"I want to be your girl," she said. "I love being your girl."

"Maybe someday, when we're older, when we've finished school, maybe it'll be more than that…"

"Maybe I'd like that." She smiled. "I was going to save this for a surprise—but what the heck. I've been applying for scholarships and university admissions. I'm applying mostly in New York."

"Near the Academy?"

"Uh-huh. I don't want to be away from you, Tom. Not any more than I have to."

"Brenda," he said, pulling her close. "That's such good

news." He slipped his hand down and put his fingers on her. "Were you timing it?"

"No, why?"

"I think enough time has passed…"

"Good," she said. "That's good. Ooh, that's very, very good."

The general, Vanni and the baby returned home on Sunday night. Tom had washed all his linens, cleaned the house, taken care of the horses and was doing homework when they arrived. Vanni appeared to be extremely tired and irritated, so he went straight to her and took Mattie out of her arms. "Was it fun?" he asked.

"Depends on your definition of fun," she said, walking down the hall to her bedroom.

Tom followed her. "What's up?"

"I asked Carol if she'd invite Paul—I haven't seen him since the baby was born. And she said sure, but she also invited another guy. She was fixing me up. It was very uncomfortable. I didn't really get a chance to talk to Paul."

"What kind of guy?" he asked, holding the baby against him.

"A nice guy. Under any other circumstances, I would've enjoyed meeting him. A doctor. A pediatrician from Grants Pass."

Tom laughed. "Well, I guess if you'd just fall for him, you could marry a guy who's really *somebody,* move to Grants Pass, be close to Granny and make her look good."

A stricken look came over Vanni's face. "God, that's it! She's trying to hook me up with a local guy—to get us under her thumb again! But then—" She stopped for a minute, thinking. "Why doesn't she try to hook me up with Paul?"

"Paul is a construction worker. He was an enlisted

Marine. Vanni—this new guy is a *doctor!* Besides." He shrugged. "Paul wouldn't put up with Carol's shit. I know him. He wouldn't. Not for long, anyway."

Carol had never approved of the fact that her son hadn't finished his degree and spent his career in the fighting Marines; she was pretty snobby about things like money, credentials, prestige. She had always intimated that Vanni's decision to be a flight attendant, even though she had a degree, was copping out. She had always asked Vanni what she planned to do *next*.

"You know Carol," Tom laughed. "The sooner she can get you fixed up to her satisfaction, the less she has to worry you'll fall for someone who makes his home in Florida. She always covers her bases. She's on top of everything." He put the baby in the crib. "How'd he do on the trip?"

"Great. He's a good little traveler."

"How's my man Paul?"

"Good. I keep begging him to come back here, but he won't commit. Hey, how was your weekend?"

He ducked his head. "Nice," he said. "We watched a movie."

"You seem pretty relaxed," she said, smiling.

"I'm not telling you anything," he said.

"That's okay, buddy. But everything around here was all right while we were gone?"

"Yeah." He left her bedroom. Then he stuck his head back into the doorway and said, "Know what I said about wishing I'd had a big brother? I take it back." Then he disappeared.

Three

Less than a week after visiting Grants Pass, Vanessa opened the front door of her father's house to find Cameron Michaels standing on the stoop. "Well, hey," she said, surprised.

"Hey," he said, showing her that sexy, dimpled grin. "I decided to have a look at this little town, see what all the fuss is about."

"No kidding? You should've called. We could have made some plans together."

"Is it too late for that? Because all I was going to do is drive around the area. Maybe drop into that bar you and Paul were raving about. If you're not too busy…"

"Kind of far to come for just a look around…"

He shrugged. "I have a couple of days off in a row, which I pay for by being on call all weekend, and I thought, what the heck? It's worth a shot. It was a very last minute idea."

She lifted one brow and folded her arms over her chest. "You didn't have any trouble finding the house."

He had the grace to laugh a little and avert his eyes, caught. "Carol," he said.

"Look, you should understand something. I respect my mother-in-law, but she can be a little pushy and—"

He put a hand on her arm to stop her. "Hey, Vanni—I asked her. And I didn't call on purpose. I didn't want to give you time to think of an excuse. I thought if I popped in unannounced, you might just cave in. Spend a couple of hours with me. You can punish me for bad manners later."

She smiled at him. "I look forward to it."

"So, do you have a little time?" he asked.

"It's not as though I'm busy, but I have a baby who still nurses a lot."

He tilted his head and grinned. "I'm pretty comfortable around babies."

"Yeah. You would be, huh. Well, come on in."

He stepped inside and looked around. "Wow," he said. "What a great place. From the outside it looks like just an ordinary house."

"My dad had the inside completely gutted and remodeled while he was serving his last tour in the Army. Last summer he and my brother Tommy came out and I joined them in the fall." She walked into the great room and found her boots sitting by the chair. She sat down to pull them on while Cameron went to the window and looked out at the stable, corral and pasture. "Do you ride?" she asked.

"I did years ago. I haven't been on a horse since I was a teenager."

"Do you like horses?"

"I have great respect for horses. The last time I was near one, he stepped on my foot. Broke it."

"Yeah, they should beep when they back up. You have to be alert." She stood and smoothed her jeans. "Mattie is due to wake up any second. I can feed him, change him, beg him to behave and we could take a little run around Virgin River. How's that sound?"

"Like just what I was hoping for."

"You're very presumptuous, you know," she said, but she smiled.

He smiled right back. Confident. "You're very beautiful, you know."

She felt her cheeks grow instantly warm. "Help yourself to something to drink from the kitchen. I'll see about the baby."

"Take your time. Put him in a good mood."

Forty-five minutes later they were underway in Walt's big Tahoe. Cameron had come to Virgin River in a Porsche and there was no room in it for a car seat. She drove him out Highway 299, through the redwoods, then out to sit at the Virgin River where there were only a couple of anglers, it not being the best time of year for fishing. She explained the seasonal sports—fly-fishing in the summer, salmon in fall and winter was best, bear and deer hunting season from September through October, waterfowl hunting season October to January. Forest fire season from June through October. In summer the hikers and campers were all over the place.

While they were looking at the sights she learned that Cameron hailed from Portland, went to undergrad and medical school at Stanford and had parents, one brother and one sister in Portland, both married with kids. He did his residency in family medicine, then decided pediatrics was his first love. "I've disappointed my parents in the area of grandchildren, but I don't think they should be so quick to write me off."

"Certainly not," she said. "Mel, my midwife, and her husband, Jack, didn't marry until he was forty—and they're expecting their second now. Jack says each one makes him feel younger. Mel frowns at him when he says that. I think the babies are a little closer together than she likes."

"Medical school and residency is consuming. I was thirty by the time I was ready to go into practice, and that wasn't simple. I had big time bills to pay off and it wasn't easy to find an existing pediatric practice in Oregon that needed me."

"And it had to be Oregon, huh?" she asked.

"At the time, I thought it had to be. I've become a lot more flexible since then."

"But you like your practice?"

"Yeah, good docs. One woman and two men—outstanding physicians."

Vanni continued the tour by driving him up into the foothills where sheep and cattle grazed, down through the valley where vineyards were just beginning to come to life and finally, as the afternoon had aged, they ended up at Jack's. By the time they got there, Matt was fussing and demanding dinner. Before she could get to him, Cam had him out of the car seat and was jiggling him against his chest. Cameron had the diaper bag slung over his shoulder as well, taking charge. It was nice, having a man do that. Not just any man could—it would take someone special to be so confident with a baby. At that moment Vanni realized she'd been feeling so alone, even with her dad's continual support. She missed her man. She would like to have a partner. She would like Mattie to have a dad.

When they walked into Jack's, she was pleased to see the dinner crowd included her people, her friends. The first order of business was to introduce Cam to Jack. "This is Cameron Michaels, Dr. Michaels, a friend of Matt's parents. And Cameron, this is Jack."

Cameron deftly held the baby against his chest while

he shook hands. "Pleasure," he said. "I've heard a lot about this place. I thought I'd drive down and look it over."

"Welcome," Jack said. "What can I get you?"

"How about a beer?"

"You got it. Cameron, meet Paige," he said just as Paige came from the back. "She's married to the guy who really runs this place—our cook, Preacher."

"Nice to meet you," he said. "Looks like the stork is on the way."

"Pretty soon now—this summer," she said, smiling sweetly.

Jack put a beer on the bar and Vanni said, "Paige, can I impose on your hospitality for a few minutes? I should nurse Mattie—we've been out driving around all afternoon and he's hungry."

"Sure. You know the way."

Vanni reached for Mattie and said, "Jack, can you introduce Cameron to the crowd? I'll be back in a little while."

She went into Preacher and Paige's apartment behind the bar, settled herself into the soft leather chair and nursed her baby. In spite of her determination to be strong about the events that shaped her days, she felt the sting of tears. This guy had driven all the way from Grants Pass on the chance he might see her. She'd had a lovely time with him. But where was Paul? She'd give anything to see him, but he didn't even call. Because, she reminded herself, I'm not a woman to him. I'm his best friend's wife; he loves me like a sister, whether he'll admit it or not. Hadn't it always been like that?

Cameron was introduced to Preacher, who was very welcoming, if a little distracted by the dinner he was working on. With him in the kitchen was Christopher, who he introduced as his son except the boy called him

John. Then there was Mike Valenzuela and Jack's sister, Brie. Cameron sat down with them for a little while and learned that Mike was a former police detective and sergeant and Brie a former prosecutor. He hadn't imagined he'd be meeting professionals with such sophisticated educations and experience in a little place like this.

He was offered dinner of pork loin, garlic mashed potatoes and green beans, but he chose to wait for Vanessa to finish with the baby. And while he waited a beautiful young pregnant woman came in, followed by an old man carrying a young child. The woman leaned across the bar to kiss Jack and then Jack took immediate charge of the child. Cameron was soon introduced to Doc Mullins and Mel Sheridan. A couple more tables were pushed together and they joined the group while Jack, with his son on his hip, fetched the high chair from the kitchen.

"Mel, I'm fascinated by your work. You deliver most of the town, I'm told," Cameron said.

"I don't know about that. I do for the women who don't have a lot of insurance. Or for special cases like Vanni. She doesn't look it, but she's kind of granola natural—she wanted to give birth at her father's house, and she did a fantastic job. Textbook. In fact, we had a wonderful birthing party."

"A birthing party?" Cameron asked.

"It kind of fell into place. When I was called out, Jack let it slip that she was in labor, so Preacher and Paige packed up dinner from the kitchen and closed the bar. Mike and Brie came out in case any of the children needed tending. With the general and Tommy, Jack and Davie, and of course Paul helping with the delivery, we were a full and happy house. It was great fun."

"Wasn't it a little melancholy? It being Vanni's late husband's child?"

"That's the thing about babies, Cameron. They give you such hope. Such joy. That's why I love this business."

He laughed and said, "You obviously take it personally."

She rubbed her swollen middle. "Not much longer. Jack promises we're going to take a break after this one. And I've promised that if he doesn't keep his word, I'm going to shoot him in his sleep."

While Doc had his whiskey, Cameron grilled him with questions about small town doctoring, asked Mel about some of her other cases and quizzed Mike about local policing. He asked Brie what kind of law she was practicing and learned that while she'd been a prosecutor in Sacramento, she was now occupied with small cases that included divorces, property closures, water rights disputes and such. The county D.A. used her as a consultant on some cases, as well. He was completely fascinated, completely enchanted. Before long Vanni joined them, Mattie full and content against her shoulder. Cameron reached for the baby across the table and said, "Get yourself a beer. Lucky for you, it's good for nursing mothers." When Jack joined them, they were ready for dinner together.

Cameron enjoyed this excursion far more than he expected to. He had hoped for an opportunity to be with Vanni on the excuse of checking out Virgin River, but it had happened that he was delighted by the town, the people and the families that gathered at Jack's.

"Are you staying at the general's?" Jack asked him.

"No, there's a motel in Fortuna that has plenty of room."

"You're welcome to stay with us," Vanessa said.

"Or, I can give you another option," Jack offered. "The cabin Mel and I just moved out of is empty and furnished, and right here in Virgin River. Clean sheets on the bed, towels in the bathroom, but no food in the fridge. If you want it, it's yours. I can even fix you up with food and drink to take with you—I'm tight with the cook."

"Are you sure?" Cameron asked.

"Absolutely. Let me draw you a map—the door is never locked."

"Hey, that's fantastic of you. Since it's already kind of late, I really appreciate it."

"I'll write my number at home and at the bar on this map," he said, drawing on the back of a napkin. "Give me a call anytime. If my family isn't visiting and using the cabin, you're welcome to it."

"What can I pay you for it?" Cameron asked.

"Don't be ridiculous. It's there for friends and family." He finished with the map and turned it around to Cameron. "Any friend of Vanni's is a friend of ours."

The night was still young when Mike and Brie said good night. Not long after Jack fetched his son out of the high chair and swept his family away. Doc Mullins said goodbye.

Cameron had enjoyed his dinner while holding Mattie against his chest; he had loved looking across the table at the beautiful and sexy Vanessa. Julia Roberts, that was what she was. Leggy, full-breasted, her hair a reddish hue shot through with blond, her smile wild and spontaneous, her laugh loud and free. He didn't think he'd ever run into a woman like this in his life.

"What do you think? Time for you and the baby to go home?"

"Yeah," she said, and she smiled as though she'd had a good time.

"Let's get going. If you're not too busy tomorrow, maybe you could introduce me to the horses before I head back to Grants Pass."

"Sure," she said. "We should go for a ride. The bear are just coming out of hibernation with their cubs, and the deer have fawns now."

"I would love that. But is it dangerous? Any worry about the bear?"

"Not for you," she said with a big laugh. "I carry a rifle. I'll take care of you." Then she laughed some more.

As they stepped out onto the porch of the bar, Cameron stopped and listened. He looked up at the sky—the magnificent clear, black sky studded with a billion stars—and heard in the background the gentle strumming and picking of a Spanish guitar. He held the baby against him with one arm, put the other around Vanessa. "Do you hear that?"

"Hmm. That's Mike. Miguel, actually. Isn't it beautiful?"

He leaned closer to her. "I love this place."

When Jack had settled Mel and Davie into bed, he crept into the kitchen and placed a long-distance call. Paul Haggerty answered and Jack said, "Hey, it's me."

"Hey, Jack. What's up?"

"What's up is that doctor. Cameron what'shisname. Down here putting the moves on Vanessa. Paul, I'm not going to tell you twice. You better not let this happen."

"Jack, listen. She's not ready."

"You sure it's not you who's not ready?"

"I was there when she met him—at Matt's parents' house. She told me—she's not ready."

"But the problem is, he's ready. Buddy, don't be stupid."

"Yeah," Paul said. "Okay. Thanks."

When they hung up and Jack went back to Mel, crawling into bed and slipping his hands under the T-shirt to feel her belly, she said, "You're doing it again, aren't you?"

He sighed. "I thought you were asleep."

"You're getting in the middle of stuff."

"Mel, I wasn't going to tell you anything. But I'll tell you, because you're so goddamn nosy. Paul loves her."

"I know."

"Well then why are you all over me?" he asked.

"Because this is for them to work out. Not you."

"But Paul loves her. And this Cameron—he's nice, he's a good guy, he's slick."

"It's for them to work out."

"Well, what the hell do you expect me to do?"

"Stay out of it."

"But what if…"

"Stay out of it. You are such a mother hen."

"We owe Paul…"

"Jack, if Paul isn't smart enough or aggressive enough or in love enough to handle this, maybe Vanni is better off with the pediatrician."

"How can you *say* that?!"

"Because I'm the wise one in this marriage," she said. "And you're too emotional."

"Aww."

"Why did you give Cameron the cabin if you don't like seeing him with Vanni?" she asked.

"Because. He wouldn't be under the general's roof tonight."

She laughed. "Jack Sheridan, you are such a *sneak*. I never give you enough credit."

The next morning Cameron was invited to breakfast with Vanni and the general, then out for a ride. It was a weekday and Tommy had school so the general was needed to baby-sit. Vanni took him out alone, just the two of them. Vanni rode Tommy's horse, a gelding named

Chico who was pretty frisky, while she put Cameron on their gentlest mare, Plenty, short for Plenty of Trouble. There were four horses in the stable, all of them good riding mounts with the general's stallion, Liberty, being the most difficult to manage. As promised, she had a rifle strapped to her saddle.

"You ride, shoot, have babies at home—I thought you grew up in the city?"

"When you grow up with the general, you learn lots of interesting things. And my mom was a farm girl."

"When did you lose your mom?" he asked.

"A few years ago. She was a real amazing, strong, beautiful woman. She did so many things—besides riding and hunting with my dad, she was also a licensed pilot and followed Dad all over the world. When both my brother and I were born, Dad was off in one conflict or another. For some of the most important times in our family, he was missing—and she never once complained or ragged on him. She admired him, respected the work he did—they were true partners. She was the strongest woman I've ever known." She took a breath. "She was killed in a traffic accident in D.C. Such a waste, such a loss."

"I'm sorry," Cameron said. "You take after her, don't you?"

"I hope I do. That would be the highest compliment you could give me."

They rode along the river for a while, enjoying the crisp air, the spring foliage. Ponderosa, fir and pine spattered with sequoia rose high above them, covering the foothills. "You're doing pretty well," she observed.

"If this old girl doesn't make any fast moves, I can hang in there."

The river trail opened up into a field and Vanni stopped. "Look," she whispered. On the other side of the field was a small herd of deer, two bucks, several doe and their babies. "It's not even the best time of day to see them." A gentle breeze caressed her; she removed her hat and lifted her hair off her neck to take advantage of the cooling. "What's not to love about this place, huh?"

"Fantastic," he agreed. "Can we take a break? Get off and walk around?"

"Sure," she said, dismounting. She led Chico toward the river edge and he lowered his head to drink. Cameron did the same with Plenty.

Vanni gazed off at the deer. She could feel Cameron move up behind her; the warmth of his body was right there, though he didn't touch her. Then one hand caressed her upper arm while the other pulled her hair away from her ear.

"This is the first time I've ever driven two hundred miles to see a woman I've barely met, Vanessa," he whispered.

Vanni bit on her lower lip. She'd been sleepless last night, thinking. She knew Cameron was interested in her, but that wasn't enough. Her mind was on Paul.

She turned around. "I'm very vulnerable, Cameron," she said by way of warning.

"I know. I'll treat you carefully."

"You're going to have to treat me patiently," she said. "I'm not prepared to be any more than friends right now."

He laughed and shook his head. "I'd sure like to see where this could go."

"Friends," she said. "Or nothing at all."

He cocked his head and smiled. "Do friends kiss? Just to see if there's…chemistry?"

She shook her head. "They do not. Not yet."

"Yet is a much more encouraging response than nothing at all. I guess friends kiss when they've gotten to know each other and there's trust. Do I have that right?"

She sighed deeply. If not for Paul, she might be attracted to Cameron. He was handsome, sexy, sweet. "It's too soon. My mother-in-law jumped the gun, introducing us and—"

"Nah, it's not Carol's fault. I'm jumping the gun because…" He shrugged. "Because you're beautiful and fun. So shoot me."

She smiled at him. "I don't think your life is in danger for calling me beautiful and fun. That's very nice. But I'm not getting involved with you right now."

"You said we'd be friends," he argued. And he reached out to stroke her hair.

"Behave like a friend, Cameron. Like a Boy Scout."

He laughed at her. "You're asking way too much. I'll behave, but let's keep this in perspective. I'm a man. You're a damn sexy woman."

"Do I have to worry you won't mind your manners?" she asked, lifting a brow.

"Absolutely not," he promised. "You're in charge."

"Then no touching until… No touching."

He put his hands in his pockets. "Whatever you want, Vanessa. I'm just going to—"

At that very moment, Plenty whinnied, backed away from the stream and bolted.

"Shoot!" Vanni said. "That little troublemaker." She pushed Cameron away, grabbed the reins of the gelding, leaped into the saddle and said, "I'll be back." She directed her horse after Plenty. "Don't go away," she yelled, laughing, as if he could go anywhere, stranded as he was. She whipped at Chico's rear flank with the end of the rein.

Vanni took off at a gallop and burst into a dead run, leaning low in the saddle and urging the horse with her heels, going after the mare. The deer lifted their heads and headed for the trees while Plenty ran across the meadow, clearly enjoying her freedom. But Plenty was no match for Chico, who was the second fastest horse in their stable. On the other side of the meadow, Vanni caught up with her, leaned out of her saddle to grab a trailing rein, pulled back on the runaway and slowed her down.

She trotted back toward Cameron, delivering his horse, laughing in spite of herself. "I forgot to mention, she's a runner. She sneaks off."

"That was no sneak. That was bold-faced."

"Yeah," she laughed. "You gotta love a woman with nerve."

Vanni had known for a long time that her best friend Nikki was in a troubled relationship and that it wasn't going to last. Cameron had barely departed, headed back for Grants Pass, when the phone rang and Nikki said. "It's over."

"Oh, honey," Vanni commiserated. "Something major must have happened. Big fight?"

Through her tears, Nikki said, "It started out as the usual fight—me saying I needed a relationship with a future and him saying he wasn't ready because of his short, terrible marriage years before we met. Then he dropped the big bomb. A couple of years ago, without telling me, without talking to me about it, he had a vasectomy."

"What?" Vanni asked. "But how could he do that without you knowing?"

"I was gone on a couple of trips for a little over a week. He only needed a few days to recover completely. I never suspected." She sniffed into the phone. "Craig was afraid I'd stop taking my birth control pills and try to sneak a baby out of him. He said he was sorry, but he didn't want a family and was tired of fighting about it."

Vanni sank into the chair by the phone. "This is just...*unbelievable*."

"He said that if what we have isn't good enough—just like it is—then it would probably be better for both of us if I just made good on my threat. Vanni," she said with a whimper. "When did he become that kind of man?"

Vanni grimaced. It was tempting to say he'd always been like that—selfish, insensitive, an egotistical bore who took a lot more than he gave. But Nikki's heart was breaking so all she said was, "Oh, honey. I'm so sorry. The creep."

"My dad helped me move out—all my things are in my parents' garage. I'm staying with them while I look for something to rent. I'm calling from the car. I don't have to work for a few days. Can I come up?"

"Of course," Vanni said. Nikki and Vanni had been best friends since they both started at the airline. They'd gotten each other through a dozen rotten boyfriends, but nothing like this. Nikki had been with Craig for five years.

Nikki had been Vanni's maid of honor when she married Matt. Vanni would have been lost without Nikki to talk to, to lean on when Matt was deployed to Iraq. When he was killed, she spent hours on the phone with her best friend. Of course she would try to comfort Nikki now.

"I feel so stupid," Nikki said. "Why'd I let myself fall in love with him?"

"Can we really help who we love?" Vanni asked with a sigh. "Just get up here. We'll eat fattening food, play with the baby, tease Tom, ride the horses and stick pins in a Craig doll. Nikki, you know it's time to move on—he wasn't good enough for you. And what he did—that was so deceptive, you could never count on him again."

"Vanni, what's wrong with us?" Nikki asked. "Why are we stuck loving men who don't love us?"

With a shock of clarity, Vanni gulped. Why indeed, she

asked herself. *And then we feel so stupid, like such failures. It was wrong, all wrong.* "We're going to work on that, my friend. Both of us."

Joe Benson got a call from his old friend, Preacher, explaining that he and Paige had done a lot of talking about their growing family. Right now they were housed in Jack's old apartment behind the bar—a small L-shaped bedroom/living room built for a single man—while Paige's son, four-year-old Chris, was sleeping in the bedroom above the kitchen that had once been Preacher's. With a baby coming and maybe more in their future, they had to do something. They thought about buying a larger house, but in point of fact, Paige and Preacher loved living right where they worked. As far as either of them could foresee, Preacher would always be the cook and manager at Jack's bar with Paige as his right hand.

Preacher had talked to Jack about allowing him to enlarge their quarters. Jack thought it was a fine idea; it would at least double the value of the property. He made Preacher a deal—if Preacher would build on, Jack would get together a contract to make him a full partner and half-owner. If the bar and grill and attached home was ever sold, the proceeds would be split.

Before any further discussion could occur, an architect would have to be consulted to see if building on was feasible. There was room; the property on which the bar sat was comfortably large. Preacher wanted to find a plan that would give them plenty of space and wouldn't disrupt business too much during renovation.

That's where Joe came in. If Joe thought it was a good idea and could draw up some plans, Preacher could begin to look for a builder.

Joe loved an excuse to spend a day or two with Jack and

Preacher. And it made him feel good when his buddies asked him for help; he always gave them a deal on the designs. So Joe said, "I'll have to see the space and the structure, do some measuring. It's not raw land, Preach. An add-on is a little complicated—the basic structure has to support additional square footage. Tell you what. I'll drive down tomorrow, stay overnight…"

"Tomorrow?! Oh, man, that's great of you!"

"For you and Paige, Preach? It's an honor."

And that's what he had done. When you're an architect with your own small firm, you make your own hours, design at three in the morning sometimes, if that's when the inspiration hits. So he made it to the bar before noon on Thursday, had a nice long lunch with Mel and Jack, Preacher and Paige and they talked about the expansion. To Joe's surprise, Preacher was the one with the most elaborate ideas—he wanted a large great room and dining room, a play area for the kids, a small office for himself, plus a total of four bedrooms. And, he wanted the family connected, not separated the way it was—right now they had to go through the kitchen and up the back stairs to get to Christopher's room. Preacher wanted it to become a house like any other house—with a clear path to all the rooms. And maybe a fireplace. The only thing he didn't need was a kitchen.

Joe got busy right after lunch, sketching, measuring, tromping through their quarters and around the yard behind the house. There were some beautiful big trees back there he'd rather not disturb and a huge brick barbecue he'd prefer not to move. He could see the potential for a nice, spacious house connected to the bar by one door through the kitchen, and with two separate entrances independent of the bar. The downstairs could be enlarged enough to hold a great room, master bedroom and bath, dining room and serving station with storage for their personal dishes and dining accessories, with a breakfast bar separating the serving station from the dining room. He could install a food-warming tray, dishwasher, trash compactor and sink in their serving station for convenience. He left the laundry room right where it was, just inside the door to the bar. The addition of a small office would square out the first floor and support additional bedrooms and a loft on the second floor. They could entertain friends and have family meals there. The stairs to the second floor could be removed to enlarge their ground space and they could put an open staircase to the second floor in the great room.

There was room upstairs for two additional bedrooms and an open loft. The bedrooms would be large enough for more than one child, with walk-in closets. Their total living space now was twelve hundred square feet and he could turn it into three thousand without even breathing hard.

The only inconvenience would be that Preacher and his family would have to move out for most of the construction. Joe knew they had some options—one of which was Jack and Mel's cabin. Small, but serviceable for four to six months.

It was almost five by the time Joe was ready to discuss these possibilities with Preacher, Jack and Paige. Since Jack was busy serving, and Preacher and Paige were busy cooking and clearing, he would enjoy a beer while waiting out the dinner crowd. He had a large sketch pad and notebook full of measurements that he flipped closed for the time being.

That's when he saw her, the profile of a small brunette with long, silky dark hair that went halfway down her back. Right beside her, leaning toward her and talking in her ear, was Vanni. For a moment Joe was struck dumb. Then, gathering his wits, he said, "Vanni?"

Vanni looked up, past the back of her friend's head and said, "Joe?"

"Yeah," he laughed.

She immediately left her beer and her friend and came over to him. Of course they'd met more than once, the last time being at her husband's funeral. Joe knew Matt; he'd met him in Grants Pass when he'd been home on leave. They'd been introduced by Paul.

"What are you doing here?" she asked, embracing him.

"A little design work for Preacher and Paige," he said. "They want to enlarge their home. You know—to accommodate the baby and then some." The thought that immediately came to mind was the conversation he and Paul had had a couple of weeks ago. Paul was in love with this woman and had messed it up so bad, he probably didn't stand a chance. Joe peered around Vanni at the woman with her, but he saw only her profile. She was exquisite. Beautiful beyond words.

"Nikki," Vanni called. "Come here." When Nikki approached, her smile very small and maybe shy, Vanni made introductions. "Meet Joe, a friend of Matt's and Paul's. Joe, meet my best friend, Nikki."

He put out a hand and she laid hers in his. "Nice to meet you," he said.

"A pleasure," she said, but then she glanced down.

"Gee, this is terrible," Vanni said. "If I'd known you were coming, I'd have made plans to do something special for you. I would have cooked dinner or something."

"I'd be glad to buy you a little of Preacher's dinner if you'll stay," he offered. "I'd really enjoy that."

"Thanks, that's sweet. But I've left my dad baby-sitting for a while and I had Preacher pack us up something to go. I'm still nursing—my escapes are very brief. I could get Preacher to add to it if you'll come out to the house."

"I wish I could, but I have to discuss building plans with these folks tonight."

"Doggone it, Joe. Next time, please let me know you're coming. I'd like to spend some time with you, too!"

"It's a promise," he said. "And I'll be back. Guaranteed." But will she be back? Joe wondered. Nikki. He wouldn't forget that name.

Right at that moment, Paige came out with a big sack holding their dinner. Vanni fished for her wallet and Joe said, "On me, sweetheart. Amends for not calling you ahead. A mistake I'll never make again." He pulled a couple of twenties out of his pocket, peeled them off, laid them on the bar and reached for the take-out sack to pass to her. "Enjoy the best food you'll ever eat," he said to Nikki.

Nikki gave her head a small nod while Vanni said, "Gee, thanks! I sure didn't expect that." Then she leaned toward Joe and gave him a kiss on the cheek. "That's very sweet."

"Enjoy," he said. "Nice meeting you, Nikki," he said, wishing that he'd had a little cheek press from her. But what he got instead was another small nod.

They left and he went back to his beer. It was quite a while before Jack was freed up enough to walk down to his end of the bar, wiping his hands on a dish towel. "How'd you do there?" he asked, glancing at the sketch pad.

"I think I have some good ideas here," Joe said. "With the right builder, this could work out nicely."

"The right builder is the problem. When I was finishing my house, I couldn't find squat around here. That's why I called Paul."

"Well, I know some people," Joe said. "I might be able to help you with that. First, we have to see if you three like my ideas. And, by the way, who was that woman with Vanni?"

"Girlfriend from the flight attendant days. I gather they're best friends who flew together for years and she's up here to visit."

"Jesus," Joe said. "She's incredible."

"Based in San Francisco," Jack said with a smile. "She's going home tomorrow."

"Well, so am I." He lifted his beer. "Here's to another close call."

Jack laughed.

Joe took a long drink, Jack wandered away and Joe thought, I've been to San Francisco five times in the past year and I never saw anyone like that. Why not? This is a town of six hundred. I shouldn't see anyone that amazing here—I should see ten or twenty so gorgeous in the city.

Jack came back with his coffee cup. Joe merely looked up at him and said, "This place. It's kind of scary."

"Tell me about it," Jack said, taking a sip of his coffee. "I found Mel here. That stuff isn't supposed to happen."

Four

Paul knew that Jack was right—he'd have to make his presence felt in Virgin River soon. He couldn't let the doctor be the only one there when Vanni came out of mourning and was ready to get on with her life. So he called the general and asked if it would be all right to come down for a weekend visit, to see the family and the baby.

He got up early on Saturday morning and made the drive in record time. He pulled up in front of the house and what he saw from the driveway gave him pause. Vanni was dressed in well-worn jeans, chambray shirt with the sleeves rolled up, boots and a Stetson, standing out in front of Matt's grave. She pulled the hat off her head and shook her hair down her back. Then she wiped at her eyes. Damn it, he thought. I told Jack she was still in that dark place.

He left the truck and, rather than going to the front door, he went out to the grave. As he came up behind her, she heard him and turned. Then she quickly turned back and wiped at her eyes with the back of her hand. He walked up behind her and put his arms around her waist. "Having one of those days?" he asked gently.

"Yeah," she said. "Every once in a while I just get so lonely."

"I know, Vanni. It's going to be okay."

"Dad's worried about me coming out here to tell Matt about it." She laughed uncomfortably. "He wishes I wouldn't do this."

"It's okay to do this," he said.

"I'm not brooding. Really. Sometimes I can't think of anyone else to complain to."

"You can always complain to me," he said.

She turned around and looked at him; for a moment her eyes flashed. "And how am I supposed to do that? I hardly ever talk to you. I almost never see you."

"I'm sorry, I meant to do better. I know I went missing for a while after leaving here. It's complicated, Vanni. I can explain."

"Any more complicated than losing a husband?" she snapped. "Oh God, I'm sorry. I don't know what got into me just now. My God, you lost your best friend—I'm sorry. Paul, you don't have to explain…"

"Yeah, I think I do. After we buried him and I stayed on for Mattie—I was kind of like a grenade with the pin out. I hadn't unloaded, and man, I really needed to. I was a little out of my head, Vanni. I didn't use the best judgment. I had to take a time out, some space—a few weeks. I had to get a grip on things, you know? And I didn't want everything between us to be about grieving over Matt. There's a lot more between us than that."

"There is?" she asked hopefully.

"Well, Jesus, we delivered a baby together." He rubbed a thumb along her cheek under her eye. "Sorry. My hands are so rough."

"No," she said. "No. Your hands are fine. Do you have any idea how much I've missed you?"

"Not half as much as I missed you. We've been through a lot together, you and me." He reached for her hand. He couldn't tell her now, here, in front of Matt's grave with the general waiting right inside the house. "Go get cleaned up. Tom's probably got a big date tonight, but I'm going to take you and your dad out to dinner."

She smiled. "Anywhere special?" she asked.

"Your favorite bar and grill. I made a reservation."

By the time Paul got the general, Vanni and baby to the bar, the few customers were finishing up their early meals and leaving. Tables were pushed together and the usual crowd gathered around. The April nights were still cold, so the fire was lit in the hearth. Jack divided his time between the tables and his favorite spot behind the bar. Paul drifted back there and said, "Look at your wife, my man. She's almost more baby than woman. And she's got a kind of wild look about her. Her cheeks are awful pink."

"I know," Jack said. "We just had a doctor's visit—John Stone said if we turn her upside down we might see the color of Emma's eyes. Stand back. She's going to go early. I've been driving myself crazy trying to keep her still. I'd like to keep this one inside at least a couple more weeks."

"She's real animated. Kind of like Vanni was that day she made me watch the childbirth movie."

"Yeah. I'm not experienced enough to know how early is too early. I thought about calling John…" Then he smiled at Paul and said, "I see you made it right down here. Good thinking. You make any progress with Vanni?"

That changed Paul's expression. "When I drove up to the house today I caught her out at the grave, crying. I told you—she's still on real shaky ground."

"My advice—which, by the way, Mel says I am not,

under pain of death allowed to give—is be sure you're around when the ground stops shaking."

"Jack, I should talk to you about a couple of things. This whole business with Vanni—it just keeps getting more complicated."

"Yeah?"

"For one thing, I have some pretty stiff competition…"

"Oh, yeah? Join the club, my brother."

"Yeah, that's right. Mel's husband was a doctor."

"Yeah," he said. "An E.R. doctor. A saver of lives who, by all accounts, was also perfect in every other aspect of his life." He swallowed. "He was neat, smart, humorous and probably great in bed. A fucking god."

"You didn't stand a chance, intellectually speaking," Paul said.

"I know it," Jack said. "And yet…"

"I need to talk to you about a couple of things," Paul said. "Maybe you'll point me in the right direction."

"Paul, you don't need my input. You just have to tell her how you feel."

He hung his head briefly. "I don't think it's gonna be that simple. I think I might come by in the morning. So we can talk."

"Come by the house then," he said. "I try not to get too far away these days. I haven't been coming into the bar until a little later in the morning."

When Paul sat beside Vanessa again, she looked at him with sparkling aquamarine eyes and he almost melted. His very next thought was how he'd probably see those eyes flash in pure rage when he unburdened himself. She had a fire in her, and he'd seen a hint of that earlier today, out by the grave. It caused a shudder to pass through him. Then he noticed her hand was resting on her thigh, right next to him, and he reached for it, holding it under the table.

It was still early when they got back to the general's house. Vanni took a little time alone with the baby, nursing him and settling him for the night. While she was busy, Walt built a fire. Then he went down the hall, leaving Paul alone in the great room.

Paul wanted a drink, but he didn't dare. He was afraid it would loosen him up, make him either talk too much or do too much. Then Vanni joined him. She'd brushed out her hair and it fell in silky curves onto her shoulders, glistening in the firelight, making him want to scrunch it up in his hands.

"Where's Dad?" she asked, curling up in the big leather chair beside his.

"He fixed up the fire and left the room," Paul said. "It's kind of early for him to turn in, isn't it?"

"Maybe he'll be right back. Can I get you anything? A nightcap?"

"No, thanks," he said a little nervously. "So—rumor has it the doctor was here last week…"

She smiled. "Mel was right. If there's anything you want to keep secret, get out of this town!"

"Did you want that to be a secret?" he asked, lifting his brows.

"No reason for that," she said with a shrug. "I didn't invite him. Yes, he came to town. I showed him around, had dinner at Jack's, took him for a ride. He's not great on a horse." She grinned.

"How is he off the horse?" Paul heard himself ask.

She laughed at him, then said, "Cameron seems to be a very nice man. But then, we knew that."

"A woman in your position—you'd probably be very interested in someone like him," he said.

"Well, Paul, I have to admit, it's nice to finally have a man pay a little romantic attention to me. It's been a very

long time. I know I haven't been widowed all that long—
but it's been almost a year since…" Her voice trailed off
and she looked away.

"Since?" he said, talking like a man who had had that
drink.

She let her gaze drift back with a mysterious half smile
on her lips. Vanni almost laughed, wondering how poor
Paul would react if she said, "Since someone melted my
bones with an orgasm…" A secret chuckle escaped her.
Paul was sweet and affectionate, but far too taciturn. She
reminded herself to treat him gently. He was very cautious
with women. If he weren't, he'd have been married years
ago with a flock of children by now. "Since anything,
Paul," she said. "Anything at all."

"Sorry," he said, dropping his chin. "I didn't mean to
get so personal…"

She laughed at him. "Paul, you weren't this shy with
me when I was delivering Mattie. What's going on?"

He took a breath. "Vanni, Vanni… I have things to
explain. Difficult things. I know I don't seem like the kind
of guy who'd have complications in his life. I seem more
like the kind of guy who has no life at all. But before
Matt… Before I came down here to finish Jack's house…
I went out sometimes, you know?"

She laughed a little. "Paul, even though you never
said anything, and I know you're kind of shy around
women, I assumed—"

"Stupid," he said, interrupting. "I'm mostly stupid
around women."

"Uncertain, maybe. But under the right circumstances…"

"Exactly," he said, almost relieved. "Under the right circumstances things can happen that you just don't expect."

She frowned slightly. "Paul, I understand you went out

with women. Why wouldn't you? You're a handsome, single man."

"It's about me being a little absent since Mattie was born… I have a situation to work out."

"A situation in Grants Pass?" she asked.

"Yeah," he said, rubbing a hand across the back of his sweaty neck. He took a breath. "Before I came down here last fall, I went out with a woman a couple of times. Just a casual thing. Nothing serious. But then the whole goddamn world shifted, Matt was killed, Mattie was due, I stayed here with you, we got a lot closer during that time. It might've been all about Matt and the baby at first, but that's irrelevant—we got real close. You and me."

"As close as brother and sister?" she asked him softly, hopeful about what could be coming.

"A lot closer than that, Vanni. At least in my mind. Then I went back to Grants Pass and not that much had changed there. I had changed, boy had I changed, but things back home were…"

"The same?" she asked. And she thought, there's a woman in Grants Pass. Someone who had perhaps become important to him. "That woman you went out with a couple of times—when did you meet her?"

"Why?" he asked, perplexed.

"When?"

"God," he said, rubbing his sweaty palms on his jeans. "I don't know. About a year ago, I guess."

"A *year* ago? Jesus, Paul. Why didn't you just *tell* me!"

"Tell you what?"

"There's a woman! All this time, there's been a woman!"

"No. No. There was just this woman I saw a couple of times and…"

She stood up abruptly. "That wouldn't be complicated."

He stood, as well. "I had a few things to figure out, Vanni—that's why I wasn't in touch for a while. And now I have an…*unexpected* situation at home I have to work out, but I'm going to get that under control and I'll be here a lot more, I promise."

"Oh, for God's sake," she spat out. "Just say it. You're involved with someone and it doesn't work into your plans to spend time in Virgin River!"

"That's not it," he said nervously.

"You know everything about me! Yet you couldn't even casually mention you were seeing someone at home?"

"It's not like that. Listen, I just need some time on this. Some patience. Because I really intend to do better by you than I have. I know I haven't been here for you like I meant to be and—"

"Stop!" she said. "I haven't asked you for anything except to stay in touch! Stop whimpering!"

He scowled. His neck got red. "I'm not whimpering!"

"Well, you sure as hell aren't talking! Man up!"

"I'm trying! But you're doing all the talking for me!"

She had a few more hot retorts, but bit her tongue against them. She pursed her lips. He had been in Virgin River for months, but he went back to Grants Pass almost every week for a day or two. He had said it was to check on the construction company he'd left in the hands of his father and brothers. And to check on *her?* It must've been pretty hard on her to be asked to understand he had to be away so much, tending to his best friend's *widow.* Imagine now, being told he'd have to make frequent trips to Virgin River to make sure the widow and baby were doing all right. Talk about complicated. Well, she wasn't interested in that kind of relationship.

"I think you're trying to tell me there's a woman back in Grants Pass who's counting on you. You have obligations there."

"Yeah," he said weakly. "But, Vanni, I have obligations here, as well. You and Mattie, you're awful important to me…"

Being referred to as an obligation should have made her want to cry, but instead it made her furious. "Well, don't worry your little head. We're getting along just fine— better every day. You have a life in Grants Pass. I wouldn't want to get in the way of that."

"You're not listening," he said, his voice raising to match hers. "I want to be here with you, as often as possible," he said. "I'm doing my damn best!"

"It sounds like you have other things, other people you'd better pay attention to."

"Listen, things can happen that you don't plan, don't expect!"

"Oh really?" she asked sarcastically. "Tell me about it," she said. She hadn't expected her husband to die, or to fall in love with Paul. If there was one thing she knew about the men in her life—her father, her late husband, Paul and all the guys who seemed to gather around him—they didn't make commitments lightly, and once a promise was made, they *never* broke an oath. "I'm sure you'll get everything straightened out," she said. She tried to keep the angry edge out of her voice, but she was thoroughly unsuccessful. "Please, you have no *obligations* here. We'll be fine. I don't know why you didn't just tell me—a long time ago! Did you think I wouldn't understand you had to get home because there was someone there? Someone who was counting on you?"

"It isn't like that!"

"You could have just told me!"

"Vanessa! For God's sake—" Paul attempted.

Walt walked into the room. He looked stricken, startled. "Are you having an argument about something?"

"No!" they both said.

"Oh," Walt said. "Poetry, I guess. Some new kind of poetry?"

Vanessa hissed and Paul just shook his head.

"I hear the baby," she said, whirling out of the room.

"I hear something, too," Paul said, leaving in the opposite direction, charging out the front door and letting it slam behind him.

Walt was left alone in the great room in front of a blazing hearth. "Well," he said to himself. "Glad to know that wasn't an argument."

Vanni cursed herself. She'd lost it. She hadn't given him much of a chance to explain, but then the time involved in him actually getting to the point might have taken a lifetime. She lay on her back on her bed, fully clothed, the back of her hand on her forehead. She kicked her feet furiously and groaned. She had a short fuse sometimes, she knew that. It rarely reared its ugly head like that, but Paul had frustrated her so much. How could you love and hate the same thing about a person? She adored that he was kind of shy and reluctant; that a woman had to mean everything in the world to him for him to speak at all, for him to embrace, smile, kiss. But she hated that he couldn't take charge! Stake his claim! He should have told her long before Mattie was born that there was a special woman in Grants Pass, and that he had to get back to her!

Vanni was not going to be like Nikki, hoping to change a man's mind. Or his feelings. More to the point, she wanted nothing to do with another woman's man!

Then, despite the fact that her cheeks were still hot with anger, she cried. Then damned herself for crying.

Paul had a hard time sleeping through the night. He'd made a half-assed and totally unrehearsed attempt to explain things to Vanni and, in his bungling, left it undone, maybe worse. Of course, having the general right down the hall, maybe ready to walk into the room right at the moment Paul announced, "She's pregnant!" didn't help. But that was no excuse.

He had to get this done, and the very thought curdled his stomach.

If he was going to be a father he would be an involved father. He was more than committed to taking on little Matt and he hoped…no, he *prayed,* Vanni could accept his child as part of the package. But he had no idea how to go about telling her. Vanni scared him to death. She had a helluva temper.

It was just after dawn and the household was quiet. Paul dressed, made a pot of coffee and took a cup with him down to the stable, thinking of having a little morning chat with the horses. Maybe he could get some advice about the embarrassing fact that he was thirty-six years old and was still trying to figure out how to get close to a woman he'd been in love with for years. Not to mention the fact that he had this little complication of another woman having his baby.

He was leaning against a stall when he heard a sound. He turned around and saw that the tack room door was ajar. His first thought was that the general might be up, so he pushed open the door. There, seated on the bench, elbows on his knees and head down, was Tom. His jacket was tossed over the bench beside him and his shirtsleeves were rolled up. "Hey," Paul said.

Tom lifted his head. His expression was troubled. "Hey," he said.

"You been out all night?" Paul asked.

"I was out late, yeah. Then at Brenda's. I got home a couple of hours ago."

"Have fun?"

Tom shuddered. It was unmistakable. "Yeah," he said in a breath. "Yeah."

"What's the matter, bud?" Paul asked.

"Nothing," he said. "Just thinking."

"Yeah? Maybe if you think a little louder, I can help."

Tom studied him for a long moment. "I sincerely doubt it, Paul."

"Try me. I'm older. Maybe I've been down this road."

"If you have and you're still single at thirty-six, I really don't want your advice," he said glumly.

"Whoa," Paul said. "What the hell's this? Thinking about marriage at eighteen?"

"Nah. Not quite that. It's just that… Brenda, man. Jesus, I love that girl. I didn't think I could love a person this much."

"Doesn't sound exactly like a bad thing so far. Unless she doesn't feel the same way…"

"Whew," Tom said. His cheeks got a little pink and he shook his head. "She feels the same way. Whew."

"So. You crossed that line, did you?"

"Whew," he said again. He stood up, turned around and ran sweaty palms down his pants. When he turned back to Paul he said. "It should come with a warning, you know?"

Paul put a foot up on the bench and forced himself to take a leisurely sip of his steaming coffee, trying to get mentally ready for just anything. He hoped to God he and Tommy didn't share the same problem. "Oh, yeah?"

"Can I talk about this? Does it make me a real jerk to talk about this? Because I was always taught men don't talk about the women they… My dad always said a real man never talks about private things that happen with his girl."

"It won't go any further. We're a long way from the locker room, Tom. I think I can be trusted."

"It's just that… Well, damn. She took her sweet time, you know? And I was real patient, even when I thought I was going out of my mind. But I just wouldn't have felt right if she wasn't sure. We had all the ground rules in place—double protection, we did a lot of talking first, were totally sure how we felt about each other. I promised I would be totally faithful to her, only her, unless she changed her mind, but I'm not changing mine. And she said the same thing to me. We love each other, Paul."

"Yeah?"

"I figured it would take a little time, you know. Getting used to. I figured it would go real slow, maybe be a little clumsy. At first."

"Yeah?" Paul asked, wondering what the hell this kid was getting at.

He ducked his head, then made eye contact. "It wasn't."

"Wasn't what?"

"It didn't take any time at all. It isn't clumsy. It's freaking incredible. *She's* freaking incredible."

Paul shook his head in confusion. "Is there a problem in here somewhere?"

"I'm leaving pretty soon," he said. "Right after graduation I go to basic, then West Point. For *years*." Then he hung his head.

"Aah," Paul said. So, the boy had tapped the honey pot and found it sweeter than life. He wanted that to be a part of every day for the rest of his life. And West Point was going to lock him up for four years—you couldn't live away from the academy, couldn't graduate if you got married. "You won't be gone forever," Paul said.

"It's going to seem like it."

"I bet it will. But if she feels the same way you do, you

have something very nice to look forward to. When the time's right." Paul took a sip of coffee. "Hey, man, even if you didn't have West Point, eighteen's just too young to do the forever thing."

"Does it ever happen? Do people like me and Brenda fall in love as kids and stay together?"

"Happens more than you might think," he said with a shrug. "My buddy Zeke, firefighter from Fresno? Married his high school sweetheart and so far they have four kids. They managed to do that even with being separated by the Marine Corps for at least two years. Phillips and Stephens were married pretty young—have nice little families. And they're still so crazy about their women, it's almost ridiculous. You'd think they just met them."

"I never expected this," Tom said. "I didn't expect it to be so natural, so awesome. Makes me feel like I can't live without her. Makes me feel sick to my stomach to even think about her ever being with another guy. I can't imagine ever being with another girl. It just has me torn up inside."

Paul chuckled in spite of himself. "Tommy," he said, putting a strong hand on his shoulder. "You're talking about the thing that makes the bucks lock horns, makes bulls tear down barn doors to get to the cow. Men go into battle for less. Makes you think you'd risk anything, give up anything, lay awake at night in a cold sweat…"

"Shew," he said. "I guess that's what they mean when they say love hurts," Tom said.

"No, buddy, it doesn't. You just said so yourself—it feels wonderful to love someone and to make love. Keep your focus—separation hurts, breaking up hurts, infidelity hurts—but love, man, that's what we live for. Because it feels *good*."

"Sounds like you know what you're talking about," Tom said. "But it doesn't look like you do."

Paul frowned and gave that shoulder a squeeze. "I know. I just haven't worked out all the details yet."

At nine Paul threw his duffel in the back of his truck. He shook Tom's hand and told him to hang in there, shook the general's hand and thanked him for his hospitality, and after checking Vanni's eyes and seeing that she had softened and wasn't going to bite him or kick him, he slipped an arm around her waist, kissed her forehead and said, "I'm going to call you when I get back to Grants Pass tonight. We have some things to talk about. Maybe without the yelling part."

She turned her sparkling turquoise eyes up to his face and said, "I'll be here."

Before heading up the highway to Oregon, Paul took a swing by Mel and Jack's. He knocked softly on the door and Jack answered, David still in his pajamas balanced on his hip. "Morning," Jack said. "Heading out of town?"

"Yeah. But if you have a few minutes, I need to talk."

"Sure. We can sit out here so we don't wake Mel. She was up half the night with her back hurting and she's sleeping in. I have coffee. Want a cup?"

"That would be great," he said, though he'd already had enough coffee to screw up his nerves pretty good.

Jack handed off David to Paul while he went for coffee and a bowl of dry Cheerios for his son. They settled in the Adirondack chairs, looking out over the valley below. David sat on the porch floor with his bowl of cereal between his legs.

"You don't look too good," Jack said.

"I'm not too good. I've really messed things up. After little Matt was born, after I went home, I was pretty shook up. All those months of hanging in there with Vanni and not really taking any time to grieve my best friend took a toll, I guess. Might've vented a little bit. There's this girl back in Grants Pass…"

"You vent on this girl?" Jack asked.

"I vented in her. She's pregnant."

"Well, holy shit. That was brilliant. What were you thinking?"

"I was thinking we were protected. I'd been with her a couple of times before. You know—before Matt was killed. How impressed are you with my timing, huh?"

"What are you going to do?" Jack asked.

"I'm going to support her, naturally. She's having the baby, so I'm going to do my part. I'm not going to marry her because I don't… Aw hell, I wouldn't be doing her any favors. I met her in a bar a while back—little over a year ago. I wasn't seeing her regularly. I feel terrible about this."

"Man," Jack said.

"What's your best advice, bud?"

"How pregnant is she?"

"It happened after I got back to Grants Pass. A couple of months now. I'm going to have to tell Vanni. Pretty soon. I tried last night, but I screwed up. And even without knowing the details, she flipped out, tore my head off just thinking I had a girl back home I hadn't mentioned. Man, that woman has a real short fuse. She's going to kill me. No figure of speech here—she's good with a gun."

"Hold on there," Jack said. "One thing at a time. You should probably get yourself tested for STDs—do that tomorrow. If you used protection, I don't know…maybe there's a chance this baby isn't yours…"

"I thought of that. Thing is, she says she hadn't been with a guy for so long, she got a little lazy with the pills and I used a condom I'd been carrying around for months…"

"She suggest marriage?"

"Yeah, that was the first thing…"

"Listen, Einstein—what if she's not even pregnant, huh? Outside chance, but possible. Before you make a lifetime commitment to support someone you don't know very well, you better get all the facts. Just don't move too fast here, pal."

"I gotta call Vanni tonight, and tell her. I've got her all confused and totally furious…"

"Paul, you can't tell her on the phone," Jack said.

"But—"

"Paul! She's gonna hang up on you! And then the next time you show your face, she's going to put a bullet in your head. And Walt will help her line up her shot."

"Well, what am I gonna do? Huh? She thinks I have a woman back home—she wouldn't give me a chance to explain any—"

Mel appeared in the doorway, her robe covering her huge pregnant tummy. Her face was freshly scrubbed, but her hair was mussed from sleep. She gave Paul a smile, then went to Jack, sitting on his lap.

"Morning," she said to Paul. "I heard that. I can't wait to hear why you're going to be shot."

"Aw, man…"

"Relax," Jack said. "Really, this is the person you should talk to. And she *never* tells. It's infuriating."

Paul went through the facts slowly, embarrassingly. It made his neck red. He was not able to make much eye contact with Mel while he spoke, but at the end of the story he was amazed to look into her crystal-blue eyes and find they weren't wide with shock. "I guess you've heard it all, huh?" Paul asked.

"Pretty much. This must be very difficult for you, Paul," Mel said. "You're worried."

"You have no idea," he said.

"Of course I do. I guess your first concern is whether you're actually the father of this baby?"

"Um, I figure I am—but…"

"You should probably verify that as soon as possible. Remember, Paul—the lady knows who the mother is. You're entitled to the same assurance. Ask her to offer that to you."

"Mel," he said pleadingly. "How in God's name do you suggest I do *that?*"

"In an honest and straightforward manner," she said. "You might be able to learn something from an ultrasound. It will at least show exactly how pregnant she is, and if you can narrow down the times you were in contact—"

"Time," he said. "Just one time."

"Then you know exactly how pregnant she is and an ultrasound will either verify or dispute the gestation. But if there was another partner involved at approximately the same time, it will require a paternity test. Blood types, DNA, etcetera."

"I don't want to upset her. Offend her."

Mel smiled patiently. "Let's see—the two of you didn't have a conversation for six months and when you did, it escalated to intimacy rather quickly—do I have that right? Paul, if she's offended by your desire to be sure you're the father of this baby before you commit yourself personally and financially, you're not going to have an easy time with this. It's a very reasonable request. If she's absolutely certain, I'm sure she'll cooperate with you."

"And if she doesn't?" he asked.

"Tell her you'll hire a lawyer to assert your paternal rights. She can be prevented from aborting or having the baby adopted, and you will be obligated to support your child, which I assume you're prepared to do anyway."

"If she's having my baby, I'll take care of her. Of course."

Mel smiled. "Of course you will."

"And Vanni?" Paul asked.

"Oh," Mel said. "She's not taking it well?"

"She doesn't know. I tried to tell her last night and I got as far as telling her I dated a woman in Grants Pass when she came unhinged because I hadn't told her sooner."

Mel made a face. "Take care of that, Paul. If you have feelings for Vanessa, it isn't fair to leave her confused and wondering. She deserves the truth."

"She's going to shoot me in the head," he said miserably.

"I doubt that. She might need time to consider the facts, however." Then she smiled patiently. "Paul, you've played around with this long enough. If you care about her, assert yourself. Explain. You didn't betray her—you didn't break the law. You have to behave responsibly toward both women—that's all there is to it."

"Yeah," he said.

"This will work out. Babies are miracles of life—no matter the extenuating circumstances. Don't lose sight of that."

"Yeah," he said again. He leaned toward her, kissed her brow as she sat on her husband's lap. "Thanks, Mel."

"Sure," she said. "Best of luck."

He shook Jack's hand, ruffled David's floppy golden hair and headed for his truck. Once he'd turned around and was headed off the Sheridan property, Mel looked at Jack to find him grinning hugely. "Melinda," he said. "Did you just get involved in someone's *relationship?*"

She lifted a brow. "Do you really want to mess with a woman who's about seventeen months pregnant?"

"I'm just saying…"

"Try shutting up," she advised. "I believe I was *asked.*"

"You did," he laughed. "You got right in there, got your hands dirty in someone's relationship. Just admit it—it's irresistible. You're just as nosy as I am."

She glared at him. "Jack, no one is as nosy as you are."

Right after Paul left, the phone rang at Jack's house. He knew who it was; it was a regular Sunday morning call. He lifted Mel off his lap and dashed for the phone, grinning from ear to ear.

There had been a boy in Virgin River who was like a son to Jack. Ricky. He'd taken him under his wing when he was only thirteen because it was just Rick and his grandmother. Jack taught him to hunt and fish, did what he could to teach him the ways of the world. He'd pridefully watched as he grew tall and strong, a young man of impeccable character who could take the toughest stuff life could serve up and hold his head up, stand straight and do a man's job. The boy had gotten close to Preacher, to Mel, to the Marines from Jack's old squad who still gathered there.

At eighteen Ricky had signed up. What was the young protégé of a bunch of tough old Marines going to do but sign up? And Semper Fi suited him. Ricky had excelled. He'd gone from Basic to Airborne to Sniper training to Reconnaissance training to SERE—Survival, Evasion, Resistance, Escape training. In every program he'd been the best. He was nineteen years old and at least six feet of proud, muscled, skilled Marine. He just phoned to say he had ten days of leave coming up in a couple of months.

And then he had orders for Iraq.

"No sniveling, Jack," Rick said. "I want you to remember when you were going—you didn't want your parents and your sisters acting like you were walking into a grave, right? So—we'll have a drink. Maybe smoke one of those nasty cigars you and Preach like so much. Tell some dirty jokes. I might even let you cheat me out of some money at poker…"

"You got it, kid. It'll be great. I'll even call some of the boys…"

"Aw, they don't have to come. They're your boys, not mine. And there's no hunting now anyway."

"We'll see. Virgin River's going to want to celebrate you a little bit. We only send our best."

"Thanks. I can't wait to see you."

Jack straightened his spine, took a deep breath and told himself they were going to have to make his leave in Virgin River memorable and positive—there'd be no whining and worrying. After all, Jack had gone into war five times and the only really bad injury he'd sustained was a pretty miserable shot in the ass. Not everyone who went to war came out crippled. Or dead. Rick was sharp. And this was what Rick wanted.

Ricky had grown up too fast. He lost his parents in an accident when he was so young, he didn't even remember them. At sixteen he'd fallen ass over teakettle in love with a girl two years younger than him and they'd had a baby together, a baby that hadn't lived.

Mel came into the kitchen to find Jack leaning on the counter, looking down. He lifted his gaze. "Ricky's coming home in a couple of months," he said. "He's got ten days."

"Oh-oh," she said, knowing something was bad about this.

"Then he's going to Iraq."

She was quiet for a moment. Her eyes misted over. She pursed her lips and then said, "*Damn* it!"

Five

Paul stopped off for dinner on his way into Grants Pass, took a run by his office to check messages and any paperwork that might be left on his desk. There were a couple messages from Terri asking him to call. When he finally got home, it was after seven and he found a few messages from Terri on his home phone, left over the weekend, asking him to call her. Then the last one—all upset, full of tears and little gasping breaths, saying she couldn't stand feeling so ignored, so alone. She mumbled something about maybe it just wasn't worth it. The time of the last call on the caller ID showed the call came in only an hour ago. He dialed her number and there was no answer, so he flew out the door and drove to her apartment. Aw, Jesus, don't do this, he was thinking all the way there. Don't go crazy on me.

She opened the door to his knock; her eyes and nose were red, her cheeks chapped, like maybe she'd been crying all day. She took one look at him and turned, walking back into her apartment, leaving the door open with him standing there. He followed her and stood in her small living room as she whirled around, flopped on the couch, drew her feet up and cried into a tissue.

"Terri, what's going on? Why didn't you answer your phone?"

"I turned it off," she said.

"Why would you leave me a message like that and then turn off your phone?"

"Because," she said, blowing her nose. "I left a lot of messages—and you ignored them all. I just couldn't take it anymore, waiting for the phone to ring. It was agony. What's the point in giving me all your phone numbers if you weren't going to take my calls?"

He sat down beside her on the couch, but he didn't get too close. "We had lunch last week," he said. "Everything was okay. Are you having problems with the pregnancy?"

"Yeah, I'm having problems! As in, I have no one to talk to and it gets damn lonely!"

"I was out of town," he said. "I didn't call in for messages."

"And your cell phone was turned off?" she asked hotly.

"There's no signal where I went—I didn't even carry it with me. I left it in the truck all weekend. I was in Virgin River, in the mountains. I'm sorry—I didn't know you'd need me. And I still don't know why you thought you needed me."

"I was upset! Didn't you say you were in this with me? I needed someone who was on my side to talk to. What if something worse was wrong? How long would it take you to notice? Maybe I should just get rid of it—it would be less trouble for you."

He reached over and touched her knee. He gave it a squeeze. "Don't do that," he said.

"You want me to have it?" she asked him. "Because you don't exactly act like it."

Paul felt an angry heat rise up his neck to his face. "If you had wanted an abortion, you would have done that already. I'd never have known. Don't threaten it now to keep me in line."

"God, I just felt so *abandoned*..." Her face melted into a pathetic, contorted mess of wrinkles. She buried her face in her tissue and let it go for a minute. Resigned, he scooted closer and pulled her against him, holding her while she cried on his chest. "So—what's in Virgin River that keeps you from even thinking about us up here?"

"Get a grip now," he said, not answering the question. "I'm not letting you go through this alone. I didn't know you needed anything."

"And what if I do?"

"I'll do my best. But we'd better establish some boundaries. I'm not going to let you do this to me."

"What are you talking about?"

"You know what I'm talking about. I'm in this with you—I'll coparent and pay support. I'm grateful you're willing to have the baby, but I'm not going to be manipulated."

"What if I give it away?"

"If you give it away, you'll be giving it to me."

"To take to *her?*"

"Who?" he asked, startled.

"There has to be a woman. Otherwise you'd give us a chance."

He sighed. It couldn't really be that simple, could it? "Listen to me," he said. He grabbed her chin and turned her face so he could look into those swollen, wet eyes. "This has to do with me and you—and the fact that even though we're not a couple, we're having a child together. We have to figure out how to make that work."

"So there is," she said.

"There is," he admitted. "But even if there weren't..."

"But there is," she said.

He took a breath. "There might not be, after she hears about this. But that won't change anything between us. Terri, I'm sorry—I'm fond of you, I care about you, I swear I'll do my best by you, but I don't love you. There are three people involved here—you, me, a baby. It wouldn't be good for any of us to try to make a marriage where there isn't real bone deep, passionate love. I wouldn't give us a year—and that would be worse than what we have." He ran a knuckle down her cheek. "Believe me."

She was quiet a moment. "You said there was no one," she whispered. "When we met, when we… You said there was no one in your life…"

"It's real complicated," he said.

"But you cheated on her. When she finds out you cheated, she's going to—"

"Terri, I didn't cheat on her, all right? I told you the truth. I wasn't with anyone."

"I don't understand. Did you just meet her? After we—?"

"Okay, listen to me. We weren't together. I knew I had real strong feelings for her, but we weren't together when I met you and I had no reason to hope we ever would be. She had no idea how I felt. I told you the truth—I wasn't with a woman and I didn't want a serious relationship. You said the same thing—you were unattached and liked it that way."

She was quiet for a long moment. "And now?"

He glanced away. "Things changed. Lots of things changed."

"Oh God," she said, falling into a fresh round of tears. "Oh God, your friend's wife! The one who just died!"

Oh, he thought, *this is going to be so much worse than I ever imagined. I swear to God, I'm never having sex again.* "Don't come unglued on me like this," he said softly. "Listen, there will be times I can't be there for you—times we're not in touch. There has to be someone you can talk to when you're upset and you can't find me. What about your mother? Is she someone you can talk to about this?"

"Not really," she said with a sniff. "She thinks I'm crazy to go through with this. She doesn't believe for one second you'll be a part of it."

He took a breath. "I'll go with you to meet her, help explain what I'm able to do to help. That might put her mind at ease a little bit."

She lifted her head and looked up at him. "Would you?"

"Sure. After we've seen the doctor together."

"Why do we have to do that?" she asked.

"I have some questions for the doctor. I want to make sure everything is going well. You know?"

"What do you mean?"

"We'll ask a few questions about your health, the baby's health, insurance, that sort of thing. Once you get through the early months, we'll see your mother and I'll reassure her that I'm going to support you. Who's your doctor?"

"Why?"

"We should make sure you have the best." He shrugged. "Who?"

"Charlene Weir."

"When's your next appointment?"

"Not for a while. I just went. Just before I told you."

"So, when?"

"A couple of weeks," she said. "Three, I think."

"Okay. You be sure to give me the date of the next appointment, okay?"

"Why don't you just tell me your questions and I'll get the answers?"

"No," he said, brushing her hair back from her face. "I want to go. I want to be a part of this."

"Okay," she said, a sentimental look in her eyes. "Will you stay with me tonight?"

"I can't, Terri. It's about those boundaries."

"Well, it's not as if I'm going to get pregnant!"

"Terri—you want me in this with you or not? I told you, I'll be an involved father and I'll support you the best I can. I hope we can cooperate, work together, be friends. I'd like us to do a good job with this—but we're not a couple, and we're not going to be intimate anymore."

"Jesus," she whispered, leaning against him to cry some more. "I have myself so upset I can't eat, I can't sleep. It's like you feel completely different about me because I got pregnant, and it's not my fault!"

"Shh. Since we were both taking precautions, it's not really anyone's fault, but it's still a responsibility we both have. You're going to have to settle down and be more rational. This isn't good for you or the baby. Try to calm down a little, okay?"

"It's just so hard," she said. "We might not have been together that much, but when we were, it was wonderful. We got along, we liked each other. I thought when you knew we'd made a baby, you'd at least give us a try. But man—you won't even *think* about it."

"Yeah, honey… We liked each other fine, got along great, had fun—four whole times in a year. I think it takes a lot more than that to make a successful marriage. Besides, if there was potential for it to be any more serious than it is, we'd have known a long time ago. But you know what I'd like?"

"What?" she said, turning her face up to look at him.

"We're going to be parents together. Not under the same roof, but still—we have to do this as a team. I'd like it if we could do that as friends. Two people who might not have what it takes to be a couple, but have everything we need to be good parents. That's going to take some practice, I think."

"You think?" she whispered.

"Yeah," he said with a weary sigh. "Lots."

"That woman," she said with a sniff. "Did you know you loved her right away?" she asked.

"Right away," he said, his arm around her.

Terri was quiet for a moment. Then she said, "I guess you probably know exactly how I feel."

He thought it made as much sense for Terri to think herself in love with him after a couple of one-night stands as it did for him to be in love with Vanni the second he laid eyes on her. And Vanni had been as unavailable to him as he was to Terri.

"Come on," he said to Terri. "Let's lay down on the bed, see if you can calm down enough to rest. I can't stay the night, though. You understand?"

"I think so, yes," she said. "I don't like it, but I get it. I'm not usually this crazy."

"It's okay. Let's quiet you and the baby down, then I'm going to leave and go home. You feeling a little better yet?"

"There's just no way for us, is there, Paul?"

"There's a way for us to have this baby and be good parents, Terri. In my mind, that's a lot."

First thing Monday morning the phone rang at the Booth household, and Vanessa lunged for it. It was Cameron and she let out a disappointed sigh that she hoped he wouldn't interpret. The man she'd been thinking about was Paul. She'd been worrying about him. Frantically, in fact. He hadn't called as promised and by ten o'clock the night before she'd left messages for him at his home and office, getting no response. She'd hardly slept, afraid he'd been hurt or killed on the drive home. It didn't feel good to have something between them yet to be resolved.

She collected herself. "Well, hello, Cameron."

"Vanni, how are you?"

"Very well, thanks. And you?" She chewed her lip a little bit. Why couldn't this just be Paul?

"I'm good. Listen, I know Virgin River is perfection, but I was wondering if you'd like to get out of town for a weekend."

"A weekend?" she asked, completely unprepared for such a question.

"There's a great seaside hotel in Mendocino, on the ocean. Lots to do around there. Very relaxing and entertaining."

"Cameron, I have a baby."

He chuckled. "I thought maybe I could bring along a pediatrician."

"But, Cameron, I'm really not ready for—"

"Easy, Vanni. We'll get two rooms. Think of it as a chance to get to know each other better, that's all. And no, I have not mentioned my plans to Carol."

"Oh. Listen—I appreciate the invitation, but I'm not sure I'm ready for something like a weekend date. That's moving a little fast for me…"

"I'll be a Boy Scout," he laughed. "Two rooms, good views, great food, a little relaxation, conversation, no pressure…"

"I appreciate the thought, really. It's very nice of you, but…"

"All right," he said. "It was worth a try. Well, then, can I wrangle another run down to Virgin River? I have Jack's phone number. I could make a reservation at that little cabin…"

"You're welcome anytime," she said.

"Maybe this weekend, since I scheduled it off?"

"Sure," she said without enthusiasm. "Let me know if you decide to come down."

It was another tense hour before the phone rang and this time it was Paul. She nearly bit his head off. "Where have you been?"

"Vanni, I'm sorry. I didn't get your message until this morning."

"Forget the message—I didn't *ask* you to call! You said you were going to! I was afraid something terrible might have happened. I worried half the night!"

"Something unexpected came up. I had to, ah, just help out a friend with something. I was home too late to call you. I didn't even check the messages until this morning."

She sighed heavily. It wasn't like her to panic, but she'd had far too many losses over the past few years, and Paul felt like one more. "If you hadn't said…"

"Vanni, I'm sorry. That will never happen again."

Taking care of the widow again, she thought. He got home, got sidetracked by the woman in Grants Pass and she was the last thing on his mind. How could he be any more clear? Still, she heard herself ask, "What was the problem that sidetracked you until so late?"

"Ah, it wasn't anything. Not as serious as it sounded at first. I'll tell you all about it, Vanni, but I'd rather do it in person. I'm so sorry I didn't call."

"I'm not your keeper," she said. "You have a private life, as you tried to explain…"

"Vanni, I don't want you to get the wrong idea here…"

"I doubt I have the wrong idea," she said. "Don't worry about it, Paul. I'm glad everything is okay. We'll catch up later."

"I'll talk to you this week," he said. "I'll see you on the weekend."

"Sure," she said. She hung up the phone and went to her bedroom. She sat on the edge of her bed. She could tell by the nervous sound in his voice—he hadn't been home too late to call—he hadn't been home at all. He spent the night with the woman. The woman who had complicated his life.

We have things to talk about.... Those were his parting words, along with the promise to call. That thing he wanted to talk about—it would be an explanation about his relationship in Grants Pass, as if she needed more of his lame attempts. What did she expect, really? He had a life before Matt was killed, before Vanessa needed him, and that life went on. She had to find a way to let go of this, of him. If she didn't, it was going to tear her apart. Worse, it would tear Paul apart because more than anything, he was faithful to Matt.

The best thing she could do for herself, for Paul, was attempt to get on with her life.

She remembered back to those old flying days when she and Nikki got each other through a dozen bad boyfriends, the pain and disappointment. "Raise your right hand and repeat after me," Nikki would say. "I will *not* be pitiful! I will *not* be pathetic!"

She checked little Matt to find he was still sleeping. She wiped at her eyes. It was so ridiculous to cry—it had been very clear for a long time. Paul was devoted to her, bonded with her in some special ways. Probably her best friend. He was loving and affectionate and genuinely cared about her—but it wasn't romantic. It never had been. She'd better get over it.

One thing she absolutely couldn't take—Cameron and Paul both in Virgin River for the weekend—Cameron trying to seduce her, Paul shyly and clumsily trying to find a way to tell her he had a girlfriend. Chinese water torture would be sweeter.

She went back to the great room and sat beside the phone for a few minutes, thinking. She picked up the receiver and dialed. "Cameron? Yes, I've been thinking about it and a little trip to the coast might be just what I need. Mattie and I would love to go. But it'll have to be two rooms. And only if you're sure you want to do this with no expectations. I don't want to disappoint you."

"I understand your position, Vanessa," he said. "Let's just have a good time."

"That sounds so nice. Can we make it early on Saturday and home Sunday?"

"Perfect."

"Good, I'll be ready." And she hung up.

She looked at Walt, whose newspaper was folded into his lap. He stared at her over the top of his reading glasses. "Vanessa, just what the hell's going on?"

"I'm…ah…I'm going on a little weekend trip with Cameron. I'll be taking the baby, of course."

He had heard her side of all three conversations and she knew it. "There seems to be a lot more to the story here…" he said. "Fighting with Paul? Making a date with this doctor?"

"It's really nothing, Dad," she answered. "You don't have a problem with me going away for a weekend, do you?"

"You're a grown woman," he said.

"Paul will be coming down for the weekend."

"And you're not going to be here to see him?"

She stood up. "He's not coming to see me. I think I'll just go for a quick ride, if you don't mind listening for the baby."

"Not at all," he said. "Don't hurt the horse."

If Cameron had hoped to impress and charm Vanessa, he certainly was on the right track. First of all, he borrowed his brother's SUV so that the car seat and stroller would fit. She had some misgivings about going away with him for the weekend, especially when her motivation was mostly to avoid Paul. But he entertained her with stories on their drive to the coast—growing up with a brother and sister close to his age, fraternity pranks, med school horror stories that made her laugh in spite of herself. She was immediately comfortable, enjoying herself, and decided there were some perks involved in avoiding Paul.

He took her to a motel that resembled a country inn; they entered rooms on the parking lot side while the back of each room opened up onto a quaint, sheltered and private patio with table and chairs that faced the ocean cliffs. Lush pots full of geraniums sat around full green ferns and daisy beds that bordered the patios. In Vanessa's room, which was joined to Cam's, were fresh flowers and fruit.

After lunch at a sweet little seaside restaurant, they put the baby in the stroller and walked along the cliffs above the ocean, finally spreading a blanket under a full, leafy tree. They talked about their youth, their pasts, their experiences, their likes and dislikes. "You have a real way about you," Vanni said. "I bet the mothers who bring their children to you fall in love with you all the time."

"I'm just waiting for the right one to fall in love with me," he said.

"You were never even tempted to get married?" she asked.

"There were a couple of close calls."

"I bet you've had a million girlfriends," she said.

He laughed. "That might be giving me too much credit," he said. "Or not enough, I don't know which. I've had some girlfriends. And many more attempts that didn't work out."

"Ah. You're picky."

He lifted an amused eyebrow. "Maybe they were."

"Come on. Haven't you been in love a hundred times?"

"Not quite. Not counting high school and college when I was in love with a different girl every week, the first one hit me in med school. I had it bad for another med student. It was very hot, very intense, very brief. Very painful. Took me off the market for a while."

"Really? I'd take you for the heartbreaker."

"No, sir," he said, shaking his head. "I realized that up to that point I'd been attracted, but not in love. I had my share of flings, but this woman I went to pieces over. I was all of twenty-four and I could've made the promises—all of them. She was with another guy before I knew what hit me. Then another and another. I lost track of her during internship when I heard she was with the senior resident in her program. My pride suffered a major blow, not to mention my perspective."

"There were more?" she asked.

"Oh, yeah," he admitted. "I lived with a woman once—but not for long. I don't think we made it three months. That was my only attempt at that." He shrugged. "I was twenty-nine and it seemed like I ought to at least make an effort to have a stable, monogamous relationship. It was awful."

"Awful? What went wrong?"

"Um, first of all, it wasn't stable. She turned out to be crazy." Then he smiled.

"Really? I mean, really?"

"You just wouldn't believe it. A total loose cannon. She threw things at me and everything. I almost went deaf from her screaming."

"You moved in with her without knowing that?"

His cheeks took on a rosy stain. "I probably should've

guessed, but I was in denial." He laughed. "Because she was really…" He swallowed. "Because she was very sexy. I thought I could handle anything if I could just…" His voice dwindled away.

"What men will do," Vanni said, shaking her head.

"Yeah. Guilty. Did you ever live with anyone?" he asked.

"Never. The closest I came was when I was going with my husband, I traveled from San Francisco to Camp Pendleton to spend every weekend with him while he was still stateside."

"In college," he said. "Who were you in love with in college?"

She laughed. "Bret McDoughal. Captain of the football team, president of the debate club. I really expected him to be a senator by now."

"What is he doing?"

"He sells used cars in Virginia. He makes sleazy, late-night commercials and wears his hair in some kind of weird pompadour. In college, he looked like he was going to take over the world. I was nuts about him."

"How'd he let you get away?"

"A lot of girls were nuts about him. He had a very short attention span."

"What a dope," Cameron said.

"Yeah? Well, I think I made a very slim escape there," she said, laughing.

He reached out and covered her hand with his. "Can you tell me about Matt? Is that too hard for you to do?"

"It's okay. I like to talk about him," she said, and resisted the memory that made one of the things about her relationship with Paul so comfortable—they could share memories. "Matt was a wonderful man, a great friend. He was so funny, so full of energy. What snagged me immediately was his sense of humor—he made me laugh till I cried. And there were other things about him—like his commitment to the Marine Corps, his commitment to his buddies, his boys as he called them—that filled me with admiration. His commitment to me," she added, somewhat quietly. "He was single-minded when it came to the things he cared about. And he was strong—not just physically. Emotionally strong, too. But you should've seen his arms and shoulders. He could do pull-ups and push-ups all day long."

"Big, like all those Virgin River men," Cameron said.

"Not really," she said. "Broad shouldered but not even six feet. When I wore heels, we were the same height. Dark haired, like you. Blue eyes, like yours. Tender and sensitive and easy to talk to." She got a little misty. "Sometimes I really miss him. I'm sorry."

He leaned toward her, sneaking up on her, and placed a soft kiss on her cheek. "Never be sorry. It sounds like you had something special. You wouldn't want to not have had that. Especially with the little guy."

"You're right, yes. I'm getting to the point where I can appreciate that—that I had him in my life, that I have his son. I'm grateful I had at least that much rather than never having known him." She inhaled sharply and looked out at the ocean. "It's nice of you—not avoiding that subject. Not pretending he wasn't...*isn't* a part of my life."

"Vanessa, he's going to be a part of your life forever."

"Yeah. I don't know if I take comfort in that or not." She looked back at him and smiled. "But I'm grateful, understand. For Matt, the baby—everything but the end."

"Let's go back," he said. "I'd like a shower before dinner and you could probably use a little time alone with your baby. Maybe a nap."

She took a breath. "That might be in order. What time is dinner?"

"Drinks at six-thirty, dinner at seven."

"Where?"

"We're eating in. It's going to be special."

"In?" she asked. "Special?"

"Once you get Mattie settled, we'll have a catered dinner on the patio so you'll be able to hear him if he wakes. Don't panic," he said, laughing. "I don't have ulterior motives—there's going to be a waiter present most of the time. I'm not trying to trap you. Impress you, yes. Trap you, no."

Paul didn't see Terri at all that week, but he called her twice to ask her how she was, and he kept the conversations short. He'd been planning to go to Virgin River, but then he got a call from Joe explaining about Jack and Preacher's add-on, and the need for a builder's opinion. This was perfect because it gave a professional purpose to the trip but he knew Terri would realize there was more to Virgin River than a construction job. He promised to call her during the weekend to make sure she was doing all right, but he didn't give her the general's number where he could be reached. This time, he would call for messages.

But she surprised him by saying, "Have a nice weekend, Paul." And he was so grateful that he suggested he might try to see her the following week, maybe for a lunch. And she said, "That would be nice, Paul."

When he got to the general's house on Saturday, Vanni was not there, and Walt was wearing a very annoyed expression.

"She didn't mention she'd be away this weekend," Paul said.

"No, she didn't, did she?" the general said. "Yet, I'm not sure why. You have any intel on that, son?"

He shook his head. "I told her I was coming. I think she was angry with me for forgetting to call her."

"She's gone away for the weekend with the pediatrician," Walt announced.

"God *damn!* Sir," Paul said. "I mean—"

"I know exactly what you mean." Walt turned away from him.

"Sir, maybe I can explain this misunderstanding," Paul attempted.

The general waved him off. "I don't want to hear it," he said. "I've heard way too much already, and I don't want to be any more confused. Seems about time you explained whatever it is to Vanessa, however."

"Yeah. Yes, sir. Ah, I have to go into town, see Jack and Preacher about building onto that bar. How'd you like to come along?"

He turned back. "As a matter of fact, I'd like to do just that."

By the time Paul and Walt got to the bar, the lunch crowd was finishing up. Both of them needed a beer, both for the same reason, though they didn't discuss it. Walt had no idea what was going on with his daughter, but he'd been real close to her for thirty years and he smelled a broken heart, yet she'd gone away with the doctor. As for Paul, he was sure his complete ineptness was causing him to lose her. Again.

After Jack served them up a couple of cold drafts, Paul said, "Joe tells me you're planning some building."

"That's a fact," Jack said. "We have to make room for Preacher's family. Now that he's figured out how to make the babies, he wants a house big enough to fill up with kids." Jack took a sip from his coffee mug. "They like it here. They like working together, living right on the property, running things their way. Makes sense to me, and Joe says it's easily done. He left some sketches, but doesn't have plans yet. He needs a builder to check out beams and foundation, etcetera."

"I can do that," Paul said. "You have someone in mind for building?"

"That's a problem around here. Until recently, there's not been too much demand so our general contractors are few and far between. Remember, I couldn't find one who could go to work within a year, but we sure have plenty of crew looking for construction jobs. And, there's been a development."

"What's that?"

"Mike and Brie. They've been looking for a house for months—nothing that works for them has come on the market. My plot's big—I can give them a parcel and they can build their own place. They'll be talking to Joe soon about a design. But they're sitting in that RV, trying to start their own family, needing space, and they have the same problem—a serious lack of builders." He shook his head. "This is one of those times I wish you lived in Virgin River, Paul."

"Let me see the sketches," Paul said, changing the subject.

Jack reached under the bar and pulled out a large sheaf of rolled papers, clipped together at one corner. "They're pretty rough sketches."

"No problem," Paul said. "I'm used to his scrawls and squiggles. He does manage to invent new abbreviations regularly, though. To challenge me, I think. Preacher in back?"

"Yeah, he's cleaning up after lunch."

Paul grinned. "Maybe I'll get started. Take care of the general, will you?"

"Who says I need taking care of?" Walt asked. "I'm as happy right now as I've been all week."

Paul drank about half of his beer, flipping through the

sketches, then dragged himself off the stool and wandered into the kitchen.

Paul knew the bar like the back of his hand, but to do the architect justice, he looked at it with a builder's eyes. He scribbled over Joe's notes. He walked through the apartment and upstairs, then stopped in the middle of the small living quarters on the ground floor. He thought with the second floor and loft added, it could handle an open-beamed ceiling over their new great room, with a fireplace. Then he walked around outside.

Before Paul could escape back to the bar, Mike saw him prowling around the yard right outside Preacher's quarters where the extension would be anchored. He walked across the yard from the RV. "Hey, Paul, did Jack tell you we're looking at building?"

"He did," Paul said with a nod. "Probably a good idea, if you're not finding anything you like."

"It sure would be great if I already knew the builder and his work," Mike said.

"Yeah, but I work in Grants Pass now," Paul said.

"There must be at least one incentive to taking a job around here," Mike said, grinning.

"I love this place, you know that. But I have commitments in Grants Pass. I left my dad and brothers for a long time while I was here last autumn." And, thought, those commitments included a pregnancy. Maybe, just maybe, Virgin River would be a more strategic place to sit it out. He could keep in touch with Terri by phone rather than having her expect him to be available to her. It would help with the matter of not giving her false hope. "Tell you what, I'll definitely think about it. But there are a lot of factors." Not the least of which was Vanessa Rutledge.

Six

At only two and a half months, little Matt had become a very cooperative travel companion. After his stroll along the cliffs, he had a nice catnap with his mother, then a bath and a little playtime. Then a long, leisurely nursing, and back to sleep. Vanni had a shower, put on a lightweight sundress, primped and waited until she heard a soft tapping at the door that separated her from Cameron. "Is he asleep?" Cameron asked.

"He is."

Cameron crept near the portable crib and looked at him. He saw Vanessa's shawl on the bed and picked it up, draping it over her bare shoulders. "I was prepared for him to join us for dinner." He laughed. "We'll keep an ear turned his way. Come here," he said, taking her hand. "I have drinks on the patio." He led her through his room onto his patio where a table had been set with china. He lifted a drink and put it into her hand. The sun was just beginning its downward path. He touched her glass with his. "To a weekend away from it all."

"Thank you, Cameron. I didn't realize how much I needed something like this."

He pulled out a chair for her, turning it slightly to face the beautiful sunset. "Sit down and enjoy the sunset. Are you warm enough?"

She pulled the wrap around her and nodded.

"Do you miss the flying, Vanni?" he asked her.

"I miss the girlfriends," she said. "We're in touch and we visit a lot, but there were four of us who bid our schedules together, so every trip was like a four-day pajama party. Two of us lived in L.A., two in San Francisco. We're still close."

"Will you go back to flying?"

"No, that part of my life is over. I can't imagine leaving little Matt for days at a time. Half of my problem is not having any idea what's coming next for me. Sitting in my father's house, a single mother?" She shook her head. "I don't know about that...."

He laughed at her. "Vanni, you're not going to do that. Carol said something about you joining her in real estate...."

It was her turn to laugh. She felt an overwhelming temptation to tell Cameron she'd rather have all her teeth pulled than work with Carol every day, but knowing their friendship preceded hers with him, she just said, "No. I already told her I wasn't interested in real estate, but in her usual fashion she wasn't listening and is probably getting a desk ready for me at her brokerage firm."

"A formidable woman," he said, giving his head a shake. "Being her daughter-in-law probably has its challenges, but I have to hand it to her—she got me my house at an irresistible price. She got the seller to bring the price way down without me even making an offer."

"She probably wore them down. She's worn me down a time or two."

"I can only imagine."

There was a knock at the door and Cameron rose to

admit a man dressed in waiter livery carrying a large tray. He was a friendly man in his fifties, delighted to be serving them. He chatted about the food as he prepared their plates, poured them wine and large glasses of water. He had a van backed right up to Cameron's hotel-room door and went back and forth to bring in the meal and, once their plates had been served, he stood silent by the hotel-room door, allowing them to talk and enjoy the meal, watching in case it was time to refill water or wine glasses.

They were served salad, pasta, chicken Marsala, crisp green beans with almonds, Chardonnay. Then came crème brûlée.

"This must have cost a fortune," she whispered across the table to him.

"It was worth every penny," Cameron said, taking a last bite of crème brûlée. "The hotel manager hooked me up with a local restaurant and I talked to the chef. He recommended the menu, said he'd have it sent over and served, and I thought it made so much more sense to be here where we could hear the baby than trying to go to a good restaurant."

"And subjecting the other diners to a crying baby?" She laughed. "I'm sure they're all very grateful."

"Crying babies are pretty much a part of daily life for me," he said.

"And for me," she added. "This was so thoughtful. I can't think of another thing you could have done to create a perfect getaway."

"Good. You've enjoyed it?"

"Immensely. And on top of it all, you've been a real Boy Scout."

"I had my instructions," he said with a chuckle. The waiter returned to the table and offered them coffee. "I'm not a nursing mother," Cameron said. "And I'm not driving—I'm having another drink. How about you, Vanni? What would you like?"

"Decaf?" she asked. And it was provided. The dishes were cleared away, a carafe of decaf left on the table. Cameron sipped his drink slowly and then the door softly clicked closed for the last time, leaving them alone.

Leaving them to talk. And talk. They went over families, friends, places they'd lived, terrible apartments they'd rented, bad cars they'd purchased, trips they'd taken. They laughed and asked each other questions and became friends, something Vanni had said she wanted. But when she said it she was only trying to keep him from pursuing her romantically. She was a bit surprised to realize how much she liked him and hoped he *could* be her friend.

She glanced at her watch; over three hours had passed. The day had been nearly perfect. It had taken her mind off all sorts of things, and had proven an ideal escape with a wonderful gentleman. "It's almost time for little Matt to make himself heard," she said.

"Does he still wake in the night?" Cameron asked.

"A couple of times, but he eats and goes back to sleep. People keep telling me he's an easy baby. Thank God. It's the only thing that's been easy lately."

"I'm glad you didn't draw the fussy card. You just never know."

She pushed her chair back and stood. "I'm going to turn in. I know it's still early for you, but after Mattie's next meal, I'll go to bed."

He stood, as well. "I'm right here if you need anything." And then he walked her to their adjoining door.

She turned and faced him. "Really, I don't know how to thank you. The day was wonderful, the evening was perfect. And you're exceptionally well behaved." She grinned at him.

"Don't give me too much credit. It's all part of a devious plan."

"Oh?"

"Absolutely. If I can show you a good time, make you feel safe and comfortable, then maybe when you're ready, I'll have a chance." He smiled at her.

She tilted her head and looked at him with a sweet smile and glowing eyes. "You're absolutely wonderful."

He shied a bit at the compliment and dropped his gaze, laughing softly. "Well, I've never had an interest in a widow with a baby before and I'm finding it has its difficult points."

"Oh?"

He threaded a hand under her hair and around her neck. "Oh, yeah. For one thing, you just smell so damn good. If your situation was different, you might have to beat me off with a club. I have a giant crush on you."

"Maybe I shouldn't have done this," she said, but she didn't pull away from his hand. "I'd hate to lead you on...."

"Come on, it's not your fault if I have a crush and a desperate need to try to impress you. Don't you have enough baggage without taking on mine?"

"Well, I'm impressed," she said softly. She leaned toward him and put a gentle kiss on his cheek. "I just don't want to let you down."

Their eyes locked and for a moment they were suspended there. And then he slowly pulled her toward him. He was going to kiss her and she was going to let him. But then the baby started to snuffle in the crib and whimper. She pulled back with a smile. "That's my call," she said quietly. "Thank you for a lovely day. And for being such a dear man, for understanding so much."

"Sure," he said, removing his hand. "I wouldn't want it any other way."

"Good night, Cameron."

* * *

Of course Vanni couldn't sleep. It stung. She wanted hands on her. She wanted a man's hot and eager body pressing her down in the bed, filling her, making her tremble and cry out. She hadn't been touched, or physically loved in so long. After Matt's death, after the baby, when her body began to come back to life, there was only one man whose touch could tempt her, really tempt her. Matt's best friend. *Her* best friend.

Oh, it made her so furious, tears came to her eyes. That damn Paul! He wasn't nearly as smooth, as romantic as Cameron! He wasn't as pretty, and Lord knew, he didn't want her like Cameron did.

Then she remembered the way he laid his head on her shoulder and wept right after the baby was born, the way he slipped his arms around her waist when she cried at Matt's grave, the way he held her and the baby close for a few long moments before saying goodbye… And the tears came. How had she let this happen? *Why can't I just want the man who wants me—instead of the man who has no room in his life for me?*

Sometime in the dark of night, Cameron was awakened by odd, faint sounds. He opened his eyes and listened. The baby, he thought. He sat up. But that wasn't a baby crying, he realized. He got out of bed and crept closer to the door that separated him from Vanni. She was weeping. Crying soft, muffled, sad tears.

He pushed gently on the door and it opened—she hadn't locked it. Maybe she did trust him, he thought. He pulled on his pants and went to her room. "Vanessa," he whispered.

She moved in her bed. She sniffed. "Cameron?" she asked.

"What is it?" he whispered.

"Nothing, it's nothing," she whispered back.

He went to her bed and sat on the edge. He looked down at eyes that, even in the darkness of her room, were filled and overflowing, her nose pink. "God, Vanessa, if I made you cry, I'll hate myself."

"It's not your fault. You're completely innocent. You've been wonderful. I think too much sometimes. I have to learn to let some things go."

"Oh, honey," he said, pulling her close. "It's all right. These things take time."

"I'm sorry," she said.

"You don't have to be sorry. I knew—we both knew— you've had so much to deal with, to try to put into perspective. It's okay." He crawled onto the bed and, on top of the coverlet, slipped an arm under her head to hold her. "You take your time, Vanni. There's lots of time."

She turned in his arms and cried against his bare chest, and he held her, understanding the pain. He ached for her. The woman had buried the husband of her heart right before delivering his child. Moving on to the next part of her life wasn't going to be that easy.

He didn't care. He was willing to go through this with her, because this was exactly the kind of woman he wanted in his life. A woman who could show commitment this powerful, emotion this deep, love this enduring.

When he woke hours later, still on her bed, he saw her across the room, her nightgown slipped down to nurse her baby. As she looked down at her son while she fed him, a tear glistened on her cheek. She was having trouble leaving her spouse behind, and every time she looked at her son it would serve as a reminder.

It was not the morning after he had imagined or hoped for. He went to his room to shower. Then he had a nice breakfast delivered to the room, but he excused the waiter so they could be alone. He held the baby against him as Vanni picked at her food and sipped her coffee. "Are you feeling any better?" he asked her.

"A little bit," she said. "God, Cameron. You don't deserve this."

"I told you, I understand. But I think we should go home. I think maybe you could use some time alone. I don't think being with me right now is helping much."

She reached across the table to touch his hand. "I don't want you to think it wasn't a wonderful weekend. For a while there, I really was far away. I needed that."

"It came with a little pain. That's the last thing I wanted for you."

"I know. I'm the one who should have known better."

"I have to believe it'll just keep getting easier."

"Probably," she said. But she didn't say it with much confidence.

The ride back from the coast was pretty quiet in Cameron's car. He attempted conversation a few times, but Vanni didn't have much to say. They had to pull into a rest stop for a while for Vanni to nurse and change the baby, so he walked around outside, giving her privacy. He stayed close, feeling protective. He reached across the console to hold her hand a few times as they drove, and she squeezed his hand affectionately, but she smiled at him with regret and sadness in her eyes and it filled him with a foreboding. He had wanted their weekend together to be just the beginning, but he had a feeling it was going the other way.

It was about two in the afternoon when they came up to the general's house. Cameron stopped short of the drive. Parked outside the circular driveway in a nice neat row were the general's SUV, Tommy's little truck, Paul's big truck.

Vanessa stared at the vehicles, gazing out the window, her mouth set in a serious line. Waiting on the front stoop was Paul. He stood as Cameron's car came into view and Vanessa's eyes were locked on him. He had something in his hand, like a pebble or sliver of wood that he tossed. He hooked his thumbs in the pockets of his jeans and looked anxiously at Vanessa. "Damn," Cameron said. "I'm such an idiot."

Vanessa turned to look at Cameron. She lifted her chin. There it was, in her eyes. All of it.

"It wasn't your husband's memory that made you cry," he said, suddenly understanding so much more than he wanted to. "Why didn't you just tell me?"

"Because," she said, tears threatening to fill her eyes. "There's nothing to tell."

"Oh, yeah? What's that?" he asked, indicating Paul.

"I have no idea why he's here. He has someone."

"I'm not so sure about that."

"I'm pretty sure."

"But *you* love *him*."

She gave a hiccup of emotion. "I'm just very confused. We were so close. Matt, the baby, everything…"

"Vanessa," he said sincerely. "You were never honest about that."

"I didn't know what to be honest about! I'm trying to move on. Really."

"All right," he said, shaking his head. "All right, don't cry. Please."

"I told you I didn't want to mislead you," she said, but then she lifted her chin, sniffed back her tears and said, "I mean nothing to him. We're just good friends."

"Well, that's obviously not true." He glanced at Paul, who was waiting for them to stop talking and pull up. "He's here. He's waiting for me to bring you back. You might've told me you had feelings for him. I've been straight with you. You know I'd like to get something started between us. You should have been clear—you're not available."

"Cameron, please, I tried to warn you about expectations. Please, don't make this worse. I don't want you to think I just used you."

"You certainly didn't do that. You could have. I would have welcomed that, but no—you weren't ready. *Now* I understand why." He laughed without humor. "God, I've made a classic fool of myself." He took a breath. "Here's what we're going to do. I'm going to check back with you later—much later. See where you are. Maybe you'll be free. Maybe not. But I'm out of this triangle."

"It's not—"

"It *is*," he said. "I could handle what I thought I was up against. I didn't know you were in love with someone else." He took his foot off the brake and coasted forward. When he stopped in front of Paul, he jumped out, went to the passenger side of the SUV and opened the door for Vanni. He then went into the back, pulled out her small suitcase and the stroller, taking them to Paul. "Hey, buddy," he said. "Make yourself useful."

"Sure," Paul said, taking them to the front door.

Cameron got Mattie out of the car seat and before passing him to Vanessa, took a long slow moment to put a little kiss on his head. Then as he passed the baby to Vanni, he placed a soft kiss on her lips. Against them he said, "I'm sorry it didn't work out better."

"It wasn't your fault," she whispered back.

"Here's your good boy," Cameron said, passing the baby.

"I had a lovely time," she said softly. "Thank you for everything."

He couldn't resist. He touched her hair, gazed into her

eyes. Out of Paul's earshot he said, "I hope I get a chance to show you I'm a better deal. I can be there for you through all this crap. I'd never let you down, never leave you to wonder how I felt. Never." He took a breath. "I hope the son of a bitch disappoints you."

She laughed hollowly. "I'm sure that's exactly what's going to happen." She held her son against her chest and put her palm against his cheek. "Thank you for being so understanding. You've been very decent."

He laughed. "That wasn't my original idea." He became serious. "You know my number, in case you're ever ready to move on. I mean, really move on."

Paul stood near the front door with Vanessa's suitcase in one hand and the stroller in the other, watching as they said goodbye. It was sheer torture. The soft kiss, the whispers, the hand against his face. It was all so sweet, so tender. *Oh God,* he thought. I've lost her forever. *Again.*

When Cameron got back in his car and drove away, Vanessa walked briskly up to the front door. Paul stood there wearing a hangdog look and rather than making her long for him, it set her on edge. Everything in her life would be different right now if he'd leveled with her from the start, if he'd made himself clear—he was committed elsewhere and she was merely a good friend. He opened the door for her and she walked right past him. "Hello, Paul. Have a nice weekend?"

"Not so much. You?"

"Lovely, thanks."

"I need to talk to you. It's important."

"What can be so important?" she asked, breezing through the foyer. "Hi, Dad," she called as she passed by him en route to her bedroom. Paul followed her with her luggage and the stroller.

"If you could just give me a few minutes. I've been waiting for you."

"Well, you shouldn't have waited," she said, laying little Matt in the crib, busying herself with his diaper. "You could have just as easily returned my calls. Or maybe made a few calls of your own." She looked at him and said, "You keep saying we have things to talk about, then I don't hear from you."

"That's what I have to talk about. I want to explain. Vanni, please."

She looked at him and saw that he was miserable and she didn't care. She hoped he was in agony. "All right. Go ahead."

He looked nervously over both shoulders. "Can we go someplace?"

"Why?"

He leaned toward her. "Because it's tremendously personal. How's that?"

"Would you like to close the door?" she asked, lifting one mocking eyebrow.

"No, I wouldn't like to close the door!" He took a breath. *Don't get mad at her,* he told himself. She was just acting on instinct. Just trying to have a life after all that death. He couldn't get mad about that. He of all people. "Maybe we could go for a ride?"

"I don't think so. I'm just back from a long ride. Let me change the baby. Then if you want to, we can walk outside. Will that do?"

"I guess it'll have to," he said in a definite pout. And then he slowly got sucked into touching the baby's head, smiling into his face and making him smile back. The diaper came off and Mattie sent up a stream of urine that appeared four feet high, which Paul ducked and Vanessa covered quickly, making them both laugh. "All right," Paul said. "We'll just take a walk outside. Is he good? Not hungry?"

"He's been fed," she said. "I'll just put him in his bouncy seat out by Dad, if it's okay with him."

"Okay. Thanks." He backed away a little, slipping his fingers into his back pockets. He had to keep doing that because he wanted to touch her so much, and this would be a bad, bad time. The look on her face indicated she was maybe inches from wanting to belt him.

A little while later, the baby settled in his seat beside Walt's chair, Vanessa and Paul walked out on the deck behind the house and down the stairs toward the stable. "Is this something you'd like to share with Matt?" she asked. "Or is this just for me?"

He sighed in frustration. "Just for you," he said miserably. He tried to grab her hand, but she pulled it away. "Listen, I'm not sure you know how I feel about you...."

"Sure I do. You've made it clear. You have a situation in Grants Pass, a woman, and you're not in touch much. It's obvious how you feel."

"Are you kidding me? Because..." He stopped walking. She stopped walking. "I care about you a lot."

"Yes, I know. I appreciate all your concern. You've been very good to me and Mattie. You've been a very good friend to Matt."

"This is not just about Matt. I thought we were close."

"I guess we are," she said with a shrug. "Like brother and sister?"

"Vanni, I have some things to explain...."

"So you keep saying. Think you'll get it out this time?"

He ground his teeth in frustration. "There's a reason I've been hanging back a little bit. Why I've been so distracted. I wanted to wait until I figured some things out, until I knew it wasn't too soon after Matt for you...but it's starting to look like I might already be too late."

They got as far as the corral and she leaned her back

against the fence, her elbows on the top rail, heel on the bottom rail, facing him.

"Can I start at the beginning? Will you listen?"

"By all means, take your time," she invited with a wave of her hand.

"Way before you came to Virgin River, way before I ran into you at Jack's, long before anything happened to Matt, I was seeing this woman sometimes...."

She averted her eyes in spite of herself. They'd gotten this far before—he'd found a woman. Still, it just wasn't easy hearing that he had a woman in his life, though it was completely reasonable.

"I met her a long time ago. We had one night together," he said. He shrugged. "Not even a whole night. I called her a couple more times because... Because," he finished. "It was casual. Not my finest hour."

"You did something wrong?" she asked.

"At the time, I sure didn't think so. Vanni, I slept with her a few times, all right? We had an understanding. You know how it is..."

"I don't, as a matter of fact. I've actually never had that kind of understanding. But you men—"

"Aw, come on! You probably had more sex over the weekend than I had last year!"

"Is that right?" she asked, lifting her chin defiantly. In fact, at that precise moment, Vanni regretted that she couldn't allow herself to do that. Men seemed to be able to do it so easily—make love when there isn't love, see it for what it was.

"I don't even care," he said in frustration. "That's not even the point. What I have to explain is *not* that I had sex last year, when you were married, pregnant and my best friend was alive, but that I had sex a couple of months ago. After I went home, after the baby, I was pretty screwed up.

Losing Matt was killing me, I didn't want to leave you, staying with you was eating me alive, and..."

He looked down, took a breath and continued, "I tried blowing off some steam with my brothers and the construction crews. But where I made my fatal mistake was I called this woman who I never had anything with but sex and asked if we could talk. Have dinner and talk. I was messed up, Vanni. I needed to tell someone what it was like, burying my best friend, helping his baby get born. I was in a lot of pain, guilty, needy. I shouldn't have called her."

"I guess it wasn't just talk...."

"'Course not," he said. "She tells me she's pregnant. From that."

She felt that icy-cold wave of dread pass through her gut. Just when she thought it couldn't get worse. "Well, my God," she said in a breath.

"At least I finally have your attention," he said. "I wasn't kidding when I said it was important. And personal."

She pushed herself off the fence. Anger shook her inside, but she tried to keep her expression passive. "You have some issues. Tell me, Paul—what does a woman have to do to get that much of you?"

He hung his head and shook it. "You won't be impressed," he said. "She was seductive, available, I didn't care... I'm not proud of that. And I apologized, but my apology isn't going to change anything."

"So, you'll be getting married I suppose?"

"No, we won't. When I left here last week and told you I'd call—I got home to this hysterical message from her and I went to her..."

"Well, I guess you had to.... It's not as though there are consequences now."

"Vanni, I didn't sleep with her. I'll never sleep with her again. I went to make sure she didn't do anything to herself, to the baby. I went to talk her down. That's what tied me up—the reason I didn't call. This woman and I— we don't have anything together except this. I didn't even talk to her last year from October to February. But if she is having a baby and if it is my baby, I have to take care of her. Them. I have to. You understand that, don't you?"

"If?" Vanni asked.

"She said she was on the pill. I wore a condom. Seems like there's still an outside chance this could be a mistake. Probably not, but who knows? It's early. I wanted to wait until I knew for sure before…"

"God, you men just can't keep it in your pants, can you?" she said in disgust.

"Well, you can damn sure believe it's behind locked doors now! You think I didn't learn an important lesson there? Now I want you to tell me something, Vanni. You and the doctor? Is that a done deal? Do you love him?"

"Not that it's your business, Paul," she said indignantly. "He cares for me very much."

"And you? You care for him very much?"

"What's the difference? You're having a *baby!*"

"Yeah, it sort of looks that way. But I'm not having a wife. I'm not having a girlfriend or a lover."

"This baby will be your priority."

"Wouldn't little Mattie? Because, Vanni, if you make a baby, whether you meant to or not, you raise a child. That's how it is."

"This woman, Paul. She must want you to marry her."

"I'm not going to marry her, Vanessa—that would be cruel. She deserves a husband who loves her, not a man who's in love with another woman."

She frowned slightly. Her mouth stood open. He took

a step toward her and she took a step back. The fence of the corral came up against her back. "What are you saying?"

"Here I've been treating you with these kid gloves," he said. "Afraid you couldn't be approached because of your grief, afraid I'd spoil my chances with you by moving too fast. And it turns out I wasn't fast enough. But, Vanni, everything I saw told me you weren't ready—being annoyed with Carol for her fix-up, crying at the grave…" He took another step toward her and she looked up, way up, into his warm brown eyes. He lowered his face closer to hers, gripping her chin in his thumb and forefinger, lifting her chin. When he spoke, she could feel his breath. "Vanessa, I've been in love with you forever."

"How was I supposed to know that?" she asked in a shocked whisper.

"You weren't supposed to know it." His other hand was on her waist, his lips close to hers. "You were married to my best friend—you know I'd never hurt Matt like that. Never. It would have been a betrayal for you to even guess how I felt."

"But—"

"That first night, I pointed you out to Matt. You were so beautiful, so full of life and energy, I couldn't even get up the nerve to talk to you. I've never really loved a woman before. I haven't since, and I tried. I tried. I wanted to be over you because I could never have you. I should have told you how I felt before I left right after the baby was born. But I was afraid you'd be…I don't know. Shocked. Horrified. That you would think the worst of me, loving my best friend's wife, that you'd never trust me again. I was afraid you'd hate me. And then the general would shoot me."

A tear escaped and ran down her cheek. "And now you're going to be a father," she said in a breath.

"Yeah, that seems to be the case. And if I'm going to be a father, I'll be the best one I know how to be." He wiped the tear away. "I'd love to be a father to Mattie, too. You know I love him. Vanni, you have to believe me—I never wanted anything bad to happen to Matt. He was my brother."

"Paul, there's a woman in Grants Pass who's counting on you! She needs you!"

"Look, I don't know if you can understand this, but it was only sex. It wasn't even my idea, the sex. It was just—God," he said, backing away a little bit, hanging his head. "I'll do everything I can for her, but we're not going to be a couple. Send him away, Vanni. Send the doctor away."

"What if I'm involved with him?"

"This isn't Matt we're talking about," Paul said. "I'm not going to bow out quietly. I'll do whatever I have to do. I'll fight for you."

"And if we made love all weekend? Me and Cameron?"

"I don't care. I don't care about anything but that you have to know the truth. I'm in love with you. I've always been in love with you—and being in love with my best friend's wife was torture."

"What if I asked you to walk away from that situation in Grants Pass if you want a chance with me? What if I said I couldn't deal with that?"

He hung his head. "Vanessa, you know I can't. I'd never abandon a child like that. If there's a price to pay, I'll pay it—but not an innocent child."

"This isn't happening," she said, shaking her head.

"Here's what's happening," Paul said. "I love you. I think you must have feelings for me or you wouldn't be so angry. There's at least one child between us, maybe two. What we have to do is—"

"Vanni!"

They jumped apart at the sound of Walt's voice yelling from the deck. Just the tone of her father's shout sent a chill up her spine. She pushed Paul out of her way, thinking something might've happened to the baby. She ran across the yard and up the small hill to the deck, Paul close on her heels. But Walt stayed on the deck and if anything had been wrong with the baby, he'd have been inside. When Vanessa got up to her father he said, "It's Aunt Midge. She passed. We have to go. You'll have to pack up the baby again. Tom's getting his things together then he can help you."

And with that, Walt turned and went back into the house.

Vanni was frozen for a moment. She shot a look at Paul and he reached for her hand.

"Vanni, I'm sorry," he said. "What can I do?"

She just shook her head. "There's nothing you can do, Paul, except go quickly so we can get on the road…"

"Vanni, tell me you understand what I told you. I can't leave anything in doubt now."

She looked down for a moment. Then she raised her eyes and locked into his. "Paul, listen to me. There's a woman in Grants Pass who's having your baby. I want you to go home. Go home to her. Try, Paul. If there was something about her that appealed to you enough to make a baby with her, maybe you can make a life with her.…"

"No, Vanni, that's not—"

"Try, Paul. Try to fall in love with your child's mother. If you don't at least try, you'll regret it for the rest of your life."

"You don't understand. You didn't hear what I said…"

"My aunt just died and I have to go," she said. "Do what you have to do, Paul."

Seven

W alt was sixty-two, but his only sibling, his sister Midge, was all of forty-four. She'd gotten pregnant at eighteen, had a six-month marriage to the father of her child and then lived her entire adult life as a single mother with her daughter. Shelby had just barely turned twenty-five. When Shelby was still in high school Midge had been diagnosed with ALS, Lou Gehrig's disease. It had been Shelby and Midge all along, so it was no surprise that Shelby ended up as a caregiver when the disease progressed.

For the first couple of years of Midge's illness, Shelby was able to either go to school or work part-time in addition to helping her mother, but it wasn't long before Midge was a full-time job. The disease had been in its final stages for a couple of years, and while Midge had been ready to go, Shelby hung on. She'd told her uncle Walt many times she couldn't say goodbye to her mother unless she believed she'd done everything she could to make every day count.

The tragedy or blessing of Lou Gehrig's is that the body withers and fails while the mind remains alert and func-tional—Shelby and Midge chose to see this as a great blessing, for their time together had rich, sentimental moments. Midge had gone into a wheelchair four years ago, finally into a hospital bed two years ago, and soon after she was completely paralyzed. Shelby got a little help from her uncle who visited almost every week once he had retired. There was a home-nursing service, and then hospice.

They were in Bodega Bay and Walt had been prepared to move there after his retirement from the Army, but it was Midge who urged him to look further. She knew she wouldn't last long and she didn't want her brother to establish a retirement home based on her location. In fact, Walt had retired less than a year before her death and even that had been longer than any of them had predicted for Midge.

The drive from Virgin River to Bodega Bay was about four hours. Tom was dozing in the backseat of the SUV with the baby while Vanni sat up front with Walt. They'd made many such visits—most often Walt went alone, sometimes with Tom, sometimes with a pregnant Vanni— but now they were all going to say a final goodbye. Mike Valenzuela had offered to take care of the horses for them while they were gone.

Vanni said nothing as they drove, but stared out the window.

"I never even had a chance to ask you how your getaway with the doctor went," Walt said. "With Paul waiting so apprehensively for the same reason, and all…"

"It was fine," she said. "I was just thinking, I never got down there with the baby to see her—and I should have made that trip the first one. Before Carol and Lance. Midge was on borrowed time.…"

"Don't kick yourself about that," Walt said. "The household of an invalid is complicated. We talked about it—it would've been hard on Midge and Mattie, not to mention Shelby. Midge understood, believe me. And

Matt's parents had a priority there. They lost their son—
it was good that we went."

"Instead of going to Mendocino, I should have gone to
Bodega," Vanni said.

"Vanni, Midge would rather you have had a nice
weekend— she was at peace with her destiny. That's the
one thing that gives me comfort. She was ready. She wasn't
holding out for anything."

"Shelby will need help now, won't she?" Vanni asked.

"Shelby has her own ideas. We've been over this many
times. She wants to sit tight for a while, continue with her
ALS support group and get her bearings. Caregivers have
huge adjustments after the end—she wants to figure things
out before she makes a big change. I think that's smart.
After all, she was only a young girl when this all started,
she hasn't had an adult life at all, at least not the usual kind.
The house is hers now, and she'll either sell it or keep it,
but it needs a lot of work and I'll help with that. At twenty-
five, it's finally time for her to start her life." Then he took
a deep breath. "Midge wasn't in pain. Emotional pain,
yes—she felt she was a burden. My little Midge—she
didn't have it easy."

"Daddy, are you okay?" Vanni asked.

"Honey, I'm relieved. She was leaving us so slowly. At
last she has her reward. At last…she can walk and laugh
again…"

Shelby had been born in the small house that had been
her widowed grandmother's and she had lived there all her
life. Her father had never showed his face during her entire
childhood and there were no support payments of any
kind—but her uncle Walt had always been there for them.
When her grandmother died, Walt refused any of the insurance benefit and took over the house payments. In

addition to that, since Shelby had no male role model in her life, she spent summers with her uncle's family where she learned to ride, shoot skeet, and had what passed for siblings with her cousins, even during Walt's Army tours abroad. Shelby had lived summers in Germany and Denmark with the Booths. Because of the Booth family, Shelby's childhood had been rich with family.

The life of a caregiver is a hard one, emotionally draining and physically exhausting. Shelby couldn't have done otherwise—her mother was her best friend. So when the Lou Gehrig's began to get bad, although Shelby was very young, her life went on hold to care for her. But hers was not a lonely life by any means—the support system for families with life-limited members was a strong one. They helped each other in every possible way and formed incredibly strong friendships. The evidence of this was obvious at Midge's memorial—nearly a hundred people turned out for a woman who hadn't left her bed in over two years. They were clearly there for Shelby.

Midge had been cremated. She had not wanted to take that wasted body into eternity. The house had become run-down during her illness and neither an open house nor a reception was possible; the living room had held the hospital bed and support equipment needed for her care, all of which had been quickly swept away within a day of her passing. Midge's wishes had been spelled out very clearly—no fuss, just kind words and friendship—but Walt and Shelby had made arrangements with a funeral parlor months preceding her departure and secured a room that was bright and spacious, and refreshments were catered in. There were a few tasteful arrangements of flowers and one large, gorgeous spray sent by Paul Haggerty.

Walt and his family arrived Sunday night and by Wednesday all the farewells had been said to Midge. He wanted Shelby to pack up and come home to Virgin River with them, but she wouldn't. "I have things to do," she said. "Important things. Not only does this house need a lot of work—most of which I can do myself—but I have a big transition to make. I'm staying with my support group until I've had a chance to adjust to the change. And," she said, "I'm not sure I want to leave Bodega Bay. I've been here all my life."

"What would you like to do now?" Vanni asked her.

"That's part of the transition," Shelby said. "I don't know yet. People in my group have talked about trying to make changes too fast—it can be devastating. I'm not going to let myself fall into that trap."

So Walt went about the business of helping Shelby make a list of repairs and renovations that should be done to make the house presentable again. It was paid off now, so Shelby could do with it as she pleased. Shelby's list contained mostly cosmetic items from cleaning and painting, to tearing out old window coverings to replace with new ones. Walt's list was a little more industrial—he thought it was time for new doors and frames, windows and baseboards, not to mention new plumbing fixtures and updated appliances. After all, this had been his mother's home. He felt a responsibility to it, he always had. He would personally contract most of this work to be done for Shelby.

Shelby herself needed some remodeling. Even though her caregiving job had been very physical, she hadn't been getting the right kind of exercise and had gained weight. Her complexion was pale and blemished, and she hadn't bothered with makeup in years. Her hair had grown long— she'd never had it cut—and she wound a single honey-colored braid around her head to keep it out of the way. Shelby had plans for some personal changes, but she didn't discuss any of that with her family because she wasn't sure where to begin. And she wasn't sure it was even possible.

The Booths left on Friday to make the drive back to Virgin River, though leaving Shelby was hard. But she was adamant—she needed the time to grieve, to be alone, to figure out how to have a life that wasn't consumed by a loved one's illness.

They were about halfway home, Tom nodding off beside the baby in the backseat while Vanni sat up front, staring out the window. "It was a sad week in many ways," Walt said. "But it's also the end of a sad time. I'd worry more about Shelby being on her own if she hadn't shouldered so much responsibility by herself for the past few years."

"She has many wonderful friends," Vanni added.

"Are you all right, Vanni?" he asked.

"Hmm, just a little melancholy, that's all."

"It's hard to tell what's bothering you most—Midge's passing or some problem you're having with Paul." She turned to look at him and he said, "Anything you want to talk about?"

She shrugged. "There's not too much to talk about, Dad."

"You could help me understand a couple of things, you know."

"For instance?"

"Oh, don't be coy—you stood Paul up to go away with the doctor and if I know anything about you, you're not that interested in the doctor. Hell, you've been in a strange mood since Paul left after Mattie was born. You knew Paul was coming for the weekend—and despite his best efforts to be circumspect, you knew he was coming for you."

"I wasn't so sure about that."

"I heard you fight with him, Vanni. Did you and Paul have some kind of falling-out?"

"Not exactly, Dad."

Walt took a breath. "Vanessa, I don't mean to pry, but it's pretty apparent to me how you feel about Paul. And how Paul feels about you. And yet…"

"Dad, while Paul was here last autumn, we got a lot closer. We were good friends before, but of course with all we went through together… Dad, before all that happened, Paul had a life in Grants Pass. One that's not so easily left behind."

"Vanni, Paul loves you, but something happened between you recently…"

"He let me know—there are complications in Grants Pass. Something he's been struggling with. It's kept him from being honest about his feelings," she said. "He has commitments, Dad."

"A woman?" Walt asked.

Vanni laughed softly. "We shouldn't be so surprised that Paul actually had women in his life, should we? Yes, apparently there was a woman. *Is* a woman…"

"Jesus," Walt said under his breath. "He's not married, is he?"

"Of course not. He wouldn't keep something like that from us."

"Engaged?"

"He says there's enough of an entanglement there to make his position difficult. That's why he wasn't around after Mattie was born."

Walt drove in silence for a while and Vanni resumed gazing out the window. After a few moments of silence Walt asked, "What about you, Vanni? I know you care about him."

"Dad, Matt's only been gone a few months. Should I even have such feelings? Should I be completely embarrassed? I'll miss him forever, but I—"

"Please don't do that to yourself, honey," he said. "Haven't we learned by now? Life is too short to suffer needlessly."

"Will people say I—"

"I don't give a good goddamn what people say," he growled. "Everyone is entitled to a little happiness, wherever that is. And I think for you, it's with Paul."

She sighed and said, "I'm asking myself why I thought I had some claim on him. He was very good to us all, I'm so grateful—but why didn't I realize that a man like Paul wouldn't have any trouble attracting the attention—the love—of a woman? I've been so angry with him for not telling me, but… Why didn't I *ask?*"

"Now what, Vanni? Is he trying to make a choice, is that it?"

"We were having a discussion, not a very pleasant one, right when the call came from Shelby. It left his intentions up in the air a bit. But there's one thing I won't do, I can't do—I can't ask Paul to choose me over a woman he has an obligation to. I tried to make it very clear, his duty to me as his best friend's widow has expired. He doesn't have to take care of me anymore."

"I have a feeling it's more than duty," Walt said. "I have a feeling it always has been…"

"He has to do the right thing," she said. "I'm not getting in the way of that. A man like Paul—he could regret the wrong decision for the rest of his life. And frankly, I don't want to be the one left to live with his regret."

"Oh, boy. You two have some talking to do."

"No. Paul has business to take care of. I have nothing more to say about this."

* * *

Paul arrived in Virgin River about midafternoon on Saturday. He left his duffel in the truck, allowing for the possibility he wasn't welcome at the Booths'. He hadn't talked to Vanni since the Sunday before—she'd been busy with the family in Bodega Bay. Besides, the conversation they needed to have wasn't for the telephone. But the way things had ended between them caused him to hit a wall. He couldn't let her get away again, or he'd never be the same. She could push him back, be angry about his screwup, but he was going to keep coming at her until he had her attention. She was going to have to tell him, convincingly, that she didn't love him, and didn't want him in her life. That was the only way he'd let go. And he was done tiptoeing around the issue.

He was greatly relieved to note the doctor's car was not parked outside the general's house. Tom opened the door for him. "Is Vanni here?"

"She just went for a ride. She'll be back in about an hour. Two at the outside."

"Mind if I wait around?" Paul asked.

"Of course not," Tom said. "You look all stirred up."

"I just need to talk to her, that's all."

"Yeah, I know. Good luck with that. She hasn't been in a real talkative mood. Coffee?"

"Thanks," Paul said. "I'll get it."

So, they knew, he thought. No surprise there—she was all worked up and angry when they parted a week ago. And she was close to her brother and father; she wouldn't hesitate to talk with them about her problems. Their problems.

As he moved toward the kitchen, he saw the general out on the deck leaning on the railing, looking out at his view. The other thing Paul dreaded was facing Walt before he faced Vanni. But he wasn't going to blow it this time; he'd lay it out there and face it like a man. Then he was going to beg Vanni to forgive him. It could take time, but he'd gladly wait her out.

He took his coffee out to the deck and, as he stepped onto the planks, Walt turned.

"You did show up here. I predicted you would."

"Well, I'm fearless, sir," he said. Then he swallowed nervously.

"You must be. She's really got her back up this time. Vanni's down at the stable, but I'd like a word with you before you go after her, if you don't mind."

I mind, Paul thought. *Do I have a choice?* "Certainly," he said.

"You know, I'll forgive a man a lot of things, but toying with my daughter's feelings, hurting her after all she's been through, that's a tough one. That would be hard, even though we owe you for all you did."

"Sir, I'm not toying with her, I'll make it up to her somehow. I just wasn't thinking real clear after we buried Matt, and after little Matt was born. My judgment wasn't keen. I'm afraid I made a mess of things."

"Well, I can't say much about that—I don't know that anyone's judgment was as good as it could have been. It's been a painful, difficult year."

"Thanks for saying that, sir. I appreciate it. I guess you could be a lot less understanding."

"Right now my only concern is Vanessa. Mind if I ask what your intentions are?"

"Not at all, sir. You have every right, under the circumstances. I'm in love with your daughter...."

"That couldn't escape my notice," Walt said, leaning his elbows back on the railing. "Yet it doesn't appear the two of you are on the same page there."

With that full head of silver hair, tanned skin and bushy black eyebrows, Walt could look downright menacing. Paul gulped. "She mentioned the situation in Grants Pass?"

"She did. She has some concerns about you doing the right thing."

"Oh, I'll do the right thing—there's no reason to worry about that. I tried to explain, the relationship wasn't serious. I'm not very proud of that, sir. I didn't see the woman very often—a few times in a year, that's all. But it is what it is—I can't deny I was involved."

"And now?" Walt asked.

"Well, sir, even if Vanessa tells me I don't stand a chance in hell, I'm still not inclined go any further with the other woman. It just wouldn't work."

Walt frowned. "Maybe Vanessa misunderstood you," he said. "I thought there was some kind of commitment."

"Absolutely, sir. I'll take care of her and my child. I'll support them and it's my intention to be an involved father. But as for the mother—I hope for her sake she can find a man who's right for her, a man who isn't in love with another woman. Regardless of that, I plan to help raise my child. It's the only way. It's the right thing to do. It's what I want to do."

Walt was speechless for a moment. Finally, in a stunned breath he said, "My God, you have a complicated life."

"Surreal. Sir."

"And when were you planning to drop this little bomb?"

"Frankly, sir, I wanted to wait until I was sure of a couple of things before I admitted to what an idiot I am. I don't know the woman a tenth as well as I know Vanni and I have to be sure there really is a child, that it's my child, that sort of thing. Since I did what I could to protect her from pregnancy, there leaves a little doubt—but I can't deny the possibility. And—I wanted to be sure Vanni knew I feel as committed to little Matt as my own child. If she'll have me with all these complications, that is."

Walt crossed his arms over his chest. "Sounds like you'll have women and children all over the place. That could be an expensive proposition. Spreading yourself a little thin, aren't you?"

"Money isn't going to be the biggest problem. I have a successful company, a supportive family. Shared custody, a situation that wouldn't appeal to any man, that'll be tough. But I'm not going to ignore my responsibilities."

"I give you credit for that," Walt said wearily, shaking his head. "I suppose you'll verify all this quickly?"

"Of course. I'm going to the next doctor's appointment and then… I just want to be sensitive. The woman is understandably upset and I don't want to suggest she's lying, but we have to be sure. Too many people are going to be hurt by my actions as it is. Once the facts are indisputable, I just hope Vanni can forgive me. Accept me with my baggage…"

Walt looked over his shoulder at a sound and both men watched as Vanni opened the corral gate, mounted Chico and rode away from the ranch, down along the riverbank. "Well, she's getting away from you. If you have a case to plead and don't want to do it in front of her father and brother, I guess you'll have to go after her."

Paul put his still-full cup of coffee on the patio table. "Can I borrow a horse, sir?"

"Knock yourself out," the general said.

"Thank you, sir," he said, clambering down the deck stairs and taking off for the stable.

Walt watched him run. Then he shook his head and said, "Holy Jesus."

* * *

Paul saddled up Liberty, the general's stallion, the feistiest horse in the stable, but also the fastest. It took a while to get him ready, though he hurried. He'd been on this horse once before and remembered him to be difficult, hard to handle. Tom, the more experienced rider, didn't mind taking Liberty and leaving Chico for Paul. But today Paul wanted to catch up with Vanni and he really hoped Liberty didn't throw him and break his stupid neck before he found her.

He took the stallion at a fast trot along the riverbank for a good twenty minutes before he saw her up ahead. He urged the horse a little faster and when he was within her hearing, he whistled. The piercing sound cut through the air and Vanni turned her mount toward him. She took one look at him, turned and kicked Chico's flank, taking off.

"Goddammit!" he swore. So, this was how it would be—not easy. He was going to have to take off the gloves. He risked being thrown by giving Liberty a snap with the end of his rein. The stallion reared. Paul hung on, then leaned low in the saddle while Liberty closed the space between them. By God, he was going to catch her, make her listen, get through to her. There was no one within shouting distance to distract them. For once in his life, he was going to finish! Even if he had to cover Vanessa's mouth with his hand!

It only took him a few minutes to catch up to her, thanks to Liberty, the champion of the stable. Pulling alongside Vanni he reached out over her hands and grabbed her reins, pulling Chico to a stop. The expression she turned on him was fierce.

"What?" she demanded.

"Listen to me!" he retorted.

"Make it quick!"

"Fine. Here's quick. I love you. I've always loved you. I loved you before Matt saw you, but I didn't have his guts and I hung back. I've regretted that forever. Now I have—"

"A baby coming," she interrupted, lifting her chin.

"Listen! I don't know much about being a father! Just what I watched when I was growing up! And you know what I saw? I saw my parents with their arms around each other all the time! I saw them look at each other with all kinds of emotions—love and trust and commitment and— Vanni, here's the ugly truth—if I made a baby, I'm not angry about that. It wasn't on purpose, but I'm not angry. I'll do my damn best, and I'm real sorry that I'm not in love with the baby's mother. I'll still take care of them— and not just by writing a check. I'll be involved—take care of the child like a real father, support the mother the best I can. What that child is not going to see is his parents looking at each other like they've made a terrible mistake. I want him to see his dad with his arms around his wife and—"

"Did you try?" she asked. "Did you give the woman who's got your baby in her a *chance?*"

"Is that what you want for her? She's a decent person, Vanessa—she didn't get pregnant on purpose. You want her stuck with a man who's got another woman on his mind? I didn't want this to happen to her—I'm not sticking her with half a husband! She deserves a chance to find someone who can give her the real thing."

"But she loves you. She does, doesn't she? She wanted to get married."

"Vanessa, she's scared and alone. It's what comes to mind. She'll be all right when she realizes I'm not going to let her down. And I'm not going to—"

"All this because you couldn't open your mouth and say

how you felt, what you wanted," she said hotly. "I wanted so little from you—just a word or gesture—some hint that you had feelings for me. Instead, you took your wounded little heart to another woman and—"

She stopped her tirade as she saw his eyes narrow and his frown deepen. He glared at her for a long moment, then he jumped off the stallion, her mount's reins still in his hands. He led the horses the short distance to the river's edge, to a bank of trees.

"What are you doing?" she asked, hanging on to the pommel.

He secured the horses at a fallen tree, then reached up to her, grabbed her around the waist and pulled her none too gently out of the saddle. He whirled her around and pressed her up against a tree, holding her wrists over her head and pinioning her there with the whole length of his body. His face was close to hers. "You never opened your mouth, either," he said.

She was stunned speechless. She couldn't remember a time Paul had ever behaved like this—aggressive, commanding.

He leaned closer. "Open it now," he demanded of her just before he covered her mouth with his. Her lips opened under his and he moved over her mouth with passion, with heat, and she responded with her own. Her gentle, shy Paul, not only filled with all this desire, but clearly aroused. He let go of her wrists and circled her waist to pull her harder against him, and with a sigh and a shiver of lust, her arms went around him, yielding. Not just yielding—inviting.

Feeling her response, he couldn't bring himself to end the kiss, but only deepened it, invading her velvety mouth with his tongue, letting his breath out slowly as her tongue came into his mouth. It was with a great deal of regret that he reminded himself they had to talk it through, get all their issues in the light and dealt with. But when he left her mouth, he stayed so close to her, he was whispering into her parted lips. "Vanessa, you have the worst goddamn temper."

"I…"

"And you're the bossiest woman I've ever known. I want you to listen to me—I can't change what I feel, what I've felt for years. I tried, because I never thought I'd have any kind of chance, I never imagined that we'd lose Matt. And even with you in my arms, finally, I'd give anything to have him back. But we can't, Vanni. It's going to be you and me now. That's all it can be. Now stop all this fucking around—because I want you so bad, my head is pounding!"

"I never knew how you felt."

"I know that, Vanni," he said quietly. "You weren't supposed to."

"I loved Matt, you know."

"I know. And he loved you." He took a breath. "And I loved you both."

"But you were the guy who caught my eye the night we all met. You. Yet you never even talked to me. Maybe if you'd talked to me…"

"He beat me to it. And once that happens…"

"What did she do, Paul? The woman in Grants Pass? How'd she manage to get your attention?"

"I told you. She was pretty. Seductive," he said. "And I was lonely. I let it happen, Vanni, because there was no reason for me not to. You belonged to someone else. Not just anyone else, but Matt."

"And later? When I didn't belong to anyone?"

"I thought you still belonged to Matt, to a memory," he said. "And I was pretty much out of my mind. It was stupid. I told you—I'm not good with women. I never have been, or you'd have belonged to me, not my best friend."

"I don't have any regrets, you know. Matt was good for me, good to me. He made me happy, he gave me a beautiful son. I'll never regret a day…"

"Vanni," he whispered, brushing that thick, copper hair away from her face. "Vanni, as much as I love you, as much as I wish I'd had the guts to pursue you before he got to you, in the end I wanted you happy. I wanted him happy. But now…" He gave her a kiss. "It is what it is. I want us to go forward. I want to take care of you and Mattie. And probably one more…"

"You're still not certain?" she asked him.

He shook his head. "Vanni, be prepared—I don't think I'm getting out of that one. If I'm responsible for a child, I'll see it through."

"I know." She sighed. "Could be a large family in the end."

"You'll stand by me through that?"

She shrugged. "You'd stand by little Matt, wouldn't you? That's how it is. We don't leave babies out there alone, without parents who love them."

He smiled into her eyes. "You're wonderful, you know. But very hard to shut up." He pressed himself against her, kissing her deeply. "God," he said in a whisper, going after her again, so desperately she laughed against his lips. "Do you have any idea how long I've wanted to kiss you?"

"If you're telling me the truth, I know exactly how long. Paul, I want you to know something—while I was Matt's wife, I didn't have one second of doubt or temptation. Not one split second. I loved him completely."

"Vanni, I know…"

"It wasn't until later, after the baby, months after Matt was gone… And I didn't think you'd ever see me as anything more than your friend's wife… I used to talk to Matt about you. I'd stand out at that grave and tell him that I'd always love him, but I was going to love again and, if he approved, he should give you a nudge. You were so much more than a friend, but you didn't seem to see me as a woman. I thought you couldn't separate me from your best friend and his death."

He ran his hand down her hair. "Oh, I saw you as a woman—too much woman for me. I was fighting for my life, I was so guilty about the way I'd felt for years. I didn't know what to do except give you time, watch you come out of mourning and plan my approach. And trust me, I wasn't planning this one." He shook his head. "The goddamn doctor got there ahead of me. The fact that you were a recent widow sure didn't slow him down."

"Does she know about me?" Vanni asked.

"She does," he said. "God, I hope she and I can work together on this. Most of all, I hope you're not making a big sacrifice because of my screwup."

"I couldn't let a child of yours go any more than you could."

"Vanni, I want to marry you, take care of you and Mattie."

She frowned slightly. "Wait a minute—is there anything else you should tell me before you propose? Any other little secret stuffed in the back of your closet?"

"Honest to God, that's it. Until very recently, I had the most boring life in Grants Pass!"

"You're sure about that? Because until last week, I thought I knew everything about you. I mean, I've known you for years, lived with you for months. We spent so many hours just talking…"

"That's it. Jesus, isn't that enough? I want to marry you and Mattie. In fact, once we get the lay of the land, I'd like to have more children. Maybe at least one that we actually make together. I'd give anything for that, Vanni."

She smiled. "Let's see how many you have so far before we make those kinds of plans, huh?"

"Then you'll marry me?" he asked, brushing the hair away from her brow.

"You're a very interesting guy, Paul. It takes you years to tell me you love me, and minutes to ask me to marry you."

"I'll wait till you're ready, but I want us to be together forever."

The corner of her mouth lifted along with one reddish brow, teasing. "Don't you think we should see how we work out sexually? See if we're good together?" she asked, grinning playfully.

"Vanessa, we'll be good together. Well, you'll be perfect and I'm sure I'll catch on eventually." He kissed her again. "Are you going to say yes or make me beg?"

"Do you think I want to live with my father and have a weekend boyfriend forever? Yes," she said. "I'm probably going to marry you."

"Oh God, thank you," he said, grabbing her to him again. "Is tomorrow too soon?"

"A little bit. We're waiting on the Grants Pass baby, remember? It won't make a difference, but I think we should know how many people we're bringing into this family."

"We'll do that. Right away. That's perfectly reasonable," he said, grinning. Then he shook his head in sheer wonder. "You've been wonderful about this. I didn't really expect you to come around so quickly. I thought you were going to drive me crazy…"

"Well, I've turned it over in my mind for a while now. When it happened, we didn't know where we stood with each other. It's not as if we said the I love you's and you went to bed with another woman."

"Yet you insisted I try to see if I could love her?"

"I had to be sure. I don't want another woman's man, even if it's you."

"You're remarkable, you know that? In fact, your whole family is remarkable. Your dad was pretty civil about it, too."

She was quiet for a moment, a startled look on her face. "My *dad?*" she asked.

"Yeah. He just wanted to be sure I wasn't playing with your feelings. And he seemed kind of interested in how I was going to manage, financially. I told him the company's doing well, that's not going to be a—"

"You told my *dad?*" she asked, cutting him off.

Paul was frozen, staring at her for a second. "No," he finally said. "*You* told your dad. Because he asked me if I planned on… Oh shit, what did he ask me? Something about whether I had commitments in Grants—" He leaned over her shoulder and let his forehead bang against the tree. "And I said, 'Absolutely, sir—I'll support the woman and my child.' Oh God."

Vanni, laughing, pushed him away slightly. "You told my *dad!*" she exclaimed, laughter shaking her.

Paul grimaced. "You didn't tell him, huh?"

"Of course not," she said, her eyes alight and her smile huge. "That's a little personal, don't you think? Plus, you said you still had to be sure it was for real."

"Oh God."

"Paul," she said, "what did you do?"

"I thought you'd told him. What did you tell him?"

She looped her arms around his neck, but she was laughing too hard to speak for a while. "I told him we shouldn't be surprised to learn you'd actually had women in your life before you came to Virgin River. That there was a woman…" And she dissolved into laughter again.

He leaned against her once more, pressing her back to the tree. "It isn't that funny."

"Are you kidding? It's *hilarious!*" She laughed a little

more and finally said, "Paul, he's a trained interrogator. You walked right into it!"

"I don't see the humor…"

"Well, if you don't have a sense of humor, I don't know if I can—"

She was cut off by his mouth finding hers. In fact, he kept her from laughing for a long time, covering her with his body. They kissed and held on to each other. Finally he released her lips and asked, "You done laughing?"

"I am. I think you worked it out of me."

He touched her swollen lips with tender fingers. "Do you think your father will shoot me?"

"Probably not," she said, smiling. "But if you hear a rifle cock, you might want to duck."

"Funny," he said, kissing her again.

"I think I have whisker burn," she told him.

"Yeah." He grinned. "Looks good on you, too."

"We have to go back. I have a baby to take care of."

"I don't want to go back…. He's going to be waiting for me.…"

"You might as well just face it," she said, and laughed again. "We've been out here a long time."

"Not quite long enough," he said, and kept her just a few more minutes, afraid to let her go.

She wiggled her hips against his. "Paul, it's pretty obvious, pinning me against a big old tree turns you on."

"I know," he said. "We need to get alone."

"Uh-huh. I need that, too. Probably more than you do. And the sooner the better."

Vanni left Paul to tend to the horses while she rushed back to the house to check on the baby. It took him the better part of an hour to get them brushed down and stabled, the tack put away. He might've been dragging his feet a little when he went back to the house. By the time he got there, Walt was standing at the dining-room buffet fixing himself a short drink. Paul had lived with the man for months; even given the untimely death of his son-in-law, he hadn't been a daytime drinker. If tragedy or depression didn't drive him to the bottle, this had to be celebratory.

Walt turned, regarded Paul and lifted one bushy black eyebrow. "Fix you a little something to take the edge off, son?" he asked.

"Thank you, sir." And mentally he added, "You dog."

"Bourbon? Scotch? Canadian?"

"Crown?" Paul answered in question.

"My pleasure," Walt said, selecting the bottle from the cabinet and pouring a short shot on ice. He passed it to Paul and said, "You didn't do much undercover work in the Marine Corps, I guess."

"No, sir."

"Obviously." He raised his glass. "Here's to me winning the game I didn't even know I was playing."

"To you," Paul said grudgingly.

After having a sip, Walt said, "I know you pretty well, Paul. Before today, I never had a doubt about you. So, I'll only ask once—you plan to treat my daughter well?"

"Like solid gold, sir. Despite everything."

"If you're her choice, that's good enough for me." And he raised the glass again.

"Thank you, sir."

"But really," he said, chuckling. "You walked right into it."

Vanni and her father were so alike it was scary. In addition, she had a fiery temper. And he asked himself, *Do I want a general for a wife?* The answer came quickly. Oh, yes. Oh my God, yes.

Eight

The general, knowing things had been resolved and were now heating up between Vanni and Paul, made himself scarce after dinner, leaving the reconciled lovebirds to the kitchen cleanup alone. But Tom didn't have the facts and caught them in a serious lip-lock while they were supposed to be washing and drying dishes. Paul had Vanni pressed up against the sink, devouring her with yet another passionate kiss.

To Paul's back, Tom said, "I guess this means you two have things worked out?"

Paul whispered in Vanni's ear, "Get rid of him, will you? Please?"

"Go away, Tom," she said a little breathlessly.

"About time, Paul. Really, I was beginning to think you were a little slow or something. I'm going to Brenda's."

"No curfew tonight," Paul said, though his voice was muffled against Vanni's neck. "Stay away all night if you want."

There was the sound of laughter, then the closing of the front door, and Paul's lips were on Vanni's again.

"Vanni, honey," Paul whispered. "Will you pack a bag

for yourself and Mattie and come away with me in the morning? Come back to Oregon with me for a few days...."

"Hmm. Good idea."

"We'll leave very early," he said. "Like in an hour…"

She laughed at him. "We'll leave at nine. I don't want to rush the baby...." She gave him a little kiss, then wiggled away from him, putting away the last plate. "I have to go give Mattie his bath, then get him settled for the night."

Paul spent what seemed to be an interminable two and a half hours in front of CNN, unable to concentrate on a word of it. After an hour he got up and fixed himself a drink, asking the general if he could get him anything. But the general declined—probably because he didn't have what was best described as bridegroom nerves. Paul was asking himself a hundred questions.

He had no idea if he was a good lover. How does a man know? He'd been pretty successful at getting the job done, satisfying the woman he was with before thinking of himself. He couldn't remember any complaints, but he wasn't a man who'd been with a lot of women. Not by comparison to some of his friends, for sure. And never with a woman like Vanni. And with Vanni, he didn't want to merely satisfy her—he wanted to bond her to him forever with the greatest pleasure of her life. He wanted their coming together to be sweet for her. Sweet and powerful. Paul wanted her to know he could be an adequate husband.

He heard the baby crying, then making sweet little noises while he enjoyed his bath. A while later he heard the tub fill again; Vanni was treating herself to a soak.

Would she cry over Matt when they finally made love? Would she remember him, long for him, miss him all over again? And how does a man handle that? Paul asked himself. He wished he'd thought to ask Jack; Jack had married a widow. There must have been special challenges. *I've held her through a million tears,* Paul thought. *I can hold her through as many more as it takes.*

He took a shower, mostly to distract himself, and when he came out of the bathroom only one light was left on in the great room, probably for Tom. There was a light under the general's door and the sound of the TV in his room could be heard.

Paul stepped out onto the deck and stood under a cool, dark sky that was riddled with a million stars. The sky was so deep and clear, it was as if one could see into the next universe. He was barefoot and bare chested with his towel slung around his neck. He looked toward Matt's grave, then toward the sky, holding on to the ends of the towel. *I swear,* he promised, *I'll do my best, buddy. I'll do my best by both of them.*

He'd give the world to hear Matt snap back some smart-ass response.

Paul went to his room, dug around in his shaving kit, then went to Vanni's bedroom door. He quietly turned the knob until it opened a crack. "Can I come in?" he whispered.

"What are you doing?" she whispered back, sitting up in her bed and flicking on the lamp. "Are you completely crazy?"

"Suicidal," he said. He entered her room, softly closing the door behind him. The first thing he did was glance at the baby to make sure he was asleep. "I have to spend more time with you."

"With my father right down the hall? With me in bed?"

"I don't care if the whole Army is down the hall. If you won't come away with me tonight, I just couldn't stop myself. Are you naked?"

She rolled her eyes and grinned at him. She was wearing a gray T-shirt with ARMY printed on it. Yet on her, it sure looked sexy. And God, that grin—it was everything. It was his world. She was so strong, so sure of herself. He should have known she was ready for him, for them, or she'd have told him she wasn't, because that was Vanessa. She didn't play around, didn't make mistakes with her feelings. She knew where she was headed; she had a will as powerful as the general's.

He grinned back at her. "You should try to be quiet," he said. And she giggled. "Vanessa! For once in your life… can you be quiet this once?"

"I don't know, Paul. What are you going to do to me?"

He smiled and knew his eyes grew hot. "I'm going to get under that Army T-shirt. Unless you ask me not to."

"Don't be ridiculous. I *want* you under the T-shirt. But really, this is way more bold than you usually are…"

"I'm turning over a new leaf. No more waiting for an invitation. No more waiting for just the right moment. I need you. God, do I need you." His mouth covered hers, his hands slipped under the T-shirt, finding her breasts, and he groaned. "Aw, Vanni. Your bottom half is totally naked."

She grinned against his lips. "Yours isn't."

"I'm trying really hard to talk sense into myself," he whispered against her lips.

"I don't think he'll break down the door and shoot you in the back of the head," she said. "He's much more direct. And he hates dealing with me when I'm depressed. But you might want to listen for that rifle cock…"

"I tried like hell not to do this," he said, lifting her T-shirt, his lips finding her nipples. "Turn that light off…."

"Not until you take off your jeans," she said.

He raised his head. "You're crazier than I am," he whispered. "Are you going to be quiet?"

"I'll try. Really. But if he comes knocking?"

Paul gave her an evil grin. "Anyone who touches that door is really going to have his hands full." He tossed the towel that had been around his neck over the back of a chair in her room. Before unsnapping his jeans, he pulled some condoms out of his pocket and put them on the night side table. There were several.

She glanced at them and lifted one tawny brow. "That's very optimistic, Paul," she said with a smile.

"It's probably delusional," he answered, pulling the T-shirt over her head and tossing it away. His breath caught at the sight of her; she was breathtaking. And not the least shy. Then he stood, his hands went to the snap and zipper and he shed his jeans quickly, kicking them away.

Her eyes grew round. "Oh my. Dear God." He was simply beautiful. A soft mat of brown hair covered his chest, his hips were narrow, legs long, and he was huge. Huge and erect.

He sat down on the bed and his expression took on an earnest look. "Are you all right since the baby? Are you worried about having sex?"

Her eyes were glued to his male parts. "I'm a little more worried about being quiet," she said thoughtfully.

Paul turned off the light, claimed her lips and slipped down into the bed with her. His hands were all over her, caressing her back, her breasts, her firm, round bottom, her lush hips. And her hands were on him immediately, examining every part of him with her fingers and palms, stroking, rubbing. "I want you," he whispered. "I want you so bad." And his fingers slipped down to that damp place where her legs were joined. "Open for me, baby." He didn't have to ask twice; her legs came apart. He slipped a finger through her silky, slick softness and inside. He whispered against her parted lips, "Oh man, that didn't take long...."

"Look who's talking," she whispered back. "You came out of your jeans ready."

"Vanni, I've been ready for hours. I tried a shower, a walk outside, a drink…"

She reached over to the bedside table for a condom, began taking it out of the foil, but she didn't quite get the job done. His fingers on her, in her, his mouth on her neck and breast, it was almost more than she could take. She began to tremble and grabbed his wrist to pull his hand away. "Stop," she whispered. "I'm already too close. Wait."

"No," he whispered back. "No waiting. Let go," he told her. "It's okay. Come for me. Hard and fast." And he kept touching her, stroking her, moving against her while he kissed her.

She spiraled up and over the top instantly, climaxing before she could even help with the condom. It was crunched in her clenched fist and she made a rather loud, growling moan and Paul covered her mouth as fast as he could, trying to muffle the sound under his lips, but he didn't let her fall alone—he carried on with his rough caresses, taking her beyond pleasure. He continued until the storm was past and she collapsed, breathless beneath him, soft in his arms. The only fear he'd had was that for some reason he wouldn't be able to do it for her—but he hadn't even gotten started and she was gone. Off like a rocket. It thrilled him.

"Aw, baby," he said. "That was special. You do that very well."

"Whew," she answered, weak. "I meant to wait for you.…"

He took the package out of her hand and applied the condom. "I should have known. You're a fireball. Let's have some more of that, huh? Let me in, baby. We're not done."

With a passionate sigh, she lifted her knees and he worked his way inside, slowly, easily, until she took all of him. "Paul," she whispered, clutching him. "Paul…"

He rose above her and began to move, slowly, evenly, deeply. He had to cover her mouth with his because the sounds she made would give them away. He grinned down at her. "You're a screamer, aren't you, sweetheart?" He moved some more and his voice was hoarse, strained. "Do it again, Vanni. Give it up." Then he covered her mouth again and pumped and she went out of her mind, over the moon, beyond the stars—and an explosion of pulsing pleasure that left her totally limp and completely spent. "That's my girl. You are *very* good at that.… I am the luckiest man alive."

"Paul," she whispered weakly. "I can't keep doing that without you. What are you waiting for?"

He pecked at her lips and she could feel his smile, she could feel his teeth. "Just once more, sweetheart, come on. It's so good."

"I can't," she said, exhausted. "I just can't."

"We'll see.…" He slipped down, kissing and licking his way down past her breast, over her tummy and, pulling her thighs apart, gave her a few hearty strokes with his tongue, right in her center. She threw her head back and moaned loudly. Paul's hand came up to cover her mouth firmly, which only made her squirm more wildly. He didn't torture her long. He rose, entered her again and shifted his hips slightly, creating a perfect friction. In the darkness of the room, he could see her eyes were wide, her lips apart slightly as she gasped in anticipation. "One more," he whispered. "One more, for us." She arched her pelvis against him, digging her heels into the mattress, and again he had to cover her gasping mouth to quiet her. "I love you, baby," he whispered against her parted lips. "I love you so much." And then she exploded, drowning him in pulsing heat.

Paul was done holding back. He'd never had a feeling like this before. He let it go with a powerful blast and believed in his heart he was making Vanessa his till the end of time—his woman, the head of his family, the love of his life. And he was hers. He released himself at her exact moment and emptied himself into her, giving her his heart, his life, his soul.

And then he held her, soft against him, stroking her hair and pressing soft kisses into her temple. "I've never had an experience like that in my life," he whispered. "You're an amazing woman. I think I might be the luckiest man in the world, to have this with you."

"Shew," she whispered, letting out her breath. "I think you're catching on...."

She was answered by a deep, low chuckle. "You make it so easy."

"Come on, Paul," she said, laughing softly. "Don't pretend you don't know—you're an incredible lover. And I know there have been women..."

"Not very many," he said. "There are things about this that are brand-new." He rose up on an elbow and looked down at her. "It's the first time I've ever made love with someone I want to spend the rest of my life with, someone I want to be my partner, my best friend, my lover until the end. The mother of our children. It's what's been missing from my life."

She was quiet for a long moment; her eyes might've glistened. "That's very sweet."

"It's very true." He gave her a kiss on the cheek, chin, lips. "Should I get out of here?"

"No. Stay with me," she whispered. "Please..."

"Okay, baby. As long as you want me here," he whispered back.

"Forever," she said. "Is forever too long?"

He kissed her cheek and pulled her against him. "Might not be long enough… Give me a second in the bathroom. I'll be back."

He grabbed the towel and wrapped it around his waist. He was lucky; no traffic in the hall. He made it a quick, quiet trip and was back in bed beside Vanessa, pulling her close. Paul lay awake for a long time, just listening to her breathe, drinking in her scent. Holding her like this, naked against him, it was like a miracle. You don't just go to sleep on miracles. You savor them, give thanks for them.

It wasn't until Paul looked out Vanni's bedroom window at dawn and caught sight of the general trudging down to the stable to feed the horses that he finally made the short journey back to his own bedroom.

Vanessa was in the kitchen in the morning with a cup of coffee, Mattie in his bouncy chair on the table beside her, when Walt came back from the stable. "Good morning, Daddy," she said brightly. She looked at her watch. "You must have had a very early start."

"About the regular time," he said, going for a mug of coffee. "I'm going to miss the hell out of Tom. I'm just starting to realize what it must have been like for him, up so early, getting all that stable work out of the way before school." He took a sip. "I'm going to miss more than that, of course."

"But you wouldn't have it any other way," she said. "We're all so proud of Tom. He's going to do well."

"That's the hard part—sending him off like this, knowing it's the best thing, even while it feels like the worst thing. And I'm losing you, too," he said.

Vanessa had no trouble imagining how the general could look scary as hell to his troops. But this morning, at the kitchen table with just his daughter and grandson, he was soft as a puppy. She reached across the table and patted his hand. He played with the baby's foot with his other. "You're not losing me, Daddy. Not ever."

"It's okay, Vanni. You're a young woman in your prime. Paul's a fine young man, despite the fact that he's fathering the nation…"

"Daddy…"

"Nah, he's a good man. His incident aside."

She leaned toward him. "You're not losing me," she said again. "But I packed a bag this morning. I'm going home with him, Dad. Just for a few days. We'll be back before the weekend."

"That doesn't surprise me a bit. I'm surprised you didn't take off in the dark of night."

Then she asked softly, "Did I disturb your sleep last night?"

He shook his head. "I suppose we're an odd family," he said. "Not quite the stiff and upright family I had always thought we were, but the facts of our lives have changed all that. Relaxed our expectations… At least mine." He looked down. "I heard you, yes. It wasn't too disturbing. In fact, those are happy sounds." He lifted his eyes. "There were other nights I heard you—and your brother. Nights of crying over loved ones lost. Your mother. Your husband. And I don't doubt there were nights young Tom, at only fourteen, wondered what to do about a tough old three-star crying in his bed over his wife's death."

"Oh, Daddy…"

"Vanni—life is rough. It can't help but be, especially for military families like ours. But we have to soldier on, be strong, do the best we can. If you tell me you're happy with Paul…"

"Oh, Dad, I love him so much. I loved him before I fell

in love with him, if that makes sense. He loves me. And—he loves you."

"Any man who would do all he did after his best friend's death—this is a man who deserves my respect."

"Thank you, Daddy. We still have plenty of time before Tom's graduation and his exit to basic training, even if I spend a little time in Grants Pass." She laughed. "Tom may have trouble fitting us in, anyway—I know Brenda is on high priority right now."

"Leaving is hard for him, too. But he'll be swept up in it in no time. There's something about being with those boys, competing, trying to prove yourself. He won't have time to miss anyone." He laughed a little. "The girl. He'll miss the girl. He's not a eunuch, after all."

She smiled but didn't say anything. Her father—he'd looked at so many young faces over his career—his read was solid.

"Paul's hoping to do some building here. We'll live down here as much as work provides."

Walt's eyes widened. "Did *you* insist on that?"

"No," she said. "He loves this place. He has good friends here. He loves coming to meet the boys. He'd like to build us a house here."

"Vanni," he said, touched. "That would be wonderful. I can let you go if it's what you want but, selfishly, I'd be so happy to have you nearby."

"He'll have details to work out. And there's that other matter—"

Before she could continue, Paul walked into the kitchen. "Good morning, sir," he said, heading to the coffeepot.

Walt stood. "Vanni tells me you're considering working here."

"Yes, sir. But don't get ahead of me—I have to talk to

the family. When we get up to Oregon for a few days, Vanni can do some grandparent time with Carol and Lance, meet my family, and I can run this proposition by my dad and brothers. I hope you're okay about me taking Vanni home with me for a few days. We'll be back before the weekend."

"Good. That's good." Walt stuck out his hand to Paul. "You should go away together for a while," he said. "So I can get some sleep." And then he walked out of the kitchen.

Paul could feel subtle changes in himself after just twenty-four hours. A confrontation with Vanessa followed by one night in her arms had taught him a few things about her. And himself. She was a strong woman—she needed a man of equal or greater strength. One who was sturdy, determined, not someone who would defer or shy away. She liked power, and she didn't crave it for herself, but rather wanted to align herself with it; she was a for-midable partner and required a man who wasn't the least bit nervous about that. If Vanessa felt overpowered, she wouldn't cower, she'd fight. But if she felt considerably stronger than her man, she'd fight even harder. She could only team up with confidence, passion and conviction. All that brought out the best in him—his self-assurance and competence. She was raised by a general—she appre-ciated brawn and nerve. Courage.

She liked his gentle side, but only in contrast. She'd been forced to shoulder so much pain and loss and had had to be tough; she couldn't partner with a man who would take her strength for granted; she needed a man she could lean on sometimes. She had a temper; she was feisty and bossy, sometimes difficult. But she was fair and just with a love that was deep and enduring. She had both a growl and a purr; Paul was committed to bringing out and adoring both.

She was perfect for him. And he realized with some surprise that he was her match. It was an incomparable feeling. The pride it fed in him honed his strength, deepened his love.

While Paul drove them to his home, to Oregon, with the baby tucked into his car seat in the back of the extended cab truck, Vanni slept as much as Mattie did. The trepidation that had kept him from speaking up earlier, that had once kept him from approaching her from across a crowded bar and sitting down beside her a few years ago, was gone. He was possessive, sure of himself, serene. He couldn't keep his hands off her, constantly reaching for her, touching her knee, circling her shoulders with his arm. He'd been inside her body, made her tremble with pleasure and beg for more, branded her, made her his. She didn't scare him anymore.

When they were nearly to Grants Pass, Vanni asked when they should see Paul's family or the Rutledges. "We're not even going to call them until tomorrow afternoon," he said. "We'll stop off at the grocery, get what we need and have a night alone, just the three of us. Monday is soon enough to get in touch with them." When Vanni started making noises of cooking him an elaborate dinner to show off some of her skills, he stopped her. "We're not spending all our time in the kitchen tonight. There's plenty of time for that," he said. Into the cart went diapers, formula for the baby, cereal, eggs, milk, sandwich and salad makings and an already-roasted chicken and vegetables.

Vanessa had seen some of Paul's work before—Mel and Jack's house, which was Joe's design and Paul's construction expertise. But he showed her his house in Grants Pass with pride. It was a masterpiece. Large oak double doors led into a spacious foyer with white marble floors.

There were a few steps down into a sunken great room with thick, light beige carpet and a large fireplace of beautiful slate. A long row of windows with French panes looked out onto a manicured lawn, and the ceilings were high and beamed. There were two bedrooms, spacious, and throughout the house were stunning built-in bookcases and cabinets and even a gorgeous built-in breakfront in the dining room, so large it took up most of one wall. Off the kitchen and dining room was a long deck with a barbecue and redwood furniture. Paul had done most of the interior work himself—he had a complete workshop in the third bay of his three-car garage; he was a master carpenter. The kitchen was a showplace—hardwood floors, white granite countertops flecked with gold, cupboards with glass doors. And it was immaculate to the point of being sterile.

"This is magnificent," she said in a breath. "I would give anything for such a house," she said.

"I'll build you whatever you want," he said.

Paul set up the baby's port-a-crib in the second bedroom while Vanni nursed him in the great room. He made a tray of snacks, poured Vanni a glass of wine and himself a beer. Then there was a little playtime before Mattie started to yawn. Paul took the baby to his bed to put him down for a nap and when he got back, he found Vanni in the kitchen, rinsing off their dishes.

He wanted to tell her things about how his life had changed in a day, but the words eluded him. It would be nice to explain that he'd been with women before, but never like this. He'd had sex. Good sex. In fact, the worst sex he'd ever had was pretty damn good. But no woman before her had taken him in with the kind of intimacy and intensity that Vanni had; he was sure he'd never been able to draw the kind of response from anyone that Vanessa had given back to him. The second his lips touched her neck or his hand glided over her soft body, she was in motion. Hotter than fire. The passion she unleashed was unbelievable. Unimaginable. The way her hips moved against him, it made him weak to even think about it. It gave him a kind of power and mastery he didn't know he had. When she was in his arms he became the world's greatest lover. There was nothing in the universe that could stroke a man's pride more than lighting up a woman with such ease; to bring her complete, exhausting satisfaction like that, over and over. She was amazing and he felt as if his heart would explode. And clearly, the most remarkable and wondrous part was that she left him without a shred of doubt—she was his. Completely his.

But instead of trying to explain how she made him feel, he came up behind her, put his arms around her and kissed her neck. He shut off the running water and turned her around. He lifted her into his arms and whispered against her parted lips, "I can't believe I can take you to my bed and love every piece of you."

She trembled and answered, "I can't believe you're not getting me there faster."

And then it began again…

Muriel St. Claire figured Sunday afternoon was a good time to check out the town of Virgin River. Everything was very quiet and she knew she could poke around without creating a huge stir. The house she'd recently bought was just outside of town and she'd never had time to do more than drive down the main street. The place was small and compact with what looked to be one very low-key restaurant and no other businesses on the main street.

The Open sign was on in the window of the restaurant, so she parked her truck and went inside. Muriel looked around appreciatively. This was a perfect little country bar and grill—everything polished to a high sheen, embers glittering in the hearth, two little old ladies sharing a table near the fire, fishing and hunting trophies on the walls. Behind the bar was a good-looking, grinning bartender polishing glasses.

She felt a little overdressed in her tailored pants, ostrich boots and fitted leather blazer over a cream-colored silk blouse. But, no worries, she'd know for next time.

The elderly women immediately started to whisper and twitter, glancing at her, then whispering some more. Well, that was quick; they might be senior citizens but they knew who she was. The bartender tilted his head and gave her a welcoming smile.

She walked up to the bar. "Nice little place," she said.

"Thanks. We're kind of proud of it. What can I get you?"

"How about a cola? Diet."

"You got it." He fixed her up with a drink and asked, "Passing through?"

"No, actually. I just moved here. Well—" she laughed "—I was born not far from here and always intended to come back."

"You look kind of familiar," Jack said. He shook his head. "I had a little déjà vu. You kind of reminded me of my wife for a second there. First time she walked in this place, I figured she was lost. Classy blonde in my bar? Couldn't be happening."

"I guess you did the right thing and married her."

"What was I gonna do?" Jack asked with a laugh. He put out his hand. "Jack Sheridan."

"Muriel," she said, accepting the hand.

"You been around lately?" he asked.

"Not lately, no. I used to visit when my folks were still

alive. But over the past few years I've just been up here on very quick trips to look at property. I've never been in this bar before."

"I take it something worked out in terms of property?"

"A ranch. Out on Silverton Road."

Jack frowned. "The old Weatherby place? He didn't die, did he?"

"No," Muriel said. "Finally decided to give it up and go live near the kids."

"I didn't know it was even available," Jack observed.

"I don't think it was. I've been working with a Realtor for a few years now, looking for property. I think she went visiting, telling people she might have a buyer if it was the right place. And this was the right place. Did you know him?"

"Nah," Jack said, giving the counter a wipe. "He was an old-timer when I got here a few years ago. He'd already sold off most of his stock, kept a couple of horses, couple of dogs and a nice garden. He was already retired. I met him a couple of times in the bar. Had a slew of kids and none of 'em stayed around." He laughed. "You know— you make it your life's dream to get your kids a big education and, in the end, no one wants the ranch." He glanced at the tittering women. "Madge and Beatrice," he explained. "They are all stirred up. Newcomers rate some attention around here."

"I suppose that's the case," she said.

"Doesn't that Weatherby place need some work?" he asked.

"Some serious restoration," she said, sipping her soda. "But it's solid, has a good barn and corral, and there's a guesthouse. What was Weatherby doing with a guesthouse?"

"As I understand it, his late wife used to like to paint,

so she built herself a studio. After she died, a long while back, he turned it into a little apartment he could rent out to ranch hands or loggers. Sort of a bunkhouse."

"Oh, that explains it," she said.

"Explains what, if you don't mind my asking?"

"It's a good little room with a lot of windows. But it was filthy. Like it was rented to men and not cleaned in between." She sipped her cola. "The Realtor got a crew to clean it up real nice. I gave it a coat of paint, decorated it in a small way, bought a big area rug and can live in it while I work on the bigger house."

"You looking for a contractor?" he asked.

"Not yet. I'm sure I'll need some help, but I've been looking forward to this for a long time and I want to do most of the work myself. I mean, I'm not crazy—I'll need help if I ever have to wire, plumb, lay flooring or put on a roof. But I'm hell with a paintbrush. And, believe it or not, I've mastered seamless wallpaper."

"What about cabinets, countertops, tile, wallboard, et cetera?"

"I'm very handy. I plan to restore it, not upgrade it. It's got a lot of spirit. Some women do needlepoint, some sand and varnish."

That got a big laugh out of Jack. Right at that moment, Mel came in with David on her hip and her big belly preceding her through the door. He lifted his chin in greeting, but before Mel could make it to the bar, she was summoned over to Madge and Beatrice, who leaned their heads together and spoke intently, glancing at Jack and the woman, eyes round.

Muriel glanced at the woman and baby; no doubt about it, that would be the classy blonde who married Jack. She smiled.

Mel passed the baby over the bar to her husband, gave

him a little kiss and then grinned at Muriel. She put out her hand. "Muriel St. Claire," she said. "Hi. I'm Mel Sheridan. How exciting."

Muriel took her hand. "How do you do. I guess you know this guy."

"Know him real well, actually." Mel laughed. "You have those women over there in a fluster. They can't believe it's really you."

"Oh, it's really me. I just moved here."

"Summer place?" Mel asked.

Muriel shook her head. "Retirement place. Permanent."

"Really?" Mel asked, lifting a brow. "An early retirement?"

"Hardly." Muriel laughed. "I'm so ready for a change of pace. Jesus, I've been making movies for forty years!"

"Okay, wait a second here," Jack said. "I'm totally lost."

"Of course you are, Jack. Muriel St. Claire is an actress, very famous, and has been since she was about…"

"Fifteen," Muriel supplied.

Jack did the math. "You're fifty-five?" he asked, his eyebrows shooting up. "Wow."

"Good maintenance," she said, brushing off the compliment. "I'm fifty-six and sick of acting. Well, not acting so much as the lifestyle that goes with it. I've been shopping for a ranch for a few years now. My parents lived in these mountains many, many years ago. I have a couple of horses and can't wait for delivery on a couple of dogs. I have a chocolate Lab being trained in Kentucky—she's a beauty. And a Lab puppy coming in a couple of weeks. Both hunters, I hope."

"You hunt?" Mel asked, trying to keep the shock from her voice.

"You hunt?" Jack asked, grinning.

"Waterfowl. Duck and geese."

"Jack shoots deer."

"I could try that," she said. "But you can't use dogs for that and I love working the dogs. I've always had a dog." She squinted at Mel. "You look familiar."

"We met once. I don't expect you would remember me—first of all it was years ago. But I lived in L.A. before moving up here and we went to the same day spa for a while. I saw you there a couple of times. I think we might've had the same aesthetician." Jack was frowning in total confusion again. "Facials," she told him.

"Fantastic," Muriel said. "Who do you use around here?"

"Well, there are some decent beauty shops in Fortuna and Eureka, but probably not what you're used to. Nothing here in Virgin River." Mel glanced at Muriel's perfect nails. "You're going to go a long way for a good manicure."

Muriel followed her eyes. "I can kiss these goodbye. I'm going to be busy redecorating."

"Really? You're planning to do some of it yourself?"

"Most of it," she said rather proudly, lifting her chin. "What brought you up here?"

"Ah, long story. I was looking for a change. I was a nurse-practitioner and midwife in L.A. and took a job here—population just over six hundred. It was supposed to be for a year, but Jack got me knocked up."

"We *are* married," he said, shaking his head at her. "Tell the woman you're happy about that, Melinda."

"Perfectly happy. Jack worked out." She grinned.

"Muriel has the ranch just across the pasture from the Booth place. About six miles by car, or a mile and a half down the river on a horse."

"Oh, fantastic. You're going to love that family," Mel

said. "Walt's a retired general with a couple of grown kids and a new grandson. Great people. In fact, Virgin River is a whole town of really nice people. I'll look forward to introducing you around."

"That's real nice of you."

"Mind you," Mel continued, "once Madge and Beatrice over there get on the phone, formal introductions won't be necessary. Maybe we should put them out of their misery. Would you like to go over and say hi before they go into shock?"

"Lovely," Muriel said.

"Ah, wait a second," Jack said. "Are we going to have a lot of those reporters and photographers around here?"

"Paparazzi?" Muriel asked. "I highly doubt it. I'm old news. The wild, half-dressed young girls are keeping them very busy these days." And then she flashed him a dazzling smile.

With Tom at Brenda's, and Vanni gone to Grants Pass with Paul for a few days, Walt faced two choices for dinner—throw a piece of meat on the grill, or get something at Jack's. He got in the car.

There were about ten people in the bar when Walt arrived, all of them sitting at tables except Doc, who was up at the bar. Walt joined him there, leaving one stool to separate them. Doc and Walt merely nodded at each other; Doc wasn't usually given to deep conversation. Jack grinned at Walt and slapped down a napkin. "Well, now. What can I do for you, sir?"

Walt peered at the empty baby pack Jack was wearing. "Lose a rider, son?"

"David's off being 'refreshed,'" Jack said with a laugh.

"How about a beer while you tell me what Preacher's got cooking tonight?"

Jack drew the draft and put it in front of him. "Sunday special—pot roast. I don't know what the man uses for seasoning, but it's so damn good. And the gravy's almost like tar, it's so dark. He cooked it with vegetables but he's serving whipped potatoes on the side. They're like silk."

"Perfect," Walt said, lifting his beer.

"You want takeout for the family?"

"Just me tonight. Vanni's gone up to Oregon with Paul for a few days, and I don't rate much time with Tom while he's on Brenda's dance card."

"Oregon?" Jack said with a lift of his brow. "You don't say? What do you suppose they'll find to do in Oregon?"

Walt smiled at him. "Funny."

Jack chuckled. "Sounds like maybe some things got sorted out. This mean we won't be seeing too much of that nice Dr. Michaels around here?"

"I think maybe that nice Dr. Michaels hanging around lit a fire under Paul," Walt said. "Good man, Haggerty. If a little slow."

Jack laughed. "Don't go too hard on him, General. I think Vanessa scared him to death. She's awful pretty. Wicked smart, too."

Walt appreciated the compliment and smiled. "Hell, sometimes she scares me."

"I'll go give Preach your order. Be right back."

Walt had enjoyed about half his brew when Mel came from the back and took the stool beside him. "Hey, there," she said brightly. "Jack said you were here."

"How you feeling, girl?"

"Ready to pop. But I'm hanging in there." Jack came out with the carrier full of baby again, holding two steaming plates. He put them in front of Walt and Mel. "Mind if I join you for dinner?" Mel asked.

"I'd welcome it. Jack's not eating dinner?"

"I've been helping Preacher all afternoon make sure it's just right. I've probably had three dinners already," Jack said. "You just missed your new neighbor by about an hour."

"Oh?" Walt said, digging in. "Who might that be?"

Mel leaned an elbow on the bar. "Does the name Muriel St. Claire mean anything to you?"

"Can't say that it does," he said. He took a mouthful. "By damn, that Preacher," he said, savoring the seasoned, tender beef. "He's got the gift."

"She's an actress, Walt," Mel explained. "Quite famous, actually. I've seen a lot of her films."

Walt hummed in response, more interested in his food. Finally he said, "What's she doing around here?"

"She says she came from these mountains and decided to return, retire here."

"Just what we need," Walt said. "Another little old lady. Is she rich at least?"

"She looked pretty rich to me," Jack said. "And not exactly old."

"Rich, retired movie star? What's she going to do with a ranch? Raise exotic chickens?"

Mel laughed. "You might be in for some surprises. She moved into that old Weatherby place on the other side of your pasture. You should bake her a cake or something. Go say hello. I told her you Booths were nice people."

"I'll put Vanni right on it when she gets back to town," Walt said.

Mel perked right up. "Vanni's out of town?"

"Gone to Grants Pass for a few days with Paul," Walt said, hardly missing a mouthful. "They'll be back by the weekend."

"Well, how about that," Mel said, smiling. "Were you expecting that?"

Walt dabbed his lips with his napkin. "Girl, the finger's been on that trigger for months. The only thing I didn't expect was how long it would take Haggerty to pull it."

When Walt got home, the house was dismally quiet. He turned on the TV for some noise and picked up a book for something to do. He wished Tom would show up with Brenda and take over the TV for a movie or something, but they probably wouldn't. If they could escape Brenda's house, they'd be buried in the woods, parking. He'd like to hear the baby fuss, or Vanni cooing to him. Paul would make decent company right about now—he could do that running commentary they had in response to CNN stories.

Out of sheer boredom, he went to the computer. He started a search of Muriel St. Claire, his new neighbor. He found several Web sites plus a Wikipedia listing. Fifty-six years old, born in Brother Creek, California. He looked it up—Trinity County, right near the Humboldt line. There was a list of movies—Jesus, almost fifty of them, not to mention television credits. When he saw a photo he recognized her, but only because she'd recently been on *Law and Order* and *CSI*. He'd never in a million years have known her name. He ran through a series of publicity photos—none in the recent past. Blond, sleek, large blue eyes. Too thin, he decided, although she could certainly hold up a strapless black dress. She always appeared to be glancing over her bare shoulder at the camera, or leaning into it with those sultry movie-star eyes. There was even a shot of her in bed, the only visible fabric being a satin sheet. And pictures of her taken at Academy Awards and the Cannes Film Festival—lotsa big jewelry.

His wife had never much liked big jewelry.

It was all Hollywood stuff, dedicated to the superficial. She'd obviously be more at home in a marble mansion with a pool. What the hell was she doing with that old Weatherby ranch house? That wouldn't last long.

"Exotic chickens, my ass," Walt muttered to himself as he shut down the computer and headed for bed.

Nine

In the early morning Vanni felt the bed dip as Paul brought her a freshly diapered and hungry baby, placing him between them.

"Well, good morning, my angel," she murmured, kissing the baby's head. He sent up a loud protest at kisses instead of milk and she snuggled him close to nurse.

Paul stretched out on the bed to watch Vanessa and the baby. His hand wandered affectionately from Mattie's little head to Vanessa's soft, mussed hair. The baby made a lot of noise this morning, which made Paul laugh. "Have you been starving him?"

"He's always starving," she said. "Time for him to get some solid food."

"I thought you said the breast only for six months? He's barely over three."

"I did, but look at him. He's ravenous. Maybe he could use a little cereal…"

"He's awesome, and growing damn fat on the breast," Paul said. "Vanessa, call Carol and Lance about a visit, find out when they can see you. Then I'll get in touch with my mom about a family thing. I'll try to get more details about Terri's pregnancy while we're here."

"I should meet your family right away," she said. "Make sure they're not all as crazy as you are. Are you going to tell them about Terri?"

"Not until I know something for sure. But I want to tell them about us—that we're getting married when we can get our plans together. Is that all right? Because I can't look at you without wanting everyone to know."

"Sure. I have the same problem," she said with a smile. "This is the part about being married that I like. Lying beside you in bed…"

"Baby between us…"

She laughed. "He has his needs. And if you want more children, you'd better get used to this."

"This," he said, stroking the baby's soft head, "is everything I've ever wanted."

"So odd that you didn't find someone to marry years ago. You're so good at it. And this thing you have for pregnant women and babies…"

"For a while there it seemed like everyone had a pregnant wife but me. Between my brothers and my friends, I was surrounded by them. Round bellies, nursing babies… Is there some rule about waiting a respectable length of time between the first 'I love you' and the vows?" he asked her.

She laughed at him. "What's the difference? We've known each other for years. We've been through things together that even some husbands and wives haven't."

"What would your father think if we got married right away?" he asked.

She shrugged. "Daddy scares everyone but me," she said. "Anything I want suits him fine."

"The person most on my mind is Tom," Paul said.

"Tommy? Why?"

"We've gotten real close. He's like one of my brothers. And the way he feels about you—he tries to hide it, but he admires you. We can't do it without him. He's leaving right after graduation, but I want him to be there. I want him to be my best man."

"How would your family feel about a fast wedding?"

He chuckled. "Relieved, believe me. My mother's secret fear is that I'll die a lonely old man."

"Paul, you can't tell your family that one woman is having your baby and you're marrying another all in the same sentence."

"I know. I'm going to get the facts as soon as possible— but, Vanni, the bottom line will be the same, whether it comes in one sentence or one month. I'll take care of them, I'll take care of you—but you're going to be my wife. Period."

"You've been thinking about this...." she said.

"There's something about lying next to you all night that disturbs my sleep."

"Funny that you didn't disturb mine," she said.

"I thought I'd give you a break. But your break is almost over."

Mattie drew in a deep sigh and fell away from the breast, satisfied and asleep. Paul leaned over the baby's head to place a soft kiss on her lips. He then kissed the baby's head and asked, "Would you like to hold him a while longer?"

"No, I'll put him down," she said, beginning to rise.

"Stay right there. Let me," he said, scooping the baby into his arms. Mattie's head fell right to Paul's shoulder and before Paul had made it out of the bedroom, a loud, sleepy belch escaped the little boy.

Vanni chuckled and snuggled into the bed. Happy. She let her eyes close, but not for sleep. For a long time she had been afraid she'd never get to feel this way again. And then her man was back, pulling her into his arms, covering her mouth in a kiss that was not soft, drawing a deep moan from her as her arms went around him.

Later that morning Vanessa phoned Carol. "Hi. I'm going to be in town for a couple of days and I thought if you had time, I'd bring little Matt over for a visit."

"You're in town?" she asked. "Will you stay with us?"

"No, but thanks. I decided to come at the very last minute and I'm staying with Paul. He was in Virgin River so I came back up here with him, since he's going right back to Virgin River at the end of the week."

"My, he's spending a lot of time in Virgin River," Carol said.

"He is, with more time there in his future. He has a couple of potential building contracts down there, if it doesn't interfere with his company up here. It seemed like a perfect opportunity to bring the baby over to see you and Lance."

"I see. Make it tonight," she said flatly. "We'll have dinner."

"All right," Vanni agreed.

"Great! Six o'clock. Do you need a ride?" Carol asked.

"Of course not. Paul will bring me."

"Good, then. We'll do something on the grill."

Vanni spent the whole day alone with Mattie while Paul went to his office, checked on his crews, saw his brothers and tried to catch up on business in general. He was home in plenty of time to shower and change to go to the Rutledges' home.

When Carol opened the door to them, she actually stepped back in surprise. "Paul!" she said with a gasp.

"Hi, Carol," he said. He gently squeezed Vanni's upper arm. "How've you been?"

"Great! Great! Come in! Will you be staying for dinner?"

"Of course he'll stay for dinner, Carol," Vanni said, totally confused by this question. "When I told you he would bring me, did you think he'd just drop me off? Didn't you expect him to stay?"

"Of course," she said, reaching for the baby. "I'll just set another place."

Vanni passed her the baby, completely baffled. There was protocol and obligation with grandparents, not to mention the promise she'd made to Matt, and she held that sacred. But Carol never failed to put her under a strain. Most of the time she didn't understand her. As they walked into the house, Vanni glanced into the dining room and noticed a table set for four. She was totally perplexed, until they stepped into the living room and Cameron stood up from his chair.

It was then she realized that Carol was at it again—and two extremely fine men were going to be made uncomfortable. She wore a sad smile as she went toward Cameron and allowed him to kiss her cheek. "How are you?" she asked softly.

"Fine," he said. "You?"

"Good," she answered. Paul came up behind her and put that hand on her shoulder, that hand that claimed her. She was sorry about how that would make Cameron feel, but not at all unhappy about how it made her feel. After wanting him so much, she loved letting the world know she was his.

"Cameron," Paul said, sticking out his other hand from his place behind Vanni.

"How you doing?" he asked, shaking the hand. "So—just in town for a couple of days?" Cameron asked.

"That's right," Vanni said. "Paul was down for the weekend and I decided to come back here with him. To meet his family. I'm staying at Paul's, Cameron...."

"Ah," he said, understanding perfectly. He turned and lifted his drink to his lips.

Lance came into the room, saw that Paul was there and welcomed him heartily. "Hey," he said, reaching out his hand. "My man Paul! How is everything?"

"Great. Never better. How about you?" he asked.

"The same," Lance answered. "Where's that baby?"

"Carol took him to the kitchen," Vanni said.

"Well, I don't mean to seem rude, but I have to have a grandson fix. Be right back," he said, darting off.

The three of them stood there, looking at each other. It was Cameron who broke the tension with a laugh. "Well. Looks like a serious miscommunication."

"I'm sorry," Vanni said. "I don't understand."

"I do," Paul said. "Carol has a very specific plan in mind and she didn't bother to consult anyone."

"We can make the best of this, can't we?" Vanni asked hopefully.

Cameron smiled at her, but it was a disappointed smile. Carol flew out from the kitchen, headed toward the dining room with a plate, napkin and utensils in her hands. She had obviously handed off the baby to Lance. "Carol, wait," Cameron said. "I'm going to have to shove off. My pager," he lied. "Thanks, but I'm not going to be able to stay."

"Oh no!" Carol said. "Are you sure?"

He put one hand in his pants pocket. "I'm sure," he said. He leaned forward and gave Vanni a kiss on the cheek. "You look terrific," he said. "It's good to know you're happy." He gave Paul a conciliatory slap on the upper arm as he passed and headed toward the door.

Paul squeezed her shoulder. He leaned down to her ear. "I'll be back." And he followed Cameron.

Cameron was making fast tracks to his car when Paul called to him. "Hey, Cameron. Buddy. A minute, huh?"

Cameron turned. "It's okay, Paul. You don't have to say anything. Don't worry about it."

"I'm not worried," he said, taking another two long strides toward him. The two men were completely different—Paul in his jeans and boots, rough, rugged. Cameron in his linen pants, silk shirt, Italian shoes—possibly the best-dressed man in Grants Pass. "I think you deserve some kind of explanation. About me. Me and Vanessa. This was a horrible setup."

Cameron put his hands in his pockets, rocked back on his heels and laughed ruefully. "It was pretty ugly," he agreed. "Maybe more terrible for you and Vanni than for me."

"I don't know what Carol told you, and I don't know why she brought you out to dinner, but I've been in love with Vanni forever. I couldn't tell her that, of course—she married my best friend. God, I'd never have done anything that wrong to Matt. But since… Well, we've been through so much together and it just got stronger. It took a long time to iron it out. Man, I'm really sorry if you were misled."

"I've only known her a few weeks, Paul. We're not exactly confidants."

"We're getting married," Paul said.

Cameron stiffened slightly, but he smiled. He nodded. "Congratulations. I'm sure you'll be very happy."

"Look," Paul said. "It isn't hard for me to understand you have a thing for her. What man wouldn't? I want you to know something—this is my fault, Cameron. I should have spoken up sooner. Before Carol set up that first meeting with you. There's no excuse. I knew how I felt. But Matt hadn't been gone long and I—" He hung his head, shaking it briefly. "I just didn't want to upset her."

"*She* could have spoken up," Cameron said.

"Well, it turns out there's an explanation for that, too. I was real scarce for a while after the baby was born, trying to give her time and to get my head together. It was real hard for me to get into Matt's territory, even after he was gone. I gave her the impression I wasn't interested in her in that way." He shook his head. "I'm not good with women. I'm real clumsy, in fact. But at least it's finally out—how we feel about each other. Now we move ahead. I'm sorry, man," he said, sticking out his hand. "You're a good guy. You have everything. There's no reason I should win this one."

Cameron gave a huff of laughter. He took the hand. "Maybe there's lots of reasons. No hard feelings."

"Thanks. This, between us—it shouldn't be hard for her. She's so sensitive. She'd hate for anyone to be hurt. I happen to know—she thinks highly of you."

"I know," Cameron said. "Don't worry about it, okay?"

"I don't deserve her, I know that. But I'm going to do everything I can to make her happy. I hope you're going to be okay."

"You could gloat, you know," Cameron said. "You got the girl."

"Yeah," he said. "Crazy woman." He laughed. "A guy like you—you won't have any trouble. The right one will come along."

"Paul. I didn't close the deal, all right? It barely got going. I might be a little disappointed, but that's all. Vanni and I—we were just friends. In case you think I'm going to be a problem for you."

"Nah, I know better than that. Didn't take me long to figure you for a class act."

Cameron smiled. "Yeah? Well, maybe I'm not the only one."

Vanessa sat in the chair that had recently been Cameron's. The baby was out of sight with Lance and so was Carol for the moment. Vanni was seething. Beyond furious. She picked up Cameron's drink and took a long, deep swallow of liquid courage and grimaced at the taste of scotch. It was another minute before Carol showed herself.

"Well," Carol said. "That was a bit uncomfortable. I didn't realize you'd invited Paul."

"You didn't? And why didn't you *insist* he be invited? He was Matt's best friend. And you *know* how much he means to me!"

Carol stiffened indignantly. "I'm not sure I do," she said.

Vanni stood to meet Carol at eye level. "Then let me be very clear about this. He means the absolute world to me. Paul was in Virgin River when Matt was killed and I asked him to stay on until the baby was born. I asked him to be with me for the birth. I've known him for years. I've always felt comfortable with him, I trust him—he's wonderful. We've always been close, closer still when we lost Matt. For God's sake, Matt asked him to take care of us if anything happened to him. How can it be so impossible for you to understand that I would come to *love* him?"

"I couldn't imagine it," Carol said, anger barely reined in. "Matt's hardly gone…"

"He's gone enough for you to try to set me up with a doctor."

Carol lifted her chin. Her mouth took on a strained line. "That's uncalled for!"

"How dare you treat Paul as if he's inferior! Shame on you!"

"I never meant that. I never meant to—" Carol swallowed. "I thought Cameron was perfect for you…."

"Cameron knew about me and Paul. What in the world did you tell him to get him here for dinner?"

"I…ah…I told him Paul was dropping you off and

you'd love to see him. I didn't think I was making it up—you said Paul coming back here from Virgin River was a perfect opportunity to visit us and—"

Vanni was shaking her head. "Why don't you just *ask* if I'd like Cameron to join us for dinner? More to the point, why don't you listen?"

"I do listen," she said, insulted.

"No. You don't listen. When I say I don't want coral bridesmaids' dresses, you buy them and dress up my girls in them. When I say I don't want to be set up, you invite the man to dinner not once, but twice. When I say I'm staying with Paul and he'll bring me to dinner, you plan your own party without asking, without listening. For heaven's sake, Cameron is a wonderful man who didn't deserve what just happened to him. And that you would humiliate Paul after knowing him for so many years, after knowing how he loved your only son, treating him like he's my chauffeur, offering to set another place like he's some last-minute addition to your private little dinner party…"

"I just couldn't imagine it. Not Paul," she said.

Lance appeared, coming out of the kitchen with his grandson cuddled against his chest, and the expression on his face was not a happy one. Carol said, "I was trying to help…. Maybe Mattie could benefit by being raised by a doctor. Instead of…" She glanced away uncomfortably.

Vanni laughed suddenly and hollowly. Here the woman was in real estate and had no concept of how successful the man who built some of the finest houses in the region might be. And that was nothing compared to the fact that Paul was the most incredible human being, and would be the most wonderful father. "Paul is such a catch, you can't even imagine, but I'm not going to waste your time. Carol, I'm sick of the way you take over and I won't have it anymore." She walked toward Lance and reached for the baby just as Paul was coming in the front door. "I'm sorry, Lance, but we're leaving. This was horrendous, and I'm never going through anything like this again." She looked over her shoulder at Paul, who stood across the room, just inside the door. In his eyes she saw warmth and understanding. Patience. Kindness. Everything was going to be okay.

Vanni walked over to Paul. She turned at the door and said, "Carol, you should be more considerate of people's feelings. What you did tonight was in bad taste, it's beneath you." And with that they left the house.

The next night was dinner with the Haggertys and Vanessa was tense. After what she'd been through with Carol Rutledge, she couldn't imagine what kind of paces these people might put her through. The fact that Paul was so down-to-earth and kind didn't reassure her much. After all, Matt had been so charming and fun, yet Carol could be a nightmare. When Paul drove up to the large, stately home in the beautiful countryside, Vanni gulped. Another big house. She knew their family business was successful, but at this point their obvious prosperity was making her nervous. It seemed to be the fulcrum on which so many opinions were balanced. Opinions that had little to do with the true quality of life.

But this was a whole different scene. Marianne Haggerty rushed to the front door when she heard them pulling up, drying her hands on a dish towel that she immediately flung over her shoulder. She was a short, round woman with steel-gray hair and a beautiful complexion. Her smile was effervescent and she had the most wonderful, engaging dimples. Right behind her was a tall, handsome man, Paul's height, with Paul's sandy-colored hair, strung with gray.

Marianne gave Paul a peck on the cheek and then quickly focused on the baby, reaching for him. "Oh my God," she whispered. "Matt's baby, how luscious. Oh, Vanessa—it's so wonderful to finally meet you! Matt was so precious to us—we loved him so. Can I hold him? Please?"

"Of course," Vanni said with a smile, handing him over.

Like grandparents, Marianne and Stan were focused on the baby, smiling and cooing and snuggling, almost ignoring Paul and Vanni. And then, surprisingly, Marianne began to tear up. Then weep. Stan put a strong arm around her shoulders, holding her and the baby against his big chest, murmuring to her, "All right, honey. Don't get started…" And then his eyes welled and a tear ran down his weathered cheek and they were wiping at each other's cheeks while cuddling the baby.

"Okay, you two," Paul said. "Let's not get going. Don't upset Vanni."

"I'm sorry," Marianne said immediately. She looked at Vanessa with wet eyes. "You'll just never know how grateful I am for this chance to see him, to hold him. We loved Matt so much. I always felt that he was one of my boys."

"Mom, if you don't get under control, I'll take the baby," Paul threatened.

Vanni laid a hand on his arm and shook her head at him, a small smile playing on her lips. This was good for her— Carol and Lance didn't get choked up like this. There was no question in her mind that the Rutledges loved their grandson, but their restraint was sometimes hard to endure, especially during those times she was feeling emotional.

"Beer," Paul said. "We need beer. And control."

Stan let go with a hearty though shaky laugh. "Great recipe for control," he said. "Beer. Come on, come on in."

He reached for Vanni's hand and pulled her into the house, wiping clumsily at his cheeks.

She was led through the foyer, past a gorgeous and huge great room with a beautiful marble fireplace, past a large dining room and huge kitchen, out onto a redwood deck that was furnished with handsome wicker patio furniture that would be as much at home in a living room as outdoors.

"This is an amazing house," Vanni said.

"We'll give you the tour later if you want one," Stan said. "A builder's house has to be a good house—people look at that. It's way more than we need, for sure, but Marianne wants room for the family. What can I get everyone?"

"I'd love a beer," Vanni said, sitting in one of the chairs outside.

Marianne followed, still clutching the baby possessively, holding him against her. "Sure, sweetie," she said to her husband without ever taking her eyes off the baby. She migrated to a chair near Vanessa while Paul went with his dad to get beer. "He's so beautiful," she said. "So sweet. Is he a good baby?"

"He is," Vanni said. "Sleeps through the night and is hardly ever in a bad mood. But of course he gets a lot of attention, so I'm sure when he's older, I'll be in for it."

"No, you can't give a baby too much attention."

"Paul tells me you have five grandchildren."

"Yes," she said. "Three boys, two girls. They're brilliant, each one. Oh, I could eat this little one up!" Marianne turned her eyes toward Vanni and said softly, "I'm so sorry for your loss, Vanessa. We miss him, too."

"Thank you. I remember your card and flowers."

"It was so wonderful for Paul to be with you when this one was born. He talks about it."

She laughed. "Does he tell you about how hard he tried to get out of it?" she asked just as Paul came back onto the deck to hand her a beer. He stood behind her chair and that hand was again on her shoulder.

"He doesn't admit to that, but it doesn't surprise me," his mother said.

Vanni reached up to caress the hand that possessed her. And it wasn't until that moment that Marianne's expression changed and she exchanged looks with her husband.

"Yes, Mom," Paul said. "Once I told Vanni what wonderful grandparents you two are, she agreed to marry me. She even agreed to more children. So you see—I'm not going to die a lonely old man after all." Vanni looked up at him and saw that his smile was soft.

"Oh," Marianne let go in a surprised breath. "Oh, how long has this been going on?"

"For me, quite a while," Paul said. "Vanni just gave up the fight a little while ago. But I think she can convince you she's happy."

Smiling, Vanni said, "I'm happy. Very happy."

Stan stuck out a hand to his son. "Congratulations, son. This is good news." Then he stooped to put a kiss on Vanni's cheek. "Welcome, daughter," he said. "It's an honor. An honor."

All Marianne said was, "Excellent. I don't have to let go of this baby for a second!" Then her face sobered and she said, "Oh, forgive me, Vanessa! I'm so happy to have you in the family." She grinned happily and said, "You *and* the baby!"

It wasn't long before the rest of the Haggerty family arrived—Mitch and Jenny and their three kids, North and Susan and their two—the women bearing food to contribute to a big family dinner. Vanni was welcomed warmly with hugs, everyone offering their condolences for Matt's death since the boys had grown up together. The baby was fussed over and passed from woman to woman. In no time Paul had charge of the baby while Vanni joined the women in the kitchen getting the meal on the table.

Dinner with eight adults, five kids and a baby is a loud affair, but Vanni felt so much more comfortable in the chaos than she ever had at the Rutledges'. Paul's mother, she thought, has such an ideal existence, surrounded by loving family, her life filled with happy noise and small children's arms around her.

This, Vanni thought. *This is what I want to do next.*

Before dinner was consumed, Stan stood and raised a glass to toast Vanessa and Paul's engagement. Excited whoops and hugs followed with questions about the when and where, to which Vanni and Paul could only answer, "The sooner the better. After all—we've known each other for years."

When dinner was over, the cleanup and female chatter continued, and Vanni pitched in happily. It was during this time that she stole a look at Paul, out on the deck with his father and brothers, jiggling Mattie against his chest, trying to keep him from getting too fussy as he waited for his mother's attention. Mattie was squirming anxiously, ready for a feeding, but Paul was completely comfortable and confident.

When the last dish was put up, Vanni asked Marianne if she could borrow a bedroom to nurse the baby. "Of course, sweetheart," the older woman answered. "But no one in this family is uncomfortable with a nursing mom, not even the children. Do whatever you'd rather—take a bedroom or sit with us, it's entirely up to you. We're kind of homespun around here."

"What about the men?" Vanni asked.

"They're even less uncomfortable." North's wife laughed. "The first time I put Angie to the breast, demurely covered by a blanket, Stan walked right over to me, lifted the blanket and said, 'Marianne, honey, come and see how good this little critter sucks!'"

"Oh, my," Vanni said. "Think they'll stay outside a while?"

"I think Stan will give you time to get used to us before he pulls his tricks," Marianne said with a smile. "Not much time, though—take that as fair warning."

So Vanni went to collect her son from Paul and chose the great room, settling with the women, who had a hundred questions about Vanni and Paul and how the whole romance came to be.

On the deck, Paul was talking to his business partners, his family. "I think there's money to be made in Virgin River and the surrounding towns. When Jack was looking for a contractor to help him finish his house, he couldn't find one, which was what brought me down there." He grinned. "That and all the overtime he paid."

"How would you prefer to do it?" Mitch asked.

"I could extend the company into another branch and we could participate in any profits, or I could use my house equity to start my own company, since the house is paid for. I leave that to you."

"You have plenty of stock in Haggerty Construction," Stan said. "If you want to cash out…"

"I don't want to pull money out of your company, Dad."

"It's not mine, son. We've all put a lot of sweat equity into this operation—it's ours. We back each other up."

"Vanni would move up here if I asked her to. But I have interests there. There are building contracts, there's Vanni's dad, who's alone now. And… Well, there's Matt. I want

Mattie to have a connection to his dad, to know everything about what a great man he was." He shrugged. "We're close to Grants Pass—it's not a bad drive. If I hang on to the house, we could come back up here to work if there aren't contracts down there. You know I wouldn't be a stranger. But God, Dad, it's a beautiful place. I'd love to raise a family there. I'd love to live there with my wife and children."

"Then we'll set you up, son. Sounds like a place primed for opportunity."

"We could provide jobs—there are a lot of people looking for opportunity in home construction. And a lot of city money comes up to us from the Bay Area. Virgin River is isolated and grows slowly, but there are dozens of towns around the area just dying for renovation and new construction. I don't think you'll regret it—but I'd rather you not shoulder the risk. I can afford it."

Stan grinned. "You saying we made you rich enough to start your own company?"

Paul returned the grin. "You did, in fact."

"Then you owe it to us to give us a piece of the action."

"I agree," Mitch said.

"I hate to lose you," North said. "If you take on a new division, we'll have to put someone in charge of building operations up here. And damn, you're the best there is."

"I've been pretty absent since last fall. A long time now."

"True," Stan agreed. "But it looks like it was a good investment, personally and professionally. Anyone around here have cigars?"

"You have cigars," North said.

"I do, don't I?" Stan said, getting up.

"You know," Paul said. "You guys have to come down to Virgin River. You're going to fit right in."

Ten

Walt had begun making it a habit to be away from the house for long periods of time when Paul was there for the weekend. He stretched out his stable chores and frequently took Liberty out for long early-morning or early-evening rides. His reward for this new behavior was a decent night's sleep.

It appeared these trips to Grants Pass during the week would continue for a while, and the kids would be back on the weekends. He looked forward to seeing them, but they also needed their space. So, after Friday night's dinner at the house, with Tom out with Brenda, Walt left cleanup to Paul and Vanni and went for a ride.

He was moving along the river trail when an animal darted down the path toward him. It wasn't much more than a streak of brown fur and Walt reined in Patriot. He could hear horse's hooves and then the air was split with a loud whistle and that chocolate streak stopped on a dime. And sat. Panting.

Momentarily, a horse galloped up toward him, a pretty woman astride. She wore a cowboy hat, but even that wide brim couldn't hide her peachy complexion, rosy cheeks, pink lips. "Good girl, Luce. Break."

The dog got out of her sit position, at ease, and wagged at her mistress.

"Sorry," the woman said to Walt. "I hope that wasn't a problem for you, or for your horse."

"We're fine. Amazing little friend you have there."

"Luce. She's a bird dog, still in training. I'm Muriel. Are we neighbors?"

"Walt Booth," he said. "I'm a little embarrassed. I've been meaning to bake you a cake and bring it over. Welcome you to the neighborhood."

She laughed. "I'll bet you were planning to have your wife do that," she accused.

"Widowed," he said, and he plucked his hat off his head in gentlemanly fashion. And curiously, he wondered what his hair looked like. That should have been his first clue.

"I'm so sorry," she said.

"Years ago now," he answered, smoothing a hand over his head. "How about you? Married?"

"Several times," she said with a laugh. "I'm trying to quit."

"You shouldn't have much trouble. There aren't so many prospects in Virgin River. What use do you have for a bird dog?"

"I've been known to hunt. I don't know how much of that I'll get in this year—I'm working on that house. But Luce needs a little time on her skills and I should get her in the water before too long. Keep her up to speed. I'd like to get a litter out of her in a couple of years, after we check her hips. She's got such a good line."

Walt looked at her hands. They weren't fancy-girl hands. Her manicured nails were short and she wore no rings.

"Do you hunt?" she asked him.

"I haven't in a while, but I'm planning to get back into it. Soon." It made her smile at him; she knew a flirt when she saw one. "I guess I thought you'd be breeding peacocks on that ranch. Or something. Not working on a house and training a bird dog."

She tilted her head. "And you would think that because...?"

"Mel told me my new neighbor was a movie star, so I looked you up on the Internet. Lotta fancy pictures," he said. And then he felt his cheeks grow warm.

"Well, God bless the Internet. Anything else you'd like to know?"

His first thought was he could probably find out who all those husbands had been, but maybe he'd resist. "I don't know much about movies. Haven't seen too many. And I don't know anything about movie stars."

"Retired," she said. "I'm sanding, varnishing, hauling trash and training my bird dog. I'm going to pick up another one pretty soon now—I picked the bitch and sire a while ago and she whelped, so as soon as they'll let him go... And I don't cook much, don't bake at all, but as it happens I have sugar for my coffee. In case you want to borrow a cup for that cake you're baking me."

"My thirty-year-old daughter has a man in her life—a good man—and they're at the house every weekend," he found himself explaining. "I have reasons to stay out of the house a lot. How much sugar do you keep on hand?"

She grinned at him. "Plenty."

"I might need some as early as tomorrow evening," he said. "That good man my daughter has is here for the weekend."

"Is that so?" Then Muriel turned her mount, facing the other way and said, "Luce!" She gave two short whistles. The Lab bolted back where she'd come from. Muriel looked over her shoulder and said, "Bring a decent bottle of red wine then," she said. She put her horse into an easy canter and followed her dog.

Walt sat there for a long time, till she was out of sight. "Damn," he said aloud.

The next evening Paul and Vanessa decided to go to Jack's for dinner, a predictable event for them. Of course they expected Walt to join them. "Nah," he said. "I see enough of Jack during the week. Tom gets dinner at Brenda's and I have no interest in cooking for one. I'll pass. In fact," he said, "I might head out to Clear River. There's a little bar over there where I'm not so well known. I might do that."

"You sure, Dad?" Vanni asked.

"I'm sure," he said. "Enjoy yourselves. I'll see you later, or in the morning."

When they were gone he showered, applied a little aftershave and poked around in the wine rack, selected a bottle and grabbed his car keys.

When Walt pulled up to his new neighbor's house, he wasn't sure that he wouldn't come off looking like some old fool, chasing a movie star. Of course, the chasing hadn't even started—this was just a glass of wine with a neighbor. But he felt every second of his sixty-two years and although the research said she was just a few years younger, she looked many years younger than he did. And far more confident than he was.

The property was made up of a timeworn two-story house with a wide porch, a smaller vintage bunkhouse, a barn and a corral. Walt didn't know where to look first. On instinct, he went to the house and knocked on the front door. "Right in here," she yelled. "Come on in."

As Walt stepped inside he was greeted first by a very

excited Luce, wagging and nudging him playfully. Muriel was up on a ladder with a trowel in her hand, which she put in a pan. She wore overalls that were as splattered as the wall. "Good. Break time," she said, wiping her hands on a rag that she had stuffed in her back pocket.

Hmm. He had showered and splashed on the cologne; she hadn't even bothered with a comb, much less makeup. She looked real good for a woman her age. "What's that you're doing?" he asked.

"Spackling. After which I'll paint and install new base-boards, and then I'm going after some crown molding."

He looked around at the mess. The place was in full remodel mode. He lifted the bottle and pointed the label toward her as she descended the ladder. "Will this do?"

She took the bottle from him. "Nice," she said. "Give me a minute to clean up my tools." She grabbed her pan and trowel, disappeared into the kitchen and he heard the water run. Momentarily she was back. "Come with me. Come on, Luce."

He followed her out of the house and across the yard to the bunkhouse. She opened the door and surprised him again. It was one whole room, but it was a big room—as a bunkhouse it could've held six twin-size beds. She had a bed in one corner, a settee and chair in front of it, a small table with two chairs and, along one wall a few appliances—a bar-size refrigerator, microwave, small oven, sink, a few cupboards and drawers. The bathroom, such as it was, occupied the corner—a toilet, sink and small shower—right out in the open.

But she had the room fixed up a little bit—fresh paint, bright colors of yellow, red, a little rose and pale green. The bedspread matched the love seat and chair cushions.

While he was looking around, she was digging a cork-screw out of a drawer. She handed him the bottle and the implement and went after glasses. "Nice little place," he said, going to work on the cork. "Hope I don't have to pee while I'm here. More to the point, I hope you don't have to."

Muriel laughed, then she grabbed something that leaned up against the end of her cupboard and, one-handed, glasses in the other hand, she erected a wooden TV tray between the chair and short couch. "Instant coffee table," she said. "Please pour."

She went to the refrigerator and pulled out a platter covered in Saran, then grabbed a big box of crackers out of a cupboard and placed it on the tray next to her platter. Sliced ham and salami, sliced cheese, olives, veggies and hummus. "Ah," he said. "You were expecting me."

She laughed and sat in the chair. "Walt, it's my dinner."

"Oh. Oh, I wouldn't want to take your dinner...."

"I sliced up twice as much, in case you came for your cup of sugar."

"You really don't cook? At all? You eat like this?"

"I have a feeling this isn't going to hold you for long," she said, picking up a celery stick and dipping it through the hummus. "Well, you'll be all right. You can make yourself a pot roast or something when you get home tonight."

And he thought—*if we begin to keep company, I will have to be in charge of the food.*

And she thought—*if we see much of each other, I'll probably gain weight.*

"From the outside, this looks like a bunkhouse or guesthouse."

"It was. Or is. First it was an artist's studio for the rancher's wife," she said, pointing up to two skylights in the ceiling. "Then a bunkhouse for hands or lumberjacks. The kitchen and bathroom facilities were an afterthought,

I believe. My Realtor had the junk hauled out, then I did some painting. I'll stay here while I work on the big house. And if you have to relieve yourself, the bathroom in the big house works just fine. The door closes and everything." She took a small sip of wine. "Hmm," she said, letting her eyes close briefly. Then she clinked his glass. "To new neighborhoods."

"This isn't exactly what I expected of a movie star. Spackling. Living in one room."

"How interesting," she said, leaning back in her chair. "You're exactly what I expected of a general."

His eyebrows shot up. "Is that so?"

"Uh-huh. Thinking anyone who isn't carrying an M16 is a wimp and women who dress up can't do heavy work. Walt, time for you to get with it. Movie stars are people. Most of them, anyway. And besides, I'm not a movie star now—I'm retired."

"What's that like, being a movie star?"

"Being a star, as you put it, is like living an imaginary life. Acting, however, is the hardest work you'll ever find. Look at me," she said, connecting with his eyes. "Closely, closely—yes, like that. Now look angry." He scowled for her. "Very nice," she said. "Now—look *vulnerable*." He frowned in confusion. "Not easy, is it? Add to that, you have to memorize one hundred and twenty pages of dialogue, be on the set at 6:00 a.m. and won't get done before 10:00 p.m., you'll either sweat or freeze, you'll stand at attention for so many goddamn hours your hips will lock and the man you have to kiss will have breath that would gag a maggot or the promising young actress who's playing your daughter will be a snotty little shit who holds up the whole production and costs everyone time and money." She leaned back and grinned at him. "It's not easy. I swear to God."

"Well, no wonder you retired."

"Why'd you retire?"

"Over thirty-five years is a long time for an Army officer," he began.

And they talked through a bottle of wine and her snacks. Walt learned a little about the life of an actress and Muriel heard about the Army and Walt's family, including the death of his son-in-law, the new grandson and Paul. Before long the wine was gone and it was almost ten o'clock. There was no kiss good-night or anything even close, but Walt said, "If I had time on my hands, could you use help with painting and such?"

"I'd never turn down a helping hand," she said. "But are you any good at it?"

"Passable. I admit, I hired tradesmen to get it done at my place, but only because I was still in D.C. and wanted the place ready when I retired. I don't want to intrude in case you're training your dog or running errands. Why don't I call ahead?"

"That would work," Muriel said. She went to the counter of her little makeshift kitchen and wrote down her number. "Or, you can always just come for your sugar." She smiled at him. "Thanks for the wine. Very nice wine."

"I have plenty of wine," he said.

"And I have plenty of sugar."

"So," he said. "We're in business."

After a weekend in Virgin River, Vanni and Paul returned to Grants Pass. On Tuesday morning, Paul called Terri.

"Hi, Terri, it's Paul. How are you feeling?"

"Fine, Paul. How are you?"

"Great, thanks. I've been out of town and—"

"Let me guess," she said tiredly. "Virgin River again?"

"As a matter of fact. I have a couple of potential

building contracts down there and I've been crunching some numbers to see if it's doable."

"Big surprise," she said with an unhappy laugh. "Kind of a strange place to go when you have a child coming you claim to want to be involved with, don't you think?"

"Both these jobs will be complete by the time you deliver. And it's not far—I can get to Grants Pass when I need to. Listen, I wanted to do this in person, but there's no point in blindsiding you—I'll be getting married fairly soon."

He heard a sound; he wasn't sure if it was a snort or a laugh.

"That won't be a problem," Paul said. "She knows all about my situation with you. She also has a child and—"

"I know," she said, cutting him off. "Your best friend's baby."

"She understands we'll be sharing custody and—"

"I'm not sure I like that idea so much," she said impatiently.

"Well, we have to deal with what we have," he said. "And speaking of that, I've been looking at the calendar. It has to be time for that doctor's appointment by now."

"What appointment?" she asked.

"The one with the OB-GYN. The one I'm going to with you."

"Oh, that. I had my appointment last Friday. Everything seems to be fine."

He took a breath. "You know I wanted to go with you," he said.

"Sorry—they called with an opening. And you didn't seem to be in town," she answered crisply.

"If I'd known there was an appointment, I would have been there." Anger began to swell up inside him and he cautioned himself to stay cool. He didn't want to set her off, though he wasn't sure what more she could do to screw up his head.

"Look," she said. "You seem to have more important things on your mind—I don't even hear from you once a week…"

He took a breath. "Can you get away for lunch today?" he asked her.

She was quiet for a moment. "Paul—forget it, huh? You don't have to meet me for lunch or for anything else. Clearly there's nothing between us. You're getting married—go have your life. I'll be fine."

"There's one thing between us. According to you."

She hung up the phone.

"Damn it!" he said, slamming down the phone.

"Uh-oh," Vanni said, standing in the bedroom doorway with Mattie against her shoulder.

One hand braced on the desk, he hung his head. "She's got me over a nice little barrel here," he said, lifting his head and looking at her. "She just gave me my out."

"I don't think that made you real happy."

"No. It didn't." He flipped through his calendar. He found the name of the doctor that he'd jotted down, then pulled out the phone book. He couldn't find Dr. Charlene Weir listed anywhere. "I don't know what she's up to."

Vanni walked toward him. "What was your out?" she asked.

"She told me to go have my life—she'd be fine."

"Oh, my."

"You know what kind of problem that is for me," he said.

"You wouldn't be happy having a child of yours floating around out there, without knowing you, without your support and protection."

"I'm sorry. I can't." He dropped an arm around her

shoulders, kissed Mattie's head. "I'm sorry to put you through this."

"Don't worry about me, Paul. Just resolve this to your satisfaction—I'm not going anywhere."

Two hours later he found himself in probably the most unlikely spot in Grants Pass—the office of Dr. Cameron Michaels.

Of course Cameron fit him in, probably hopeful that his visit had something to do with Vanessa. Something that could benefit the good doctor. When Paul explained himself and what he needed, Cameron couldn't keep from laughing outright.

"I'm sure you find this hilarious," Paul said grimly. "But the fact is, I don't have many places to go for a little assistance."

"I have to hand it to you, Paul. You're not as clumsy around women as you think. For an unlucky son of a bitch, you sure land on your feet."

"How's that, exactly?"

"You've got this mess to straighten out and Vanni still wants you. Damn."

"Stop grinning. This isn't easy for Vanessa. But if it's mine, I want to take care of it. I have to. If I'm going to be a father, I'm going to be a decent father."

Cameron shook his head. "I'm sure you didn't mean to, but you stumbled into the right place. I'd love to tell you there's nothing I can do to help you out of this mess—but I'm a children's doctor. And it isn't easy to deal with the number of babies who come into this world with parents who don't give a shit, don't even want them. At least you do. I'll hook you up for an ultrasound, which might give you some answers, if you can get her cooperation. You can follow through with a court order for an amniocentesis if you need one to check DNA and confirm paternity. Not for you, not even for her. For this baby she's carrying." He flipped through his BlackBerry. "Then you can tell her, if she needs a good pediatrician, you know one."

Paul went from Cameron's office to the law firm at which Terri Bradford worked. For the first time he considered the fact that she worked for an attorney. She would know he had legal rights.

Terri was clearly surprised to see him. When she looked up from her desk, her eyes were wide and her expression completely baffled. "What are you doing here?" she asked.

"We have to talk. Right now. Today. Have you eaten?"

"Yes, and I don't want to talk. You're getting married—you'll be far too busy to think about me. It's time for you to walk away from this, leave me alone." When she stood up from her desk, he noticed the tiniest rounding of her middle and he tried to judge whether it was approximately three months or if maybe she'd just gained a little weight. Her breasts were definitely larger, straining at her blouse.

"You'd better talk to me, Terri," he said sternly. "I'm not going away and if I have to, I'll get help. Legal help."

She leaned over her desk, whispering, "What am I supposed to tell my boss?"

"Tell him it's a family emergency. Because it is."

She sighed, shook her head and went into her boss's office. She came right back and fished her purse out of the bottom drawer of her desk. As she walked toward the door, he grabbed her elbow with a soft hand, escorting her. She was small—much shorter than Vanni. Her shoulder-length dark hair was shiny and her blue eyes large, surrounded by tons of thick lashes. There was every reason in the world to be attracted to someone like Terri. He noticed her body had changed with her pregnancy; she was fuller, rounder—she definitely hadn't been lying about the fact she was pregnant. The thing missing was that glow a woman carrying seemed to have—but that could be explained by her lack of a partner with whom to bring this baby into the world.

They weren't even to the parking lot before she stopped walking, turned her eyes up to his and said, "You can let this go. It's not yours."

"What? How do I know for sure?" he asked her.

"What the hell does it matter? I'm not holding you responsible for anything!"

"I know," he said. "I'm holding me responsible." He looked around. Across the street was a small park. "Come on," he said, leading her there. There was a bench under a big tree and not too many people around. "Sit down," he told her. "We're going to get this straightened out once and for all."

"I don't know what your problem is," she said, sitting down, shaking her head.

"Yeah, you do. I can't be sure which lie is the truth and which truth is the lie."

"So?"

"So, if there's any chance you're carrying my child, I want to be its father. Is that too crazy for you to understand?"

"Even though you want nothing to do with the mother?"

"That's not true, either. It's not like that. If you're the mother of my child, that comes with respect and support. I wouldn't ignore your needs."

"Oh? And how does the woman you plan to marry feel about that?"

"She'd expect nothing less."

Terri laughed. "Jesus. Aren't you all just so goddamn *decent*."

He nearly flinched. "I need to be sure. I'm not walking away from this without some confirmation. I'm not going to miss out on any time with a child that's mine."

"Look," she said. "It was close enough. I didn't have anyone and you and I—I thought we worked pretty well. I thought I could pull it off, all right? You caught me. I knew I was pregnant before that night with you. I was thinking of ending it, the pregnancy, but I didn't want to. I've made a lot of mistakes. I'm not going to let this be one of them."

"Can you prove this to me with an ultrasound that shows you are further along than three months?" he asked.

"Oh, Jesus," she groaned. "I don't have to!"

"Yeah, you're going to have to. I'll hire a lawyer. I'll sue you for my paternal rights, and to get me off your back, you'll have to have a test."

"What kind of test?" she asked, shocked.

"Amniocentesis. DNA."

She went a little pale. "Does that involve a needle?"

"Yeah, it sure does. Unless we can get some easier answers from an ultrasound."

"I don't have another doctor's appointment for three weeks. Maybe I can convince her to do an ultra—"

"You said your doctor was Charlene Weir. Who, by the way, isn't in the book."

"God, you remembered that?" She laughed. "Charlene Weir is my girlfriend. I just tossed it out there. I didn't want you going to the doctor with me."

"We're not waiting three weeks, Terri. I have a place to take you for an ultrasound today. Will you go? Or do I have to hire a lawyer?"

"How can you waste money on something like that?" she asked, perplexed.

"It wouldn't be a waste. I have to know for certain."

"Is your fiancée making you do this?"

He stood up. "Not at all." He held out a hand to her. "Let's do it."

She sighed, put her hand in his and let him draw her to her feet. He drove her to the offices of Mary Jensen, M.D. They filled out a lot of paperwork, Paul put his credit card on the visit and a very kind and gentle woman doctor fired up the ultrasound. Since Dr. Jensen, a friend of Cameron's, knew the purpose of the visit, there wasn't much talking in the room. It took only moments for the doctor to establish that the pregnancy was closer to four months than three, perhaps a few weeks advanced of Paul's contact with Terri.

But something happened to Paul as he watched the life inside her, moving around, kicking and squirming. For a big tough guy, things like this were his undoing. Pregnant women were beautiful to him; he hadn't been great with women but he'd always wanted a wife, a family. Knowing that baby wasn't his didn't really give him the relief he expected. Had it been established that the baby was his it wouldn't exactly have made him proud, either—he'd been trying to keep Terri safe from that complication. He was ambivalent. And he felt a deep sadness for Terri, who despite all her attempts to mislead him, was in a very difficult position. He had sad feelings for the baby, who would not have the love and protection he could offer as a father. The urge to keep the vulnerable safe, to protect the weak with his strength, was natural for Paul.

Terri said nothing at all. She walked ahead of him out of the doctor's office and jumped in the truck. As Paul got in and started the engine, she looked into her lap, silent. There, she seemed to be saying without words. Done. Over.

He was also quiet as he drove her back to her office.

When he got to the law firm's parking lot, however, he didn't turn in. He drove around the block and, instead, pulled into that same little park they'd visited earlier. He got out of the truck, went to her side and opened the door for her. He put out his hand. "What are you doing?" she asked. "What *now?*"

"Let's talk a minute," he said softly, gently.

"Paul," she said, tears brimming in her eyes. "Please. Enough. I'm sorry."

"It's okay. Come on," he said, pulling her out of the truck. He dropped an affectionate arm around her shoulders and led her back to the bench, and as he did so she leaned against him and began to softly cry. "Sit down, Terri," he invited her. "Tell me something. Does the baby have a father?"

"Obviously," she wept, digging around in her purse for a tissue.

He pulled a clean handkerchief from his pocket and handed it to her. "I mean, a man who is standing by. Supporting you. Ready to take his share of responsibility."

"'Fraid not," she said, accepting the hankie and dabbing her eyes.

He ran the back of his finger along her cheek, wiping away a tear. "Is that why you told me it was mine?"

She turned liquid eyes up to him. "Partly," she said quietly. "There's more to it than that...."

"Was it about money?" he asked.

She laughed without humor. "No," she said. "It was because neither of us had anyone in our lives—at least that's what you said. It was because of the way you are—telling me that story about how you were with your best friend's wife when her baby came, and it tore you up but it was the most beautiful thing you'd ever seen. It was the way I felt when I was with you." She shrugged. "I thought you'd be a good father. A good... Never mind."

"We weren't together very much," Paul said, shaking his head.

"I know. It was stupid. But I thought if you grew to love me…" She leaned against him and let the tears flow. "If you thought I was having your baby, maybe we'd be together more. And if we were together, maybe…" She wiped at her eyes. "I thought I'd… I thought we'd be safe with you. I felt a lot more for you than you did for me. But what I did… It was wrong. I'm sorry."

He put an arm around her and held her. "Terri—you had to know I'd find out eventually…"

She shrugged and sniffed. "Maybe not. At least not until we'd had some time together. And if you got attached, if there were more children… It was a stupid risk, I really don't know if I'd have been able to go through with it." She looked up at him. "I'm not a dishonest person. I probably would have told you the truth before…" She took a breath. "It took me a while to accept that you just weren't into me," she said. "You didn't call, you left town all the time. You were right—there wasn't much between us. But that didn't keep me from wishing there was."

He put a large hand over her barely swollen middle. "And this little one's father?"

"Not interested, either," she said.

"Does he know?"

"I told him. He could care less. He told me I'd have to sue him to— Well, it didn't take me long to decide I was better off."

"Loser," Paul muttered under his breath. "How did this happen?" he asked.

"I've always been bad about those pills. Missing them, forgetting. And he didn't use anything. It's my screwup. All mine. I'm pretty lucky a baby is all I got from him." Her eyes were large and round. "The condom didn't fail,

Paul, and I was tested at my first appointment. I didn't give you anything."

He didn't share that he already knew that. Acting on Jack's advice, he'd been checked out. "Are you going to be all right?" he asked her.

"I'll manage," she said, wiping her tears away.

He lifted her chin. "Is there anything I can do to help you now?"

"You're off the hook, Paul. You don't have to do anything."

"Do you still have that card I gave you? With the phone numbers?"

"Yeah. Somewhere."

"You can find me easily. I work for a family company headquartered in Grants Pass. My family. If I'm not here, they can reach me. If you ever need anything…"

"Paul," she said, laughing through tears. "I lied to you. You don't have to…"

"Terri," he said sweetly. "It's true we're not a couple. That we never were. But I don't go to bed with women I don't have any feelings for. God, I'm not that bad. Even if we weren't in love, I thought of us as friends, at least. We had a real important connection. You were good to me. I tried to be good to you."

"God, you're incredible… After what I tried to do to you!"

He smiled at her. "I was wrong to call you when I got back to Grants Pass. It set up a series of events that were unfair to you. But I remember it so damn well—I was in a lot of pain. It was a bad, bad time for me. That night, I was a pretty miserable, desperate guy and you got me through a rough spot. You were kind to me. Sympathetic and sweet. Loving. At the time, I was very grateful. I wouldn't be a gentleman if I didn't tell you that."

She leaned against him, the tears dry now, and he put his arms around her in comfort. She sighed. "I thought I loved you, that I could make you happy if I had a chance," she said. "I didn't lie about that." She lifted her head and looked up at him. "You're an easy man to fall for."

He tightened his arms a bit. He knew something about love now. It filled him up inside, made him feel like the luckiest man on the planet to have Vanessa. He would do anything for her, and if she had come to him with another man's baby and asked him to take her with that burden inside her, he wouldn't even have to think about it.

"Is there anything you need?"

"Yeah," Terri said with a sad little laugh. "I need to find a man like you. Then I'll be set."

He sat with her for a long while, his arms around her, giving what small comfort he could. He dropped a tender kiss on the top of her head. "You'll find the right man," he said. "And you'll be a good mother. This will work out."

"Paul, I'm sorry if I hurt you, if I complicated your life. It was so selfish of me...."

"We'll get past that, no problem. Desperate times sometimes bring out desperate measures—I'm not angry. And I know a really good pediatrician, if you're looking for one..."

Eleven

Vanessa had just finished nursing the baby when the doorbell at Paul's house rang. Holding the baby, she went and glanced out the window beside the door. There stood Carol, looking every bit the chic and sophisticated businesswoman she always did. Vanni opened the door somewhat reluctantly.

"I didn't know if you'd be here," Carol said. "I didn't want to call. I wanted to see you and I wasn't sure you'd agree."

Vanessa opened the door. "I haven't been in touch, Carol, because I thought we could use some time to think things through. Both of us." Vanni held the door open. "Come in, since you're here."

"Is Paul at home?" she asked, stepping across the threshold.

"Not at the moment." She looked at her watch. "I guess he should be coming soon."

"I'm sorry, Vanessa," Carol said uncomfortably. "Lance is furious with me. Terrified we won't see much of the baby because of what I did."

"Come in and sit down," Vanni said, leading the way

to the dining room. She put Mattie in his bouncy seat on the table and pulled out a chair. "So," she said bravely. "Lance didn't like that little meeting you tried to arrange?"

Carol was caught looking around at Paul's house. By the rather surprised expression on her face, maybe she wasn't expecting anything quite so beautiful, so tasteful. Maybe she thought Paul made his home in a construction trailer?

"Carol?" Vanni asked.

She shook her head. "No," she said. "Not from the beginning. He blustered about it, but I didn't think I was doing anything harmful. You know we care about Paul for many reasons, but after getting to know Cameron, I just thought the world of him. And… Oh hell," Carol said. "I didn't know about you and Paul."

"That's exactly why you should make it a policy to ask if your plans are acceptable. Had you asked me in the first place if I'd like you to invite a single man to dinner, I would have asked you to wait on that. I was missing Paul, wanting to see him. Cameron's a great guy, but I'm not interested in him romantically," Vanni said. "In the end, both men were hurt. You have to stop doing things like that."

"I always think I'm helping," she said. "I always feel like I have the perfect solution. Really—I wouldn't…" Her voice trailed off. "You and Paul…?"

"That's right. We're getting married. I love him. He'll be a wonderful father to Mattie. You can't imagine how much he adores this baby. How grateful he is that there's a little piece left of his best friend."

"And you're happy?" Carol asked, her brow furrowed. "This is what you want?"

Vanni reached out a hand to touch Carol's. "When we lost Matt, the pain was so great for both me and Paul—

for everyone—I didn't know if I could ever be happy again. I imagine there were times you felt the same way."

"Sometimes I miss him so much," she said, and her eyes glistened. She reached for the baby. "May I?"

"Sure. Go ahead."

Carol picked up the baby and held him against her, her eyes wet. "You have no idea how fast the time goes, and how much goes with it."

"When Matt had that videoconference before his death, Paul was at the house. God, Matt was so happy to see his face, to talk to him. I think he was as happy to see Paul as me. Carol, this would make Matt happy."

Carol laughed through some tears. "Oh, I'm sure that's true. Matt and Paul always spent more time at the Haggerty house than ours. A whole crowd of messy boys with big smelly feet never threw Marianne. She somehow knew just what food to toss at them. Our house was too sterile. I was strict about neatness."

"Well, I guess if you have three of them, one more hardly matters," Vanni said.

"They were just boys," Carol said. "Who can blame them. They weren't interested in how hard I had to work to buy a certain lamp or how much trouble it was to keep up the landscaping. Before the Haggertys built that big house, while the boys were young, they could barely keep grass in the yard." She smiled a bit forlornly. "All the boys played soccer."

Whew, Vanni thought. It wasn't just that Carol thought Cameron was a better choice for her. She didn't want to compete with Marianne and her mother-earth qualities. "I suppose Marianne always had cookies when they got home from school, too," Vanni said, testing out her theory.

"I'm sure. A trampoline, drum set, all kinds of stuff. They let the boys set up a kind of band in the garage—

electric piano, guitars, the whole bit. Noisy enough to split your skull." She laughed a little. "Not one of them had a lick of talent, thank God. Or else they'd all be tattooed rock stars."

With his usual fabulous timing, little Mattie barfed curdled milk right down Carol's back and predictably she said, "Ewww."

"Oh no!" Vanni shot to her feet, a diaper she used as a burping cloth in her hand. She reached for the baby.

"No, please don't take him," Carol said. "Just put that over my shoulder."

"Carol, it's silk!"

"Oh the hell with it. There are dry cleaners, you know."

Vanni wiped her off as well as she could, then draped a clean diaper over Carol's shoulder. She was pretty stunned that Carol didn't fling the baby away from her, but she held him close, snuggled him.

Vanni chewed her lip for a second. *Carol's afraid of another generation that belonged to her by blood preferring the Haggerty family. Because she's rigid, not warm and fuzzy, and she knows it.* Then Vanni said, "Each one of those Haggerty men turned out to be successful and hardworking. Someone in that house must have insisted on study."

"Probably Stan. He's always been business-minded." She cuddled and kissed the baby. She seemed to have already forgotten about the wet patch running down her back. Facing the thought of being separated from her only grandson had created a shift in Carol. Maybe not a total personality change, but definitely a small conversion.

"There's something I want to talk to you about," Vanni said. "It's early, I know, but Paul and I, when Mattie's a little older—we want more children. I really want more children. I'd like it if you welcomed them as much as little

Matt. Along with us, of course. I know Mattie's special, your biological grandson, but it would be so nice if we could count on you and Lance to open your hearts to any of his siblings." Carol raised startled eyes to Vanni's face. "Don't worry—I certainly don't expect you to turn your beautiful home into a clubhouse. I don't intend to live that way, no matter how many boys come along. But of course, there could even be girls. I hope so—you'd be perfect for little girls…"

"Do you mean that, Vanessa?" Carol asked, her eyes a bit wide.

"There will be boundaries," Vanni said. "You have to check with me before you make any plans that affect me, my son, my life, my relationship, my—"

"Of course."

"If you get any little granddaughters' ears pierced without my permission, you'll pay," Vanessa said, lifting one brow meaningfully.

"Oh heavens, of course I wouldn't…"

"And you'd better show Paul the gratitude he deserves—he's *still* a wonderful friend to Matt."

"I'm sorry I said that," Carol said. "Thinking a doctor would be better for my grandson…"

Vanni surprised herself with a laugh. "I guess you're not the first mother or grandmother to try to hook up your loved ones with someone as prestigious as a doctor. And Cameron is wonderful—smart, sensitive, kind. What I'd like you to see is that Paul is at least his equal. And that you have a great gift in Paul as Mattie's stepfather— because Paul will do everything to keep Matt alive for him. Paul was so loyal to Matt, so committed. That's something no other man can give us, Carol."

"I guess I can see that. Are you still angry with me?" she asked.

Vanni shook her head. "You should make amends with Paul."

"Is he furious?" Carol asked, snuggling the baby close.

"He hasn't said a word. But still—he deserves much better than he got. Long before I fell in love with him, he was wonderful to me, to your grandson. You should apologize."

"You're right, though I dread it," she said. And as if planned, the door from the garage to the kitchen opened and Paul came in.

"Well, this is a surprise," he said when he saw Carol. He went first to Vanni, dropping a kiss on her forehead and again, that possessive hand on her shoulder. "How are you, Carol?" he asked.

"Repentant," she said. "I'm sorry, Paul. I didn't realize what was happening."

Paul gave Vanni's shoulder a reassuring squeeze. "It's behind us, Carol. Let's move on."

"That's decent of you under the circumstances. Any chance I can squeak in another attempt at dinner before you leave town again?"

"I'm afraid that isn't going to work out," he said. "We have plans and I'd rather not cancel them. But we'll be back next week and try again then. Of course you're always welcome in Virgin River—you know the general would make you welcome anytime."

Vanessa frowned, not knowing they had any plans before leaving town. She wondered if maybe Paul was more angry than he'd allowed to show.

"I guess I'll have to live with that," Carol said, jostling the baby close to her.

"I'm going to leave you women to your visit. I need a shower," he said, heading for the master bedroom.

After about twenty minutes, Vanni felt for the first time

since she met Carol that they had reached an understanding. Pleading the need to get ready to go out—a complete lie—Vanessa escorted Carol out the door. She then carried the baby with her to the bedroom and put him in the porta-crib. The shower had stopped and she stepped into the master bath. Paul had a towel around his waist and was brushing his teeth. When he saw her he gave a spit and a rinse, wiping his mouth on another towel.

"Something's wrong," she said.

He smiled. "Depends on your perspective. And how did you get to know me so well, so fast?"

She shook her head. "I feel like I've been with you forever. What is it?"

"It's not mine. The baby. She's closer to four months than three."

"You know this for certain?"

He nodded. "We had an ultrasound. Your friend Cameron made arrangements for me. And he found the situation very humorous, by the way."

"Wow," she said, taking that in. "Did he hope you'd learn it was your baby and I'd toss you by the side of the road?"

"No, Cameron's actually a much more decent guy than that. He has a real soft spot for responsible parents. He didn't do it for either of us, but for the baby in question. A child deserves parents who care." He opened his arms. "Come here. Press yourself against me."

She walked into his arms.

"It was very sad," he said, holding her close. "She was sorry, of course. I forced the issue of the ultrasound for positive proof even after she swore up and down it wasn't mine. I threatened with legal action. I had to be sure."

"You don't seem relieved," she said.

"Oh, I am. It wouldn't have been easy to be a halfway-decent father, not being partnered with the mother. But the fact is, she isn't going to have any father for that baby. I don't know her very well, so I don't know much about her friends and family, about what kind of support she'll have. But I know she doesn't have a man in her life. That has to be hard."

"It is," Vanni said, a fact she knew only too well. "Maybe she'll get lucky like me, and one will come to her."

"I hope so. There's no question—she stands a better chance of having that in her future without me in the mix." He kissed the top of her head. "I can't ever love anyone but you. I'm all in."

"But you felt sorry for her. Even after she tried to trick you," Vanni said.

"I did," he admitted, holding her, tightening his embrace.

"Out here, you're all muscle, a hide like leather," she said, running her hands over his upper arms, shoulders and chest. "You have a soft underbelly. You're a soft touch."

"I know. Mush. Nothing but mush."

"Tell you what I'll do for you," she said, looking up at him. "When Mattie's a little older, I'll have this IUD removed. We'll get you started on your own small herd."

That made him smile. "That would be nice, Vanni."

"Will you be all right? No regrets now?"

"One regret," he said, looking down into her eyes. "I wish I hadn't told your father about it." She laughed at him. "Now he's got that on me forever."

"Well, he tripped you up. I told you—he's very good. Tom and I learned early not to try to slip anything by him. Welcome to the family." She grinned. "You didn't want to try to have dinner with Carol and Lance while we're still in town?"

"Nope," he said. "Believe it or not, I'm dead tired. I'd rather spend all day on a roof in the hot sun than do the kind of business I did today. It wore me down. I feel better now, after a shower—if you'd like to go over there, we can call her, tell her we had a change of plans. Just say the word."

Vanni thought briefly about explaining to Paul that she and Carol had turned a corner, that much of Carol's attitude had to do with being afraid she might lose another generation of her offspring to Paul's nurturing and homespun mom. Maybe someday, she thought. For now it would be enough to give Carol a chance to demonstrate she could stop controlling everything.

"No. I think it might be a good idea if Carol begins to understand she's not in charge of everyone's life. We'll catch up with her early next week." She smiled. "It isn't likely I'll ever pass up a night alone with you. Except," she said, hearing a little fussing from the bedroom, "I do have another man in my life, and I think he's drenched."

Paul and Vanni were back in Virgin River Friday night for another weekend. Paul and Walt turned some hamburgers on the grill and Walt seemed especially jovial. For the first time in such a long time, Vanni asked herself if her dad was ever lonely. It had probably been a long, quiet week—she and Paul out of town and Tom spending every second with Brenda—and it seemed as though Walt was relieved to have them home.

After the dinner dishes were done, Vanni went to settle the baby in bed. Paul found the TV on in the great room, but Walt was out on the deck with a cup of coffee. Paul stuck his head out the back door and said, "Sir, if you can spare a few minutes from that sunset, I'd sure like to talk to you about something."

Walt turned. "By all means." He threw an arm wide and indicated Paul should precede him to the great room. Walt clicked the TV off and chose the chair facing Paul. "What's on your mind, son?"

Paul scooted forward a bit. "Well, it's no secret I'm in love with your daughter. I want to marry Vanni. Do I have your blessing? Your permission?"

Walt shook his head and chuckled. "Haggerty, you sneak down the hall after I'm in bed every night—you'd damn sure better marry her. In fact, it might make sense for you to put the baby in that bedroom you're not using—save a trip or two, let the child have some space…"

Paul felt a stain creep to his cheeks and thought, *I'm over thirty-five—how the hell does this man make me blush?* "Yes, sir. Good idea, sir. Thing is—we've been talking…"

"How about that little mess up in Grants Pass?" Walt asked.

Paul scooted forward a little more, surprised. "Vanni didn't tell you? A misunderstanding, sir."

Walt let go a laugh. "That must've made your day."

Paul hung his head briefly. "Actually, it's a sad situation and I regret that I… Well, I'm relieved Vanni doesn't have to deal with it." Right then Vanni came back to the great room. She went to Paul and sat on his lap. "We've been talking about getting the wedding done the weekend before Tom leaves. It's quick, but neither of us wants anything flashy—just a simple ceremony with friends." He squeezed Vanni. "We're anxious to make it legal, and we want Tom with us for that. Do you have any objection to that idea?"

"You realize that's only three weeks away?" Walt said. "Think you can do it that fast?"

"We do, Dad," Vanni said. "We've talked out some of the details. We'd do it right here, if that's okay."

"What about your family, Paul?"

"I think we can count on them, sir. In fact, there's another thing regarding my family—my dad and brothers support the idea of starting a Haggerty Construction division here, serving the towns around here. I think there might be enough work to keep me busy—and if that's the case, we can make our home in Virgin River permanently. Of course, I won't know till I try—but while I'm looking for building contracts, I have the Middleton and Valenzuela jobs to keep me going."

"And if there isn't work here?" Walt asked.

"There will be," Paul said. "But until it's established, I'll keep the house in Grants Pass. If I have to, there's always a lot of work for me there. But, General, people have such a hard time finding a contractor around here, I have a feeling there will be too much work, once my name gets out. We have a good reputation in Grants Pass."

"Hmm," he said. "Just how many houses can you build at one time?"

"We've gotten pretty big in Oregon," he said with a shrug. "We've gotten up to a dozen or two structures in progress at a time, depending on the size, whether they're commercial, family units or multifamily—apartments. Our specialty has been custom homes from the beginning—I don't know how much of that I'll find around here. But there's lots of renovation work. How long did it take you to renovate this house?"

"Almost two years," Walt said.

"See, that's it—we could've had it done in a few months, even if we started with a lean-to. Six at the most. I sense a serious market."

"Can you make a living on a few a year? Renovations or custom homes?"

"A damn fine living," Paul confirmed.

Walt hmmed again. "Give me a second." He left the

room and Vanni and Paul exchanged confused glances. Then Walt was back. He held a thick, folded document. "This was impetuous of me, and if it doesn't appeal to you, there will be no hard feelings. But then again, if you like the idea, you can consider it an early wedding gift." He handed the pages to Paul.

Paul unfolded the document. At the top was printed, in boldface, DEED.

"I have a lot of land here. I wanted a lot—in case the surrounding acreage sells off at some point. I need space to ride. I thought a couple of acres on the other side of the stable might work out for you. If you're interested, that is. If you'd rather scout around for your own land…"

"Oh, Daddy," Vanni said, so deeply moved that her hand rose to her throat and her eyes swelled with tears.

"It's going to belong to you and Tom one day anyway. I have Shelby taken care of. If you're inclined and want to keep your own horses, we can always enlarge the stable and corral." He grinned. "I know a builder."

Gently, Paul pushed Vanni off his lap and stood, facing Walt. "This is very generous, sir," he said.

"It's very selfish, Paul. I wouldn't mind having my daughter and grandchildren nearby. Frankly, a year ago I didn't think that was an option." Then he looked at Vanni and asked, "Honey, can you be happy in a little town like this? Your husband building around the area, nothing much to occupy you but children and horses?"

She laughed a little emotionally. "You're kidding me, right? Dad, not many people even have the opportunity for this kind of life. The only complication is whether there's enough work here for Paul." She reached for his hand. "He loves building houses. And he's brilliant at it. We have to keep him at it."

"Well, here's the thing, Vanni," Paul said. "Before approaching my dad and brothers with this idea, I called around. I said I had house plans and needed a company to build—the soonest I could get someone was a year. There's plenty of work if they're backed up a year, plenty to spare." He looked at Walt. "I'd be willing to call Joe Benson in the morning, tell him we're ready to discuss our own plans. If you're sure…"

"You're holding it in your hand, son. It's your future wife's property. I'm sure."

Twelve

When May arrived in Virgin River there was love in the air. Paul and Vanni had been back and forth to Grants Pass for a couple of weeks, unable to be apart for even a few days. Paul was working out a deal with Joe Benson and his family business to build Preacher's add-on, and Mike and Brie's house. Then there was Tom and Brenda— young lovers, too hot to touch, getting ready to say goodbye for Tom to go to basic training and then to West Point. It was prom weekend and Vanni and Paul were back again to see the prom couple.

Mel Sheridan made it to May with that new baby girl still growing, and she was damn happy about that. One morning she woke up at 5:00 a.m., well before Jack. That almost never happened, especially when she was pregnant. But she was up and full of energy, so she started her day by making her husband a pot of coffee and began cleaning out the refrigerator. She would routinely bring home groceries and they would inevitably rot while they took their meals together at the bar, or packed up some of Preacher's delicious meals to take home.

Just getting rid of the old food wasn't quite good

enough. Mel was on a roll, so she filled the sink with soapy water and began to scrub the inside of the fridge.

"What are you doing?" Jack asked as he wandered into the kitchen.

"I'm cleaning out the refrigerator," she answered. "I'm going to stop bringing food into this house—we let too much go to waste."

She heard David start to stir and lifted her head like a doe smelling a hunter.

"I'll get him," Jack said. "He's heavy."

"Okay. I'll get his breakfast ready. Would you like me to make you an omelet or something?"

"How old are the eggs?" he asked.

"Hmm," she said, looking. "I don't think they're deadly yet."

"I think I'll pass, thanks."

"Coward."

David had his Cheerios, then his playtime in the great room with all his toys while Mel started the laundry and Jack went outside to spend a few minutes on his favorite morning activity of splitting logs. By next fall there would be a nice huge stack of firewood ready for the winter. Some of the trees that had been felled to widen the driveway were stacked at the tree line on their property, and he was working on turning them into fuel for the fireplace.

Mel wiped down the kitchen cabinets with lemon oil. Paul and Jack had truly outdone themselves on the kitchen with its gorgeous oak cabinets, black granite countertops and stainless-steel appliances. The house was absolutely magnificent, and much more than Mel had dared allow herself to expect. Compared to that little cabin she'd lived in for almost two years, it was huge—over three thousand square feet—but she'd managed to fill it up very quickly with furniture and accessories.

Once done with the cabinets, Mel did another laundry shuffle, then got a clean diaper for Davie. She followed that by getting to work on the shutters with the lemon oil. Then she busied herself with a special cleaner for the leather furniture, followed by one more load of laundry. When Jack checked in on her before lunch, she was pulling the tags off new little pink things that she'd had for a long time— gifts for the baby from Jack's sisters and her sister. Mel laundered and folded all these infant garments, something that probably should've been done weeks ago.

Having babies barely a year apart creates a need for two nurseries—she cleaned David's room and gave the new baby's room a little cleaning, too, putting away the clothes and getting out the newborn diapers and bath towels.

By afternoon Jack found her down on her hands and knees scouring the bathroom floor around the toilet and tub. "For the love of God," he said.

"What?"

"What the hell are you doing? If you want the bathroom cleaned, why don't you just tell me? I know how to clean a goddamn bathroom."

"It wasn't all that dirty, but since I'm in the cleaning mood, I thought I'd whip it into shape."

"David is ready for his nap. Why don't you join him."

"I don't feel like a nap. I'm going to vacuum the area rugs."

"No, you're not," he said. "I'll do that if it has to be done right now."

"Okay," Mel said, smiling.

"I've been tricked."

"Only by yourself, darling," she said, whirling away to get the Pledge and Windex. After that was done—and there was a lot of wood and glass and stainless steel to occupy her—she was sweeping off the porch and back steps. Not long after that, she was caught dragging the cradle into the master bedroom.

"Melinda!" he shouted, startling her and making her jump.

"Jack! Don't do that!"

"Let go of that thing!" He brushed her out of the way and grabbed the cradle. "Where do you want it?"

"Right there," she said. He put it beside the bed. "No," she said. "Over there, kind of out of the way." He put it there. "No," she said. "Against that wall—we'll put it where we need it when she comes." He moved it again. "Thank you," she said.

The phone rang. "I'll get it," he said. He picked up a pencil and put it in her face. "If you lift anything heavier than this, I'm going to beat you." Then he turned and left the room.

He has cabin fever, she thought. *Spending too much time at home with me, making sure I don't pick up anything heavier than a pencil. He should get out more, and out of my hair.*

When Jack was done with the phone, she was on her knees in front of the hearth, brushing out the barely used fireplace. "Aw, Jesus Christ," he said in frustration. "Can that not wait until at least frickin' winter?"

She sat back on her heels. "You are really getting on my last nerve. Don't you have somewhere you can go?"

"No, but we do. Go shower and get beautiful. Paul and Vanessa are back and after they view the prom couple, they're going to the bar for dinner. We'll all meet there, look at some pictures."

"Great," she said. "I'm in the mood for a beer."

"Whatever you want, Melinda," he said tiredly. "Just stop this frickin' cleaning."

"You know I'm not going to be able to do much of this

after the baby comes, so it's good to have it all done. And the way I like it."

"You've always been good at cleaning. Why couldn't you just cook?" he asked. "You don't cook anything."

"You cook." She smiled. "How many cooks does one house need?"

"Just go shower. You have fireplace ash on your nose."

"Pain in the ass," she said to him, getting clumsily to her feet.

"Ditto," he said.

An hour later the three of them were on their way into town. "So, you did it," she said. "You got Paul down here staking out his territory. And now they're together."

"You should at least give me a little credit for trying to get a couple of people together instead of trying to keep them apart." Then more softly he added, "Like I did Preacher and Paige, Brie and Mike."

"I should—apparently it all worked out just fine…" she said a little dreamily, rubbing her hands over her tummy.

"Do you feel all right?" he asked, glancing at her. "You're a little…pink."

"I feel fantastic. Probably just the calm before the storm."

"Probably," he said. "You do that again tomorrow and I'm tying you down. You make me crazy sometimes."

"Jack…" She laughed. "When did you get like this? You're so *annoying!*"

By the time they got to the bar, Brie and Mike were there and of course Paige and Preacher and Christopher. Doc came in, but before he could get comfortable his pager went off. He made a phone call from the kitchen and headed out for a house call. Next, Vanessa, Paul and the baby, along with a bouncy baby seat, had all arrived. The crowd was treated to digital pictures of Tom and Brenda and another couple all dressed up in their fancy clothes.

"Aw," Mel said, clicking through the pictures. "Look at how gorgeous they are. Aren't they the cutest? Don't they look so in love?"

"*So* in love," Vanni said. "I never thought I'd see my little brother like this."

"Where's the general?" Mel asked.

Vanni frowned and shook her head. "He said you see enough of him all week when we're in Grants Pass. He said he'd stay home tonight."

"Really?" Mel questioned. "I haven't seen much of him at all lately. In fact, I've been wondering what he's been doing with himself. I assumed he'd had Tom and Brenda for dinner every night."

"Hardly." Vanni laughed. "If they can escape the parents, I believe they have important making out to do. Gotta cram in as much of that as possible before Tom leaves, you know."

"I imagine so," Mel agreed.

The bar had few customers that evening, so Jack divided his time between the pushed-together tables and his favorite spot behind the bar. Paul drifted up to the bar and said, "You seem a little unhappy tonight. Is it because your wife is about to explode?"

"Nah, that's only part of it. We got a call from Rick a while ago. He's got ten days of leave coming up—after which he goes to Iraq."

"Aw, man. You doing okay?"

"Hanging in there. I mean—we went, right? It's just that Rick…"

"Feels like a son—and it's different."

"That's it, I guess." Jack had known all along that Rick wouldn't play it safe—if he was going in, he'd be part of the fight. "At least he'll be around for a while—I'll see if some of the boys want to come up, I think."

"There will be four of us for sure," Paul said. "How's Mel doing?"

"She's nesting," Jack said. "She's been after it all day. I've heard her talk about her patients and their sudden burst of energy. I saw it today up close and personal. Any second, trust me."

"Damn, it'll be great. I'd love to be here for it."

"You're really getting into this baby business...."

"I'm not as far into it as I was," Paul said. "After talking to Mel, I followed through, had an ultrasound with the woman and the baby's not mine." He shook his head. "Something's wrong with me, man. I'm relieved, but almost sorry—because there's a baby coming and no man to take care of them. It would almost be better if it had been mine. I'm a sick SOB—you should get more rational friends."

Jack leveled him with a serious look, a slight frown. "I can think of twenty reasons why you don't get married if it's not the right match, but I can't think of one reason why you'd walk away from your own kid."

"I offered to help her anyway," Paul said. Then he shrugged. "She's a good person. This is gonna be tough on her."

Jack gave him a half smile. "That doesn't surprise me, Paul. She take you up on it?"

"Nah. Like I said, she's a decent person. I'm sorry she's going through this. Glad Vanni isn't going to have to put up with it, but sorry—"

But Jack wasn't listening anymore. His narrowed eyes were on Mel. It was like he sensed it; smelled it. She got up from the table and was heading toward the bathroom back off the kitchen. She paused when she got to the end of the bar, gripped it to stabilize herself, made a noise that only her husband heard, bent slightly over her huge belly and let go with a gush of amniotic fluid that splashed to the floor.

"I knew it," Jack said, going to her at once.

Silence fell over the dinner crowd. Paul edged back to the table, sat down beside Vanessa and said, "Jack said she's been nesting all day."

"Is it happening?" Vanessa asked.

"Oh, yeah," Paul said.

Jack braced Mel from behind, his hands on her upper arms and asked, "Contraction?"

"Boy howdy," she said, a little breathless.

"By the time you got to cleaning the bathroom this afternoon, you had completely given yourself away," he told her.

"Yeah, I suspected this would happen today. But I didn't want to get my hopes up. I don't think we have a whole lot of time to screw around. She's here, Jack."

He turned her around to face him. "Have you been having contractions all day?"

"Not really. A couple. A few." She inhaled deeply. "Yeah."

He lifted her immediately into his arms and started barking orders. "Someone bring Davie to the truck and ride home with us. Preach—call John Stone and tell him it's now and it's gonna be quick." Then he carried Mel out the door to the truck.

Brie quickly picked up her nephew, the diaper bag, and followed. Preacher went to the kitchen to use the phone. Everyone waited tensely. When Preacher came back to the room he said, "John's on his way."

More silence lingered. Then Mike said, "What are we waiting for? Let's wipe up the floor, pack up some stuff and join the party." Everyone got busy cleaning up, gathering food, drink and even cigars to go to the Sheridan house to stand by for the birth.

* * *

Before Jack got Mel home, she was already having hard contractions, two minutes apart. "Breathe," he was telling her. "Don't even think about pushing."

"I'm fine," she insisted.

"You'd better be. I should've known. I should've kept you home. I should've brought Doc along."

"Lighten up, it's only a ten-minute drive. And Doc's on a call… Uhhhh," she added, bending over her belly.

"Aw, Melinda… Okay, baby. You just breathe, don't worry about a thing."

"I'm *not* worried," she rasped out.

When they got to the house, he lifted her out of the truck into his arms and smacked her head on the door frame in the process.

"Ow!"

"Sorry," he said.

"You've done this to me before!" she accused.

"I know. I've always been real smooth," he said, remembering a time long ago, before they were married, when he was carrying her home in much this same manner, though not pregnant, and while his mind was on sex, he damn near gave her a concussion, which sort of precluded any kind of sex. His mind was definitely not on sex right now.

Jack carried Mel to the bedroom while Brie took charge of David. Mel had already prepared the bed with a rubber mattress protector so all that was necessary was helping her to undress and climb in, which Jack did. He added a couple of soft, clean towels under her. Then he went for a flashlight from the kitchen and Brie shouted, "What's that for?"

"I have to see how close she is," Jack responded, moving quickly.

"Oh my God," Brie said. "We need some professionals here!"

"Try Doc Mullins's pager. The number's inside the cupboard door. And get out a bottle," Jack said.

"You're going to have a *drink?*" she asked, appalled.

Not a bad idea, he thought. "For Davie. Get him ready for bed and give him his bottle."

"Oh. Sure," she said, rattled.

Back in the bedroom he said, "Let's have a look, honey."

Mel's knees came up and Jack clicked on the flashlight, shining it right on her pelvic floor. "Good. I don't see anything yet." Then he looked over her knees. "You gonna wait for John this time?"

"With any luck," she answered breathlessly.

He rolled his eyes. "Where's your bag?"

"In the truck."

"Fine," he said. "I'll get it. I'll wash up. Pant." And he disappeared again.

He didn't stop to chat with Brie as he ran through the house, but he noticed her eyes were round and a little scared as he passed her with Mel's medical bag. He was rushing around like a madman, getting clamps, scissors and suction out of her bag, spreading out towels and baby blankets at the foot of the bed. He shone the flashlight on her again and said, "Pant!" Then he headed for the bathroom, rolled up his sleeves and began to scrub up to his elbows. He'd been down this road before and he wasn't thrilled about doing it again. Doctors and midwives should deliver babies, not men who knew nothing about it. He'd been lucky once, but there was no guarantee he'd be lucky again. It took him ten minutes to get set up and washed, then he was back at her side, flashlight in hand. He gave a look. "Oh God," he said.

"She's crowning," she confirmed.

"You're incredible. How can you do this so fast?"

"I don't have the first idea. I'm a breeder, Doc says."

"Pant," he said. "If you push, I don't know what I'm going to do."

"You know, you get so pissy…"

"Yeah, I keep trying to avoid this part. All the rest of it, I'm game. I hate doing this. I should've had you tested or something—to see why you just dump 'em like this, like there's nothing to it. Holy shit, Melinda—what if I screw up? Huh? Have you thought of that?"

"Jack," she said weakly, "you aren't going to screw up." And then she was seized by another contraction.

He suddenly realized he was thinking only of himself and he got down on one knee beside the bed, took her hand in both of his and said, "I love you, baby. More than my life—you know that. Right?"

"Not now, Jack," she whispered. "I'm busy."

"It'll be okay."

"Sure it will," she said. "Maybe *you* better pant."

"I should never have let you do all that cleaning."

"Shh… Just breathe…"

He heard the sound of voices outside their bedroom. Brie stuck her head in the door. "Need anything?" she asked.

"A basin or bowl. The baby bathtub of warm water. John Stone would be nice."

"Oh, he's here. He's scrubbing up in the kitchen sink."

"Tell him to get in here now. Tell him she's *here!*"

"Not quite here," Mel said. "But she's coming…" Mel looked at Jack. She reached out a hand and touched the hair at his temple. "You're getting a little gray here."

"Big surprise. I really didn't know you'd be such a handful."

"I'm the best thing that ever happened to you."

"Yeah," he said in a breath. He leaned down and kissed her brow. "Yeah, baby. You sure are. And you're a reproductive genius."

John came into the room, all smiles. "You have a nice little birthing party going on out there, Mel. What've we got here?"

"We're ready," Jack said, getting up.

John lifted the flashlight with a clean towel, fixed the light on Mel's pelvic floor and said, "Yup. We're ready. How about you two? You ready?"

"John, I'm so glad to see you," Jack said.

"And I'm just so glad to be here. Jack, why don't you glove up, help me out here."

"Sure," he said. "Sure. I can do that. How you doing, baby?"

"I'm ready," Mel replied.

"Hey, Jack," John said. "Why don't you go ahead. I'm right here. Go ahead, bring her out."

"No way, man," he said, backing away.

"Come on—you know you want to. Might as well. You did the hard part. You put up with this for nine months."

"Hey!" Mel objected. "Ex*cuse* me?"

But Jack got a funny, dreamy look on his face and said, "Yeah. Let me bring her out. Let me. Since you're right here…" All these months of insisting this wasn't what he wanted and suddenly it was *all* he wanted. He'd pulled the last one right out of her body and he felt as if he'd gone to heaven, it was such a trip. He gloved up real fast. "There won't be anyone for Mel's back," he said.

"I'll take her back, and I'll coach you," John offered. "But you're okay, you know what to do. Go for it, man. It's your baby."

"Okay," he said, getting himself settled on his knees, right at the foot of the bed, and waited through a few more contractions, and then she delivered the baby's head.

Without even being told, he checked around the neck for the cord. John left Mel for a second to look over his shoulder to be sure. Then Jack supported the baby's head with a large hand and John told Mel to give them a little push. The baby came out slick and easy, mucky and screaming.

Jack held another life he'd produced in his hands. No one should be this lucky, he thought. No man on earth should have all this.

John spread the baby towel over Mel's belly and Jack placed the baby there and began to dry her off so he could wrap her in a clean, dry blanket. He clamped and cut the cord.

"Okay, I'll take care of the placenta," John said. "You get that little girl to her mother, then to the breast."

Now Jack was on terra firma—he'd done this before. He wrapped her, moved her into Mel's arms and got down on his knees to watch as his baby daughter nuzzled against Mel's warm flesh for a little while, then rooted and finally latched onto the breast, suckling. "Aaah," he said, smiling. "Another genius."

He pulled off the gloves and ran a couple of fingers along Mel's cheek, then over the baby's head. She turned her watering eyes up to his face. "You're getting pretty good at this," she said in a weak whisper.

"I am, huh. So are you. Mel, she's gorgeous. Positively gorgeous. She's going to look like you." He leaned over the baby to put his lips against hers. He moved over her mouth lightly. "God, I love you."

"She's smaller than David," Mel whispered.

"She's a good size," Jack said, as if he knew. "God, she's gorgeous."

"Jack?"

"Yeah, baby?"

"You do this to me one more time without my permission, you're a dead man."

"Sure, honey. I'll be careful…"

"And all those people out there?"

"Yeah?"

"You get out there and tell them, if they mess up my clean house, they're going to pay. *Pay,* do you hear me?"

He grinned at her. "I hear you, Mel."

Walt Booth was just dishing up dinner—two plates of fish he'd steamed in foil packages on the barbecue, wild rice and fresh broccoli—when the phone rang. The answering machine was in the kitchen and he decided to listen before picking up. "Dad? Dad, are you there?" Vanessa asked.

He picked up the phone. "Right here. Everything all right?"

"We're all at the Sheridans'. Mel's in labor! We're waiting—and according to Mel it isn't going to be long. Want to come over?"

"Hmm," he said. "I'm just about to eat some fish I cooked. I'll be along…"

"Good," she said. "I'll have Paul save you a cigar." Then she hung up.

Walt looked over the kitchen counter at Muriel, who was still on one of his bar stools with a glass of wine. She tilted her head and smiled at him. He brought the plates to the table. "I think you're about to have your debut," he said.

"You think so, huh?"

"Mel, the local midwife, is in labor, and it's kind of a tradition around here for friends to gather at the house, see the baby fresh out of the chute, have a drink and a cigar. It's a girl, I hear. We should go."

"I've met Mel. Just as I thought," she said. "You didn't tell your daughter you were having me to dinner."

"Of course not," he said, sitting down opposite her. "Vanessa would have stayed home. That didn't fit into my plans."

Muriel laughed and dipped into her fish—sea bass that Walt had seasoned wonderfully. She sighed and let her eyes drift closed for a second in appreciation.

"There you go," he said, smiling. "You could do that. I could teach you."

"I'll pass."

"We'll enjoy dinner, leave the dishes in the sink and then run out to the Sheridans'. How does that sound to you?"

"I'd love to see the baby," she said. "I'd like to meet your daughter and little grandson. After all, I introduced you to Luce."

"The thing is," he said, "this is going to get Vanessa a lot more excited than Luce was when she met me."

"I don't know if that's possible," Muriel replied, thinking of her Lab's wild reaction every time she saw Walt.

Thirty minutes later they were en route in Walt's SUV, having left Muriel's truck at his house. Their timing was perfect; the little baby girl was just making her first public appearance. And when Walt walked into the house with Muriel, Vanessa's chin almost dropped to the floor. "Vanni, meet our new neighbor, Muriel St. Claire. Muriel, this is my daughter. And this," he said, turning toward Jack, who held a small pink bundle in his arms, "must be the new Sheridan."

"Oh my God," Muriel said. "Oh my God, look at her! I've never seen a baby this new! She's *amazing!*"

"Want to hold her a second?" Jack asked.

"I don't even know how," Muriel said. There was that

look, Walt thought. Vulnerable. He'd remember that. "Puppies and foals I can handle—human newborns... Maybe I shouldn't..."

"You'll be all right." Jack laughed. "Support her head." He shifted the baby into her arms. "There you go. It's not that hard."

Vanni was still staring openmouthed at her father, but Walt was completely oblivious to his daughter. He had a dreamy smile on his face as he watched Muriel. He had learned that there had never been children for Muriel, that she wished she'd had a long marriage like his and maybe a couple of kids. He hadn't asked her a lot of personal questions about her relationships because he was a little afraid of the answers, but he knew this was new territory for her. It warmed him to see her experience this for the first time.

"Dad?" Vanni whispered, sidling close to him. "Were you spending the evening with Muriel?"

"I was cooking her dinner," he said. "You should see the way she eats. Wouldn't keep a rabbit alive."

"But, Dad, you didn't mention anything about—"

"Of course I didn't, Vanessa. She's a new neighbor. Only been in that house a couple of months. In fact, I didn't even know she was around till I ran into her out on the trail. She has a couple of horses. Nice woman. You'll like her."

"Dad?"

He finally turned to look at her. "What?" he asked.

"Dad, do you realize that's Muriel St. Claire? The actress?"

"Uh-huh. She mentioned that, yes. Nice woman, you'll like her."

Vanni just shook her head in confusion. But her attention was drawn back to Jack as he presented little Emma to the rest of the gathering, giving each one a chance to admire her.

"I'm sorry, Vanessa," Muriel said. "I should have said how pleased I am to meet you—but I was completely distracted by the baby." She put out her hand. "It's very nice to meet you."

Vanessa took the hand, but she said, "You and my father...?"

"Are neighbors," Muriel said with a smile.

Then Jack took the baby back to his wife and invited the women to follow. They all did, including Muriel.

Muriel went straight to Mel, leaned over the bed and with a smile said, "Congratulations. Excellent work—she's magnificent."

"Muriel!" Mel exclaimed tiredly, clearly surprised.

"I was having dinner with Walt when the call came. I'm so glad I got to be a part of this. I held the baby," she added a little conspiratorially.

"Ah," Mel said. "I'm glad to see you again. But we'll have to meet under other circumstances from now on. We're not going to keep doing this. Jack has strict orders not to knock me up again without permission."

"Very smart," Muriel agreed.

Shots were poured for the men, and Doc showed up right about then as if he'd whiffed the whiskey. John Stone abstained because he had another woman in early labor, but he accepted the cigar. The women stayed with Mel in the bedroom, but Muriel stepped out onto the porch with the men. They all turned to look at her with puzzled expressions on their faces as she joined their group.

"I heard there would be a drink and a cigar," she said with a shrug. "Isn't that right?"

They all stared at her dumbly except Walt—he was

somehow not at all surprised by this. "I can take care of that," Walt said. He went into the house to pour her a drink and brought it back to her. By the time he'd returned, Mike Valenzuela had snipped the end of a big ugly cigar for her. She accepted her drink and waited her turn for the lighter. Once she had her cigar going, she lifted her glass. "To you, Jack, and to your amazing wife, and to the newest Sheridan. Congratulations."

It was almost midnight when John Stone reached into his pocket and pulled out his pager. "I've got another one coming. They come in batches," he said, jogging off to the ambulance. "Full moon," he yelled over his shoulder. And with lights flashing on top of the Grace Valley ambulance, John was gone.

A few minutes later the birthing party packed up, leaving the Sheridans to themselves. When Walt and Muriel got back to his house he turned to look at her before opening the car door. "I'd just like to say one thing, Muriel. I thought it was going to be a real challenge, the way you eat celery and yogurt and little bitty slices of cheese, but damned if you aren't a good time."

She laughed at him. "Well, thank you, Walt. You're not that dull, yourself. Your daughter's going to have a lot of questions for you."

He grinned at her. "She can ask all she wants. I don't really have too much to say."

"Walt, there *isn't* much to say," she reminded him.

"Yeah. Not yet, there isn't."

Thirteen

When Brie pulled up to Jack's the early morning after the birth, she found her brother and nephew out on the porch. David was having his Cheerios, Jack was having his coffee. "Morning," she said, getting out of the car. "Did you sleep at all last night?"

"I can't sleep within twenty-four hours of a baby. Mel's out like a light. And David wants her, of course. That's why we're out here."

"Well, I'm here to help you out," Brie said. She planned to spend at least the morning with her brother and sister-in-law, if not the whole day. She would take care of David and help around the house. "When I left last night there was a lot of laundry waiting."

"Mostly done. But by this afternoon, I'm going to need a nap."

She laughed. "I'll cover for you," she said. "How's everyone doing?"

"Okay. We're about due another feeding. Can you handle Davie? Morning bath and stuff?"

"You bet," she said.

Jack took his coffee cup with him back to the bedroom and pulled the rocker next to the bed.

Mel looked a little pale to him. The second baby was supposed to be easier and she sure came faster, but this one had been hard on her. Mel was weak and shaky when she roused to nurse during the night. In the cradle beside the bed, Emma started to fuss. She was going to need to be fed, but his wife wasn't stirring yet. He wanted to pick up the baby, but it was better if Mel heard her—that snuffling from the baby helped with the breast milk. It was just amazing to him the way a woman's body responded to all this, the way something like the baby's cry could cause the milk to let down and drip like a faucet.

He reached out a hand to touch his wife's brow and found her clammy. "Mel," he said softly. Maybe there were too many blankets on her.

Emma made her demands known a little louder, but Mel still didn't stir. "Mel," he said more loudly, giving her shoulder a little shake. She didn't wake. "Mel," he said. Nothing.

Jack felt something squeeze his heart and hit his gut like a punch. He pulled back the covers and under his wife was a large, spreading pool of blood.

"Brie!" he screamed. "God! Brie!"

He picked up the phone and called John at home. Before the phone rang through Brie was in the doorway with David on her hip. She saw the blood, her sister-in-law motionless, and she ran to put David into the safety of his crib.

Susan Stone answered the phone.

"Susan, Mel's hemorrhaging! She's unconscious!"

"Oh, Jesus. Start massaging her uterus, like you saw John doing after delivery. Press down from the top, cup your other hand just above the pubic bone to support the uterus. Stay with me now." Then without putting down the phone, he heard her pick up the other line and in just seconds she was asking for emergency airlift transport. "Jack," she said, "give me your coordinates."

A man who'd built his own house knew every detail, and he rattled off his latitude and longitude. Phone cradled between his ear and shoulder, he said, "Help me, Susan! Blood's coming! What can I do?"

But she was repeating the location information into a second phone and responding to some questions. A moment later she was back on the line with Jack. "We're so damn lucky," she said. "John had an emergency and was airlifted to Redding a couple of hours ago—the helicopter is nearby, en route back to Eureka, and they're diverting to you. Jack, are you massaging?"

"Yeah, but…"

"Does she have a pulse?"

He put his fingers to her neck. Blood from his fingertips left a garish streak on her neck. "Yeah, it's weak. Soft."

"You'll have helicopter transport in less than five minutes. Are you alone?"

"Brie's here," he said, kneading Mel's lower belly.

"She needs Pitocin. Methergine. Where's Mel's bag?"

"Here," Jack said. "Right here."

"Thank God. Show Brie how to massage. Jack, I need you to draw a syringe of Pitocin. Jack? You there?"

"Jesus," he muttered. At that moment Brie ran into the room. "Brie. Massage her uterus like this," he said, showing her. "Damn." He tried to shake the fear out of his head. "I have to give her something," he said. "Susan?" he said into the phone.

"I'll walk you through it. Find the vial of Pitocin and a syringe. We're going to give her Pitocin first. Her blood pressure has never been high, so we'll follow with Methergine. She's bleeding from the uterus and it needs to contract."

"Susan," Jack said into the phone as he watched Brie squeezing Mel's lower abdomen. "Blood's coming. Clots."

"I know, Jack. Right now, get the drugs."

He dug around in Mel's bag and found what he was looking for. "Ready," he said. With the phone cradled against his ear he followed her precise directions, drew the Pitocin into the syringe first. "I don't know if I'll find a vein...."

"You're going to inject in the muscle, Jack. Just roll her a bit to the side—"

"I know," he said. "I know where. I've had plenty of shots...."

"Pull back on the syringe to check for blood return," Susan said. "Don't waste time. The paramedics will have more of what we need. She'll need a few doses."

"Done," he said.

"Now the Methergine," she said, walking him through it. "Time is short here. Once the paramedics get there, they can open a line and Pit her. Keep this phone line open in case you need me—do what I told you, Jack."

"I'm doing it," he said.

"Check the uterus. Can you tell if it's firming up a little?"

He brushed his sister's hands out of the way and resumed the massage. "I don't know. Maybe a little. Yeah, a little... But blood's coming. More clots."

"I know. Just keep massaging. You're doing great."

He moved away and, on instinct, Brie took over. Jack dug through Mel's bag again, looking for more Pitocin or Methergine. "Susan, there isn't any more.... We used everything she had!"

"They'll be there any second. Just don't stop massaging. While we're waiting for the chopper why don't you put the baby to the breast."

Jack dropped the phone.

He plucked the wailing Emma out of the cradle and positioned her against the breast, slipping an arm under Mel's shoulders to raise her a bit. He held them both. He squeezed and tickled Emma's little cheek with the nipple, the way he'd seen his wife do it. "Come on, baby. Come on. We need you to—" Emma found the nipple and began to attempt to nurse. She wasn't a hearty nurser yet and she was still upset from crying, but she did manage to get hold of the nipple, though not with great strength.

"Is it slowing? The bleeding?" he asked Brie.

"I don't think so, no."

"Mel," he said. "Mel, baby, come on. Open your eyes for me, baby. Oh *God*, don't do this, Mel."

Her eyes fluttered open. She looked up at Jack and in a weak whisper she said, "Uh-oh."

"Baby, you hang in there. The helicopter's on its way and it's close. You stay with me, Mel." Then, "Come on, Emma. Come on." But the baby was having trouble, probably because of the panic. Terrified, he slipped his arm out from under his wife, put the crying baby back in the cradle and, kneeling beside the bed, he began to massage her breasts in the way Mel would if she were pumping. He remembered then—remembered when David was born and he handed her the baby to nurse. *Come on little guy,* she had said. *Bring out the placenta and stanch the bleeding.* Then he leaned over her, put his mouth on her and drew gently, suckling, and the warm, sweet milk came into his mouth. And tears threatened to blind his eyes.

He felt her hand, weak and light, touching his head, threading fingers through his short hair. He nursed from her, and prayed it would help.

"It's slowing," Brie said. "It's definitely slowing. But damn, Jack, there's so much…"

He lifted his head from Mel's breast and saw that her eyes were open just a bit and there was a faint, almost imperceptible smile on her lips. "You stay with me, Mel. Goddammit, you stay with me!" He suckled a bit more. To Brie he said, "Keep massaging her uterus." Then he bolted from the house, leaping off the porch steps and racing to his truck. He opened the storage locker in the bed and pulled out a flare, ripping it open to burn and tossing it in the dirt driveway as a guide for the helicopter. He was back on his knees beside his wife, drawing on her breast again in less than thirty seconds.

Emma was crying, David was screaming and Mel was passed out again.

He put his lips on her forehead and prayed. *God, I'll do anything. I'll do anything. Don't take her from me!*

He repeatedly checked Mel's pulse, suckled and prayed. It was the longest two minutes of his life until he heard the sound of rotor blades. For a moment he was thrown back in time, almost an out-of-body experience—he was surrounded by dust and smoke as the choppers came into the rocky desert to pick up his wounded. His eyes glazed over, he was back there in Iraq, desperate to save his men.

He forced his mind through the maze of flashback. He said, "Don't stop," to Brie as he ran from the room to the porch just as the helicopter landed in the clearing in front of his house. He thought back to the last battle he'd fought—a battle he'd fight a thousand more times if it would save his wife. The medics had a saying—if we can get you to the chopper, you're going to live.

He saw two medics jump out and run toward the house with a stretcher. "This way," he yelled. "I've given her two doses of Pitocin and one of Methergine," he yelled as he jogged back into the house with them on his heels. "I think the bleeding slowed a little, but it's still heavy. Real heavy."

They followed him into the master bedroom and immediately took over. An IV was started. He'd watched Mel do it a dozen times, but this was the fastest work he'd ever seen. They were shouting orders—Ringers, Pitocin, blood pressure seventy over forty, pulse one-sixty and thready, diaphoretic, respirations shallow. "Let's boogie," one of them said, throwing a towel between her legs as they lifted her quickly onto the stretcher, leaving behind a blood-soaked bed. "Load her and go, go, go!"

"Brie, get Doc out here with formula for the baby." He grabbed Mel's bag and followed them out, jogging behind them toward the helicopter. They were airborne in seconds.

Jack held Mel's hand on one side of the stretcher while on the other side an inflight nurse monitored blood pressure and IV fluids. "We used all the drugs in her bag," he said. "Two Pitocin, one Methergine," he repeated to the nurse.

"Her bag?" the nurse asked.

"She's a midwife. I left the syringes behind, but threw the empty vials in the bag. The OB's wife, a nurse, talked me through it."

The nurse relayed that to the pilot and after a minute the pilot shouted back that he'd been radioed a second order for Methergine and the nurse plucked the ampoule out of their supply, drew the syringe and pushed it into the IV. Another few minutes passed; Mel opened her eyes, looked at Jack and mouthed, "I love you, Jack."

He put his lips by her ear. "Melinda, you are my life. You are my whole life, baby. You stay with me. John's at the hospital, honey. We're going to the hospital. You hang on. You're going to be all right."

Jack heard the pilot radio the hospital that they were inbound and relayed that there was an OR team and anesthesiologist standing by. The nurse pulled back the blanket to gently part Mel's legs and look at the bleeding. "I think we're gonna make it," she said. Then she said softly, "Dear God, let us make it."

If Jack weren't so terrified, he'd be impressed by how fast the team could move. When they touched down, the nurse and EMTs on board had that gurney out of the chopper so fast they almost knocked Jack out of the way. Waiting for them were emergency nurses and a doctor. They ran into the hospital where someone was standing at the elevator, holding the door open. Jack stayed with them, but he was stopped as they flew into the surgery.

Jack stood outside the doors, staring. He had no idea what to do, but he wasn't leaving her. He couldn't even sit down. His heart was pounding, he was sweating, hyperventilating, dying inside. He'd faced his own death with more calm than this.

Five or ten minutes passed before a nurse came out to talk to him. "Mr. Sheridan, she has a uterine hemorrhage and has lost a lot of blood. Dr. Stone took her immediately into surgery to try to stop the bleeding. It's possible he'll have to do a hysterectomy. It's going to be a while before we'll have anything more to tell you."

"She's going to make it, right?"

"Her situation is life threatening, Mr. Sheridan. But Dr. Stone is very, very good. He's being assisted by Dr. Larson, an excellent surgeon."

"Yeah," he said, running a hand over the top of his head. "God." Confused and terrified, he turned around in a complete circle twice. Then to the nurse he said, "I'm going to the chapel, but I'll be right back."

Jack made one phone call, to Brie. Then he found the chapel and though he had no idea what good it did, he lit a bunch of candles. His shaking hand made the light flicker so much he almost couldn't make contact. He didn't even have a wallet with him to leave money in the box but he was thinking, *If she lives, I'll write this hospital a check for a million dollars.* Then he went into the second pew, got on his knees, leaned his elbows on the pew in front of him and prayed.

God, I know you're sick of hearing me beg, but this is my woman, my wife. My best friend! No, she's so much more than that—she's the other half of my heart. I've waited my whole life for her—I'd give my life a hundred times to keep her safe! A thousand times! She's every breath I take, every single beat of my heart. I don't think I can live without her now. Not now... Please, God. Please. Oh God, please...

A half hour later he was back upstairs, sitting outside the surgery. He saw the second hand pass through every minute for two hours before John finally came out of surgery. Jack stood up.

"We made it in time, Jack—we got so lucky. We had a helicopter in flight, not far from you—a miracle in itself. She got critical drugs in time, thanks to you digging through her bag. But, Jack—I wasn't able to save her uterus. I'm sorry. I know you wanted more children."

Jack fell into the chair, his elbows on his knees, his head in his hands. His shoulders shook briefly as relief poured out of him, and when he looked back up at John, tears ran down his stubbled cheek and he said, "Man, the uterus doesn't mean *anything*. I can't live without her."

John put a strong hand on his shoulder. "You have many years with her left to you, my friend."

"God, thank you. Thank you, John."

"You and Susan made a good team, then putting that baby to the breast to nurse," John said, shaking his head in wonder.

"It wasn't the baby," Jack said weakly, wondering if his

legs would ever hold him upright again. Remembering his fear that his last memory of his beloved wife would be taking her milk as he tried *anything* to keep her alive. "Emma wouldn't nurse. I did it."

"Hmm," John said. "You might've given us the couple of minutes we needed to save her life."

Jack called Brie to tell her Mel was out of surgery, then he stood at the recovery-room doors without moving for another two hours until he was allowed in. A unit of blood dangled above her, but her skin was still pasty white, her eyes dark and sunken, her lips so dry they appeared cracked. She looked so tiny, it was scary. He bent over her, slipping an arm under her shoulders, lifting her a bit. He pressed his lips against her forehead and her eyes opened weakly. "Jack," she whispered.

"Aw, Mel, you scared me just terrible," he said.

"There won't be any more babies, Jack," she said.

"We have all we need. Two perfect, healthy kids."

"I know you were going to try to sneak one more by me…"

"I wasn't going to," he said. "I promised you time to enjoy your kids. I have more with you and them than I ever thought I'd have."

"Well," she said, a weak laugh escaping her. "As long as you're within reach, I'm destined to never have a period."

This was so like her, to joke around with him when she'd nearly died. "Close your eyes and rest, Mel. I'll stay with you. I won't leave you."

"I want to be with my children," she whispered, her eyes closing.

"Pretty soon, Mel. Shh. Pretty soon I'll take you home."

He held her like that, stooped over her bed rail, for another hour. The nurse tried to urge him away to check her bleeding, but he wasn't inclined to go. John came up to the three of them and said to the nurse, "I got it." He pulled the curtains around the bed. "They don't understand about you," John said to Jack. "I guess if you can deliver your own children, you're all checked out on peri-pads."

"All checked out," Jack said, dropping another kiss on her brow. "You going to stay all day?" he asked John.

"I haven't figured out how I'm getting back to Grace Valley yet. Plus, I want to run in another unit of blood. I'll stick around for that at least."

"You aren't hanging around because she's in any danger, are you?"

"Nope. I'm hanging around to keep you from being thrown out." He lifted the sheet and as he gently pulled apart her legs, she roused briefly. "Good," John said. "Looking much better."

"Better," Jack told Mel.

"You should think about getting back to your kids," John suggested. "Once I figure out the transportation, I can take you."

"Not until she's fully conscious and knows why I'm not here. Preacher would come for me. We'll work that out," Jack said.

"I'm going to turn her over to Larson, and he's going to keep her a few days," John said.

"You have to get her a breast pump. You know how she is about nursing. And Emma's the last one—you know how she is."

"She'll get a pump, don't worry."

Another hour passed, Mel rousing from time to time, Jack holding her all the while. John came in again and said, "We're going to take her to her room now, and there's someone out in the hall to see you. Meet us upstairs—306."

"Okay," Jack said, gently lowering Mel's shoulders to

the bed. "I'll be with you in a minute, baby. You're going to your room now."

When Jack walked through the swinging doors there stood Doc, leaning heavily on his cane, looking both frazzled and exhausted, as if he'd aged years in a few hours. Doc had driven all the way over that mountain pass to get here. It would've taken hours. Jack stepped up to him and put out a hand. "It was close," he said.

Doc shook his head. "Thank God. We can't do without her now."

"No," Jack said. "We can't."

"When can I see her?"

"Come with me, Doc. We'll go up to her room."

"John says she's going to be all right now," Doc said.

"Yup. We have her back. No more babies, though."

"How do you think she's going to feel about that?"

Jack was remembering how pissy she'd been when she found out she was pregnant with Emma. Then how, later, she'd said, *I sure love carrying around a little piece of you.* "She's going to be fine. We have each other. We have David and Emma, two more than we thought we'd get. Did Brie call you?"

"Uh-huh. The whole town is standing by." When they got to her room, Mel was slightly elevated in the bed, taking a sip of water through a straw. Doc seemed to be limping a little more than usual as he entered the room. He went straight to her and did something he'd never done before. He leaned over the bed and kissed her on the forehead. "You're a lot of trouble, Melinda. I knew from the start you would be."

"I keep you young," she said tiredly.

"You do, at that. But I think you're wearing Jack down."

Taking care of the Sheridans was a family and community affair. Brie and Mel's sister Joey took care of the babies so Jack could go to the hospital; Paige and Preacher made sure there was food ready for every evening meal. At the end of the day, Mike came to the house to be with his wife and wait for Jack to come home with his daily report. Jack got up very early to make that long drive over the mountains to Redding, stayed all day and came back to Virgin River late, after dark.

On the fourth such day, Brie sat in the big leather chair holding Emma close with her bottle while Mike was in the rocker with David and his bottle. The door opened and Jack came in, looking exhausted, carrying his little cooler that would contain the breast milk Mel had pumped. Brie lifted her chin in greeting and he lifted a hand in response, then went to the kitchen. It was easily six hours of driving each day, but he wouldn't even consider not being with Mel every day. Brie had been very worried about him being sleep deprived as he drove over the pass.

Once Brie and Mike had their charges settled, they joined the gathering in Jack's kitchen and found that Preacher had dinner almost complete and was setting up a couple of drinks for himself, Mike and Jack. "How's our girl?" Brie asked.

"Feisty," he said. "They're going to kick her to the curb tomorrow. She's giving them fits. Nurses make lousy patients."

"If you don't mind me saying so, you look whipped," Brie said.

"Thank you, precious," he said, lifting his glass. "Whoa, that helps. My thanks." He put the glass down and said, "I'm going to go kiss my kids and I'll be right back."

The kitchen was quiet for a moment. Preacher broke the silence with, "I can't believe how close we came to losing her."

"It's very unusual for something like that to happen," Brie said, trying to reassure him, given Paige's pregnancy.

"It reminds you, though, what a serious business this is." He pulled Paige close. "We have to take this real serious."

"I'm not going to let you do this, John," Paige said. "We had a close call, everything is okay now, and we're not going to panic. We're going to enjoy this pregnancy. God knows we worked hard enough for it." She turned to her son. "You about done there, buddy? Ready for your movie?"

"Yeah, Mom," he said sweetly.

"Let me," Preacher said. "Come on, cowboy," he said, taking his little hand. "I'll help you get comfortable." As he walked out of the kitchen Preacher was heard to ask, "What are we watching tonight?"

"*Incredibles,*" Chris said.

"Don't we watch that almost every night?"

"Almost."

Joey looked at Paige. "He's a wonderful father, isn't he?"

"Just amazing. I still can't believe how lucky I've been."

When Jack came back to the kitchen, Joey said, "I've been wanting to ask you something, Jack. How's Mel with the hysterectomy?"

He dropped his gaze and lifted his drink. "Disappointed," he said. "For all her bitching about being pregnant all the time, she actually wanted to be pregnant some more. It defies understanding. She carried on about Emma coming too soon, threatened me with certain death if I did it to her again, kept reminding me how old I am, and yet—"

There was a moment of silence.

"Being able to reproduce is a funny thing," Brie said. "We just want to control it."

"And in my experience, it's one of those forces of nature with a mind of its own," Jack said. "When you want it, it doesn't come. When you'd like to take a break, it's all over you."

"How are you with it?" Joey asked him.

"You're kidding me, right?" He lifted his drink. "I'm so grateful to have Mel come through this, it doesn't even cross my mind. Besides, I have two healthy kids. I'm a rich man. A very rich man."

"To rich men," Mike said, joining the toast.

Only a week after Melinda's hysterectomy, she was getting around very well. She had some surgical soreness and tired easily; she didn't wander around the house much. She dressed in a comfy sweat suit and stayed mainly on the big king-size bed, the cradle close at hand so she could nurse Emma as often as possible, trying to get her caught up. All she had to do was give Davie a little boost under the bum and he could climb up to the bed with her.

With Brie and Joey in charge of the house during the day, making sure Mel had everything she needed and was getting plenty of rest, Jack was able to spend a few hours at the bar in the afternoon. Then he could take dinner home to his wife.

He didn't get a lot done at the bar. He didn't dare go on supply runs, it would take him too far from Virgin River. But he added up receipts and inventoried, finding, unsurprisingly, the bar ran just fine under the watchful care of Paige and Preacher.

In that little space of time after lunch was finished, and before the dinner crowd began to drift in, when the bar was typically very quiet, often deserted, an old familiar ghost in his Shady Brady wandered in. Jack had had some traffic with this guy in the past; some good, some not so good. He was a known illegal grower from somewhere around the mountains and Jack had refused to take his money once because it stank of freshly cut marijuana. But he'd materialized out of nowhere one night when Paige was in danger and saved her life.

He came up to the bar and for once made actual eye contact with Jack. A first. "Hey," he said somberly. "How's the family?"

"Getting by," Jack said.

"Heineken and Beam," he said. "If it's not too much trouble."

Over the man's shoulder, Jack saw Mike come into the bar. He stopped short, obviously recognizing their friend from the broad expanse of his back and the familiar hat. Jack looked back at his customer. "We've been over this," Jack said. "You know what kind of money doesn't work in this bar and I'm not comping you. I'm in no mood."

Mike sat up at the bar, just one stool separating him from the stranger. "I got that, Jack. I'll have a beer. Take care of my friend here." Mike pulled out a few bills. "It's my pleasure."

"You sure about that?" Jack asked Mike.

"Yeah. I'm sure."

Jack set them up with drinks, then went back down the bar to where his trusty clipboard with inventory sheets waited. There was no conversation between Mike and the Shady Brady. Just silent, serious drinking.

Paige came into the bar carrying a fresh stack of towels. She recognized the man, was paralyzed for a moment, then gave him a very slight nod before escaping back into the kitchen. Mike half expected to see Preacher right away, but nothing more happened. Then there was a low, rumbled comment from the man next to him. "Things worked out then," he said, having noticed the obvious pregnancy.

Mike chuckled in spite of himself. "Oh, yeah. Just

fine." He looked at the man and lifted a brow. "Once more on that boilermaker?"

"Nah. I don't want to put you out."

"Jack," Mike called. "Fix up my friend here."

Though Jack scowled disapprovingly, he served the whiskey and refreshed the beer. It was a strange situation—Jack appreciated the help the man had given them in an emergency, but he wanted nothing to do with growers. They were trouble. And he wouldn't have their money in his till. He went back to his clipboard and counting, leaving the men to finish their drinks.

It wasn't long before the stranger scraped back his stool to stand up. He looked at Mike and tipped the brim of his hat.

Mike pulled a hand out of his jacket pocket, put something on the bar and slid it toward him, turning his black eyes up at the standing man. He took away his hand and there, on the bar, was a padlock.

Shady Brady glanced over his shoulder toward Jack, finding him occupied with counting bottles beneath the bar. He slid the padlock off the bar and into his pocket. "Thanks for the drinks," he said to Mike.

"Hey. Don't worry about it. Even a private sort of guy like you should catch a break sometimes, huh?" He jutted his chin toward Jack. "He's not real flexible." Then Mike looked back into his beer.

For the first time ever, Shady Brady gave a quick, short grin. He touched the brim of his hat again, though no one was watching him. Then he quit the bar.

Mike smiled into his beer. There, he was thinking. Mike knew and Shady Brady knew he knew. Something about him was iffy—but not all bad. Their business was done. At least for now.

Fourteen

Once the Haggerty family had been told a wedding was imminent, Paul called Joe. "How are those plans coming for Preacher and Mike?"

"Close to ready for you, buddy," Joe said.

"Maybe you could sketch up another house and we could talk about design…"

"Yeah? What you got?" Joe asked.

Paul took a breath. "You'll never believe it," he said. "It didn't go the way we thought it would. Vanni—she didn't let me down easy. Turns out I was a little slow, which shouldn't surprise you. We're getting married."

"Whoa! You serious?"

"Why wait?" Paul said. "It's not like we need time to get to know each other."

"But what about that little problem we talked about?"

"It turns out, it's not my problem after all. And Vanni—God, man. She's been just wonderful about everything—me taking so long to come clean, having a serious complication to work out, everything. We're gonna get it done before Tom leaves for boot camp in two weeks. I thought maybe, if you had some plans lying around, it might be a good time to visit Virgin River. And if the plans work for your clients—I could stay right here and build."

"Who's the third set for?"

"Me and Vanni," Paul said. "The general gave us a nice big parcel on the other side of the stable and, brother, having our own house down here sounds better all the time. Might as well build it before I get real busy."

Joe laughed. "Good for you, man," he said. "Any idea what you're looking for?"

"Oh, yeah—Vanni loves my house in Grants Pass. But that's set up for a bachelor or a couple without kids— sunken great room, that kind of thing. Raise the floor and level it, add a bedroom, more kitchen… You know what to do."

"I know what to do." Joe laughed.

"And come down for the wedding. It's gonna be small and quick, but Jack tells me he's calling the boys and there could be poker."

"Deal me in."

There was enough going on in Virgin River in June to create a great deal of excitement. First there was high-school graduation and the following weekend Vanni and Paul would be married. Somewhere between the two, Rick would be home on leave before shipping out to Iraq and for both his leave and the wedding, the rest of the marines would hit town.

Vanni had been busy in her father's kitchen whenever she wasn't tending to the baby, trying to prepare hors d'oeuvres for a Saturday-evening open house for Tom's graduation. The youngsters would be roving from party to party and would barely make an appearance, but Walt still insisted Tom deserved a celebration of his own, not just one coupled with the wedding the following weekend.

And he was right in this—Tom had graduated with honors and an appointment to West Point was a huge achievement. Even though Tom had a three-star for a father, it still required a near-perfect GPA and a congressional recommendation.

Vanni took a short break and, wiping her hands on a dish towel, walked out on the deck for some cool air. What she saw took her by surprise. Paul was standing in front of Matt's grave. Memories of standing there herself came flooding back, and she walked down the deck stairs and across the lawn, up onto that small rise. "Paul?" she asked.

He turned, saw her there and gave her a small, sad smile, lifting his arm. "Aw, Vanni, Vanni…"

"Are you all right, Paul?"

"Sure," he said, giving her shoulders a squeeze.

"You know, if we both start brooding at this grave, it's going to drive Dad nuts."

"I'll try not to make a habit of it. Listen, can I say something? Just once, then I won't again?"

"Paul, you can say anything to me. Are you missing him?"

"I'll always miss him, honey. Sometimes I think about when we were just boys together and I can see it so clearly, it's like being back there. When we were kids in high school, we never even talked about the Marine Corps. We talked about girls, sports, girls, tattoos, girls, trucks… He had all the girls, though. I never had any nerve. I wouldn't have even had a prom date if Matt hadn't made it happen. Who knew the crazy fool was going to make himself into a lifer." Paul turned and held her upper arms in his big hands, looking down into her eyes. "Do you have any idea how much I love you?"

"I do," she said, smiling.

"Well, I'd give my life for you, that's how much. I've

never been happier than these past few weeks. But I was just telling Matt—I'd give it all up and live alone and miserable and jealous till the end of time if I could get him back. He was the most amazing man, the most incredible friend. It would probably kill me, but I'd give this up if it meant he could live."

Vanni put a hand along his cheek. "He knows that already, Paul. He always knew that."

"You have to be real sad sometimes, honey. Even now. You don't ever have to hide that from me. I'll hold you through the tears now, just like I did before—and I won't feel cheated. Not by a long shot."

"Paul, I wouldn't hide anything from you," she said sweetly. "Not long after Matt and I met, I lost my mom—and she was the best friend I ever had. And then I lost my husband to a war. Do you have any idea what a gift I have in you? It was like being rescued. I didn't know I could feel like this. I thought every day would hurt forever. It's probably not really stronger than what I felt for Matt, but coming after all that loss and pain, it sure feels like a miracle to me. Oh—I'll always miss him, too. I can't help that. But I'm so grateful to have you in my life. I'm not giving you up."

"I just wish there was a way I could know— I wish I knew he was okay with this—you and me."

"Remember, I told you," she said, smiling. "I ran it by him already. A few times. Before you ever let me know how you felt."

"I wish I could know he forgives me for—for wanting you all those years you belonged to him…"

She laughed softly, sweetly. "I think you're being silly now. You showed him such incredible respect, never letting anyone know. Paul, there's nothing to forgive."

"The night Mattie came, I was out here talking to him.

Jack came and got me—he said Matt had moved on. He said we each have our destiny and Matt's took him somewhere else."

"Yeah—wherever he is, he's tearing the place up, making people laugh, feel good. Paul, this would make Matt happy. You know how much you love him? He loved you that much or more. I can't think of anyone he'd rather have raise his son."

"I'll do the best I can with that, honey. I'd sure like to make Matt proud. I'll try to be as good a husband as Matt was...."

She shook her head and smiled at him. "You're not going to have to try. As far as I can tell, you're a natural."

Jack stood on his front porch with his morning coffee. He saw something in the distance that caused his pulse to pick up. He looked out over the valley to the northeast and saw a thin column of gray smoke that wound its way to a plateau in the sky and he hoped, beyond hope, it was nothing to worry about. It had been an unusually dry spring.

Mel came outside and he dropped an arm around her shoulders as she snuggled close. "What is it?" she asked.

"Fire. Could be a controlled burn, could be wildfire. It's been awful dry."

"Has Virgin River ever been threatened by fire?"

"Not the town, no. There was a big one just north of here a few years ago. Right after Preacher showed up. Everyone pitched in. We dug a lot of ditches, hauled drinking water, drove trucks. Then we got certified in training so we could be ready."

"What would happen?" she asked. "If a fire got too close?"

"Well," he said, his arm tightening around her. "We're sitting in the middle of a forest, Mel. This place could end up looking like the face of the moon." He lifted his eyes to the horizon. "We need a good, solid rain. And there isn't any forecasted. This forest is pure kindling."

Tom graduated with honors and the general and Vanessa hosted a party at their home, open to all their friends and all of Tom's friends. The young people were on the move—they'd spend the entire weekend going from one open house to another. Tom and Brenda and some of their friends spent about an hour at the Booth home before taking off for other graduation parties, but the adults didn't mind a bit that they were left to themselves.

Everyone dropped by to pass along their congratulations, including Muriel St. Claire.

"Can we count on you to come to the wedding next Saturday?" Vanessa asked her.

"Oh, sweetheart, thank you for including me. Actually, I'm driving to Sebastapol to pick up a dog. A little guy named Buff. Another Lab—this one is yellow. I've got a good hunter already—Luce, my little girl and best friend, a year and a half and brilliant. But no dog should grow up alone." And then she grinned. "But I hope to see you soon after the wedding. It would be lovely to have dinner with you and Paul. I'll speak to Walt about that, since I can't cook."

"At all?" Vanessa asked.

Muriel shrugged. "At all. I'd like you to know, though, I have other talents. I can paint, hang paper, sand and varnish, grow vegetables, hunt duck and tell jokes. Besides, I heard there's great takeout at Jack's."

"There is." Vanni smiled. "And you ride, too."

"I do. I have two horses with me. We should go out for a ride sometime. We can meet midway between our houses along the river."

"I would like that so much," Vanni said. "We have a lot to talk about."

"Yes, we do," Muriel agreed, then gave Vanessa a conspiratorial wink.

As he was leaving the party Tom took Paul aside for a minute. Just outside the closed front door, Tom asked, "So. You ready to take on Vanessa?"

"More than ready, pal."

"Great, man. I couldn't have planned this better myself."

"Good. I hoped you'd say that."

Tom took a matchbook out of his pocket and flipped it around in his hand. "There's an all-night graduation party tonight that Brenda and I are going to," he said. He put the matchbook in Paul's hand. "Except we're not going to it. Someone should know where we are, in case there's any kind of emergency. Someone who can keep his big mouth shut."

Paul looked at the matchbook. The Brookstone Inn. He met eyes with Tom.

"Someone who isn't going to ask me one more time if I have a condom in my pocket."

"Why would I ask that?" Paul said. "You're way outta my league, brother."

"Just in case someone has a heart attack or something."

"Thanks," Paul said, slipping the matchbook in his pocket. "I appreciate that you think smart. Have a good time."

"See you tomorrow." And he was gone.

When Paul went back in the house, Vanni was waiting for him. "What was that about?"

Paul leaned close to her ear. "Just asking your brother's permission to be his brother-in-law," Paul said. "It's official. I'm welcomed to the family."

* * *

Tom checked into the Brookstone in Ferndale while Brenda waited in the car. The way it had gone lately, they'd make wild love, and then there would be some tears about him leaving, and then they'd make wild love again, then they'd have a few more tears. There hadn't been any long nights together since that first time at his house, but there had been some remarkable sessions, here and there, especially evenings at the Booth house when Vanni was in Grants Pass and Walt was down at Bodega Bay with Shelby.

"Before you start crying again, I have something for you," he said.

"You do?"

"I do." He leaned over the bed and dug around on the floor for his pants, pulling a box out of the pocket. He passed it to her. "It's how I feel about you."

She opened the box and there, curled around a velvet circle, was a sparkling diamond bracelet. She was speechless. "My God," she finally said. "My God."

"Here's how I feel. If we somehow manage to keep it together, through separations and school and all that stuff, I want to be with you forever. I didn't want to get you a ring—that would be too crazy. I mean, a senior in high school wearing an engagement ring? A senior like you who practically aced the SATs and is going all the way—you can't be wearing an engagement ring. I want you to be thinking about yourself now—you're just a girl." He took the bracelet out of the box and put it on her wrist. "But you can wear this. To remind you that I love you. And I'm not leaving you to be away from you, but to start building what we're going to have."

"Oh God," she said again. "Is it real?"

He laughed. "It actually is."

"How could you afford this?"

"I have a couple of bucks and college is paid for by the Army. It's not the best diamond bracelet ever made and the rocks are real little, but for your first one, it's okay. Later, I'll get you better diamonds, I promise. Brenda, I love you, honey. And I need you to stop crying. Leaving is hard enough. I'll be back in August for a little while, before I start West Point. You can make it till then, can't you?"

"I can make it as long as you need me to," she said.

"It's not going to be easy, you know. Even if you go to school in New York. We're going to be mostly separated for four years, maybe five while you finish—"

"No," she said. "Four. I'm going to finish college in three." She stared at her bracelet, then when she lifted her eyes to his, she raised one light brown brow and smiled. "Do you have any doubt I can do that?"

He grinned at her. "None whatsoever."

"Then I'm going wherever you go, Tom."

"The Army is going to keep me from getting married while I'm at West Point. This next four years, this is when we're going to find out what we're made of, because Army life isn't easy. It's good, and it's strong, but it's not easy. My dad always said that sometimes the Army spouses have to be tougher than the soldiers—my mom was left to raise us alone so many times. I know she was lonely, sometimes scared, and she was probably pissed some of the time, but she was so proud of my dad's work. You'd never know it was hard for her. You have to know that going in, it's just not easy. If you change your mind, if someone else comes along that can offer you—"

She put a hand against his cheek. "What if someone comes along for you?" she asked.

"Brenda—I think all I'm going to get in the Army are sore muscles and a completely worn-out brain."

"You never know—there could be some really sexy drill sergeant," she said with a laugh.

"Right," he said. "Listen to me now. My mind is made up, but I want you to promise me—keep your options open. Have fun, be a single girl and enjoy yourself. Take a good hard look around you, a long look at the world. When this four years is up, you have to be sure. You have to think I'm your best choice—not your only choice. I don't want you to ever think you made a mistake, betting on me and this life. Because if you're still my girl, I'm going to marry you the first day I can, and then I'm not letting you go without a fight."

"I'll keep my eyes open, Tommy," she said. "But I bet my heart will only be able to see you. And I'll miss you so much, but I'm proud of you. I know we're pretty young—but I'm not too young to know I have to marry a man I can be that proud of."

It made him smile. "I'll work on making sure you always feel that way."

"Yeah, I know you will."

"I used to hate my dad for coming up with Virgin River," he said with a laugh. "Now I'm thinking of putting him in my will."

Jack drove to Garberville to pick up Ricky from the bus early the next Wednesday morning. He was thinking about the phone call he'd had from Ricky a few weeks ago. It changed his world, but it was something he could have predicted.

The boy stepped off the bus not in uniform, but in his jeans and boots. Even so, that jarhead haircut branded him as a marine on leave. Jack's chest swelled with pride. Boy? This was no boy. Here was a man, a fighting marine, who had matured and grown even stronger in the months he'd been away. His grin, however, was the same young, infectious, optimistic smile as when he first rode his bike up to Jack's years ago.

It took willpower not to run to him and fetch him up in his arms, but Jack stood stock-still, letting the boy—the young man—come to him. They grasped hands and brought themselves shoulder to shoulder. Rick had grown yet taller. He was every bit the six-two Jack was. "Hey, man," Ricky said.

"Damn, boy. Look at you. You're almost as old as me."

"Hardly." Ricky laughed. "Look at *you*. You're getting gray, what's this?"

"Melinda, naturally. She's working me over. You should be careful, Rick. Strong, sexy women? They'll kill you slow."

"What a way to go, huh?"

"Yeah, I can't complain. It's turning out to be a big weekend here, man."

"Yeah?"

"Paul's getting married. I'll catch you up on all that— but the two events, your leave and Paul's wedding—it's bringing the boys to town. We're going to have us a time. They'll start arriving in a couple of days."

"Good. How's Mel?"

"Getting around a little slow, but don't worry—she's bossing me around like crazy, which tells me she's fine. She can't wait to see you."

"And Preach?" Ricky asked.

"About to be a father, in a month or so."

"Damn," Ricky said. "When I first laid eyes on him, I would never have put money on that."

"Tell me about it. By the way, your grandma is doing well. And from what I hear from her aunt Connie, your girl is excited about your leave."

"Yeah, I called Lizzie. She's a little freaked about Iraq, but it'll give her time to finish school. It's been a real headache, getting her through school…"

"She still trying to marry you?" Jack asked.

"I'm sticking to my guns, man. Four years, that's the deal. Down to three now. But holy Jesus, I love her like crazy. I can't wait to see her."

"You going to have time for the rest of us?"

"I can cut you a few minutes," he said with a grin that was all boy. "Try not to jam me up too bad, huh? I've been totally faithful to this girl for nine whole months and I am in bad shape. Bad."

Jack cracked out a big laugh. He put an arm around Ricky's shoulders. Something he couldn't help but wonder was how his life might have been different if he'd met his Melinda when he was sixteen. They'd be broke and have twenty-seven kids by now. But he said, "Iraq. What shit is that?"

"It's just the usual. I'll be fine."

"Of course you will. There are some people I want you to meet. Paul's new wife—she's something else. And I want you to meet her younger brother. He's slated for West Point. Daddy's a retired Army three-star and the kid's a year younger than you. Good kid. Sharp. He's been seen around with Brenda Carpenter this whole past year."

"Brenda? No kidding."

"You two—you should meet. Talk. For both of you, Virgin River will always be your base, you know?"

"Yeah, Jack. As long as you're here," he said.

"I hooked you up with some wheels."

"Yeah?" Rick asked.

"Mel's not able to work yet, which leaves Doc the Humvee and his truck sitting idle. He says it's all yours."

"Perfect," Rick said. "I think I'll check in with my

gram, then head over to Eureka to find that girl. I mean, first things first, Jack."

By noon on Friday the first of the marines arrived in the person of Joe Benson from Grants Pass. He had hooked up Paul's fifth wheel as his home away from home for the weekend and walked into Jack's with rolls of parchment under his arm and a big grin on his face. He had preliminary architectural drawings for Paige and Preacher, Mike and Brie, sketches for Paul and Vanni. Tables were pushed together, coffee was poured and plans were spread out.

Only Preacher and Mike were available to scan the drawings as Brie was at Jack's helping Mel with the babies and Paige was sharing Christopher's nap.

"How's Mel doing?" Joe asked Jack.

"She's doing great, but she hates being stuck out at the house all the time. Brie's bringing her and the little ones over later on, once most of the boys are here."

"She feeling okay now?"

"She gets tired real easy—and you can imagine how that pisses her off," Jack said. "Wait till you see her. She doesn't look like someone who damn near bought the farm three weeks ago. I'll tell you what, buddy. That about did me in."

"Bad, huh?"

"Boy howdy, as she would say."

By two, Paul came into the bar and the reunion continued. For Joe and Paul, who hadn't seen each other in at least a few weeks, there was a hearty embrace, robust congratulations to Paul. "I didn't figure to see you until much later," Joe said.

"There's a maid of honor at the house," he explained. "I was told I was in the way. Which suits me fine. And I think the general and Tommy will be kicked out pretty soon, too."

Next to arrive, Josh Phillips and Tom Stephens from the Reno area, pulling up in a nice cushy RV, a new purchase for Tom. Finally, Zeke, which made the crowd almost complete. "Corny's putting in a no-show," Jack explained. "He's got a baby coming in a couple of months and has to save his time off for that. Number three. He's still chasing that boy."

Beer was set up and at about four, Paige came out of the back and walked right under her husband's arm. Zeke was the first to spot her and sent up a whoop of excitement, rushing toward her with a huge grin on his face. "Whoa, baby, look at you! Damn me, girl—you're cooking a good one there!" He rubbed a big hand over her belly. "Preacher, you dog—you did fine work here!"

"Yeah, I sure did."

"You're about to pop, girl."

"Pretty soon," she said, grinning. "How's your wife doing?"

"She's great," Zeke said. "I thought I could sneak one more kid by her, but she says I'm all done. I don't know what her hang-up is. We only have four. You think four is enough?" he asked Paige.

"I think that's more than I'm having." She laughed. "I don't know how you tricked her into that many."

"What can I say." He shrugged. "The girl's been lightin' my fire for almost twenty years now—since the first time I saw her in that cheerleading outfit." He whistled. "Those pom-poms just knocked me out."

"To say nothing of that short skirt," someone supplied.

"And those itty-bitty panties," someone else remarked.

"I am so cut off," Preacher grumbled.

"John," Paige warned, though she couldn't help but

laugh. Joe was next, hugging her, checking out the stomach. Right behind him, Josh. "All right, all right," Paige said. "One at a time! You guys," she happily admonished. This crowd of men, each one of them what would be called a man's man, so driven in the masculine pursuits of soldiering, hunting, fishing and the like, loved women, pregnant women especially, and the babies they brought. It was uncanny. And tremendous fun.

Doc turned up for his whiskey, the general and Tom finally came in. Jack pressed a beer into Tom's hand.

"Where's the cop?" the general asked with amusement. "This kid's underage!"

"I get around that by giving it away," Jack said. "In fact, when this crowd's here, I end up giving away the bar!"

"Hey, where's Rick?" someone asked.

"He went over to Eureka to fetch Lizzie," Jack said. Then he grinned and added, "Wednesday."

The place was soon throbbing with the noise of men, and Paige made her escape, but not without the plans Joe brought. The barbecue was lit, the party spilled out onto the porch when Doc's old truck rumbled into town and stopped in front of Connie and Ron's corner store across the street. A hush fell over the crowd. The marines who hadn't already been outside quietly gathered there as Rick got out, helped his girl out to go visit her aunt and uncle, but not before pulling her to him for one last kiss. The moment their lips met, the marines sent up a wild cheer.

The couple bolted apart in surprise. Rick saw them and his face was split in a huge grin. The cheering and jeering continued and with his arm still around Lizzie's waist, he obliged the crowd by pulling her against him again to finish what he started. Then he let her go, gave her a little pat on the rump and sent her into her aunt's store.

Tom leaned toward Paul and said, "I hope Brenda stays indoors until these whack jobs leave town."

"Aw, don't worry, Tom. They wouldn't do that to you."

"No?" he asked.

"No way. You're Army." He grinned. "It's just not the same stuff, Tom."

To the welcoming cheers, Rick walked across the street and stopped in front of the bar's porch. "You guys are so frickin' rude," he said with a smile.

"Hey, jarhead," someone yelled. "Last I heard, Eureka was only a couple hours away."

"Make a stop or two, buddy?"

"He looks pretty loose to me."

"Come on up here, pal—we don't have much time before the invasion of women! I wanna hear about recon training. They scare you?" Rick was asked.

"They did," he replied. "Reconnaissance rappelling looked like a suicide mission to me, but then I just couldn't stop doing it. It's such a rush. And I got pushed out of an airplane a few times—that really turned me on."

"I don't know," Zeke said, shaking his head. "Airplanes make me throw up. Well, not regular airplanes. But when I'm in one painted up in camouflage with about a hundred and fifty pounds of gear on my back, it just does something to my stomach."

"'Cause you're a sissy," Rick said, laughing.

The next to arrive to a huge and affectionate welcome was Mel and Brie and Jack's babies. Jack took immediate charge of David, but couldn't hang on to him long as he was passed around and admired. Next came Vanni and her girlfriend Nikki. "Hey," she said, smiling. "Is this some kind of bachelor party?"

Joe Benson was sitting up at the bar when these last two women walked in, and he was brought instantly off the stool and to his feet. Nikki, small and dark-haired with big dark eyes and a small pink mouth, knocked the wind out of him for the second time. He had to shake himself. He'd met her briefly a couple of months ago and the memory hadn't let him go. There was something about her that made his mouth drop open and his eyes shine. He couldn't stop staring at her.

Paul hung on to little Matt for Vanni so she could be welcomed and introduce her maid of honor. Steaks were turned on the grill, salad tossed, potatoes baked, ears of corn buttered and some of Preacher's finest pies set out. There was feasting and laughter. Toasts were made to Rick, Tom and the wedding couple. Women disappeared to nurse babies and reappeared as the sun slowly set.

The general found Paul. "You ready to take the plunge, son?"

"Sir, I've been ready for a long time. I promise you, I'll do right by her."

"I have no doubt. Nice group of men you have at your back."

"They are, sir. The best. Thanks for making them welcome. Thanks for sharing Tom's going away with all of us."

"It's an honor, Paul. It's good for him to see this—he'll have this in no time, a crowd of brothers, shoring him up. I'm going to miss that boy."

"We'll all miss him, sir."

"Think you'll ever just call me Walt? Or even Dad?" he asked.

Paul smiled. "I don't know, sir. I think I'd kind of miss the edge."

As the evening aged and dinner was done, Joe stepped out onto the porch, pulled a cigar out of his pocket and snipped the end. He struck a match against his shoe, when he heard a sound and looked up. Nikki was leaning on the porch railing. "Oh, sorry," he said, shaking out the match. "I didn't know anyone was out here."

She smiled at him. It seemed a shy smile, maybe a sad smile. "Vanni's nursing the baby," she said, then looked upward again. "I couldn't figure out what she saw in a little town like this. But then I had a look at this sky."

Joe stepped up beside her. "It's something, all right. Nikki, isn't it?"

"Yes. And you're Joe. Paul's friend from Oregon."

"That's right," he said with a smile. She remembered him. She remembered him? "You must be a city girl."

"San Francisco. What's Grants Pass like? Big? Small?"

"Small, but not this small. Twenty-three thousand, some of the most beautiful sunsets in the world."

"Have you lived there a long time?"

"Pretty much all my life. I have a big family there."

"Lots of kids?"

"No kids." He shook his head. "No wife."

She frowned at him. "Still single?" she asked.

"Divorced."

"Oh. Sorry."

"No problem. It's been a long time. You?"

She looked away. "Single," she said. "Recently broken up, actually."

"Oh, then I'm the one sorry," he said. "He must be an idiot."

She laughed. "He is. You can have your cigar. It doesn't bother me."

He slipped it into his pocket. "It'll keep. How long have you known Vanni?"

"We started flying together eight years ago. She stopped flying when she got pregnant, so we don't see each other as often as we used to." She looked out at the sky again.

"This is the second time I've been her maid of honor. She promises it's the last."

"I think you can trust her on that. She can be yours next time."

"I doubt that'll ever happen," she said, looking down.

"Don't be ridiculous," he said. "You're young. You even thirty yet? And beautiful. It's just a matter of days, probably."

She just sighed. "Imagine, Vanni finding two wonderful guys like that in such a short period of time. You knew Matt?"

"Very slightly. We grew up in the same town but went to different schools, and I didn't serve with him. I met him through Paul later, after I started designing houses for Paul's company. If Matt was on leave, home for a visit, we'd run into each other for a beer when he was out with Paul. Good man."

"These all seem like good guys. Does this happen often? Gatherings like this?"

"It used to be a lot of hunting and fishing, but lately these old boys have been tying the knot a lot. First Jack, about two years ago. Then Preacher last year. Mike, just a few months ago. Now Paul. Bunch of bachelors who no one could catch, everyone real slow to find the right woman, then all of a sudden there's a rush on. The only one who found his girl real early was Zeke—he's been married since he was about seven. Four kids. Now it looks like I'm the last one left."

"They're all so good-looking. I mean, *you're* all so good-looking—it's pretty amazing you weren't snapped up early."

"That turned out to be my fatal mistake." He laughed.

"How long have you been divorced?"

"Over ten years," he said.

"I guess you've recovered your bachelorhood."

"Yeah," he said. "I guess. Can I get you anything? Something to drink, maybe?"

"No, thanks. I think I'll just enjoy the stars."

"Mind if I enjoy the stars with you for a while?" he asked her.

She looked at him and tilted her head slightly. His question finally coaxed a smile out of her, a real one, and he thought, damn. This girl is beautiful. "That would be nice, Joe."

Jack was the first to leave when he noticed Mel was looking tired. He collected his son, said goodbye to his boys and took Mel out onto the porch. They passed Joe and Nikki and said good-night as they left. Next to leave was Brie, giving Mike a kiss good-night on the porch before walking across the yard to their RV. Paige disappeared for good as she tucked herself in with Christopher for the night—advanced pregnancy requiring rest. Next was Vanessa, out on the porch looking for Nikki. "Hey, you can stay as long as you like—there are plenty of people around to take you home."

"I could do that," Joe offered. "I'd be glad to do that."

"No," Nikki said. "A maid of honor's work is never done."

Finally it was the general and Tom. Rick walked outside with them. Tom shook his hand and said, "Come out to the house tomorrow. Bring your girl."

"Thanks, I might just do that. But not till after the wedding. No way I can let Lizzie see a wedding."

By the time Rick walked back into the room, the tables were pushed together, the cards were out and the cigars were being snipped. "Get over here, boy," Zeke said. "Get out your money."

Rick laughed. Someone pressed a cigar on him and he said, "God, do I have to smoke this ugly thing?"

"As long as you get your money out, you can do whatever you want."

"I don't have that much money, guys," he complained, but he was sitting down.

"Don't worry about it, kid. We'll take whatever you've got."

Fifteen

The general's house was a busy place on Saturday. The nuptials were scheduled for 4:00 p.m. with a party to follow. Sunday night would belong to Tom, his family and his girl since he'd be leaving early Monday morning.

Caterers arrived in the morning, setting up a trellis strung with white drape in the yard behind the house. Fifty folding chairs were unloaded, champagne chilled, flowers placed around the house and yard. Paul's family arrived just after noon and his mother gratefully took charge of Mattie so the bride could primp. The general was happy to host the Haggerty men and Tom out on the deck while activity around the house and yard kept them out of those regions.

The next to arrive was Shelby. She drove up from Bodega Bay. It hadn't been that long since her mother's passing, but she was already changed; she'd dropped a few pounds, wore her shiny, honey-colored hair free, flowing down her back, and for the first time in years, she wore makeup. She looked so great that when Tom saw her, he grabbed her up in his arms and whirled her around, making her laugh. "Look at you," he said. "What have you done to yourself?"

"Not so much," she said, smiling. "I just have a little more time now, that's all."

"It's more than that. You're looking *hot.*"

"Thanks, honey," she said. "That's nice. I've never been hot in my life."

Next it was Paul to lift her off the ground and make a fuss over her, and finally she was pulled into the circle of women with Vanni exclaiming over how wonderful she looked. The only one not surprised was Walt, who'd been making regular visits to Bodega Bay since his sister's passing. As they were getting the house back into shape he'd been watching the slow and startling transformation of his niece as she found her footing, making her way into a new life.

Paul was showered before noon so he could clear out of the bathroom, finally putting on his suit at three, as did the best man and Walt. When the guests began to arrive, cold champagne was pressed into their hands as they were directed to the chairs in the yard. The minister, Harry Shipton of Grace Valley, was more than happy to accept his champagne with the rest of the gathering. Right at four, Vanessa and Nikki stepped out onto the deck from the house, making their way to the yard where the vows would be spoken.

Paul felt his knees almost buckle when he saw her. Now, he knew this was one fine-looking woman, and since he'd been the best man at her last wedding, it wasn't as if he'd never seen her all dressed up. But it felt like the first time. She was usually found in jeans or a simple sundress, and in those she was almost too much for his heart. Today she was resplendent in green so pale it was nearly white. It was a shimmering, clingy silk, her reddish-gold hair lying in full curls on her shoulders and down her back. Her turquoise eyes were alive with love, sparkling brightly, and her peach lips were curved in a smile.

"Holy shit," Tommy said. "Look at my sister, man."

"I see her," Paul croaked. "God above."

Tom laughed. "Well, go get her," he said, poking him in the ribs. "God, I hope I'm cooler than you when I get married."

"Yeah," Paul said in a weak breath. He unstuck his rooted feet and went to collect his bride and bring her into the gathering. She was greeted with lots of hugs and kisses, a glass pressed into her hand. Paul's arm was around her waist and he couldn't make himself let her go. He felt his chest swell with cocky pride, having her at his side. No way he should be getting a woman who looked like this. And she was all his; she couldn't even glance at him without confirming that with her gaze.

"Let's get started, shall we?" Harry asked, stepping up in front of the trellis.

Paul and Vanni went to stand before him, followed by Nikki and Tom.

Paul's eyes were riveted on his bride, but she was hardly the only beautiful woman present. Mel was looking very fine on this occasion, color in her cheeks again and that sparkle in her eyes. Paige was stunning in her last trimester of pregnancy, a glow around her as she clung to her husband's hand. Brie was a vision in lavender, her man reluctant to let very many inches separate them. Shelby was looking awful cute in a fitted pantsuit and heels to bring her up to five-five, her thick hair free and glorious, her smile bright.

And there was Nikki. The dark-haired beauty wore a closely fitting pale pink dress with a demure slit up one side, not visible unless a soft breeze caught the silk and lifted it. Her black hair fell down her back in a breathtaking contrast to the pastel. She wore a beautiful smile for her best friend's vows and had no idea how closely she was being watched.

The vows were exchanged quickly, without a single mistake, and it was finally time for Paul to take Vanni into his arms and cover her mouth with a searing kiss that suggested he wished they were alone. The gathering cheered and applauded the bride and groom until they had no choice but to break apart.

As the couple made their way slowly through the gathering and toward the house where the party was laid out for the celebrants, Joe saw his chance. He grabbed a glass of champagne off a tray and pressed his way toward Nikki. He offered it and said, "You look very beautiful today."

"Thank you," she said, accepting the drink.

"There should be dancing at this party," he complained. "Otherwise, how am I going to get my arms around you?"

"Are you flirting with me?" she asked him.

"I am. I think it's the dress."

She laughed at him.

"It's an amazing dress," he went on.

"Into fashion, are you?"

He shook his head. "I wasn't before today." He put out a hand to escort her. "Let me take you to a party."

Not long after the food was put out, Walt realized he'd misplaced Shelby. He looked around the house and yard and then, on an impulse, he went to the stable. He found her there, all dressed up and fancy, stroking Plenty's neck. She looked over her shoulder at her uncle and smiled. "It's been years since I've seen this girl."

He stepped toward her. "Looks like she remembers you."

"I don't know about that, but Liberty's as self-centered as he ever was. And I sure like this new guy, Chico. I can't wait to get back on a horse."

"You know where they are," he said. "Visit us whenever you can. Ride. Enjoy the summer along the river. It's wonderful."

"The whole place is wonderful, Uncle Walt. It lives up to all the pictures you brought."

"I'm a lucky man."

She turned around and leaned back against the stall. Plenty nuzzled her hair, making her laugh. "You're going to have an extra bedroom when Tom's gone to boot camp and West Point," she said. "I'll have to fill it up for you on weekends."

"I would love that, honey."

"Vanni says Paul's building them a house. He's going to start right away—try to get them in by Christmas even if there's still a lot of work to finish."

"That's his plan as I understand it." Walt chuckled. "I think he's anxious to get his new wife out from under my roof."

Shelby stepped toward her uncle. "I'm not sure yet what I'm going to do next. Probably go back to school, but it's really too late for me to get accepted for the fall semester. Besides, I think I need a little more time to unwind. To think about what direction I might take."

"Fortunately, you have lots of time."

"I'd like to spend it here...."

His eyes widened in disbelief. Hopefully, he said, "Do you mean that, honey?"

"You'll be lonely without Tom. I can help with the horses."

He reached out and stroked her shiny hair. "What about Bodega Bay?" he asked gently.

"I've decided to let it go," she said. "I'll be sure the work on the house gets finished, but I've already talked to a Realtor. I'm going to sell it, Uncle Walt. I think I want to move on. I don't think it will take longer than a couple of months to sell. It's a good little house."

"Sure you don't want to just rent it for a while? Keep a grip on it just in case you decide that's where you belong? You've been there your whole life...."

"I know. I think it's time for a new life. Don't you?" She smiled. "While I'm thinking about where that new life is going to be, I'd like to be here with you, with my family. If it's okay."

"Shelby, nothing would make me happier. Honey, I never even dared hope you would come here for a long stay."

"I hope you still feel that way when I've been underfoot for a while. I'm leaving early tomorrow, Uncle Walt. I'm going to shop my way back to Bodega Bay. I haven't bothered with things like new clothes in years." Tears came into her eyes. "Do you have any idea how happy that would make my mother?"

Walt pulled her against him and held her. "Shelby, sweetheart, I have an awful lot to be proud of, but I don't think anyone in my life has made me prouder than I am of you. You're an amazing young woman."

Joe tried to keep tabs on Nikki throughout the party, even though she spent a great deal of time mingling among the guests. When it looked as if she wasn't engaged in conversation, he found a way to get next to her, ask her if she was having fun, how long she would stay in Virgin River, when did she have to get back to work—anything that would keep her attention, keep her talking. Apparently he hadn't lost his touch; she seemed to enjoy his flirting.

He wondered what the hell was going on with him— she wasn't typical of the sort of woman he was attracted to. No, it was leggy blondes he liked, and this woman was small with that long sheath of satiny black hair. Her waist was so tiny, he thought maybe he could get his hands around it. That pink mouth, the same color as the dress. Her ankles, narrow. Calves, slim but firm; tiny feet with pink toes. When did he start caring about ankles and toes? He watched her laugh, the way she tilted her head back, an action that sent ripples down her curtain of hair.

Joe was a little confused. When he developed one of those physical attractions, he couldn't seem to pull his eyes away from a woman's butt, her breasts, her thighs. This was a whole new thing—the way she laughed, her little feet. It was nuts. It was like a schoolboy's crush.

He kept watch, looking for a moment to spirit her out under the starlight, maybe steal a kiss or something, wondering why he would bother. First thing in the morning he was headed to Grants Pass and she would take off for San Francisco. Still, he watched her every move. When he saw her walk down the hall and slip into the room that had been given to her for her stay, he briefly gave up the vigil and went to the bar for a drink.

The hour was still early when some of the guests began to leave and Joe was caught up in saying goodbye to friends. "I'm going to open the bar for the guys who are staying over," Preacher told him.

"Thanks, but I'm just going to bunk in the trailer out front and leave first thing. I have some work to get done before Monday morning," Joe said.

The marines started to filter out, headed back into town, maybe thinking along the lines of cards, and Paul's family—parents, brothers and their wives—were going to drive as far as Fortuna to stay the night before going on to Oregon in the morning. Vanni and Paul would pass their wedding night right here, to spend as much time with Tom as possible before he left.

She was gone, Joe realized. The house was beginning to empty of guests, the night was dark but for a sliver of a moon and a billion stars, and the girl he'd had a fix on all day was missing. He looked around the great room, the kitchen, and then, braving rejection, walked down the hall to her room. He tapped lightly on the door, but there was no answer. It was not gentlemanly, but he pushed open the door because he had to find her. She wasn't there. How'd she get by him? There was no one in the hall bath; the door stood open. He had to at least get her phone number. He felt a trip to the Bay Area coming on.

"Have you seen Nikki?" he asked Vanessa.

"I haven't. I thought maybe she turned in."

"Maybe she did," he lied. "I just wanted to say good-night—I'll probably be out of here real early in the morning."

Damn, he wasn't ready to give up on that one. He hadn't been drawn to a woman in a while, but this one had hooks in him like grappling. He wasn't exactly sure why, but it was fierce.

The party was dwindling to just a few people—Rick and Tom and their girls, the bride and groom, the general, Mike and Brie, Shelby. The caterers were packing up and cleaning the kitchen. Joe stepped outside onto the now-dark deck. He took out a cigar, clipped the end, struck a match on his shoe—and it illuminated her. She was standing at the far end of the deck, out of sight, out of the light from within the house, her back to him.

He started to get excited at having found her, feeling a crazy lift in his chest. The match burned down to his fingers and he shook it out with a muffled curse. He took a breath and walked up behind her. "The stars again?" he asked softly.

"Something like that," she said, her voice teary.

He slipped the cigar back into his shirt pocket and gently grabbed on to her upper arms. "What's the matter?" he whispered.

"Nothing. I'm fine," she said. Then she sniffed.

"Nothing? Fine but for the tears?" He gave her arms a squeeze. "Don't cry, now. I can't stand it when a woman cries. Wipes me out."

"Go back inside," she whispered. "Go on."

"Can't," he said, leaning toward her a little, inhaling her scent. "I'm kind of stuck here now."

"Just go, okay? This is sort of embarrassing."

He turned her around slowly. He looked down into those dark, liquid eyes, a trace of tears on each cheek. "All this wedding crap, huh?"

"I don't want Vanni to think I'm not happy for her."

"She wouldn't think that. She'd understand."

"Someone told you."

"I asked Paul why a woman as beautiful as you seems sad. Bad breakup, he said. I don't know the details, but I'm sorry that happened. He's certifiable, the guy who let you go." He pressed his lips first against one of those tear tracks, then the one on the other cheek.

"What are you doing?"

"The only thing I can think of is kiss the tears away. I don't want you to cry anymore, but if you do, I can take care of it."

"You shouldn't. We don't really know each other."

"You know, I've been thinking all day—we should get to know each other better." He put his hands on her waist. "I've been wondering about this all day," he said. "I can get my hands around your waist." He lowered his lips to hers, barely touching them. "I think there was a small tear there," he whispered.

"There wasn't."

"There was," he insisted. He put his lips there again. Barely touching. He ran his tongue along her upper lip. "Tear," he said. "I'm sure of it."

Her eyes closed and another tear squeezed out and ran

down her cheek. He was right on it, kissing it dry. It took many soft kisses. "No one should make you cry like this. Tell me who he is. I'll kill him for you."

"I wasted so much time on him," she said with a hiccup of emotion.

He kissed her eyes. "He's a dick," he said. "Worse. He's a stupid dick."

She responded with a small, whimpering laugh.

He pulled her closer, slipped his arms around her and lowered his head to kiss her neck.

"There are no tears there," she said in a whisper.

"I know that now," he said. "Do you have any idea how good you smell?"

"Of course. I meant to smell this way," she said. Her hands were on his arms. Not embracing, but not pushing him away. "Do you do this a lot?"

"I've *never* done this before," he said.

"You're such a liar," she said softly. "I bet you pick up girls all the time."

He lifted his head. "I try," he admitted. "It doesn't work that often. And I swear, I have never found a beautiful woman crying over some jerk and kissed her tears away. Never. But I think I like it. And I'm getting good at it."

"Not too bad," she said with a sigh, laying her head on his shoulder. "For an amateur."

He chuckled. "Nikki, you're beautiful and sexy. And funny. You shouldn't be treated badly by anyone. No one should make you cry. Ever."

"Believe me, I want you to be right."

"Oh, I'm right." He touched her lips again, a little more firmly this time. He moved over them tenderly. "I think you're starting to feel a little better."

"Not yet," she said, her eyes closing as she leaned into his kiss again.

Something happened inside Joe's head, inside his chest. There was a kind of lightness and fullness at the same time. He opened his lips as he kissed her, tasting her mouth, and she was delicious. In fact, she tasted even better than she smelled and he was falling headlong into her. Whoa, he thought. I'm wanting this girl, this woman. I want the maid of honor. She opened her lips under his and allowed his tongue inside and it brought a thrilled, lusty moan from him. He held her close against him, probing the inside of her mouth. No way he was letting her go, now that he finally had her in his arms. Her arms went around his neck, yielding to the kiss, making small noises that were not associated with crying. He found himself thinking, *Paul is going to kill me. I'm thinking carnal thoughts about the maid of honor and how to get her out of this pink dress and Paul is going to kill me.*

But I will die happy, he further thought.

He pulled away from her just a bit, whispering against her lips, "That's what you needed. You needed to be kissed."

"Possibly," she whispered.

"We should be sure," he said, covering her mouth again. And again, tongues played, lips moved. He ran a hand down her hair and found it felt as soft as it looked—pure silk. The softest thing he'd ever touched. He scrunched up a handful at the base of her neck. "God," he whispered, in awe of the texture. "God."

"We hardly know each other," she said again, but she said it while her lips were still in contact with his.

"Yeah…but that's a short-term problem. We're going to get to know each other lots better."

Like an answer to a prayer, she came to his lips with hunger, thrusting her small tongue inside, moaning softly as she did so. He ran his hand down to the small of her back and pulled her against him. He devoured her lips for a full minute, for two full minutes. Three. A light from the great room inside the house flicked off, leaving the deck that much darker and he became intoxicated with the taste of her, the feel of her small body molded to his. With a will of its own, his hand brushed against her breast and if he wasn't mistaken, she kissed him harder, deeper. He could feel an erect nipple under the silk of her dress and he ran his thumb over it, bringing a sigh from her. She didn't push his hand away. His lips slipped to her neck. "Yeah. You're starting to feel better I think."

"Maybe. Just a little."

He couldn't hold it back any longer; he was aroused. Erect. Damn. This was going to put him in a tough spot, because this reaction always made it a lot more difficult to think straight. It was a real challenge to be sensible. Logical. Thoughts of Paul killing him for making love to the maid of honor fled from his mind, replaced with obsessive thoughts of what his lips around that nipple would feel like. He lowered his head to check. He was absolutely right—it felt perfect. Even through the dress.

"Maybe we shouldn't get any more worked up," she said in a whisper.

"Whatever you say," he replied, but he was agonizingly unable to lift his head. He was busy putting small kisses on her breast, her neck, her shoulder. He ran a hand down her back, over her bum, down her thigh. He accidentally found that slit in her dress and before he knew it, his hand was inside. "Oh God, Nikki. I'm a dead man."

"You're not doing too bad for a corpse," she said.

"Nikki, you have no panties on, and I'm a dead, dead man."

"Then take your hand out of there," she advised breathlessly.

"I. Can't."

He put his lips back on hers for a long, deep, wet kiss that lasted two minutes at least. But, he proudly thought, he was somehow able to keep his hand from wandering any farther than her naked bum. One large hand on one small, round, perfect cheek. He had cast a mental image of Crazy Glue holding him there, because if he slid it any farther south all the blood would drain from his brain and he would faint. And then came the danger zone. She pressed against him, rubbed against him. She gyrated her hips a little and moaned softly. She knew he was hard and ready to burst. She knew he knew she knew. He lifted his head. "Nikki. Let's," he said.

"Oh God," she said. "We shouldn't."

"Let's make love."

"How tacky is that? The maid of honor having sex with a marine on the deck?"

He chuckled in spite of himself. "I'll take you somewhere."

"By that time, I will have come to my senses," she said.

"It's not far. I drag my bedroom around with me."

"Wow. Talk about always being prepared…"

He kissed her again. Hot and hard kisses that lasted forever. "It's not really mine. I borrowed it from Paul. There aren't exactly rooms to rent around here.…"

"That funny little trailer?" she asked him.

"The door locks," he said against her lips. "It's very comfortable."

"Listen," she said, pushing him away a little bit. "I haven't ever—I mean, I'm no nun, but I've never done anything like this. This one-night stand thing. Never."

"It's not, I don't think," he said.

"Hmm?" she said, yielding to his lips again.

He wasn't going to bother saying something that was just going to sound like a line, even if it seemed entirely true. He felt something. He'd been feeling it since the moment he saw her in the bar with Vanni a while back, felt it again the second time he saw her, had been feeling it all day today and he had absolutely no idea what it was. But it sure didn't feel as if he was going to be cured of it in one night. "It's just the first night," he said.

"Talk me into it," she pleaded.

"No. No way," he answered, pulling away a little. "It's up to you. If you want me to, I'll make love to you. If you don't, I can step away right now." He kissed her again. "It wouldn't be easy, but I could let go of you."

"But what will people think—"

"Shh, people don't have to know if you don't want them to. This—it's just about you and me. It only matters what you think, what you want. Don't do anything you don't want to do." He made a derisive sound deep in his throat. "That was really hard advice to give, by the way."

She answered by kissing him deeply, pressing her body up against his, and he was only further weakened. Or maybe he was further strengthened, because he was feeling more and more sure that he had to have this woman next to him, in his arms, in his life. There was some terrible curse on this place that turned fine, upstanding, confirmed bachelors into ridiculous, desperate men who tripped over a pretty girl and began to instantly think life would not go on if they didn't have her forever. They hadn't even been intimate and he already couldn't imagine letting her go. He tried to tell himself that by morning that feeling, that compulsion would be gone, but he doubted it. He'd wanted before, but he couldn't remember wanting like this. Like he was drugged. Like he was glazed over and totally out of his mind for this one person.

She pulled away. "I want to," she said.

"Sure?"

"Sure." She drew a ragged breath. "I'm really sure."

He smiled down at her, took her hand in his, and they walked down the steps into the yard and around the house, stopping every few feet to embrace, to kiss and fondle. And then he opened the door to that funny little trailer.

It was a little awkward at first, stepping up into that tiny trailer, because Joe was tearing the place apart looking for a condom. And she asked him, hadn't he brought any? And he told her he never expected something like this to come up while he was in Virgin River. "We usually just hunt. Play poker. Drink a little too much." And then he found a box of condoms in the drawer under the microwave and said, "Ah! God bless Paul."

After that discovery, the awkwardness passed as he began to seduce her and became seduced by her. There was nothing under that pink dress but Nikki, and she was exquisite—tiny, firm, beautiful, sensual. Despite his condition, which was one of being so worked up and turned on he was afraid he might embarrass himself, he managed to make a decent study of her body and make long, slow, delicious love to her. Love that he was sure was completely satisfying to her as well as him.

Then they lay in each other's arms and talked for a while. "Don't tell me about him, I don't want to know. But tell me more about you. Where you came from, what you like to do, how you want to spend the rest of your life."

He learned that she had grown up in the city, gone to private schools, disappointed her parents by choosing to fly as a cabin attendant rather than becoming a neurosurgeon or astronaut or something. She liked to travel, ride horses, read. She was a good cook. What she wanted was to have a family, which was why she ended up with this guy who finally made it clear he was completely opposed to that idea. She had no idea it was really going to come to that. "Whoops," she said. "I think that might've been about him."

"That's okay," he forgave. "Let's put him away for now." And he made love to her again.

There was something about loving her that surpassed the sex. He could easily move her around, she was so light, and as he did so, he forgot that he had been dying to experience her. The only important thing became her pleasure, giving her everything he had. Working her up, getting her so hot she was begging. Long, slow, deep strokes that made her sigh and moan. And when she let him know it was time, deep and strong thrusts that made her gasp and hold him tightly to her. When her orgasm came, he felt proud, as if he'd taken good care of her. Maybe it was her response to him, the way she was swept away, her release leaving her breathless and gasping. If he had anything to say about it, this would go on forever and she would never be disappointed in his arms, in his life.

What he hadn't been prepared for was how loving and sexual she was toward him, acting as if his pleasure was the most important thing as well. Unwilling to lie back and receive his lovemaking, he felt her lips on every inch of his body; she pushed him back on that small bed and tortured him so beautifully it almost brought tears to his eyes. She was a woman who could give as good as she got and it filled him up with emotion so strong, he was sure he'd never felt that way before.

And again they talked—this time about Joe and his small town up north, the houses he designed, the Marine Corps and the friends for life he'd made. He told her all about his Virgin River experiences, including the first time Jack called on the boys to help him clear the woods of dangerous men, to the time they'd come together to help Paul lay his best friend to final rest.

Then more love. Deeply satisfying, wondrous, phenomenal love. Joe honestly didn't know if he'd suddenly become better at making love than he realized or if this woman, Nikki, was simply so astonishing, she made him look good. So responsive, so sweet. It didn't matter to him—he was sublimely grateful for every orgasm she had, and more grateful that he was able to give her more than he took for himself.

"Nikki," he whispered. "I think finding you was the luckiest day of my life."

Then they talked about the others. Not the one who was making her cry, because Joe didn't want any more crying. Since stepping into that funky little trailer, there hadn't been any tears. Soft laughter, whispers, deep sighs, no tears. They talked about the other ones that just didn't work out, starting with his year-long marriage at the age of twenty-five. "*She* left *you?*" Nikki asked, as though stunned.

"Yeah," he said. "It killed me."

Joe told her he'd always been kind of prepped for marriage and family, given his parents' long marriage, the successful marriages of two brothers and one sister. And maybe he was gun-shy, that he hadn't fallen in love again after that. He was surprised to find himself this old and still unattached; he thought he'd be settled and have a couple of kids by now. Once he saw some of his buddies find it late, he had renewed hope that maybe it wasn't outside the realm of possibility for him.

Nikki, it turned out, had had an affair or two go south before the one who made her cry. She dated an airline captain for a while without realizing he was actually married. And then, to her supreme embarrassment, she continued with him for a while after knowing. "I don't know what I was thinking," she said, but she'd been really young then. "I regretted that, you can't imagine how much. He's been with quite a few single women since, though still married."

Lots of intimate talk, lots of wonderful, sweet but powerful sex. The sun was starting to peek over the mountains when Joe nodded off with Nikki close in his arms. It was high up when he heard the sound of an engine and bolted upright, finding the bed beside him empty. He couldn't believe she'd sneak away without saying goodbye. Then it occurred to him she might've escaped into the house, into her guest room, to keep her private life private from her hosts.

He dressed, shaved, ran a comb through his hair and hoped to meet her at the coffeepot in the general's kitchen. He had to get with her one more time to plan their next meeting, to tell her he wanted to call her, talk to her, find out when she would allow him to come to the Bay Area. He was already missing the sound of her voice. The smell of her skin.

When he got into the house, he found Vanni in the kitchen, the baby in his bouncy seat on the table. "Morning," he said, headed for the coffeepot. When he got back to the table and sat, he was met by her glare. "What?" he asked, perplexed.

"I cannot believe you did that," she said.

"Did what?" he asked.

"My best friend. You know she's been through a hard time."

He looked around a little frantically. "Vanni, what? Where's Nikki?"

"Gone," she said flatly.

"Gone?" he asked, rising out of his chair. *"Gone?"*

"Yes," she affirmed. "What were you thinking?"

He gave a huff of unhappy laughter. "I was thinking I'd just found the woman of my dreams," he said. "She *left?*"

"In tears," Vanni said, her mouth set in a grim line.

"Tears? Vanni, I did *not* make her cry!"

"Didn't you have sex with her all night long in that little fifth wheel?" she asked, anger in her tone.

Hoo-boy. You don't talk about that, especially when it's meaningful. "Vanni, I swear to you, I didn't do anything to hurt her."

"Didn't you find her on the deck, crying, and kiss her and seduce her and take her to that little trailer?"

"Well… Yeah… I did that part…." And he was thinking, was there a felony in there somewhere? Because all through the night the only thing he had tried to do was show her how much she could be loved. And it was wonderful; *she* was wonderful. Spontaneous and aroused and ultimately quite satisfied. And *happy.* He'd heard her sigh, he'd heard her laugh. There was absolutely no crying.

"Didn't it occur to you that after her heart had been broken, that was probably not a great idea?"

He got a little angry himself. He leaned his hands on the table, got a little bit in her face and said, "No. I thought it was a terrific idea, and so did she. I wanted to be good to her and I was. I treated her with absolute respect, and she consented one hundred percent. Now, give me her number. I need to talk to her as soon as possible."

"She said absolutely no."

"What? No, I have to get in touch with her. Vanni, this isn't funny."

"No, it's not. I just don't know what went through your mind."

"Wait a minute here, I didn't talk her into anything! I was a perfect gentleman, I swear to God!"

"Don't you know anything about women?" she asked him.

"Apparently not!" he answered hotly.

"She's just spent five years with a guy who wouldn't come through. What do you suppose she thinks you're going to do after one night?"

"She could give me a frickin' chance!"

Vanni's mouth was set in a firm line. "She said absolutely no."

"Oh, for God's sake. Vanni, this is cruel and unusual. Listen, I have feelings for her. Really."

"After one night?" she asked, a definite superior tone to her voice.

"*Before* the night," he said. "Will you ask her to call me? Please?"

"You knew her for what? Ten minutes?"

"Shit," he said. "Okay, it was fast. Okay? I admit it. But by the time we'd spent a night together it seemed…" It seemed as if he'd been with her for years! Jesus, his voice was quivering. He was losing his mind. He should be saying, fine—if that's the way she wants it, fine. But in his head, his heart, his gut, he was feeling desperate. Driven. He was not letting this woman get away.

His good sense said give it up. She's a nutcase. A whole night of magnificent love, intimate talk, something deep and meaningful going on and she splits? Like that? Never wanting to hear from you again? Give it up. Let it go. Move on. She's probably crazy. Joe had had one or two crazy women for excruciating but short duration, and he didn't want another one.

But he said, "Vanni, I have to talk to her. I won't do to her whatever he did to her. I won't make any promises I can't keep and I never did or said anything that wasn't a hundred percent sincere."

"Ha," she said.

"Oh fuck," he answered. "Where is your husband?"

"It won't do you any good," she said. "He's under orders."

"Where is he?"

She inclined her head toward the stable.

He left his coffee on the table and made fast tracks for the stable. Hadn't they all just had a perfectly nice wedding and reunion? He had no idea what had gone wrong. It had been the luckiest chance meeting of his life—that beautiful, sexy, soft and sweet Nikki had been there. And she had opened herself up to him in ways that led him to believe she found it to be her luckiest chance meeting as well. In his mind everything had gone right and could reasonably lead to many days, weeks, months, years of more nice stuff. He knew he had to invest the time before he could get a clear picture of the future—he'd been as burned as Nikki had—but you don't bolt when things are going *right*. And he looked forward to nothing so much as investing the time. With her.

He found Paul and Tom brushing down horses in the stable. He stopped short and took a few deep breaths. "Hey, boys," he said. "Tom, you mind? Can I have a minute with Paul? I'll take your brush if you want."

Tom looked at him grimly, though there might've been a little sparkle in his eye. "I heard you did the maid of honor."

"You know," Joe said somewhat irritably, "I was busy keeping private things private. I thought she might've appreciated that."

Tommy grinned. "I'd congratulate you, man, but I think you blew it."

"So I'm hearing. But if you'd been there…"

"Kinky," Tom said. "Sure I can't stay? You could think of it as part of my education."

"Take off," Paul said.

"Killjoy," he said, passing Joe the brush and leaving the stable.

"You gotta help me, man," Joe said to Paul. "I didn't do anything to her. I mean, I only did to her what she totally... She should *not* have left in tears. I swear to God."

"Yeah? Yet, she did. She was all shook up. Vanni was worried about her driving like that—all messed up."

"No, you have to understand. I—" He stopped. He didn't like the desperate sound of his own voice. He was not going to do this—he was not going to tell Paul that he held her and loved her all night long and that he was gentle and she was sweet. That they had also been a little wild—beautifully wild. That their bodies had meshed perfectly and their words just as well. That in addition to sex too hot to imagine, there had been tender words, too soft and lovely to explain. He couldn't tell a *guy* that. It was beyond him.

"Paul, goddammit, you have to help me with this. I have to get in touch with her."

"She says she doesn't want to hear from you."

"I have to hear that from her. Jesus, I don't even know her last name."

Paul stopped brushing and looked at Joe over the rear end of a horse. "I don't think I'd admit that again." He groaned. "Jesus, Joe. You screwed the maid of honor without even getting her *name?*"

Joe lost it. He dropped the brush, grabbed Paul by the front of his shirt and slammed him up against the stable wall with a huge bang. Paul could easily have hammered him if he wasn't so completely shocked. "I didn't do that," Joe said in a fierce, angry whisper. "I didn't *screw* anyone! I made excellent love to her and she made incredible love right back to me and it was almost too good to believe. I used six of your condoms and I—" He stopped. He let go of Paul and stepped back. "This isn't happening to me," he said.

"I think you might be a little out of control," Paul observed.

"Aw, come on! Help me out here!"

"Seriously, I don't think I'd admit again that you don't even know her last name."

"What the fuck is it, you jerk!"

"Jorgensen, but you didn't hear it from me. Okay? I'd like to have sex again in my life."

"Sex. Sex. It's all about sex." Joe shook his head.

"Wasn't it?" Paul asked.

"Only about half the time," Joe said. "Paul, will you listen to me a second? It was perfect—the kind of perfect that just doesn't come along very often. You hear me? It was wonderful. It wasn't just sex, but don't get me wrong..."

"You're going down the wrong road again, buddy. Women don't want to hear about how great they were in bed."

"Now you're an expert? Married twelve hours and you know everything?" He hung his head. "I have to find her, man. She gets two chances—she has to tell me twice that it's nothing. Twice. Then I go away quietly. I'm no stalker. But man..."

"Whew. You got it bad," Paul said. "She is way under your skin."

"Just tell me you don't know what I'm talking about, Paul. You of all people."

Paul was quiet for a minute. "Unfortunately, I read you."

"Help me out here. She's... Don't make me say anything more, please. It's private, okay? Help me out."

"Here's what I'd do. Write her a letter," Paul said. "I'll ask Vanni to send it to her. But I can't guarantee anything," he added.

"You are so frickin' whipped."

"Yeah? What are you right now?"

"Out of my head, that's what."

Paul lifted two eyebrows. "Six?"

"Aw, bite me!"

Before leaving Virgin River, Joe sat in the fifth wheel he'd borrowed and wrote a letter on a lined yellow pad, a letter in which every word embarrassed him. But he forced himself. He went through roughly fifty drafts to come up with one he could live with, and he still found it horribly inadequate.

Nikki—

I had a wonderful weekend with you. You left too soon and broke my heart. I want to talk to you again, see you again, and according to Vanni, you don't want to be contacted by me. I don't know what went wrong. For me, everything went right, and I thought it went right for you, too. I know you're still recovering from a bad breakup, but it didn't seem to have anything to do with you and me. Call me. Tell Vanni to give me your number so I can call you. I hope I didn't do or say anything to hurt you, to make you feel bad, but if I did, at least give me a chance to apologize. Nikki, it was one of the nicest weekends of my life. Come on, baby. I'm dying here.

Love,

Joe.

He gave the letter to Paul because he didn't trust Vanni just yet. However, when he took Vanessa into his arms to give her a kiss goodbye he said, "You have to believe me. I didn't hurt her. I want to hear from her. Please, tell her that."

"I'll tell her. But I don't know that it'll change anything."

"Just tell her. Please."

Sixteen

Tom had his gear packed by Sunday afternoon. He took Brenda out for a long ride and she held it together real well. She stayed for dinner with the general, Vanni and Paul. His dad was taking him to the bus at five in the morning. He drove Brenda back to her house at about 8:00 p.m., but he didn't get home until 4:00 a.m. He found his dad was up.

"You didn't keep Brenda out all this time, did you, son?"

"No, Dad. We were at her house. Her parents were home."

"She okay?"

"Yeah, she'll be okay. You haven't been up all night, have you?"

"On and off."

"I hope you weren't worried," Tom said.

"Not at all, son. I knew you'd be with your girl to the last minute. Unfortunately for you, there's no time to sleep."

"I'm not interested in sleep."

"You will be." He draped an arm around his son's shoulder, gave a squeeze and said, "It's what I would've done, too. She's a wonderful girl."

"She is a wonderful girl," Tom agreed, a sadness at leaving her in his voice.

"Let's get you some breakfast. Maybe a shower. Then we'll take off."

"Vanni and Paul getting up?"

"Oh, I'm sure. Come on, kid."

Walt scrambled eggs and fried bacon and the sounds from the kitchen brought the others. An hour later they all stood out on the front porch and said goodbye. Tom kissed his sister and little Mattie. While his dad waited in the car, he embraced Paul. "Watch out for my dad, Paul," Tom said. "He likes to act like this is no big deal. Be sure he's handling me being gone okay."

"I'll watch," Paul said. "I'll take care of your family, boy. You just knock 'em dead in boot camp."

"I'll do my best."

Ricky's time was spent with the four most important people in his life. His grandma, Lydie, his girl, Liz, Jack and Preacher. Liz stayed in Virgin River for the ten days he was on leave and some afternoons, Jack took him fishing.

Standing out in the Virgin with Jack, watching the lines arc over their heads as they cast, Rick felt it was where he had always belonged. It was here, at the river, that all the important growing-up talks of his life had taken place, and always with Jack. It was here that Jack had that big talk with him about sex, for what good it did—Rick had still ended up getting his girl pregnant. What a tough time that had been. Later, while Rick was doing his best to stand by her like a man, it was Jack who encouraged him, coached him, tried to keep him on the right path to avoid even more disaster. And after the baby was stillborn, Jack and Preach held him up, helped him shoulder the pain.

"Thanks for everything you've done for me, Jack," he said.

"I didn't do anything. People tend to come out to celebrate their friends."

"I wasn't talking about this week—which, by the way, has been great. I was talking about the last few years. You were like my dad. I kind of always thought of you as my dad. I hope you don't mind that too much."

Jack felt his chest tighten up. "Mind? That would make me damn proud, Rick. If I could have another son, I would have it be you."

"You gotta do something for me, Jack. If anything goes wrong over there—"

"Rick. We don't like to talk that way...."

"Jack! We know what it is over there. Now listen, if anything goes wrong over there, will you make sure my grandma and Lizzie get through it okay?"

Jack looked at him, at his profile, because Rick looked straight ahead. "You know you don't have to ask that. We take care of each other's families."

"I know. And, Jack? I just don't want to leave anything important unsaid. I love you, man. You're my best friend ever. You got me grown up. Nothing would've turned out without you."

Jack swallowed. When he spoke, his voice wasn't real strong. "There's still lots of fishing to do, Rick. I'm counting on that." He put his hand on the boy's shoulder. "I love you, too, son." But he was thinking, *If you don't come back, who's going to get* me *through it?*

"I want to tell you something I did. I know I'm only nineteen, Liz only seventeen—both of us still too young. But I bought her a necklace with a diamond in it—a nice-size one, too. I told her it was my promise to her, but I also told her it didn't hold her to anything."

Jack lifted an eyebrow. "Big step," he said.

"Half a step, really," Rick said. "Call it a first step. I love the girl, there's no question about that. I've loved her since she was fourteen—it was my undoing. But there were so many complications for us, some real hurting times. If there's a better guy for her, I won't hold her back. But if there's not a better guy…"

"Then what, Rick?"

"I'm driving her crazy, talking about school all the time. She's gotta finish high school—that's just one more year. And I'd really like her to get a little college—I asked her to at least try. When I'm done with this gig, I'm going to school. I'm not saying I'll give up the Marine Corps—I don't know about that yet—but I'm going to college. If it works out for us, if we get married, I want us to be smart, educated people. I want a family real bad—probably because of the one we lost, huh?"

"I guess that would set up a real strong desire, yeah," Jack said.

"Well, if I get another chance at that, I'd like us to be smart enough to earn a decent living and have a couple of kids raised by educated parents." He turned and grinned at Jack. "I think that kind of talk got her attention—she said she'd try to get good grades her senior year and she'd at least go to community college." He sobered. "She said she'd do that so I'd be proud of her. Man, I'm already so proud of her—look how she holds up, huh? She buried her baby and said goodbye to me, and did she fall apart? She's been solid. She's been real brave, real strong."

"You both have, Rick. A diamond, huh? How'd you save enough for a diamond?"

Ricky laughed. "I'm not doing that anymore, buying things like that with my per diem—I'll save it for something a little more practical, like a down payment on a house or a car. But Liz deserved to have something beautiful that says I love her, that I couldn't think more of her. Don't you think?"

It made Jack smile. "You think she stood by you while you were gone?"

"Every day," he said. "She gets real lonesome sometimes, and she misses all the stuff the girlfriends do—homecoming dance, prom, all that stuff. I told her to go—I could deal with that. But she said she couldn't do that. It might lead someone on. She said if she's still with me in the end, that stuff wouldn't even be important. She writes me letters almost every day—longer ones when everyone but her is going to prom. Damn… There are a lot of times I wish I was more like you—totally free and not caring about any woman until I've had a chance to really live, see the world, experience the world—and then have Liz come along later, when I'm like thirty, or forty…"

Jack chuckled. "And there are a lot of times I wish I'd met Mel a long time before she'd hooked into that first husband, started our family when we were both a lot younger, before I started getting gray. I think if you're lucky enough to find the right person at all, you don't have a right to complain about when, how." He put a hand on the kid's shoulder and gave a squeeze. "I hope it works out for the two of you, son. You buried a baby together. It would be sweet if you could bring a couple of healthy and strong ones into your lives together. But I'll say this—I think you're smart to tell her to take her time on that commitment. Believe me, when you make those kinds of promises to a woman, you want her to be absolutely sure."

"That's what I think."

A large fish jumped across the river and they were silent; he was huge. "King," Rick finally said. "I haven't seen one that size in a long time."

"He must be lost," Jack said, casting in that direction.

Rick took a few paces downstream, changed out his fly and threw a line. They played with him a while, then Rick hooked him and yelled, "Woo-hoo!"

"Lead him, let him take out line, tire him out before you—"

Rick laughed. "I know how to catch a fish."

"Don't screw around, get too anxious and lose him," Jack said.

"You milking this cow?" Ricky asked him.

For the better part of an hour Rick played him, letting out line, letting him run, pulling him back, walking up and down in the shallow part of the river when the fish ran, and all the while he had Jack in his ear. "That son of a bitch is big. Let out more line. Don't spoil him, he's a fighter. He's getting too far from your control, reel him back." And on and on and on.

Rick finally brought him in, a great big Chinook, over thirty pounds. And that was more than enough fishing; Rick's ears were ringing from Jack's mother-henning.

When they got back to the bar, Preacher whistled in admiration and loaded the fish on the scale. "Thirty-seven point four. You catch him all by yourself, Rick?"

Rick made a face at Jack. "Not exactly."

When Jack took Rick to Garberville, they sat in the truck for a minute, waiting for the bus to board. "Got any last-minute advice?" Rick asked him.

"Yeah. Trust your gut. Follow your orders, but trust your instincts."

"I want you to know that I'm not afraid of it. I'm not. In fact, I might be a little excited. It was the right thing to do, Jack. For me."

"I believe you."

"You take good care of Mel and the kids, huh?"

"You bet I will. I'll write every week," Jack said. "Nothing will happen in Virgin River that you won't hear about."

"Whoopee," he said, and laughed. Jack went to tousle his hair the way he used to, but it was shaved down so short, he knuckled his scalp instead. "I'm going now," Rick said.

Jack got out of the truck and met him around the front. He gave him a robust hug. "Take care, son. Be safe."

"I will. Now you get outta here. Don't hang around and stare at the bus, like you did last time."

Jack couldn't stop himself—he grabbed him and hugged him again. "This time next year, Rick. I'll get the boys to come. You bring your friends."

"Sure," he said. Then he turned and walked to the bus, straight and tall, his duffel over his shoulder. He never turned around to look back.

June grew old and hot. Small fires dotted a mountainous landscape that had remained dry and dangerous, while in Arizona, Nevada, Colorado and Utah several big fires had threatened to run out of control and, it being early in the season, this didn't bode well. Northern California had escaped the big ones so far, but it was a frightening prospect as the rains continued to elude them. Cal Fire and Department of Forestry was patrolling campgrounds like crazy, making sure fires were only lit in designated areas and with permits, in many cases prohibiting fires of any kind.

Mel was keeping a very close eye on her husband. The first days after Ricky left found Jack a little on the quiet side, but he was coming around. He talked about the young man a lot, read the newspapers and had a satellite TV installed in the bar so he and Preacher could keep up on CNN reports of the war. He had the Chinook mounted, taking down his big, ugly sturgeon and replacing it with Rick's fish. He had also written about a dozen letters already, and let her read over some of them while they were in progress. "Jack," she had said, laughing. "Do you really think Ricky cares what Preacher made for dinner, or how many temper tantrums Davie threw today?"

"I think he wants to hear everything. I remember."

Of course he did, she thought. He remembered every long night he spent in battle zones, often in the same landscape, the same country where Rick served this very minute. He remembered every face of a young marine, every wounded man, every letter from home. For Jack to have been through it himself and let Rick go with such pride and confidence made him, in Mel's mind, the strongest man alive.

"I have an idea," she told him. "Go ask your sister and brother-in-law if they know any news that should be sent Rick's way."

Jack's eyes briefly widened, then he walked briskly out the back door of the bar, across the yard to that RV, and banged on the door. Mel watched from the window as Brie stepped outside. A short conversation ensued and then she could hear her husband's loud whoop of excitement just as he lifted his sister off her feet and swung her around and around. Then he was back, lifting Mel off her feet, bringing her face up to his. He covered her mouth in a searing, demanding kiss—but she found herself laughing against his lips. "Jack, *she's* pregnant, not me!"

"It's almost as good," he said. "They want a baby so much. This is wonderful news." Then he scowled a little bit and said, "Did you just leak some confidential medical information?"

"No," she said. "Brie said I could tell you."

"Then why didn't you just tell me?"

"This was much more fun. Are you done kissing me already?"

"Baby, I want to way more than kiss you. I'll be very careful. How about it?"

She played with the hair at his temple. Not many women knew what it was like to have a man like this. A powerful and lusty man like Jack. He always put her needs and feelings ahead of his own, always looking to care for her in every way, keeping her safe, making sure she knew how loved she was. How wanted. In his love, in his arms, she always felt beautiful and sexy. Desired. Cherished. She kissed him on the lips and said, "Later. And you don't have to be all that careful—I'm all right now."

"But your poor little body has been through so much," he said.

"John Stone was just here this morning, so he gave me a little check. I have my operator's license back."

"Oh, baby," he said in a breath.

"But, Jack, you are not to write Rick about that!"

He grinned at her and said, "Just as well. I could never put it into words, what I feel with you."

This was a kind of union Mel hadn't even dared fantasize. The level of their intimacy, from the physical to emotional, was so deep and intense, it was impossible for either of them to tell where one ended and the other began. She could read his mind; he could sense her feelings. They anticipated each other in so many ways. It was as if his heart beat in her breast. She had never known another human being as she knew her Jack. And she made herself just as accessible to him, holding nothing back.

As July arrived, Paige's time grew near. Mel was checking her by the week and she was progressing normally, ready for labor anytime. She had decided to have her baby at Doc's because her small quarters weren't really conducive to a home birth. And there was Christopher, only four. Lots of Mel's rural patients had children around during deliveries; they'd come from families who had been having home births for generations and it was all part of the life cycle to them. For Paige and Preacher, however, this was a very new thing. In fact, Mel would have expected her to choose Valley Hospital and a sterile labor-and-delivery wing. But Paige was very determined—the only person who could deliver her was Mel.

Joe Benson was putting the plans together for Brie and Mike's house, Paige and Preacher's add-on. He also had some preliminary sketches ready to show Paul for his house, but felt hesitant. Since the incident with Nikki, their relationship was strained. Vanni seemed to be over her anger with Joe, but Joe wasn't nearly over his disappointment in all of them. He supposed it would just take time.

What he would've liked was a little support. Maybe they could have gone to bat for him with the woman. Let her know that Joe was an okay guy, that he didn't use and abuse women. Reassure her, maybe. Encourage her to at least get in touch with him. To maybe take a chance on him.

Joe hadn't talked to Paul or Vanni about Nikki for a while. What he had done, however, was send notes to Vanni for Nikki about every other day, hoping to break through the barrier. Short, one- or two-sentence notes. "Please call me, Nikki. I want a chance to show you I'm a decent guy." "Call me or write me and tell me you are absolutely not interested in seeing me again—but don't do this. Don't ignore me." "I care. I thought it was clear in my actions that I'm sincere." It took him a while to make himself stop; he began to feel like an idiot. And the more like an idiot he felt, the worse his mood. He hadn't been passing notes like that since he was totally, insanely, ridiculously in love with Jodie Ferguson in the fourth grade. Blond, brilliant, distant Jodie—the first girl to get boobs in his class.

Although he had managed to kick his habit of note writing, he found a Nicole Jorgensen in the San Francisco phone directory and when he called that number, the voice on the answering machine was unmistakably hers. "Ah, Nikki, it's Joe. From Grants Pass. I'd love to talk to you. No, I really *need* to talk to you. Please. I've been trying to reach you since the wedding. Come on, Nikki, we have things to talk about. I'm totally confused."

Of course she didn't call. Fortunately he left only the one message. It took great restraint on his part not to call that number several more times, just to hear the sound of her voice. That sweet, sultry voice that had caressed his mind with every word that had come out of her mouth. But her caller ID would show repeated attempts, making him look out of control, so he held himself back.

It had been a few weeks. He was done. No more note writing, no more calls. Even he wouldn't date someone this desperate. He was going to start looking like a stalker when what he was, was in love with her. It embarrassed even him to think like that. How could you be in love with someone you'd met twice, but you knew for only twenty-four hours? It was impossible. There must be some other explanation for dreaming about her, smelling her, tasting her, hearing her voice, feeling her hair against his cheek when he was waking up in the morning. Some sort of mania or hallucination. An obsessive-compulsive disorder.

He called Paul. "Yeah, hi. If you're ready, I can bring

down the plans for your two properties this weekend. We can go over them with the owners, walk the land, make adjustments, get moving on this."

"That would be great," Paul said cheerfully. "Want to stay with us while you're here?"

"Thanks, but I'm making some other plans."

"How about the trailer? Want to borrow it?"

He laughed uncomfortably. "For sure, no. But thanks for the offer. I think I'm going to stay at Jack's this trip."

"Whatever works. I'm really looking forward to seeing you, buddy."

"Yeah, me, too," Joe said.

Joe asked Jack if that little cabin in the woods was still available and Jack told him it was. Jack mentioned his worry about the small forest fires that seemed to be springing up all over the countryside across five states due to drought and extreme dryness. Joe was able to see firsthand what that was about when he made the drive south. He passed a couple of small pockets of fire that came dangerously close to the roads he traveled. There were not too many controlled burns out there when the weather was so dry, but he supposed some of the small plumes of smoke he saw in the distance could be fires set by Cal Fire to keep the landscape under control—spacing the clumps of forest to give them an advantage in a fire, to keep it from spreading.

He was a volunteer in the Grants Pass Fire Department, but had only been called once, years ago. There was nothing quite as ominous as driving through the lush green hillsides staked with towering pines and not be able to see very far in front of you because of smoke. Or worse, driving down a road that was bordered on each side by the charred, black skeletons of once-majestic trees. When a fire had passed through, the hillsides could look like that for years and years and years.

Joe was glad when he reached the redwoods, untouched and pristine. And then past the Virgin, wide and wild, flowing over rocks and down natural waterfalls. Another few months would bring deer hunting; deer hunters. Fishing in the Virgin would start to get real good. The boys would come down in a few months to catch the end of hunting season; Mel would throw a fit, but it wouldn't do her any good. And then she'd cry if they shot any deer. The memory of it made him smile—she was so sentimental, and Jack was so tender with her. But he'd hunt anyway.

He walked into the bar with his plans rolled up under his arm. Preacher was waiting for him, but the bar was empty, as it often was in the middle of the afternoon. Joe got his usual bear hug from the big man. "Ready to be a daddy, my man?" Joe asked him.

"Whew, you can't know. Paige, she's big as a—" He stopped himself. "Mel says that baby's ready to walk out of her."

"Get the girl," Joe said. "You're going to love the house."

"Yeah, I'll get her. And I'll give Brie a call—they're excited to see their plans. How about Paul?"

"I told him I'd get here by early afternoon. I'm sure he'll show up."

When Paige came out of the back, Joe's eyes warmed over at the sight of her. She was ripe as an overdue melon. Plump and rosy and big. "Aw, honey," he said. "You're so beautiful."

"Thanks, Joe," she said, reaching for him.

He pulled her into his arms and while he hugged her, the baby kicked. "Whoa," he said. "What do you have in there? A football team?"

"A feminine little girl," she said. "Dana Marie."

"She's got big feet, I guarantee it," he told her. "You want to see your new house?" he asked.

"I can't wait."

He barely had the plans laid out on a table when Brie and Mike came in. More hugs and warm greetings. "And I understand you've put a little rush on the building?" he asked. "To make room for a newcomer?"

"Right around Christmas," she said.

"I can already see it in your eyes."

"What you see is me getting past the first trimester. It's relief, Joe. We're not getting any younger."

"I feel younger, that's for sure," Mike said, and if Joe wasn't mistaken, his chest puffed a little bit.

"Okay, we got your house pretty close to ready, and Paul and I will walk the property this weekend. Come over here."

Joe had Paige and Preacher seated at one table, going over plans, Mike and Brie at another, and he walked between the two with a pointer and a pencil, answering questions, penciling in adjustments.

For Preacher, he had added to the existing apartment. Downstairs the current quarters were enlarged into a great room with fireplace, no need for a kitchen but a serving area with sink, counter, dishwasher and cupboards for their own dishes and glassware that fronted a large dining room. They would use the bar's kitchen for their cooking, but should have a private place for meals. He designed a big master bedroom and enlarged the existing bath. The larger downstairs could support two more bedrooms upstairs, a Jack and Jill bath and a loft, connected to Christopher's room by a short hall. There was a wide-open staircase from the great room to the loft. It turned those little quarters into a real four-bedroom, three-bath house that could be filled with family and friends.

For Mike and Brie, twenty-five hundred square feet of living space, another five hundred attached to the house as office space for Brie with entrances from the outside and inside. Four bedrooms, a great room, a spacious kitchen, three baths including the master, and some beautiful features from vaulted ceilings, a large marble shower without doors, granite counters, stone hearths in the great room and master, slate and hardwood floors, a long, deep deck.

By the time they'd gotten familiar with the designs, Paul arrived. Joe felt awkward until he saw his old friend, and then it was natural to grab him, give him a hearty greeting with slaps on the back. "I've really missed you, man," Paul said.

"Yeah, me, too. Hey, I brought some drawings for you and Vanni to look at. Maybe something will work. I did it based on what you said she liked about your Grants Pass house."

"Bring them to dinner."

"I don't want to impose…."

"You're kidding, right? Joe—we gotta get past this. Seriously. It wasn't anyone's fault."

"Maybe it was mine," he said, dropping his head briefly. "Whatever, it's in the past. It's over. We should try to move on."

Paul glanced at Brie and Mike, Paige and Preacher. Seeing they were absorbed in their house plans, he quietly asked, "Have you moved on, brother?"

"Yeah," Joe answered with a laugh that even he knew was insincere. "Sure."

"Come to dinner," Paul said. "Please."

"Okay," he said. "But you have to take the plans home first, give Vanni a chance to have a look before I get there. So she can work up her questions and complaints."

"We've got the homesite all picked out," Paul said. "We can build right on the other side of the pasture, along the river. We'll share the stable."

"Have you surveyed it?"

"Done."

"When we have a design you like, we'll walk it. Maybe tomorrow before I leave."

The back door to the bar opened and the sound of someone carrying supplies into the kitchen could be heard. "That'd be Jack. He went out for supplies so I could stick around Paige," Preacher said, getting to his feet.

"Let's do it," Joe said, and all the men present went through the kitchen to help unload Jack's truck. Work done, they settled in for a beer and a little catching up. At around four, Joe shoved Paul out the door, telling him to take the plans and drawings home to Vanni and he'd see him in a couple of hours.

It wasn't long before the dinner hour approached, which brought Mel and the little ones to the bar. Joe held the baby for a while, had a few words with Doc, said hello to Hope McCrea while she had her Jack Daniel's, passed the time with Doug and Sue Carpenter, Brenda's folks from just down the street. He checked his watch, asked for a cup of coffee from Jack and sat up at the bar.

"Business good?" Jack asked.

"Great," Joe said. "I'm staying busy."

"This stuff down here—is this extra?"

"Yeah, but it's nice to have it. It's great that my friends want my designs. Good for my ego," he said.

"So then," Jack said, "what's eating you?"

"Not a thing, my brother." He sat up a little straighter, took in a deep breath.

"*Who's* eating you?" Jack said.

"You're missing the signals, man. I'm good."

Jack lifted his coffee cup. "Whatever you say."

Joe knew what Jack was seeing. Joe had always been carefree. A grinning fool, a quick laugh, a lot of jokes, nothing in the world bothered him. He had a good family, good business, women when he bothered, plenty of money, lifelong friends like the boys. He knew there was a smudge on his personality, a sadness that now occupied his eyes and hadn't been there for a long time, not for a good ten years.

"It's just that, it seems like something's bothering you," Jack said.

"Yeah, maybe. Not a big deal. It'll pass."

"You ever want to talk, you know where I am."

Joe smiled. "Thanks, buddy."

Jack shrugged. "Maybe she'll come around."

"Who?" Joe asked, a little stunned. He would be genuinely pissed if Paul had talked about this.

"Whoever she is. Men have a lot of looks, pal. They have a look for business worries, family worries, ego worries. Combat worries—I got good at spotting that one. And there's a real special look when a man wants a woman and she's out of reach."

It made Joe laugh. "Is that a fact?"

Jack sipped his coffee. "I've worn that look a couple of times."

"I must not have been around," Joe said.

"You might've been. Mel made me work pretty damn hard for her. It was excruciating. Excuse me—I have to load up the family. I stay late now that Paige is so close. Mel has to take the kids home, get them in bed."

"I'll help," he said.

They got Mel and the little ones settled in the truck. Jack leaned in the window to kiss her and Joe was overcome with longing. This was torture, watching his best friends, his brothers, with their women. By the end of a hunt, they were talking about getting home to their beautiful, lush, ripe women, bringing them children and love. Joe hadn't been so worried about the fact that he hadn't found this yet until recently, until he held a woman that made him feel that full, that in love, and immediately lost her.

Vanni loved her house plans. She was animated and full of life, and in that, very affectionate toward Joe. If he was reading her right, she was forgiving Joe's dalliance with her best friend. The general got into the mix, making suggestions, arguing with his daughter about what she should be doing differently. Joe was good at this sort of thing— he listened while they batted around ideas and waited until the dust settled. Then he could step in with one minor adjustment and bring the whole thing together.

For Vanni and Paul, Joe designed a larger version of Paul's house, but with changes that although slight, gave it a different appearance altogether, so it didn't look like a copy and was better suited for a growing family. The features they loved were there—the wide hallways, spacious rooms, high ceilings, large garage. And it had to have more bedrooms—Paul was going to fill her with babies.

He spent the night in the cabin, then in the morning he drove out to Jack's property—to the parcel he'd given to Brie and Mike. It wasn't far from Jack's—they'd extended his road another quarter of a mile to their homesite. Paul had already set up shop and was hiring construction crew, quite successfully. He had the requisite trailer for his office and a Porta Potty for his crews. Now that there were plans, Paul could have the foundation poured. The septic tank would go in and the well dug. Then the plumbing and frame and wiring. "Then it's game on," Joe said. "Let's go walk your property at the general's," he said.

This, too, was ready to move. The first order of business

was the grading of the road, which would be a three-quarter-mile stretch, but no major excavation would be required, no trees to bring down. In ball cap and jeans, Joe paced off the perimeters of the foundation and pounded in some temporary stakes with red flags on them. He took a can of spray paint and outlined the house on the ground, bringing it up close enough to the river for a nice backyard view from a deck, far enough away to avoid problems with possible flooding. "I have indoor sprinklers in the design, which I recommend, but understand that in a wildfire, they aren't going to do the job. It's a precaution for a home fire."

"I understand," Paul said.

"You can pour both foundations at the same approximate time. Do Brie and Mike's first, since they have a bun in the oven, then get over here and pour yours. You can get started on the extension at the bar and as soon as Preacher's baby is a couple of weeks old, we can relocate them to the cabin. We'll tear out some walls—and you should move fast on that one to keep the bar working. You can stagger your crews—move the framers from the Valenzuelas' property to this property, et cetera."

"I've built more than one house at a time." Paul smiled.

"I know. Just talking," he said, smiling back.

"We're going to need finalized architectural drawings," Paul said.

"Two weeks?" Joe asked.

"Perfect," Paul said, sticking out his hand. "I'll order concrete."

Joe shook it. "Pleasure doing business with you. I'm going to head out."

"You want to say goodbye to Vanni?"

"Tell her I said goodbye and thank-you, would you?"

"You know, this is probably none of my business—but

this thing we're not talking about? It might help your case a little if you could just tell Vanni you're sorry."

Joe shook his head in a silent laugh, looking down. He put his hands in his pockets. "I couldn't do that, pal," he said. "Not honestly." He took a breath. "The only thing I'm sorry about is how it turned out."

Paul was quiet for a long moment. Then he said, "Gotcha."

Vanni had nursed the baby and put him down for the night. She heard her dad walk down the hall to his room at about nine-thirty, but her husband didn't come to bed. Finally she went to the great room to see if he was hooked on something on television. She found him sitting forward in a chair, his elbows on his knees, a drink in his hands.

"What are you doing?" she asked.

He sat back and patted the chair beside him. "Thinking."

"Is it keeping you up?" she asked, sitting.

He gave her a wan smile. "Do you know how great my life is? How happy I am?"

She put her hand on his knee. "You've done a real good job of making sure I do, Paul. I'm just as happy."

"I want to tell you something. Think back a few months. A long while back, the first night you surprised me by walking into Jack's. When all the boys got together to hunt and I had no idea you were here, in Virgin River, and you surprised me. Remember?"

"I do." She smiled.

"That very night, overcome just by seeing you, I might've had one too many."

"I think you told me that, Paul," she said.

"I got tanked. And I made this drunken confession to Jack, about how I'd seen you first but Matt got to you ahead of me. No one else heard me, thank God. But Jack knew what was going on. Later, then, after Matt was killed and the baby was born and a certain pediatrician was chasing you, Jack called me one night and told me not to be an idiot. He said if I wanted you I'd better get down here and find a way to say so."

"He did? I never knew that."

"And I came as fast as I could. Because if I hadn't, I was going to lose you. And I loved you. God, I loved you." He took a breath. "Before I ever held you or kissed you, I was so in love with you, sometimes it was awful. I try to imagine what it might have felt like if we'd been a couple, for even one night, and you didn't want me anymore."

"You don't have to ever imagine that, sweetheart," she said.

"I have what every man wants—a woman he'd die for. A woman who owns him, every piece of him. I really never thought I'd be this lucky...."

"Stop," she said. "Don't go crazy on me." She put her hand along his cheek. "Just pick up your dirty underwear like a good boy and I'll reward you in many remarkable ways."

But Paul wasn't laughing. "Did you see my friend Joe? The guy is in pain. He's dying. He had one night with a woman who obviously fulfilled every wish buried in his subconscious. She put a hex on him, then rejected him. Did you see him?"

She took a deep breath. "Paul, his timing was bad. We can't help that...."

"So was hers. I've known the man for fifteen years. He might be smooth, but he's not disreputable. He wouldn't take a woman to bed if she didn't want to go. If Nikki had expressed the least hesitation, he wouldn't have touched her. I know him. I know him as well as I knew Matt."

"So? She made a mistake. What are you getting at?"

"She shouldn't make a bigger one," he said. "They just don't come any better than Joe. There must have been some reason she said yes that night."

"I've sent the little notes from him. She hasn't changed her mind. You want me to talk to her?"

"No, honey. I'm going to talk to her."

"I don't know if you should do that," she said nervously.

"But I'm going to. I've been thinking about it all day and I'm calling her. Right now. You want to listen in or go put your head under the pillow?"

She sucked in a breath. "I'll listen," she said. "But please, don't let on I'm here. I feel really strange about this."

"I want you to trust me," he said, picking up the phone. He dialed the number. "I have to do this."

Nikki could no doubt see the number on the caller ID because she picked up. She answered, "Hi, sweetie."

"It's not sweetie," Paul said. "It's Paul."

"Oh. Hi."

"I have to talk to you. About Joe."

"I thought we settled that," she said.

"Yeah, I guess it's pretty much settled for you," Paul said. "Not quite settled for me. Just for my peace of mind, Nikki, I have to ask you something. See, I've known Joe a long time now and I've trusted him with my life. Literally. I went to war with the guy. I've seen him with women, and this guy—he's always been a classy guy. I've never known him to treat a woman badly...."

"He didn't treat me badly, Paul," she said softly.

Paul let out a breath. "Well, thank God. That's a relief. I was afraid, I don't know... Afraid I didn't know him as well as I thought I did. I mean, you were really upset—and then I found Joe to be just as upset to hear you left here in tears. He wouldn't tell me what went on between you two, but he insisted he hadn't done anything to hurt you."

"It's okay, Paul. You can let this go."

"Good. Because I just couldn't stand to think he'd treat a woman wrong. He's not that kind of guy. You'll be glad to know, finally he seems to be putting this whole thing behind him. It was killing him for a while there, but I think he's getting better."

"Better?"

"Yeah, a little bit. Trying to get over it. Over you. He was up here this weekend. There were architectural plans he had to bring me—I'm going to build three of his houses. Vanni told me he was writing notes, leaving messages. I guess he had it pretty bad, but it's not like Joe to bother a woman who doesn't want to be bothered. You'll probably be shed of him pretty soon. Maybe you already are."

"Oh," she said quietly. "Good. Then."

"I don't exactly know what has him so jammed up. I'm sure he gets the message by now. That you don't want anything to do with him. Ever. Again."

"Maybe he wanted to apologize. It's not necessary," she said.

Paul hmmed. "No, I don't think so. I suggested he might get some points with Vanni if he said he was sorry. He said he couldn't do that—he wasn't sorry. Just disappointed by how it turned out."

"I thought it was best," she said. "After all, it was brief…"

"Yeah. God forbid something like that should ever happen again…"

"Paul, I gave a man five years and he was lying to me the whole time. He kept saying he needed more time before making a commitment and then finally admitted he'd never get married, never have a family. It was like I didn't know him at all."

"I know, Nikki. That was bad, I'm sorry. My friend Joe? He's not that kind of guy. A lie would turn into acid in his mouth. If he wasn't going the distance, he'd say so."

"It's better this way. Better to let it go now, before… I wouldn't want to go through something like that again."

"I guess you know what you're doing. Joe, he's still a little roughed up, but he'll get over it. You probably know better than anyone how that feels, right? Trying to get over someone?" He lifted his eyebrows toward his wife.

"Yes," Nikki said.

"There you go. He said we all have to move past it, get it behind us. That's what you want, right? For him to forget about you?"

"Yes," she said, her voice weak and quivering a little.

"God, I hope you're right about this, Nikki," he said. "That this is a man to put behind you. I did that once, you know. Different circumstances—I was up against Matt. But I fell in love with Vanni so fast it was ridiculous. No one would believe it—that I took one look at her and man, it just hit me. When Matt made his move, I backed right off. I let her go, I wasn't going to compete with my best friend for a woman. I have to tell you—I started to regret that ten minutes later. For years all I could think was why the hell didn't I walk right up to them and say, 'Out of my way, buddy—I saw her first!'"

Silence answered him.

"But I guess we don't have much in common there, huh? There was no competition, except maybe Joe was competing with a rotten memory. If there was anything about him you thought was worth a damn, you never would have let him get away. So. I just hope you're right.…"

She whimpered a little bit. "It was one night...."

"I think maybe the crazy fool loves you," Paul said.

"That's impossible," she said, but there were tears in her voice.

"Nikki," Paul said softly. "You said yes, right?"

"Of course I said yes," she sniffed. "He didn't *force* me. He didn't even insist. He's not that kind of guy."

"Yeah, that's what I'm saying. You know, it's probably none of my business, but it just doesn't make sense to me—two people trying to get over each other because something good happened, something both of you wanted to happen. But I guess you know what you want. And don't want. Huh?"

"I don't want to get hurt again."

"I hear ya, Nikki. I understand, I do. You'll be strong enough to take a chance again someday. When you are, I'm sure you'll stumble on a good man. There are probably a million of 'em out there. Just wanted to be sure nothing bad happened."

It took her a minute to respond. "Nothing bad happened."

"That's good enough for me. You take care, Nikki."

He hung up the phone and looked at his wife. He smiled.

"That was very sneaky," Vanessa said.

Seventeen

The dry heat of July brought passionately anticipated action to the Middleton family—labor pains. Preacher was back and forth from the kitchen to his quarters no less than every ten minutes. "How is it now?" he asked Paige.

Paige was reading to Christopher. "John, it's going to be a very long day for you if you can't relax a little. I'm still having contractions ten minutes apart."

"But it's going to be today, right?"

"This could go on for twenty-four hours," she said. "They're not real hard." Then she turned to Chris. "Why don't you read this page, honey. You can do it."

"'Kay," he said, and proceeded to read, but whether from identifying the words or from memory, it was hard to tell.

Preacher went back to the kitchen, his head hanging. "Still ten minutes," he told Jack.

"I have an idea, buddy. Let's get some food ready for dinner tonight and tomorrow night, just in case you don't feel like cooking. I'll hold down the fort."

"Should we call Mel again?" he asked.

"No," Jack said. "We should let her catch a nap, in case she has to be up all night with you."

"Okay," he said.

Jack chuckled under his breath. His own experience with his firstborn had definitely lacked this edge of anticipation, it having come upon him so fast. Maybe the nice slow buildup wasn't so great after all. Preacher was going to be a wreck by the time this baby finally made an appearance.

As the afternoon dragged out, and the contractions not any closer together, Jack gave Brie a heads-up when he saw her. "I have a feeling I might need some child-care assistance at the house," he said. "If Paige needs Mel during the night, can you and Mike come out to my place, stay with the kids, so I can stay here with Christopher? When Mel's working at Doc's, I like to be close by."

"Sure. How's Paige doing?"

"Early labor. She's been trying to rest to save her strength, but I think Preacher's driving her crazy," Jack said.

"Aw, he's excited."

"Excited doesn't touch it."

Jack was jotting all this down in a letter for Rick, between serving drinks and meals to his customers. He thought he was turning out a very humorous running commentary on Preacher's nerves, Paige's slow progress and growing annoyance with her husband. The dinner hour came and Preacher, who had never held frequent or long conversations with patrons, told everyone who came in that her pains were down to eight minutes apart.

Mel arrived, carrying Emma and holding David's pudgy little hand as he toddled in the door. He spied Jack and said, "Da!"

When Jack saw her, his eyes grew warm. It hadn't changed for him since the first day she'd walked into his bar. She was so damn beautiful, so sexy, even with a baby on her shoulder and a toddler in hand. And though she was still complaining about her figure since Emma was born, the jeans she was wearing sure didn't look any larger to him—those jeans just set him on fire. He was pretty sure that when she was old and gray, he still wouldn't be able to keep his hands off her.

He walked around the bar and crouched for David. He put out his hands. "Come on, cowboy. Come to Dad."

Mel let go of the hand and watched as Davie literally flew into his father's arms. She laughed at his eagerness, his clumsiness, and her eyes glowed as he fell into his father's arms. "So," she said, "I heard someone's trying to have a baby around here."

"I hope you were able to get a little nap," he said.

"I slept for a couple of hours. It was nice. Can you hang on to him so I can just look in on Paige?" she asked.

"Sure. Take your time."

When Mel got to their quarters, she found Paige pacing back and forth. "How's it going?" she asked.

"I'm trying to walk them down to five minutes," she reported. "But I'm not moving very fast. It was like this with Christopher. A long early labor, all in my back."

"That's the way some women like to do it," Mel said. "Are you uncomfortable?"

"Nah, not really. I can walk and talk through them. If they're no different after dinner, I'm going to bed early and see if I can get a little sleep, but with John asking me every five minutes how I'm doing, that could be hard."

She smiled. "Please, clear soup for dinner. Nothing heavy. Just on the off chance you get sick during delivery. That happens to some women during transition."

"I had John make up some broth and Jell-O."

"Good idea. May the Force be with you." Mel laughed. Sensing it could be a middle-of-the-night event, Mel got her children and herself settled early. At about ten o'clock she roused briefly as she felt her husband slip in beside her. She instinctively turned into his waiting arms, cuddling up against him. He slipped his big hand under the T-shirt she wore and she said, "You have to let me sleep. You know Preacher is going to get me up soon."

"I'll let you sleep," he said, kissing her brow, pulling her close.

"Did you happen to get an update as you were closing the bar?"

"Oh, yeah," he said. "We're still at eight minutes. And Preacher is growing weak from the strain."

She laughed in spite of herself. "God, this is going to be a fun one," she said. "Now snuggle me close and put me to sleep."

The call came at midnight. When she heard the phone ring, she rolled over and moaned. "I knew she was going to do this. Some women just aren't happy unless they labor all night." Jack lifted the phone and passed it to her. "Evening, Paige."

"I'm sorry, Mel," she said. "I'm at five to seven minutes now."

"How do you feel?"

"Pretty good, but they're getting nice and strong, lasting a minute."

"Hmm. It sounds like I might have time to nurse Emma while I wait for Mike and Brie to come."

"Sure," Paige said. "I'll meet you across the street in a half hour. How's that?"

"It's a date. If anything changes, call me. I can always rush and get there in ten minutes."

They were in motion, the midwife and her partner. While she headed for the nursery, Jack called his sister and put fresh linens on the bed so the babysitters could crawl in and sleep. No reason for them to sit up all night. And while no one expected Jack to be up all night, it was his routine to be awake and available when Mel was delivering at Doc's house. About thirty minutes later, they pulled up to the bar. They kissed goodbye and Mel went to Doc's while Jack went into the bar, which was lit up like a church.

Preacher was pacing. "What took you so long?" he asked.

Jack looked at his watch. "We're right on time, Preach."

Paige stood up from the table. "Jack, I'd like you to pour John a shot."

"No, baby. I want to be alert."

"John, you're way beyond alert. And I don't think I can take another minute. Do as I say!"

Jack went behind the bar. "My man, when a woman is having a baby, you do everything she says, and you do it fast." He brought down a bottle. "Just a little something to take the edge off."

"I don't know," Preacher said.

"Preach, you're six-four and weigh at least two-fifty. A shot isn't going to do nearly enough good. Mel should probably have you on Xanax." He tipped the bottle of Preacher's preferred whiskey over a glass. Reluctantly, Preacher picked up the drink and threw it back.

"Okay," he said. "Let's go."

"Christopher all tucked in and asleep?" Jack asked.

"He is. He'll be fine till about seven."

Jack walked around the bar. He leaned down and kissed Paige on the head. "Have a good delivery, honey," he said.

She smiled up at him. "I'll do my best." Then she dropped back into the chair, holding her tummy as a contraction got her. She started out breathing slowly, then as the pain threshold heightened, she began to pant and her face took on that look. She was starting to struggle. Jack smiled, watching. As the contraction eased, her features relaxed and finally, taking a deep breath, she smiled up at him. "They're getting pretty good."

"You're doing great," Jack said, putting out a hand to bring her to her feet.

"Aw, man," Preacher groaned. He walked over to Paige and swept her up in his arms to carry her to Doc's.

"Ah, Preach, don't do that," Jack said. "The minute she gets to Doc's, I bet Mel is going to have her walking. It helps speed up the baby."

"Fine," he said. "Mel will do what Mel will do, I will do what I will do." And out the door he went, carrying his wife to have their baby.

Jack's shoulders shook with laughter. He hoped Mel didn't knock Preacher over the head with a big club before morning.

Paige's labor was not fast, but it was efficient and perfect in many ways. It took until three in the morning to get to six centimeters, but then the action picked up. Mel broke her water and by 5:00 a.m., she was almost fully dilated. She managed the discomfort very well.

Preacher, however, grew paler and weaker with every contraction. Before letting Paige begin to push, Mel brought a chair into the room. "John," she said, "I want you to sit, and if you start to feel the least bit light-headed, put your head between your knees. If you faint, there's nothing I can do for you—I'm busy with Paige."

"I'm not going to faint," he insisted. "I've been waiting forever for this."

"John, you don't have to stay," Paige told him. "I'll be fine."

"I'm staying," he insisted.

For a man like Preacher to see his little wife struggle and have pain was obviously torture. He was much more comfortable in the role of protector. Mel knew immediately that he wasn't going to be much help.

When Paige finally delivered the baby's head at 6:00 a.m., Preacher leaned over his wife, took a look and collapsed into the chair with a groan. He put his head between his knees.

"Okay, Paige, pant. Give me just a second, we have a little cord issue. I'm going to be able to handle it fine. There we go—just pant for me, honey." Mel slipped the cord over the baby's head easily. "Okay, small push now. We're there."

"You sure?" Paige asked.

The baby, not out yet, began to cry. "Hear that? I'm sure. Bring her out, Paige, easy does it." The baby slid neatly into Mel's hands and screamed bloody murder. "Oh boy, she's strong! Listen to those lungs! And big!" She put the baby in her newborn towel, placed her on Paige's belly to dry her off. That done, she clamped and cut the cord. Preacher stood on shaky legs, watched the cutting of the cord and slid weakly into the chair again, groaning. Mel tried not to laugh.

She rewrapped the baby and passed her to Paige. After a little snuggling, she helped Paige settle her baby to the breast, since Preacher wasn't going to be able to do it. "John, I want you to keep your eyes up here, on your wife and baby. All right?"

"Why?" he asked.

"Because I still have delivery work to do, there will be blood, and I don't want you to faint."

"I won't faint," he said.

"You do as I say," Mel told him.

"Here, John," Paige said softly. "Look at your girl. Isn't she beautiful?"

Mel was massaging the uterus when she heard a sound. She looked up over Paige's raised knees and saw a most stunning sight. Big old Preacher was resting his lips against the baby's head and crying his eyes out. Huge tears ran down his cheeks and dropped onto the newborn's head. He slipped a meaty arm under his wife's shoulders, holding her and the baby as one, and sobbed.

Remarkable. Paige just smiled and touched her husband's face with gentle, loving fingers. Mel was moved almost to tears herself by the big man's emotion. He worshipped his wife, his little family, and he was so grateful, he was overwhelmed. It was so gratifying to help bring a child into a union of such devotion. It was what she lived for.

Her work was not done; the placenta had not delivered. A midwife friend who was older than Mel by twenty years had given her a tip years ago that seemed like sheer magic, yet worked. Mel looked at Paige and said, "Paige, time to let go of the placenta, please." Then she got back in her position, massaged a little more and, remarkably, the job was done. She shook her head and chuckled to herself. People who didn't do this all the time would simply never believe it.

Mel finished her work, let the baby suckle awhile to get the uterus contracting and stanch the bleeding. She examined her patient—no stitches necessary—then covered her and took the baby. "Let's clean her up," she said softly. "People will want to see her soon."

Preacher sniffed back his tears, wiped at his face. But when he spoke, his voice was still weak with emotion. "God, Mel—thank you. Thank you so much. You took such good care of her. Of them."

"They did most of the work. Help me, Preach. Help me wash the baby."

She unwrapped the newborn and placed her in Preacher's palms; his large, soft, gentle palms. Mel coaxed him to lower her into the bath and carefully ran a warm cloth over the little body, cleaning her off.

"Look at those big feet," Preacher said. "Look at that tiny little head."

"She's gorgeous." Mel held the towel. "Right here, Preach," she said.

Preacher laid the baby in the clean towel and Mel wrapped her. "Take her out in the hall to show Doc. But please, stay upstairs for now. I'm going to do a little cleanup and you can bring her right back in."

Mel didn't want Preacher in the room when she handled the cleanup of his wife, the changing of bloody sheets. And she didn't want him carrying the baby down the stairs in case he got light-headed again. She worked faster than usual. "How are you feeling?" she whispered to Paige.

"Like I've been up all night."

Mel palpated her uterus. "You're already contracting like mad. That uterus is getting nice and firm." She smiled at her patient. "He'll be okay now, I think."

"Poor John. That was harder on him than me."

"The bigger they are…" Mel laughed.

Her work was done by 7:00 a.m. Preacher was seated at Paige's side, holding his baby daughter. Mel went downstairs and stepped out into the fresh, bright morning. She stood on Doc's porch and heard the sound she loved. *Thwack, thwack, thwack.* Jack was splitting logs behind the bar. She walked across the street.

She leaned on the corner of the building, watching him. Her mind wandered back in time to her first delivery in this town—a one-hundred-percent-successful delivery much like the one she had just assisted. Then, as now, she had crossed the street and watched Jack as he hefted an ax over his head and brought it down. Watched the muscles in his arms and shoulders at work and admired his hard good looks.

When he saw her, he leaned the ax up against the stump

and went to her. She smiled and walked into his arms. He crossed those arms under her bottom and brought her up to his face. "It was perfect," she said.

"I love the way those babies light you up."

She kissed him deeply and his arms tightened under her.

"How are they doing?"

"Preacher's a little wobbly, but Paige and the baby are great."

"He's been looking forward to it for so long," Jack said.

"He might've gotten himself a little too worked up. Maybe he peaked too soon," she said. "Did you sleep?" she asked, touching his hair.

"I don't sleep when you work," he said, touching her lips again. "Can I get you anything? Breakfast?"

"That would be nice. My children will be awake by the time I get home."

"Was it hard, baby?" he asked. "After the hysterectomy?"

She shook her head and smiled. "That wasn't the hard part. There is nothing sad about bringing a new life to a couple as in love as they are." She kissed him again. "I admit, I was thinking of one more, down the road a bit. I tend to think like that after ours are settled in bed and quiet...."

"We have a lot more than either of us thought we'd get," he said.

"I'm dealing with it pretty well. I'm telling myself not to be greedy. As long as I have you—"

He laughed, a rich, deep rumbling sound. "As if you could get rid of me now."

Joe used to look forward to trips to Virgin River—it was such a welcome respite from his demanding work. Usually he was going with a purpose that included his friends—either a gathering of the boys for sport or someone in need of help. In fact, if it hadn't been for certain memories that were hard to shake, this trip would be a celebration. Preacher's baby had arrived, and Joe liked babies—he'd been an uncle five times. He'd always thought that by now he'd have a couple of his own.

The drive seemed longer than usual, but he made it before Saturday noon. He went straight to Jack's bar and once there, his first order of business was to deliver a large bouquet of flowers to Paige. There was no one in the bar and he didn't even glance into the kitchen, but went straight to the apartment. The door was standing open, so he tapped lightly and went in. He found Paige sitting on the couch with the cradle nearby, folding clothes into neat little piles. "Joe!" she said, her face brightening when she saw him. "Oh my, are these for me?"

"Of course they're for you, sweetheart. Aren't you the new mom?" She opened her arms to him and he held her a long moment. "You sure look wonderful for someone who just had a baby."

"I've been very spoiled this week. Lots of help. When you need something, anything, this is the place to be."

"You're feeling good?"

"Fantastic. And she's a good little girl."

He peered into the cradle. "Ah, then where is she?"

"I'll give you three guesses. I can't get John to put her down."

He chuckled. "Is he holding her while he's stirring a pot?" Joe asked.

"Lord, I hope not. He said he was going to see if Christopher would lie down for a little nap and took Dana upstairs with him. The one who could use a nap is John. He must surely be exhausted."

Joe laughed. "Here, honey—sit down. Tell me about it. Did you have an easy time?"

"I had a very long time. It wasn't so much hard as it took forever. I was starting to think she'd never come. And John almost drove me out of my mind. After about twenty hours of labor, I was afraid he was going to go in after her."

"He must have been pretty wound up," Joe said. "Is he pestering you for another one yet?"

"Oh no, I think he's going to lighten up on all those children he thought he had to have. The birth was kind of hard on John."

"Really?" Joe said, surprised.

"Yeah, he doesn't like to see me uncomfortable. And it turns out that this big man who can shoot and dress animals or carry wounded soldiers off the battlefield doesn't do too well if there's a drop of blood within ten feet of his wife."

"He's a little on the protective side," Joe confirmed. "Think you're going to be able to move out to the cabin soon? As soon as you do—we pour the extended-foundation slab and start tearing out walls."

"Oh—I'm ready," she said. "I can't wait to get going on this building. We're just going to move clothes and toys and the computer. Paul will cover everything, right?"

"It will all be protected—either in storage or pushed up against a safe wall and secured, but you'll be able to get to it."

A few minutes later, Preacher wandered in. He was holding the baby in the crook of his arm and she looked small enough to fit in the palm of his hand. Her little pink blanket was wrapped neatly around her, her bald head sticking out of the top, and he handled her as if she were attached to the inside of his forearm. "Joe!" he said, but he said it with quiet enthusiasm. "Great to see you, man."

Joe stood and reached for the baby. "My turn, buddy. Let's see what you made here."

Preacher handed over the baby and Joe brought her into his arms. "God, she's beautiful. I think you lucked out, Paige. I think she's going to look like you."

"John's been worried that she'll be six-four and three hundred pounds. I tried to explain that would take a lot more testosterone than she'll have."

"I want her to be sweet and beautiful like her mom," Preacher said.

"How much did she weigh?"

"Eight-ten. Nice and big."

"She looks like a five-pounder in your husband's arms," Joe said. "You two do good work."

"My man, it was the hardest work I've ever done," Preacher said.

"Um, John," Paige said.

"I didn't mean you didn't work hard, baby, you know that. But I damn near worried myself into the ground. Mel almost had to give me something."

"Was it everything you thought it would be?" Joe asked.

"It was way more than I thought it would be. I cried like a baby."

These two, Joe thought. He wondered if they had any idea how cute they were. "We have to call Paul, tell him I'm here. And Brie and Mike. I think we have the plans final and I'd like to get out to the properties today so I can leave early tomorrow."

"You have to take off so soon?" Paige asked.

"I'm afraid so," he said. "I could have had the plans delivered, but I didn't want to miss a chance to see the baby. And if Paul's building schedule goes as planned, you'll be in your new apartment in no time at all. You shouldn't have to spend even six months in Jack's cabin, which puts you back home before Christmas. Plus, if Preach can cook during the day in spite of the noise, the crews should be able to leave the property by dinnertime. I don't think the bar will have to be closed much at all."

"I can't wait," Paige said.

Phone calls were made and everyone convened in the bar to look at house plans. When everyone seemed in agreement about their plans, Joe and Paul went out to the general's house so that Vanessa could comb over her plans, which took a couple of hours.

"Okay, let's walk your property first," Joe said to Paul. "Then you're good to go. We'll get the Valenzuelas on the way back to town. You have concrete ready?"

"Coming this week. Will you come back for dinner?" he asked Joe.

"I'll take a rain check," Joe said. "I want to visit with Jack and Mel a little bit tonight, so I'll take dinner at the bar. Then I'm on the road early tomorrow morning."

"Aw, I was hoping to get a little more time with you," Vanni said.

"Next time, okay? It's a quick trip for me."

"Joe," she said, laying a hand on his arm. "I can't help but feel we've had a big misunderstanding. And it's affected our friendship. Five minutes before Paul asked me to marry him, he told me I have the worst goddamn temper…and that I'm really hard to shut up. I think I might've overreacted."

He chuckled in spite of himself. "The misunderstanding must have been between the woman and I." He shrugged. "I still can't figure out what went wrong. Our friendship is okay, Vanni. Be patient with me. This will pass."

"I hope so, Joe. I'm sorry you were hurt. I'm sorry I jumped to conclusions."

"Hey," he said, laughing it off. "What could you do? It's not like I'm going to help you out with the details. Whatever she says is her business, but I've already said more than I like. I don't want to betray her privacy."

By five, Joe had left the drawings in Paul's very capable hands and was headed back to Jack's, where he found Mel and the kids waiting for him. Before long everyone but Vanni and Paul had gathered. There was a humorous debrief on Paige's delivery that had them all laughing while they enjoyed Preacher's broiled trout with rice.

Not long after Mel and the kids left, a group of Hot Shots, USDA federal firefighters, came in—a hand crew of about ten of the usual eighteen—getting everyone's attention. Most of the firefighters used locally were inmates, felons, but since these guys were not, Jack and Preacher pushed tables together and set them up with beer as well as dinner in exchange for news. There had been a fire back in the Trinity Alps and these boys had been working it for two days. It looked to be contained and they were released to go home and wouldn't be recalled. They were starved for decent food and a cold beer.

"I can't believe I wasn't even aware of it," Jack said. "I can see for miles from my front yard."

"Winds have been from the southwest, it's up the mountain and we've had it curtailed to a slow, dense burn for twenty-four hours. I think we've got it now. We can't be recalled for at least twenty-four hours, so we're probably done with that fire. We'll be headed to the Mogollon Rim in Arizona, if it's still hot in two days."

"Where exactly was this last one?" Jack asked.

"Only about twenty-five miles back there. Just over the mountain."

Twenty-five miles was uncomfortably close; Jack and Preacher had a lot of questions for them about the winds, the weather forecasts, any controlled burns in the area. "There aren't any controlled burns near the redwoods right now," one of them said.

Jack set them up one more time, given they were on the way home and wouldn't be going back into the forest. Of course he wouldn't take a dime from them. "You keep our towns safe—you eat and drink on the house anytime you've been working a fire. It's the least we can do. As long as you have a designated driver..."

They all laughed, a couple of them slapping one comrade on the back. "We always try to keep at least one Mormon on the crew—the designated good influence."

As the hour grew later, Jack kept the bar open a little while longer so the firefighters could unwind. Joe sat up at the bar facing Jack. "You can pour me one good-night pop, then I'm getting out of your hair."

"Sure you're okay at that cabin?" Jack asked, pouring him a shot. "There's room at the house."

"Oh, Jack—it's terrific. I'll have the sheets washed and back on the bed in the morning before I leave. Then we'll get Preacher's family in there and start tearing up his apartment."

"It's really not necessary to do laundry. There are a lot of women around town who like a little housekeeping work...."

"Nah, I'll handle it. I appreciate the hospitality."

"And that other matter?"

"What other matter?"

"The woman. The one who has you all fucked up."

He laughed. "No change," he said. "I'm still fucked up. But I'll get over it. I have experience getting over women. I had a wife I loved once—she ripped me up good."

"I'm sorry, Joe. There's practically no one I'd rather see happy..."

"You know, that's one of the problems with this place," Joe said. "You guys. When you opened this bar, there were five of us at loose ends, and not looking to settle down. The only ones settled with women were Zeke, Corny, Phillips and Stephens. The rest of us were getting well into our thirties, pretty damn happy to be single. Plenty of women out there to keep us busy for a little while. Then you guys— Jesus. You not only hooked up, you found these in-credible…"

Jack poured himself a shot to join his friend in com-miseration. "We got lucky," he said.

"It goes way past luck," Joe said. "Some god was smiling on you." He looked into his glass. "I'm just an idiot. I had my arms around this woman for one long, in-credible night and I thought—this is what I've been waiting for my whole life. And she slipped away from me that fast," he said, snapping his fingers. "I woke up alone." He lifted his drink to his lips.

Chairs scraped back as the Hot Shots got up to leave. They all hollered their thanks, a couple of them coming forward to shake Jack's hand, then filed out the door.

Alone in the bar, Preacher in the back with his family, Jack said, "How about going after her?"

"I tried. She's gone."

Jack leaned on the bar. "I'm sorry, man. I thought that was going to happen to me with Mel. From the second she hit town, she said she was leaving."

"When did you know? Or think you knew? With Mel?"

"Oh, man," he said, and laughed. "It was real slow. Took me five or ten minutes. It was the jeans. Have you ever noticed how my wife looks in a pair of jeans? Maybe you shouldn't answer that…"

"With me it was a pink dress…"

Jack's eyes widened. "Whoa, damn."

"You shouldn't give me alcohol," he said. "Makes me talk."

"Nikki," he said, and it wasn't a question. "Yeah, buddy. I saw her. And I think I saw you see her." He shook his head. "I feel your pain."

"Vanni was furious with me. Paul was sympathetic but pissed. Well," he amended, "they're getting over that now. But the girl won't talk to me. Won't return calls. I can't figure out what I did. I was as good to her as I knew how to be."

"Whew, that bites," Jack said. "But, buddy, that doesn't mean there isn't someone out there, just waiting for you to find her. I was forty, man. I thought I was way past having this life. Mel—she makes me feel like a teenager."

"Yeah, maybe it'll happen. But not while I'm like this. I'm stung. I have to get over this before I can dip into the market again. You know?"

"Hang in there, pal. It's going to be okay."

"Yeah," he said. He threw back the rest of his shot and stood. "You should get home to the family. I'm going to borrow your porch for a cigar, since you have the sand can out there, then to the cabin to get some sleep."

"Sure. I'll lock you out and take off from the back. There's coffee in the fridge, but that's it. Want a beer or bottle to take to the cabin?"

"Nah, I'm good. I'm good and tired," he said. "And I'm planning to get out of here early."

"You bet. And, brother? Don't lick this wound too long, huh?"

He shook Jack's hand. "I'll be fine."

Joe stepped out onto Jack's porch and looked up at the sky. He heard the door lock behind him; the Open sign clicked off. The stars were fewer, dimmer, and he hoped it wasn't smoke in the sky. He pulled out his cigar from his shirt pocket, clipped the end and struck a match on his shoe. It flared.

And illuminated her.

She was wearing tight jeans and high-heeled sandals, a little blue knit shirt, a gold necklace. She leaned against the porch post in the corner, legs crossed, arms crossed, that shiny black hair resting on her shoulders. He took a step toward her, bewildered, and the match burned down to singe his fingers.

"Ah!" he said, shaking it out. He put his boot over it, crushing it for sure. Then he lit another match and took another step toward her.

There wasn't much light besides the match, but he could clearly see the tracks of tears down her cheeks, her large dark eyes shining in the glow of the match. He shook it out. He put the cigar back in his pocket. "This is about where we started," he said, not getting too close.

"I know. Do you hate me?"

"Of course not," he said, but he kept a safe distance.

"I was embarrassed," she said. "And scared."

"Embarrassed?" he repeated. "Scared?"

She gave a deep sigh. "I couldn't imagine what you thought of me. I jumped into bed with you so fast…"

"You could have asked me. I jumped into bed with you pretty fast, too."

"Men can get away with that."

"I didn't," he said. "My punishment was pretty brutal."

"Yeah," she said softly. "I guess it was. I'm sorry about that."

"Okay," he said. "Scared?"

"Oh, Joe… I was so damn scared. I thought about morning coming and you giving me a whack on the butt and saying, 'Thanks, baby.'"

"What did I say or do to make you think it could be like that?" he asked her.

"It wasn't you, Joe. It was me. I guess I just wasn't ready to move on yet."

"Did panic come with the morning?" he asked.

"Yeah. It was a nice night. A night like I'd like to have again, and I thought about what it would feel like to look forward to it and be—" She lifted her chin and sniffed. "Not in the cards."

He laughed without humor. "So you ended it to keep me from ending it? Jesus, Nikki, all I wanted to do was make you feel like you were headed for something good. What the hell happened between us to make you think that way?"

"It was just my past," she said, shaking her head. "You were wonderful to me."

"And so—you never want to hear from me again?" he asked, totally stumped. "You didn't want to even see if there was something more there? Scared of that, too?"

"I was afraid to go any further. We don't even know each other! I want something permanent, I want a family."

"Weren't you listening? I don't have any idea if that's going to happen with us, you and me—we're too new. But wasn't I clear? I'm not avoiding that."

"Joe, I think I might be clueless when it comes to love. Afraid I wouldn't know real love if it bit me in the ass."

He chuckled in spite of himself. "Been there," he said. "Pretty recently, in fact."

"I thought I was probably mistaken. At the time it seemed to me you were showing me something good. Sincere. Loving. But it could have just been… You know. Sex."

"No complaints about the sex, then," he said.

"It was so much more than that. For me, it was so much more than that."

It was a huge relief to hear her say that, he actually let out a slow breath. He reached out a hand and wiped a tear from her cheek. "And you didn't think it could've been more than that for me, too?"

"I just didn't know."

"But you came back here?"

"Well, Paul called me."

"Paul?" he asked, astonished.

"Yeah. I think I've been played."

"How's that?"

"He called to tell me not to worry about you—that although you admitted you had it real bad for me, you were working at getting over me and I'd probably be free of you in no time. He said you wouldn't bother a woman who didn't want to be bothered."

"He did that? Why'd he do that?"

"To make me think about what I might be giving up, maybe." She wiped the other cheek. "So. You're over me?"

"Not quite," he said. "I'm still working on it." He looked down for a second, thinking. "What did you come back for?" he asked her. "To clear the air? Get it over with? More sex? After which you'll take off before I'm awake?"

"Then Vanni called me. She told me she'd been thinking about things, and decided I must be out of my mind. She told me a lot of the same things you'd already told me—about coming together to help your friends, about being there for Paul while he buried Matt. She knew that if she ever needed your help for any reason, you'd be there for her. And I thought, what the hell's the matter with me? I've always wanted to be with someone who thinks like that, acts like that." She looked up at him with those wide, damp eyes. "She told me you'd be here—bringing Paul the plans. Should I have stayed away? Would that have been for the best?"

"I don't know, Nikki," he said, shaking his head. "I'm not going to kid you—the way you ran out on me… That was awful. Then I wrote you that it broke me apart and you still wouldn't respond. What am I going to think, huh? You're not the only one who doesn't feel like getting hurt again."

"You wouldn't know it by the way I acted with you, but I'm inexperienced. I've never done that before. It turns out I'm lousy at one-night stands. All paranoid and spooked."

"Yeah? Me, too," he said. "I never thought of it as a one-night stand. Not even that one night. I was destroyed to find you gone. More destroyed to hear it made you cry. I couldn't believe anything happened to make you cry. I'm still having trouble with that."

"Look, here's what happened to me. He said he loved me. We lived together for years. I kept saying to him, I need a commitment, I want a family. And he kept saying, I might need a little more time on that. And then he finally told me—he had a vasectomy behind my back a couple of years ago because he was afraid I'd get ahead of him, stop taking my pills and sneak a baby out of him. That's when I knew—there was no love, no trust. He was a liar and he was just using me. It was a horrible thing to face up to."

"Jesus," Joe breathed, almost speechless.

"I thought he loved me and was trying to come to terms with the whole forever thing," she said. "He'd been through a rocky divorce about ten years back. It made sense to me that he'd be nervous. I didn't know he was lying."

"Nikki, I'm sorry. That was bad, what he did. He should've been honest."

"Yeah. And then there was you. In five minutes I knew you were more honest and straightforward than he was, but I doubted the signals. I wanted to fall for you—but I don't know you."

He reached a hand toward her shining black hair. So soft. "By morning, there wasn't an inch of me you didn't know."

"You have a big mole on your butt," she said. "You should probably get that looked at. And a scar on your shoulder. And I think you had your appendix out."

He smiled at her. So, she had been paying attention. He wasn't the only one, then. "I was twelve."

"What happened here," she said, reaching out to his shoulder.

"I got shot in Fallujah. Mike Valenzuela kept us all alive till Jack could get us out of there. Six of us were bleeding all over the place, there were snipers everywhere, but we got out. Paul gave up a spleen. It was ugly. It ended the Marines for me—I'm out of the reserves now. Paul too." He smiled. "See? You know things about me."

"Not enough," she said softly.

Joe leaned toward her and kissed the path of a tear on her right cheek. He threaded a hand around the back of her neck and kissed her temple. "Here," she whispered. Her finger was touching her lips. "There's a tear."

He leaned his lips toward hers and barely touching them, ran his tongue over her upper lip. "No, there's not," he said. "I think you're done crying now." He put his hands around her tiny waist and pulled her onto his mouth, kissing her deeply and tenderly. She answered him with desire, hot and strong, opening her lips under his. He thought he might feel tears in his own eyes, she felt so wonderful in his arms, tasted so magnificent on his lips. He wondered if this was just another of his fantasies; he further wondered if it was real, if it would disappear once again before he could grab on to it. Feeling her body against his, her tongue in his mouth, her hands running up and down his back, he hoped beyond hope that she was real and he wouldn't wake up and find she'd just been another dream.

"I thought you were gone forever," he said against her lips.

"I wish I hadn't gone. I wish I'd stayed...."

He covered her mouth in a deep, desperate kiss that lasted forever, holding her so close he was afraid he'd crush her. He wanted to say things to her, but that would mean releasing her lips, and he couldn't bring himself to do it. All those weeks, all those long nights of wishing he could have made things different for them. All that regret, thinking that if he hadn't moved so fast, he could have brought them together differently, with more success. He should have taken his time, courted her, wooed her. He was a fool, not getting her phone number and last name before he got her body. He should have brought her slowly and confidently into his heart, erasing her doubts. And yet he couldn't imagine how it could have been different—they'd both been so steamed up. So ready.

He was ready again.

"Nikki," he whispered, "you're doing it to me again." He covered her mouth and kissed her, deep and long. He touched her breast. "God," he whispered.

"Take me somewhere," she said.

"No," he whispered. "Not until you understand a few things."

"Hurry then. Tell me what I have to understand."

"I'm not interested in one night. I want it all. If that's too much for you, tell me right now. If it's going to scare you off, I want to know."

"All?"

"I want to go to bed with you, and wake up with you." He kissed her. "Then I want to do that again." He kissed her. "And again. And again."

"Okay," she said breathlessly.

"I'm an idiot, but I'm in love with you."

"How do you know?"

"Because I've never felt this bad before."

"Isn't it supposed to feel good?"

"It does, when you're in my arms. When you're not, it's just awful."

"Okay," she said. "I understand."

"You're going to give it a chance?"

"Yes," she said, nodding.

"I realize that sometimes things don't work out the way we want them to. I've been down that road and so have you. But I'm not going to string you along. I'll never lie to you. Do you believe me?"

"I do. Do you believe me?"

"You're not going to run out on me again, without any explanation?"

"I won't do that again, no."

"You can do anything else, you know. You can tell me you were mistaken. Tell me you changed your mind and you don't feel it anymore. Anything but disappearing without a word. If it's over for you, you have to finish it. Do we have a deal?"

"Deal," she said against his lips.

"Where do Vanni and Paul think you are?" he asked her in a hoarse whisper.

"With you," she said.

"And are you?"

"Yes. Yes, Joe. I'm with you."

He lifted her off her feet, kissing her. "If you want me to make love to you, I will. But only if you want me to. And only if you think it can be the beginning of something, not the end."

She locked her hands behind his neck and smiled.

"You're something, you know that? You're not a regular guy. Usually this is about the time the guy says something like, don't try to pin me down, baby. Guys don't usually start right off saying they want a chance at something that lasts."

"Yeah?" He grinned. Then he shrugged, thinking about his boys, his friends. There was a time almost all of them were that other guy—the kind who's dodging commitment. Now look at them. "You over that idiot who let you go?"

"I'm so over him, I could laugh."

"Good." He chuckled. "Let's go someplace we can wake up together."

It amazed Joe he could sleep at all, but he did. Holding Nikki in his arms through the night, feeling her sweet, warm body against his, he was at peace. When he woke beside her, it was as though the future had been decided for him. He was dead in love with her, amazed at the way he had only to touch her, kiss her, and she would unfold, wanting him as much as he wanted her. Now it was only a question of what she would decide about them. But he trusted their pact—they would be honest with each other. No more running away.

Joe slipped out of bed in the predawn, the sun barely rising. He thought he'd start the coffee, make love to her again while it brewed, and they could watch the sunrise together. They could talk about when they'd see each other next. He started the coffee. He stared at the coffeepot while it began to brew. The smell of the pot was suspect—he wondered if it was old. Then he lifted his head. He looked at the clock on the microwave. Nine-thirty. He sniffed the air. Oh shit. He unplugged the coffeepot and ran out onto the porch, naked. He thought it was predawn because the sun streaming through the windows was so dim—but it was smoke in the air. "Nikki," he yelled, running back into the cabin. "Nikki! Wake up! Fire!"

Eighteen

The town had become a base camp for firefighters and the acrid odor of smoke hung in the air. When Joe pulled into town, he had to park back beyond the church. He held on to Nikki's hand and ran with her to the center of town. There were many Cal Fire trucks, Hot Shot transports, Cal Fire firefighters and dozens of firefighters who Joe knew at a glance would be inmates trained in firefighting. There were flatbeds loaded with gear, water tenders and trucks for hauling firefighters, paramedic rigs, dozens of men in hard hats and yellow turnouts, boots, packs of gear on their backs, and a tent pitched in the middle of the street, beside it an ambulance. The street was wide enough for a helicopter to land for medical airlift.

On the porch, among many men Joe had never seen before, were his friends. Jack was pulling on yellow turnouts, slipping the suspenders over his shoulders.

"Joe," he said. "I wasn't sure you were still here. I knew you intended to leave for Oregon at the crack of dawn." He glanced at Nikki and couldn't suppress a quick grin. He gave her a nod.

"Still here. What's happening?"

"Wind shifted. It's headed this way."

"What are we doing?"

Zeke stepped forward and handed him some gear, which he took. "We're getting in it, bud."

"What are you doing here?"

"I've been watching it from Fresno. Just after midnight it looked like it could threaten my favorite hunting grounds, so I fired up the truck and started driving."

Stephens walked out of the bar, already dressed out, a big doughnut in his hand. "Not before he got everyone out of bed," he said.

Joe immediately started getting into his gear. He pulled the suspenders over his shoulders. Zeke and Josh were professional firefighters and paramedics, the rest of them trained volunteers—Cal Fire could use them. It would be a lot of fetching and carrying, digging, removing vegetation, but every hand helped.

"What are you doing?" Nikki asked Joe.

"I'll do what I can to help. You want to go home? Go out to Vanni's?"

Before she could answer, Mel stepped onto the porch. She was wearing a white doctor's coat, something Joe had never seen her do before. There was a stethoscope around her neck. "What's this?" he asked her, lifting his chin toward her as he pulled heavy gloves out of the pockets.

"We're helping in the first-aid station set up here. Since these guys don't know us—me and Doc—we have to be identifiable by uniform."

"Where are the kids?" he asked.

"Little ones are having morning naps in the back," Jack said. "I think Christopher is standing watch. Paige is in charge of the kids while Mel works medical and Brie attempts to keep the food and water coming."

"I'll help her," Nikki said. She put a quick kiss on Joe's

cheek and whispered in his ear, "I love you, too. Please be careful." Then she headed quickly into the bar while he followed her with his eyes, a stupid grin on his face.

"There's help from Cal Fire if Brie and Nikki can't keep up with it," Jack said. "If necessary, they'll evacuate the town. We're hoping that won't be necessary."

Before long, Preacher was on the porch, already dressed in his gear. Paige was beside him, holding their new baby. He bent down, kissed his wife and daughter, and headed down the porch toward the waiting truck. Jack walked after him, snagging his arm. "Maybe you should stay, Preach. In case these women and children have to be taken out of here."

"There are people to help them out of here. I don't let you go in anywhere alone."

"I'm a big boy," Jack said.

Preacher straightened and glowered. "Me, too."

Mel walked off the porch and toward the truck that would carry the volunteers away. She watched as the marines climbed on—Zeke, Phillips, Stephens. Mike, Paul, Preacher, Joe and Jack followed them. A truck came flying into town, horn honking. Corny, also a professional firefighter, climbed out and yelled, "Hey! Forget anyone?"

Greetings ripped the air. "What about that new baby?"

"Aw, she's not so new anymore. We had her two days ago."

"And your wife let you out of town?"

"You're kidding, right? She *told* me to get my ass down here and help." He grinned, pulling his own gear out of the truck bed. "She's got her mother—I'm just in the way now. I have years with those kids."

"Another girl, huh?" Jack said.

"Yeah, but I know I have a boy in me. I just know it."

"You better keep that to yourself for a while, pal," someone advised.

There were also locals—Doug Carpenter, Fish Bristol, Buck Anderson and two of his sons. All certified volunteer firefighters.

Everyone but Jack was in the truck. He went to his wife, leaned down and kissed her lips. "When they tell you it's time, gather up the kids and get out of town."

"It's not going to come to that, Jack. It can't. I don't know if I can leave this place...."

"You do it. Keep them safe. And have someone get Ricky's grandma out."

"I'll watch out for Lydie, but I'm waiting for you," she said. "I'm waiting right here. I'll be here when you're done and Virgin River will be fine."

"Melinda, don't you dare take any chances."

"Don't *you*," she said. "You come back as soon as you can."

He smiled at her. "You know you can't get rid of me." He slipped an arm around her waist and pulled her up to his mouth. "You taste too good." He grinned. "Behave yourself."

Jack climbed into the truck and sat next to Joe. "Looks like maybe you got some things straightened out," Jack said.

"Might have a start on it. How'd you round up all these old boys?"

"Five of us were already here," Jack said. "I just can't believe these other guys. They must never have to work."

"The few. The proud," Phillips said. "The soon-to-be jobless if we don't knock this shit off."

It took a half hour to get to their area, the fire spreading toward them. Here there were steam shovels, trucks and water tenders parked along the road. All the firefighters, including the volunteers, had their gear on their backs—food, water, survival gear. They were assigned jobs—chain saws for cutting down trees or removing branches, Pulaskis and drag-spoons. They were herded up an old abandoned logging road with the rest of the hand crew. The farther they went, the thicker the air got, the more sparks were flying. They were organized into a line, some of them felling huge trees while hand crews were cutting boughs off felled pines to decrease the fuel to the fire. Still others were digging a wider gap to separate the tree line from the burning forest, digging out vegetation, throwing dirt on small pockets of spreading fire. Water tenders were driving farther back to spray down the small fires started by blowing sparks and embers. Jack walked all the way up to the end of the line and started turning earth. "I'm getting too old for this shit," he said, throwing dirt to cover the felled trees and chopped boughs.

"We all are, man," Paul said. He looked up. "You think we could get one frickin' cloud in the sky?"

"Go ahead and pray," Jack suggested.

The general drove up to the bar and walked inside. The first thing he saw was Brie, her baby niece swaddled in a carrier around her front, setting up pitchers of water on the bar for firefighters. He heard the sound of a baby crying in the back, in Preacher's quarters. He went behind the bar and dived right in. "I have an idea," he said. "Why don't you and Paige take the kids out to the ranch. It's surrounded by flat land and river—no danger there. I'll handle the bar."

"Mel can't leave and I have her nursing baby right here," Brie said. "She's been treating minor injuries with paramedics and has to be on hand for more."

"The air here isn't the best for these kids. I have someone I can call to help. You should get the little ones out of here."

"Well… Let me ask her."

Brie took the general's suggestion to Mel and she thought about it for less than a minute, then nodded. "The kids will be safer there. Can you, Paige and Nikki load them up?"

"Sure. But I hate to take them away from you."

"They should go, he's right. You can set up a nursery there, with Vanni. We'll be fine here with Walt's help."

Mel watched from the first-aid station while the women carried the children to Preacher's and Jack's trucks with Walt's help, moving car seats around and tucking them in. Into the back went a playpen, port-a-crib, infant seats and baby swing, diaper bags and paraphernalia. Little Davie and Emma, Christopher and Dana Marie. Then they pulled slowly out of town.

Mel hoped it would occur to Paige or Vanni to nurse little Emma; Emma needed the breast. She was young and vulnerable and Mel wouldn't hesitate to nurse a friend's baby at a time like this. Mel felt a tear run down her cheek as they went. She wiped at it impatiently. This was an emergency; they'd have to make do. Vanni, Brie, Nikki and Paige would keep the babies and Christopher all safe. That was the most important thing.

Then Jack will be home and we'll go get them, she told herself.

The morning flew by with trucks full of firefighters passing through, stopping for first aid or food and water. They'd be driven out and another crew would pass through. Sometimes the firefighters were new and wearing clean gear, sometimes they were dirty, exhausted, parched and hungry men. Most of them were inmates, felons trained in firefighting with plenty of law enforcement on hand, backing up Cal Fire. Mel had often wondered how many of them tried to run away while on this duty. But then, this program would likely come to an end if many did.

She took a break to walk into the bar. To her surprise,

behind the bar she found the general and Muriel. The woman gave her a bright smile.

"Hey, girl," Walt said. "What can I get you?"

"Ice water, thanks, if you still have ice. I'm so dry. I think it's the smoke in the air. It's not exactly thick, but it works on the nose and throat."

"How are you, Mel?" Muriel asked.

"A little tense today. Thanks for coming to help."

"It's nothing," she said with a shrug. "I'm glad to. You have quite the circus out there."

Mel gratefully drank down half her water. "We do, at that," she said.

"I'm going back to the kitchen. I've been making sandwiches, the only cooking I'm capable of. I just about have a big tray ready to bring out. Cal Fire has rations, but they're running low and we can pitch in. How about if we set up on the porch, along with water?"

"Perfect," Mel said. "Hang on to the bottled water till the well runs low—we might need it later. I'm going to call the ranch, see how the kids are doing."

She went to the phone. While Vanni assured her everyone was fine, she could hear Emma crying in the background. Amazing, she thought, how you knew your baby's cry. It almost made *her* cry. Worse than that, it made her milk let down and she had to make a dash for the bathroom, open her shirt and lean over the sink. Women's bodies, she found herself thinking. It was a miracle, the way they worked. *Come back, Jack,* she thought. *We have to get back to our children!*

"Mel," Muriel was calling, tapping at the door. "Are you all right?"

"Fine," she answered. "I'll be right out." When she opened the door, she found the older woman standing there, waiting, a concerned frown on her face.

"I saw you run for the bathroom, and I thought maybe you were sick. All this smoke in the air…"

Mel chuckled. "I called Walt's house to check on the kids and heard Emma crying. It's been too long since I nursed her. In seconds, I was dripping," she said, pulling aside the white coat to show a large round wet spot on her breast. "I hope they get this fire under control before I explode."

Muriel smiled. "I didn't have children. And I guess you need to get back to yours."

"I'm sure it won't be much longer. Really, this has to be resolved soon. Don't you think?" Mel asked.

"I don't know, Mel," she said, shaking her head. "There's a lot of wood out there. It's scary."

"Yeah," Mel said weakly. "Yeah it sure is."

Walt was making sandwiches with Muriel. "You know, I've been hanging around your place, riding with you, throwing the stick for your dogs, and I never asked you about the husbands. Like, how many? And why you think it didn't work out?"

"What makes you think I feel like telling you?" she asked.

"Aw, you'll tell me," he said. "You're just that kinda gal. And I told you about my wife."

"Okay," she said, still slapping sandwiches together. "The synopsis. The first one was fifteen years older than me, my agent. He's still my agent—he married the talent, not the person I was. He was very ambitious for me, for us both. He still thinks I divorced him because of his age, but I divorced him because all he cared about was my career. I don't think he could tell you my favorite color…"

"Yellow," Walt said.

Her head snapped around and she stared at him. "Yellow," she said.

"That was easy," he said. "It's all around and you wear it a lot. Red's important, too."

"Right," she said, shocked. She shook herself. "Okay, number two hit, number three cheated, number four had a child he failed to mention, number five—"

"All right, wait," Walt said. "Is this going to go on for a real long time?"

She grinned at him. "Didn't you look it up on the Internet?"

"I did not," he said, almost insulted.

"We're stopping at five. He had a substance-abuse problem. I didn't know about it beforehand, obviously. I tried to help, but I was in the way—he needed to be on his own. That's when I decided that, really, I should quit doing that. Marrying. But please understand, it's not all my fault—Hollywood doesn't exactly have a reputation for long, sturdy relationships. I did the best I could."

"I have no doubt," he said.

"Do you say that because you have no doubt? Or are you being a sarcastic ass to a poor woman who had to go through five miserable husbands?"

He chuckled. Then he slipped an arm around her waist and kissed her cheek. It was the first time he'd been that bold. He'd been riding with her, showing up at her house to drink wine while they sat on lawn chairs in front of the bunkhouse, even talking to her almost daily on the phone, but he hadn't gotten physical. "The Army was rough on families, too. I was lucky."

"Hmm," she said. "Maybe you're just better at it than me."

"I suppose that's possible, too," he said. Then he smiled at her.

The men fighting the fire grew dry and tired. They'd worked their way into the forest along a line that had grown wide and deep. Jack leaned against his shovel as Mike Valenzuela passed by with a chain saw, headed up the line to cut boughs from more felled trees. He paused for a drink and took a few deep breaths before bending to his job of turning earth, tossing dirt onto a growing pile that formed a small dike against the forest. Mike moved down the line of men, out of sight. Jack wiped his forehead and put the shovel back to the ground.

Then something subtle happened. The slight breeze that Jack had been feeling on the back of his neck changed to a hot wind that hit him full in the face. Frowning, he began to walk up the line and around the curve in the direction Valenzuela had gone, looking for the source of that sudden heat. As the logging road went deeper into the trees, the volunteers thinned out and the professionals were the ones moving closer to the fire.

A murmur went up among the men and sparks filled the air. The line of men that had been winding around the hill to his left began to move toward him, then past him. Jack didn't see Mike anywhere, so he walked a little farther. He quickly saw that there was no one back there. Behind him, from where he had been, he heard, "Move out, move out, move out!"

Firefighters who had been behind him were beginning to jog down the road. He heard a roar, sparks filling the air. The fire that they'd been chasing was coming toward them, hard and fast. In front of him was dense smoke, behind him—the logging road from whence he'd come, and to his left, a deep ravine. He turned to move out down the road when there was a blast—an ignited tree that had been burning exploded about ten feet into the forest and sent a shower of sparks and debris over the road in a huge flash. A two-hundred-foot sequoia was on fire not five feet away from where he stood. He took a dive in the direction of the ravine and began to crawl madly toward it as a burning tree came down and flames shot over his head.

At the command to move out, the firefighters and volunteers were being quickly herded back down the hill to the road, where trucks were waiting to evacuate them. Paul was craning his neck, looking for Jack. He'd seen him move into the trees, but he wasn't back yet. Then sparks began to fly and a roaring sound could be heard. Mike Valenzuela jumped up on the truck beside some of his boys. "Where's Jack?" Paul asked him.

"Haven't seen him." He looked around. "One of the other trucks?"

Paul jumped out of the truck and started back up the road, but he was grabbed by the crew chief and pushed toward the truck.

"One of our boys is in there," he said.

"There's no one in there," the chief said. "Everyone was cleared out."

"I saw him go in that direction!"

"There's no one back there, buddy."

"I saw him!"

"If there's anyone there, they'll get him," he said, pointing to a long line of firefighters making fast tracks out of the burning forest. Right at the back of their column was an explosion, sending debris and sparks flying over their heads. Paul found himself shoved into the truck, landing in a heap, while their captain yelled, "Let's go! Move out!" And the truck jerked into motion.

Paul sat up in the bed of the truck and watched as all these yellow-clad, hard-hatted men scrambled into the next truck, and then a third, and as each one filled up, they drove pell-mell down the logging road to the asphalt. He had to be in one of those other trucks, Paul thought. He had to be.

Two planes flew in low, dumping retardant on the fire, a bright red powder. Flames leaped toward the aircraft as they disappeared over the forest.

When they got to the safety zone, the marines began looking for Jack, going to every truck, but he was nowhere. Paul told the captain what he'd seen, that Jack might still be back there.

"Buddy, if he didn't get out with that last crew, he might not've gotten out."

Panicked, Paul said to Joe, "We have to find him, man."

"Where are we going to look, huh? It's coming this way."

"He's got to be around here somewhere." Paul grabbed the firefighter's arm. "Was there any other way out?"

He just shook his head. "I'm sorry, buddy."

"There has to be another way out. He wouldn't do that—he wouldn't go in there if it was too hot. He's too smart for that!"

"Pal, the wind shifted and ate up acres in minutes. We're just going to have to wait it out, see if he turns up. He's not the only one unaccounted for. Search and Rescue is on it."

"Aw, *fuck,*" Paul said. He got tears in his eyes. "That wouldn't happen." He looked at Joe. "After all we've gotten through? That wouldn't happen, would it?"

"Nah. Couldn't."

The firefighters and volunteers moved down the line to a new location, but now that the fire was moving in another direction, away from Virgin River, other crews to the northwest were taking over. A few hours later, the sun setting, the chief was ready to pull his camp out of Virgin River, relocate the base camp and send the Virgin River volunteers home.

"Can't leave," Preacher said. "Not till we figure out where he is."

"No one came out the other side, Preach. And he's not here. I think maybe—"

"No," Preacher said. "No. He made it out, we just can't find him. We'll just keep looking. We'll go back to where we saw him last, as close as we can safely get, set up a perimeter, look for a trail. We keep looking. That clear?"

It was quiet for a moment until someone said, "Clear, Preach. That's what we'll do."

By five o'clock, the firefighters were moving out of Virgin River, but the men had not returned. The acrid smell of smoke was dissipating, finally moving in the other direction. By six o'clock the town had grown eerily quiet and by seven, clouds began to roll in from the coast.

Paige, Brie and Nikki brought the children back to town and Mel was at long last able to nurse Emma and cuddle David for a while. She settled them into playpens and makeshift beds in Paige's quarters. Walt and Muriel continued to work the kitchen and bar, keeping an eye on the TV for local news updates, convinced that the men would return soon, hungry. By ten o'clock, still no word from their men, Mel saw the first few drops of rain fall on the dusty street outside the bar. She leaned out of the porch with her palm up and smiled as it grew wet. She stayed on the porch and watched, the smell of rain like the answer to a prayer.

She sat in one of the Adirondack chairs on Jack's porch and remembered the early days, before she married Jack, before the babies came. Back when she was alone and sure she'd never have love in her life again. Jack, so large and powerful, could have swept her up in his strong arms and devoured her, but he'd been patient, so gentle. He'd waited for her to say it was time, that she was ready to feel something that didn't hurt. And then his hands on her, his lips, had drawn from her the most amazing response she'd ever felt. A love so sure, so dependable, so constant. Jack didn't do anything halfway. He'd been a carefree bachelor, a lover of many women, until Mel. And then he belonged only to her. A committed partner.

You should never be afraid of anything while you're my wife. It's my job to make sure you're never afraid.

I'm a little afraid right now, Jack, she thought.

At midnight, she stuck her head into the bar and found Muriel slumped in a chair with her head on the table while Walt still stood behind the bar, watching the news on the new TV. Ready. Waiting. "Go lie down somewhere, Mel," he said. "I'll call you the second they come back."

"Have you heard anything on the news?" she asked.

"They're saying the fire's contained. And now, with the rain, they should be on top of it before long."

"Then why aren't they back?" she asked.

"Maybe they're still needed for something," he said. "Maybe cleanup or something. Go. Sleep."

Jack never slept while she worked, just in case she needed him—which she sometimes had. She shook her head. "I won't sleep until I have my man back," she said. "He's on his way." Inside, she could feel each step he took toward her, though her heart was beating suspiciously fast. But she was sure. He was on his way. Maybe he was out there looking for someone…

She remembered the first time she'd met these remarkable men, these marines who would never abandon each other. She fell instantly under their collective spell—their humor, camaraderie, pure zest for life, these men who loved their women and the life they could bring forth. They were fun and lusty, brave and loyal. Jack had proudly sent Rick off to become one of them.

Jack had fathered Rick in every way he could, with as

much devotion and strength as he would give the fruit of his own loins. She remembered how he had held the boy against the grief of losing his own child, his heart breaking into pieces. Her man, he had so much love inside him, it was amazing his chest didn't explode.

I'll never let you go, Mel. I want you to trust me, you know you're safe with me.

"I trust you," she said aloud, though there was no one to hear. "I love you. I trust you. And I know you—you'll never give up."

He had saved her life when it was bleeding out of her after Emma's birth. She was only semiconscious, but she heard his desperate, pleading words. *You're my life! Don't do this, Mel. Stay with me. Don't you leave me!*

"Don't you leave me," she whispered. "Don't you dare!"

As if you could get rid of me now.

Dawn found her still sitting on the porch, alert. She had spent a very long night thinking about her husband. He had so many faces; a fierce and dangerous expression for an enemy, a threat. A soft and tender expression when he turned his eyes to her. A sweet pride when he held their children. A joyful gleam when he was with his friends.

She remembered when he had first talked her into those stolen kisses, deep and meaningful and passionate. It had been hard to resist him, his allure was so penetrating. And how fortuitous, because that same desire had given her the children—she just couldn't say no to Jack. His love was blinding, it was so bold.

Finally, finally, a truck pulled into town, a farmer's truck. In the back sat their men, dirty and exhausted. She stood on the porch and watched as one by one, they crumbled out of the truck. Mike came up the porch steps. The black ash on his face was split by damp tracks of tears.

"Where's Jack?" she asked.

"Mel," he said. "We can't find him, Mel. We looked all night."

"What are you talking about?" she asked with a nervous laugh. "You lost him?"

"They were evacuating the area and he didn't come out. There was a sudden explosion. Fire swept over the road." He grabbed her upper arm. "Mel, he might have been trapped. Three firefighters were lost in a blast of fire when the wind shifted."

"But not Jack," she said, shaking her head. Her eyes were perfectly clear. "No, Jack's coming."

"Baby, I don't know." He pulled her into his arms, but she kept hers at her sides. "I don't think so."

Preacher came up the steps. His eyes were bloodshot, weary and sad. His face was covered with soot, as were his turnouts. He stood before her and hung his head as if ashamed. She knew him so well—he wouldn't be able to live with himself if he thought he let Jack down.

"It's okay. He's coming," she said. "He's going to be pissed, but he's coming."

One by one they approached her, touching her, hugging her, some of them with tears running out of their eyes. Before long the general was on the porch and, seeing the men, went to rouse Muriel and the younger women. But Mel was unmoved. "No," she said over and over. "You don't understand. If anything had happened to him, I'd know it. I'd feel it. He's coming."

"We're going back out there after some fluids and rest," Paul said. "We'll figure out what happened. No matter what, we'll bring him back." Then, hanging his head, he walked into the bar. It wasn't long before the sound of Brie's cry split the dawn and caused Mel to stiffen her spine. But she grabbed on to Joe's arm as he passed and said, "Tell her. Her brother's all right. He's coming. Tell her."

Joe pulled Mel against him and held her. "Honey, I'm not sure about that."

"You don't understand," she said. No one understood. If Jack were gone, she would feel it—there would be a deep, dark, hollow place in her. For just a second she was reminded that when her first husband, Mark, had been killed, she hadn't had any kind of premonition. There had been no warning, no deep feeling. But she banished the thought—it was different with Jack. It had always been different with Jack. "He's on his way."

Nineteen

Jack sat by the side of a deserted farm road at dawn, his ankle a mess, his face scorched. He was dehydrated, weak. His turnouts were covered with flame retardant, peppered with little holes from flying sparks, and he wondered how long he should rest before he just started walking again. Make that limping—he'd wrecked the ankle pretty bad. The area had been completely evacuated and it was unlikely anyone would be driving along this road until either Forestry or Cal Fire came this way. By that time he could be passed out, if not dead.

Then, against all odds, he saw the dust from a moving vehicle. He dragged himself to his feet, but he was dizzy and wobbly, his dehydration made worse by the dryness from smoke in the air. He placed himself in the center of the road. He decided he'd rather get run over than passed by. Who would pass someone in firefighter's turnouts? Only the devil himself.

Then the devil himself in a dark pickup with tinted windows came to a stop just inches from him. "Son of a bitch," Jack muttered to himself, his mouth dry as cotton.

The grower who'd crossed his path too often in the last couple of years opened the driver's door and stepped out. "Jesus. You're like a bad dream," the guy said to Jack. "You look like hell."

"Yeah? You're not exactly my favorite person, either," Jack returned thickly.

"How bad are you hurt?"

"Thirsty," Jack said. "Just thirsty. Just let me siphon out of the radiator tank and you can go," he said, insane though the notion was. He was insanely thirsty.

The guy, minus the Shady Brady and a little smudged with what could have been ash, sighed deeply and walked around the front of the truck. He opened the passenger door and said, "Get in."

"You got water?" Jack asked.

"Yeah! I got water! Just get in!" Jack limped toward the truck. "You said you weren't hurt," Shady Brady said, eyeing the limp.

"I'm mostly just thirsty," Jack said, walking very badly.

"You break it?"

"Nah. You ever hear a sprain's worse than a break? We're gonna find out…"

Shady Brady laughed in spite of himself. "Christ, you're a piece of work. Get in."

Jack wearily pulled himself into the truck, not easy— it was high, he was weak and the ankle was real bad. He'd hurt it right off, taking that dive into the ravine.

When the driver was settled behind the wheel, he reached behind him into the extended cab and grabbed a bottled water, handing it to Jack. "Take it slow or you'll puke in my truck."

"I know how to do this," Jack said, then guzzled the water fast enough to make the concern a reality. In fact he belched and hiccuped a few times and lowered his window. But it was okay; the water stayed down. He leaned his head back and said, "Oh man. Long night."

"How'd you end up here?"

"I got separated from the crew. Wind shifted, a tree exploded, I had to take a dive and run for it. But with no stars because of the smoke, I have no idea where I am. I walked all night." He guzzled more water. "What are you doing out here?"

The guy laughed. "Getting the hell out of here. Listen, I'll leave you by the county road where you'll get picked up. I'll leave you water, but I can't go back that way. I'm all done there."

"I've heard that before...."

"Well, this time it's the real deal. I'm so outta here. You'll be all right. No one's going to drive by a firefighter, even though you could just as easily be an inmate on the run. Especially the way you put yourself in the middle of the road—nice touch."

They drove in silence awhile; Jack rehydrated himself and Shady Brady just drove at a dangerously high speed on the deserted road. It was only about fifteen minutes before he came to an intersection with the county road; it would have taken Jack most of the day to get this far on his ankle—if he didn't collapse or drop dead first.

"There will be cars along this road, don't worry." He reached behind him and grabbed a couple of bottled waters. "Stay off the ankle, go slow, ration the water—"

"I've been in the desert," Jack said irritably.

"Yeah, I know. Just wait for a ride. I have to go, man. That's all there is to it."

Jack narrowed his eyes. "Why can't you be just a

hundred percent good or a hundred percent bad? Why do you have to keep me all confused all the time?"

He laughed. "My specialty—confusion. Listen—that fire was set. I can't prove it, but all I'm lacking are the facts. People died. Far as I'm concerned, death is against the rules."

"I don't know what you are, man," Jack said. "Half the time I see you, you really piss me off. The other half, you come through. And you're a marine—I saw the devil dog on your arm. But there are shitty marines out there, so I didn't let that influence me…"

"Just get out," he said. "Stay off the leg as much as possible, I guarantee a ride will come along. Since we won't see each other again, it would be better for me if you didn't talk it around that I picked you up. I'd really like to go up in a puff of smoke right now. So to speak."

"I should tell the police what you said, about it being set…"

"You know what? When they find the source of that fire, there will be a body. That body had nothing to do with me. You do what you have to do—but if you gossip a lot about this free ride, like I was there, and get some local growers looking for me, I'm going to die. And like I said, I consider that against the rules."

Jack grinned. Okay—here was a guy who was an illegal grower, but couldn't seem to resist saving lives like crazy, and didn't mind if the police heard what he'd been up to, but didn't want the other growers in the area to catch wind… He must be in deep kimshie with some growers. Now, what kind of guy would he have to be to fear the growers more than the cops? "No reason I have to say anything, pal. Appreciate the ride. Slow down a little, huh? You're frickin' dangerous."

"I'm in a hurry."

"Yeah. You wanna get there? Thanks for the ride. Try to stay out of trouble."

Once the truck door was closed, he peeled out, leaving a cloud of dust in his wake.

The drizzle continued, steaming up the ground; it was still so hot. The hottest summer ever, made hotter by the burning forest.

Mel wouldn't leave the porch. Doc came to the bar, touched her forehead and asked her if she wouldn't lie down for just a few minutes. "No," she said. "I'm waiting for Jack."

"The boys said Search and Rescue are combing the area and they're getting ready to leave again, to look. We can wake you the second something is found."

"Doc, it's all right. I wouldn't be able to sleep anyway."

Muriel tried to press a brandy into her hand, but she shook her head. She wanted to be sure she could feel everything, because she could still *feel* him. He might as well have his arms around her. And then she remembered her very first night in Virgin River, the horrible cabin, the torrential rain, and the brandy from Jack's bar that warmed her. She had snapped at him that she didn't find him amusing, she'd had a terrible day. And he had only grinned and said, "Good thing I have the cork out of the Remy, then."

And later, when he'd held her as she cried over her dead husband. Then he undressed her, dried her off, gave her that brandy. She'd had a huge emotional meltdown. *If you're going to go down, go down big. You should be proud.*

His pride in her was the greatest gift. He told her often he was proud of the care she gave, proud of her commitment to helping wherever help was needed. When a man like Jack is proud of you, it means everything. She felt herself smiling.

The volume on the TV in the bar was turned up. She'd never heard it so loud. She knew Jack's boys weren't resting, but glued to the news, hoping to catch something about the lost firefighters. They took turns on the porch with her, afraid to leave her alone, because they thought she was losing it. Quietly and stoically, but losing it. "I'm fine," she told them. "Really, I'm fine."

Inside, the men were gearing up to leave again, stuffing down sandwiches for fuel, guzzling water to rehydrate. Mel accepted water, had her baby brought to her to nurse, held her son for a bottle, but she was determined. She stayed on the porch. She never once asked if there was any news of Jack.

The morning news reported there were three firefighters confirmed dead in the blaze, names being withheld pending notification. Talking quietly among themselves, the men conferred about how some notification could be on its way soon, and they would stay on in Virgin River as long as necessary, be there for Mel. They would help her lay him to rest and for as long as she needed them, someone would be there.

The men had had a break of a couple of hours, food and water, called their families to report that they were unharmed, and were almost ready to take their personal vehicles back to the area and continue the search. Joe and Paul each sat on either side of her, occasionally reaching for her hand. She stared straight ahead.

The sound of a vehicle brought her to her feet and she stood on the porch. The rain had stopped, the ground was wet, and an old pickup pulled into town, stopping in the middle of the street in front of the bar. "Holy shit," Paul muttered, rising to his feet. Joe stumbled running into the bar.

Jack spilled out of the back, a huge smear of red flame retardant staining his body. He balanced on one foot, his other leg disabled in some way. As he reached back into the pickup for his gear, Mel serenely walked down the porch steps toward him. He tossed his gear to the ground and the pickup drove off with a toot of the horn. His face was black with soot, his eyes red and tearing, his lips pink and cracked from dryness. The turnouts he wore were speckled with holes made by flying embers.

Mel walked right into his open arms.

"You're late," she said, looking up at him.

He lowered his lips to softly kiss her forehead. "Sorry. I was held up. Goddamn truck left without me." He smiled down at her. "Do you have any idea what you look like in jeans? Melinda, you just do it to me in jeans."

"Everyone thought you were dead and you're talking about my butt again."

He grimaced. "They're going to wish I was dead. I've been walking for twenty-four hours and I'm in a real mood." He brushed the hair back from her brow. "Were you scared, baby?"

"No," she said, shaking her head. "I knew you were coming."

"You did?"

She touched her chest. "Your heart beats in here. If it had stopped, I would have known. It did beat a little fast sometimes. Was it close, Jack?"

He chuckled, tightening his arms around her. "It was so close, I have blisters on my ass."

"I spent all night remembering every time you touched me. Every one."

"You don't have to make do on memories. I'm going to touch you for many more years."

"I knew you'd never leave me."

"Baby, I'd walk out of hell to get back to you."

"I know, Jack. You hurt yourself."

"My ankle. I took a fall into a ditch. I'm not as agile as I was. I might've really screwed it up, running on it. It really slowed me down—and I was so ready to feel you against me."

"What's this?" she asked, wiping at the gooey red stuff on his shirt.

"Flame retardant. It got dumped right on me. Knocked me down—but there was a path out. Then I had to run on this damn ankle. It was awful. And then I got lost. You can get even worse lost at night when you can't see the stars because of the trees and smoke. I think I'm going to give up firefighting."

She touched his face, which appeared to be sunburned beneath the soot and ash. He winced. Then he bent down and crossed his arms under her bottom and lifted her up to his face. "Kiss me. Gimme a taste." She lowered her lips to his for a kiss that was deep and strong. Behind them, a cheer went up from all the marines gathered on the porch. But Jack took his time, moving tenderly over her lips, grateful to dive into her sweet love once more. He'd been wanting to kiss her for twenty-four hours and he wasn't going to be rushed. Not by them, not by anything. He hated the thought of letting her go, as in love with her today as that very first day. More.

"You taste like soot," she told him.

"I know," he said. "You taste so good." He jerked his head in the direction of his bar, his boys. "I hate when they do that."

"I think I'm starting to get used to it." She smiled. And she kissed him again.

* * *

As anxious as Jack was to get home, he needed a few minutes alone with Mike Valenzuela. They sequestered themselves in the RV behind the bar. Jack told only Mike the details of his rescue, and stayed there while Mike called the sheriff, repeating the story as well as the license-plate number. When Mike hung up, he slowly turned to look at Jack.

"Well, they were ahead of you. A couple of growers—partners—had a little lover's spat. One was shot, the other set him on fire to conceal evidence, thus the fire. They're investigating a drug-related murder covered by arson. A suspect was arrested trying to get away," Mike said.

Jack swallowed. "Was it our guy?"

"I'm guessing here, but if it was our guy, he would not have stopped for you. In fact, he might've put a bullet in your head to keep you from talking to the police. He definitely wouldn't have told you anything about the fire. Jack, that guy isn't what we think."

"What do we think?" Jack asked.

"That he's an ordinary grower. He might even be law enforcement, and if he is, they'll pull him in, relocate him and we'll never know."

Jack stood up. "Well. I guess that's it, then. The way he was driving, he probably wrapped himself around a tree before he got out of the county. I'm going home."

"Have a good sleep."

"Long sleep. And, Valenzuela. Thanks. For looking for me."

"It's just what we do. What you do. I'm just glad we didn't have to bring a crispy critter home to Mel."

"Yeah. Me, too."

Jack, Preacher, Mike and Paul went to their homes, their wives, to their showers and then their beds for a long, clean sleep. The others had too much of a drive ahead to think about just taking it on after no sleep in twenty-four hours. Phillips and Stephens were headed for Reno and went over the mountain pass with a big thermos of strong coffee from the bar and two sets of eyes to stay on the road. Zeke and Corny took the night in Jack's guesthouse before tackling their long drives. Joe took Nikki back to the cabin.

That left Muriel and Walt with no instructions and a bar on their hands.

"I'd say we're done here," Walt said. "We didn't exactly clean the place, but the food's put away and the dishes done. We did our part."

"I did my part," Muriel said. "By now Buff has exploded in his kennel and although Luce is an angel, it's possible she had a few accidents and ate my house out of boredom. She's a Lab. These things are inbred."

"Preacher left keys. What do you say we lock up and give up."

"Let's," she said. "I'm wrecked."

"I bet you're tired."

"Wrecked," she repeated. "That goes beyond tired."

Walt put a hand to the small of her back and escorted her out, locking the door behind them. He stood on the porch for a moment, looking at the sky. "I don't know how to thank you for coming to town, helping like you did."

"It's my town, too, Walt. Now. And it was worth it. These are my guys, too, now. Not just yours."

He laughed. "True. If you feed 'em, they're yours." He dropped his chin. "You know, I've been in some real hot spots over the years. I came here for peace and quiet, but today wasn't either one."

"I grew up in these mountains," she informed him. "It gets dicey sometimes. It's not an easy life all the time.

Beautiful, but there are issues. In the end, it's usually worth it. But, Walt, you shouldn't get the idea it's simple. It's not. It can get rugged."

"You saying beautiful isn't always easy?" he asked her.

She grinned. "I'm not sure that's exactly the message, but I guess so."

"I'll be sure to remember that."

"See that you do," she said. "I've been away a while. I had almost forgotten," she added. "This can be rough country. Fire's the worst, I think. We live in the middle of a lot of wood."

"Did you wonder, just for a second, whether it was worth it?"

"Hmm?"

"When Jack came back, all scraped up, scorched, and picked up his little wife like he did, almost as if he'd been late from the store or something, it reminded me about what I love about this—that these people face this stuff like it's just part of the package. They just man up, even the women. Everyone dives in, gets it done. It reminds me, if I'm going to belong to a group of people, I want to belong to people like these. They're tough and resilient. They don't quit early. They can count on each other. They hang in. That's why I loved the Army."

"Walt," she said, putting a hand on his chest. "We're just mountain people. We take what comes. The fact that it doesn't come easy? There's really not so much more to it than we don't give up. We fight. There's a lot to fight for here."

He looked down into his movie-star girlfriend's eyes. He smiled. "I'm going to sleep tonight. Then tomorrow night, why don't I bring groceries to your place and fix you a decent dinner."

She smiled at him. "Afraid you'll get celery sticks and hummus for food if you just come over?"

"I just think we deserve a good dinner, alone. And I might stay late." Then he grinned.

"I might let you. I'll do the wine. Will you tell your daughter where you'll be?"

"I don't know. I'm having an awful lot of fun saying nothing about us."

She lifted an eyebrow. "What is there to say about us?"

He leaned down and kissed her brow. "Let's revisit that question after dinner tomorrow night."

"Why, Walt," she teased with a smile.

He gave her fanny a pat. "Rest up," he said. "Because now that I think about it, I'm damn sure I'm going to stay late."

* * * * *

MILLS & BOON

LET'S TALK

Romance

Follow us:

 millsandboon

 @millsandboonuk

@millsandboon